"So you are Vayl's . . ." Disa raised an eyebrow, gave me *that* look.

The one that said, *Hey, even vamps who're trying to blend gotta get their blood from somewhere. So what about it? Are you Vayl's very own, personal Slurpee?*

I gave her empty eyes as I said, "I'm his assistant," then zoomed back in on Binns. He was beginning to relax. Starting to believe his *Deyrar* would tow him out of this jam. His gaze dropped to his front pocket just before his right hand tried to follow suit. So I shot him.

He staggered. Stared down at the bolt sticking out of his left shoulder. Looked up at me in shock. "Why did you do that?"

"Hair trigger," I said.

Praise for Jennifer Rardin:

BY JENNIFER RARDIN

Once Bitten, Twice Shy

Another One Bites the Dust

Biting the Bullet

Bitten to Death

One More Bite

Bitten to Death

A JAZ PARKS NOVEL

Jennifer Rardin

www.orbitbooks.net

NEW YORK • LONDON

Orbit
Hachette Book Group USA
237 Park Avenue, New York, NY 10017
Visit our Web site at www.orbitbooks.net

First Edition: August 2008

Orbit is an imprint of Hachette Book Group USA. The Orbit name and logo are trademarks of Little, Brown Book Group Limited.

Library of Congress Cataloging-in-Publication Data
Rardin, Jennifer.
Bitten to death : a Jaz Parks novel / Jennifer Rardin.— 1st ed.
    p.   cm.
ISBN-13: 978-0-316-02208-8
ISBN-10: 0-316-02208-X
    1. Parks,   Jaz   (Fictitious   character)—Fiction.   2. Assassins—Fiction.
3. Vampires—Fiction.   4. Murder for hire—Fiction.   I. Title.
PS3618.A74B59 2008
813'.6—dc22   2008005078

10   9   8   7   6   5   4   3   2   1

RRD-IN

Printed in the United States of America

*This book is dedicated to the memories of my babies,
Tessa and Ivan. Where there is love, even a brief life can
change you for good.*

Bitten to Death

Chapter One

I stood in the moonlit courtyard of a Greek villa so old and enormous it would've made me feel like Hera herself if I hadn't been so pissed. I'd just pulled Grief, the Walther PPK that Bergman, my tech guru, had modified for me. So I had no problem keeping a steady bead on my target. Since he was a vampire, I'd pressed the magic button, transforming Grief into a crossbow. Which my mark was taking pretty seriously. The only reason he was still pretending to breathe.

Beside me, my boss played his part to perfection. He'd already made the leap from faked surprise that I'd drawn on one of our hosts, to faux acceptance that I'd once again dropped him into a socially precarious situation. Maybe Vayl slipped into the role so smoothly because he was used to it. I did tend to make his existence . . . interesting.

He turned his head slightly, his short dark curls indifferent to the late-April breeze coming off the mountain at our backs. Managing to keep an eye on my target, as well as whatever vamps might come pouring out of the sprawling sand-colored mansion to check on him, Vayl said, "Are you sure you recognize this fellow?"

"He's the one," I hissed. "I just saw the report on him last week. Name is Alan Binns. He's wanted for murder in three countries. His specialty is families. The pictures were—" *Gruesome*, I thought, but I choked on the word. The twitch of Vayl's left eyebrow told me I was on a roll. Thing was, at the moment, I didn't give two craps about our little game.

The Vampere world might be all about superiority, which was why we'd needed to make a power play the minute we crossed their threshold. But I'd have popped this bastard just to erase another monster from our hit list. In fact, that we should personally benefit from his takeout made me feel almost dirty. I know, I know. As assistant to the CIA's top assassin, I shouldn't make moral judgments. But that had never stopped me before.

"You can't prove anything," snarled Binns, whose dirt-brown, shoulder-length hair did nothing to disguise his bulging forehead.

"I don't *have* to, you idiot!" I snapped, wishing I could break my rage over his head like a vase full of cobras. "You *others* have so few legal rights they could fit on the back of my passport photo. That leaves me free to smoke you if I feel you're a clear and present danger to society. Which you are."

"What is the meaning of this? What are you strangers doing in my courtyard at ten o'clock in the evening!" demanded the woman who steamed out one of the villa's blue-framed back doors, all four of which were flanked by solar lamps made to resemble antique streetlights. The elongated sleeves of her black chiffon gown batted the air behind her, making her resemble an enraged homecoming queen candidate—one whose friends had voted for the other, uglier girl. Though her mega-gelled version of beauty could have landed her a closetful of pageant tiaras, her psychic scent hit me between the eyes so hard I felt like I'd been drop-kicked into a garbage dump. What the hell kind of vamp *was* she?

Vayl turned to intercept her, placing the tiger-carved cane he always carried firmly on the gray pavers between them. She stopped three feet from it, rearing back like she'd hit an invisible wall. Her eyes, the liquid brown of stale coffee, widened as a how-dare-you look tried to settle on her face. It faded almost immediately, as if she'd undergone a recent Botox treatment and couldn't sustain any expression that might leave evidence of emotion.

I struggled not to stare. My job did require some concentration, after all. But her scent, combined with the eye-strafing she gave Vayl, tempted the busybody in me. I forced my gaze back to Binns. He'd taken half a step forward. I smiled at him. *Come on, asshole. Make it easy.* He stopped.

"What are *you* doing here?" the woman snarled.

For a second I thought Vayl was going to freeze her like an MRE, his powers spiked so suddenly. Then he said, "I heard you were dead."

Out the corner of my eye I saw her throw her head sideways, as if to dodge a bitter memory. "Hardly," she replied, her voice higher and tighter than before. "Hamon and I might have had a slight . . . disagreement. But that was settled years ago."

"Where *is* your *Deyrar?*" Vayl asked.

I searched my mental dictionary, my limited Vampere vocabulary coming up with one of its few complete definitions. The *Deyrar* was the supreme leader of a secretive vampire community called a Trust. He was like a king, only less prone to gout and gambling addiction.

She drew herself up to her full height, maybe five-foot-one, and said, "*I* am the *Deyrar.*"

Vayl and I don't have a psychic link. But we're close enough to say a ton with one stricken look.

Are we screwed? I asked him with puckered eyebrows.

A valid question, Jasmine, his narrowed gaze replied. *Obviously she was not expecting us. Which means she knows nothing about the deal.*

Well, shit.

Our agreement had been with Hamon Eryx, the (deposed?) leader of the vampires who packed the mansion before us. Together they formed one of a network of worldwide Trusts. Vayl himself had lived with this particular group nearly a century ago.

We'd been asked to come to Patras by Eryx himself, a canny old sleaze who'd promised us safe passage in return for a shot at Edward Samos, aka the Raptor. Samos had either attempted or committed enough acts of terrorism in the past few years to raise him to the top of our department's hit list. He'd also written to Eryx offering an alliance. Eryx wasn't interested, but because he knew everyone who refused Samos's advances ended up dead, he'd asked Vayl to intervene.

Now the *Deyrar* had been replaced, which meant our whole mission could be junk before it even came out of the box. Plus, we were standing in the middle of a well-established Trust. Any minute now we could be surrounded by fifteen to twenty vamps and their human guardians, who'd be psyched to have an excuse to disembowel us. Those goofy Vampere. Anything for a giggle.

As if he'd read my mind, a Mr. Universe candidate burst out the same back door the *Deyrar* had just exited. His appearance made me seriously consider smoking my target just so I could stand and stare. He went shirtless, though Grecian springs are cool and the temperature currently hovered around sixty degrees. From the look of that sculpted bod I estimated his workout took a three-hour chunk out of his daily schedule. It wouldn't have made a difference if he was a vamp. But he was all man. The kind photographers feature on the covers of books with titles like *Forbidden Folly* and *Wesley's Wench*.

"Disa, the party's ready to start," he said eagerly. He looked at Vayl, starting slightly, as if he'd only just seen him. "Who're you?" he demanded.

"I am Vayl. And this is Lucille Robinson."

"My mother's name was Lucille," said Binns.

"Shut up," I said.

"Did you know I killed her?" he sneered. "I kill everybody I meet named Lucille, Lucille. Lucy Lucillia Robin—"

"Shut the fuck up before I cut out your tongue!" I snarled.

His teeth clicked shut.

I blew my breath out through my nose, trying to keep anger from shredding my better sense. Because I knew what he was trying to pull.

Vayl had explained that in the Vampere world, knowing someone's name could give you power over them. Which was why Hamon Eryx had insisted on trading birth certificates. Vayl had, in turn, demanded that Eryx keep my personal info secure. Meaning everyone else in the Trust should get my favorite fake ID. I sure as hell would've picked another if I'd known it was going to set Binns off. Not because it disturbed me. But because I didn't want to kill him out of anger. So unprofessional.

Cover Boy, noting Disa's displeasure at my foul mouth, asked, "Do you want me to kill them?"

I tried not to gape. After all, I was holding a loaded weapon. Could he *be* that dumb?

"No, Tarasios," Disa said tiredly. "Get the rest of the Trust." As he bobbed his head and went back inside, she turned her glare to me. "So you are Vayl's . . ." She raised an eyebrow, gave me *that* look. The one that said, *Hey, even vamps who're trying to blend gotta get their blood from somewhere. So what about it? Are you Vayl's very own, personal Slurpee?*

I gave her empty eyes as I said, "I'm his assistant," then zoomed back in on Binns. He was beginning to relax. Starting to believe his *Deyrar* would tow him out of this jam. His gaze dropped to his front pocket just before his right hand tried to follow suit. So I shot him.

He staggered. Stared down at the bolt sticking out of his left shoulder. Looked up at me in shock. "Why did you do that?"

"Hair trigger," I said. Maybe not, though. He liked to torture his victims before he killed them, half of whom had been under the age of twelve. And the more I obsessed about his MO, the less control my brain seemed to exercise over my hand. "I suggest you stand very still now. Wouldn't want you to have a nasty accident before I settle on your future plans." In the deep silence that followed, all I could hear was the whir of well-oiled machinery as Grief automatically loaded another bolt into my crossbow.

I glanced at Disa just in time to see her eyes go through major changes, moving from brown to black, red to orange and bright yellow before fading back to brown. It happened so quickly it felt like watching a retro rock video in fast-forward. *Psychedelic, man. And kinda nauseating.* The only other vampire I knew whose eyes transformed with his emotions was Vayl. Did that mean the entire Trust had the ability? Or had he and Disa—*naw, don't be silly, Jaz. You're just being suspicious because . . .*

Well, because on our last mission Vayl had nearly gone off the deep end. Had almost trashed whatever future we might hope for by taking the blood of an Iranian Seer named Zarsa. We'd survived that seismic shift. That didn't mean another wouldn't destroy us.

"How dare you attack my *knaer?*" Disa demanded.

Why can't we all speak English today? Seriously, I'm going to have to get Bergman started on some kind of universal translator. Now, what did Vayl say a knaer *was? Some kind of jelly roll? No, dipshit, that's what you ate for breakfast. This has something to do with Trust hierarchy. That's right, power-wise, the* knaer *operate at about twenty-five watts. Only the humans put out less heat than them.* I'd picked the right vamp to harass.

I gave Disa my most intimidating stare. "Alan Binns is an enemy of the people I'm sworn to protect," I said. "And *you're* harboring him. Makes me wonder what other filthy secrets you're hiding."

She swung her head around, probably searching for something to throw. Luckily they hadn't left much in the way of portable Jaz trashers in the backyard. I watched her fists clench and hoped the next phase would involve stomping and screaming. My entertainment quota for the month had already fallen way below par.

Unfortunately, before Disa could wind it up a notch, her vamps and their human guardians came pouring through the villa's back doors, exclaiming angrily when they saw their wounded bud and pinning me with hostile glares when they realized I'd done the deed. Again the balance had shifted. I glanced at Vayl. He gave me a nod and the slight lift of his lips that passed for a smile. Warped souls that we are, we kinda love it when our odds dip. Because that's when the real fun begins.

Chapter Two

When Vayl gathers his powers it feels like I'm standing next to a glacial whirlpool. But it doesn't hurt. As a Sensitive I'm mostly immune to vamp abilities. One of the perks of cheating death—twice. Plus, I was wearing my black leather jacket over matching jeans and boots with my fave new shirt—a bright yellow tee with an artsy black graphic that reminded me of battling minotaurs—so my shiver rose out of anticipation more than cold. Yup, definitely time for something big.

Since my health might depend on it, I cemented the scene in my mind. Mount Panachaikon loomed like a giant ogre over the groves of olive trees and gnarled lines of grapevines that dotted the surrounding acreage. Growing like a melanoma from its big toe was the seventeenth-century building housing Vayl's former Trust. Only Cole, my wannabe beau and sometime shooting partner, could've described the villa correctly. He'd have taken one look at its massive block-on-block-on-block design with multiple outer staircases, random balconies, and tiny shuttered windows and said, "This is definitely a LEGO house. The haunted kind. Are they building another amusement park here?"

The mansion's stone-walled front entrance discouraged visitors. Its path led, not to the lane where we'd parked our green metallic Range Rover, but northeast down a steep hill to a warehouse-sized building surrounded by weeds. So we'd come around back, through the double-doored gate to our right, which still stood wide open. Vayl had expected Eryx to open the way for us, but now the walk-in kinda made you wonder about their security.

Behind us a long mosaic-topped table surrounded by teak chairs ran the length of a jasmine-covered pergola that had been built off a three-car garage. Its quaint wooden door was also framed by vines. To our left someone had arranged another seating area, almost restaurant-like in its scattering of round metal tables and director chairs. Large planters filled with miniature orange trees softened the stone wall that formed the perimeter of that section of courtyard.

Between us and the villa, the Trust members formed a united front. At first glance anyway. Six vamps and five humans, all dressed in special-occasion duds, ranged themselves in a rough semicircle around Disa except for two human guards, who stood like giant totem poles behind her.

The vamps' combined powers, as intense and unpredictable as a lightning storm, practically made the air crackle. Vayl had warned me about this, but words fell way short of the reality. Facing them felt like opening up the door of an air-conditioned SUV and stepping into the heat of the Sahara. My cheeks burned as I experienced the force of a unified Trust, something Vayl had said even he might have difficulty resisting. Especially if we had to stay any length of time. We were going to have to watch each other's backs every second on this one.

And damned if a couple of vamps didn't try to move behind us just as the thought crossed my mind. But a jolt of Vayl's arctic strength stepped them back. That and his pronouncement, delivered in his clear baritone. "We come at the invitation of Hamon Eryx. He signed a blood oath guaranteeing us safe passage in return for a boon to the Trust. Do you honor your *Deyrar*?"

"*I* am the *Deyrar*!" Disa screeched.

"So the *Vitem* has decreed," said a busty, tavern-wench type as she laid her hand on Disa's shoulder.

Vayl had either sketched or found pictures of the major players still likely to be, as he put it, "walking in the Trust." I recognized this one as Sibley. A member of Eryx's *Vitem*, which my boss had compared to the president's cabinet, she'd been his most conservative adviser. Now her role seemed to have morphed to ass kisser and morale booster. But she didn't seem comfortable in it. As soon as she touched her leader, Sibley yanked her hand back and brushed it down the skirt of her long red dress. In that moment I saw a whole lot of white in her eyes.

Since she stood closest to Disa, I'd tagged Sibley as the most powerful member of her *Vitem*. Otherwise I'd have assumed that honor went to the dude standing next to her. His silver hair, pulled back in a tight ponytail, accentuated his smooth, fine-boned face. I guessed an age, added twenty years for the hair, and decided he'd been turned sometime after his fiftieth birthday. Given his maturity and office, he could've puffed and strutted like an elder statesman. But the way his eyes darted around the scene reminded me of a chipmunk ready to jump for cover the second he spied an owl. *This guy's gotta be Marcon.*

It was easy to pick out the other *Vitem* members from the fact that they lined up on the other side of Disa, each with his own set of groupies. The vamp directly to her left kept glancing at her and nodding whether she had anything to say or not. I figured he had his head so far up her ass he should probably learn sign language. But then, Vayl had already given me the lowdown on his old nemesis, Genti. To give the toady credit, at least he was a simple soul. All he wanted from life was the quickest route to Easy Street.

He and his crew looked to have raided Bob's Costume Supply before rushing out to confront us. Genti wore a furred, feathered top hat and a purple velvet smoking jacket over leopard-print pants.

The other male vamp was dressed like the gunner for a WWII bombing crew, while the female seemed to be impersonating a homeless woman. Since I didn't recognize either of them, I decided they must have arrived after Vayl left the Trust. Their human guardian, while beautiful in a Californian blonde sort of way, wore her hair in dreadlocks. Ick.

The last *Vitem* member caught my interest because, of the entire group, he seemed the least scared. And he was the first vamp I'd met since Vayl who didn't smell of the grave. I'd begun to believe this meant something significant for their souls. It was just a theory, though. And really, who knew?

Vayl's psychic scent reminded me of a walk through a pine forest. This guy I'd put more in the area of . . . freshly picked grapes. I studied him as closely as I dared, considering I was still covering a wanted felon. Though his hair hung longer, straighter, and redder than mine, it somehow accentuated the masculine planes of his face and the iron gray of his eyes. A sleek blue-silver pinstripe suit complemented his slender build and his height, which equaled Vayl's.

So this must be Niall, I thought. Though Vayl hadn't said so, I'd gotten the feeling he and Niall had been friends before the break. Niall's partner, a Greek stud named Admes, was a fierce warrior, according to Vayl, and absolutely loyal to Niall. A human in his mid-forties rounded out their group, his quiet, alert demeanor telling me if I ever wanted to get to the vamps, I'd have to mow through him first.

"The Trust has always respected the wishes of its *Deyrar,* both past and present," said Niall, whose accent put his birthplace somewhere in the vicinity of Dublin. It made me wonder how a son of Eire had wandered so far. Or if he'd been exiled from his homeland just as Vayl had been over two hundred years ago. "What was the boon Hamon asked of you?"

"What does it matter?" shouted Genti. "Vayl turned his back on the Trust. He deserves nothing from us!"

Vayl had told me Genti's roots lay just north of Greece, in Albania, though he looked like a native with his coal-black hair and dirt-brown eyes, which were starting to cross with rage. I couldn't decide if he and his group were genuinely pissed at Vayl for leaving, or if they despised him for returning. Only the human's message was clear. And the come-get-me look she sent Vayl made me want to grind her face into the ground.

Niall gave the Albanian a slap on the shoulder that seemed friendly. It made him wince. "Honestly, G-boy, do you ever stop shouting long enough to hear what's actually being said to you?" he asked. "Because it sounded to *me* as if Hamon was after something from Vayl."

"My name is Genti Luan, you Irish hound, and if you do not say it with the respect it deserves, so help me I will pin you to a cross and watch you sizzle!" As soon as Genti revealed his whole name, Niall darted his eyes at me, his lips quirking. *Hmm, interesting.* In this place, where knowing someone's full name gave you real leverage, Niall had just handed me a weapon.

"You will have to excuse Genti, here, Ms. Robinson," said Niall. "He was born without the ability to carry on a civil conversation."

Genti stuck his chest out so far he looked like he'd just snapped himself into a pair of child's pants. "While you obviously believe the Trust has nothing to lose from Vayl's reappearance, I beg to differ. To allow strangers here, ever, is risky. But now? I say it is insane!"

Was he talking about Samos? Or something even more sinister? Before I could decide, a blur of movement demanded my full attention. Binns, sensing major distraction, had decided to jump me. Ignorant creature. Did he really think I'd panic when I saw him coming at me a million miles an hour, sure death in his blood-filled eyes? Naw. I just channeled that jolt of attack-inspired adrenaline into my arms, raised my crossbow the necessary three inches as he leaped at me, and shot him.

His jaw gaped in utter disbelief as the finely polished maple pierced his heart. And then he faded. Wafted into the night while his clothes and the last bits of his material remains dropped to the stone at my feet, some of it scattering on the toes of my boots when I didn't step away in time. I resisted brushing them against the backs of my jeans and dropped my arms with relief as Grief rolled another bolt into the chamber.

"You killed him!" cried Genti's Bomber boy. Though he'd probably been smoking stogies before my Gramps Lew learned to crawl, he looked young enough to be rapping his pencil against his desk as his driver's ed teacher walked the class through the dos and don'ts of lane changing. I learned later his name was Rastus and he'd only joined the Trust six months before. He slapped the back of his black-nailed hand against Genti's lace-covered chest. "I say we tear her limbs off and beat her to death with them!"

Before I could blink, Vayl had unsheathed the sword that rode inside his cane, closed the gap between himself and Rastus, and rammed it straight into his throat.

I laughed. Yeah, I know, wrong reaction. What can I say, my timing sucks. In my defense? Gaping vamps look hilarious. Like big, stupid bats with great tailors.

"So," I said, turning to the group at large. "Where were we? Oh yeah, I believe someone was discussing the merits of beating me to death with my own severed limbs." Stab of fear on my part — typical delayed reaction. *Ignore it, Jaz. If these predators smell weakness, you can kiss your ass goodbye.*

I shook my head and forefinger at the same time. "Not a wise choice, as you see. Vayl can go left or right with that sword, but if we find we can work together, I'm sure he'll be willing to yank it straight out. Plus, where's the fun in dismemberment? I'd definitely bleed out before any of you got off on it."

"In addition," Niall said, "Rastus has not walked in the Trust long enough to have earned a voice."

Hmm, should I point out the irony of that comment, or does everyone already get it? Deciding I'd better make my point before somebody with an actual vote suggested an even grislier end to me, I said, "Edward Samos wants an alliance with you." I maintained eye contact with Niall and Disa. Niall, because I sensed in him a potential ally. And Disa because she clearly had the final word. "Eryx knew that *really* meant Samos wanted to absorb you. Eat your autonomy and then flush it for all time. He also knew if you refused Samos's offer he'd destroy your leadership and replace it with his own." I paused. Let them wonder . . . had it already happened? Admes and the female vamp in Genti's crew both sent curious looks in Disa's direction. "So Eryx contacted Vayl," I finished.

"And who are you to speak within these walls?" demanded Genti.

"She is my *avhar*," said Vayl.

He'd prepared me for the Big Announcement. I guess vamps have problems hooking up at the *sverhamin* level, so the reaction to those who do is usually pretty red-carpet. Ironic that we'd be viewed as celebrities among Vayl's peers, creatures who called their own communities Trusts but rarely pulled off the *avhar/sverhamin* connection.

Not that *I* was completely at ease in the relationship. I still hadn't read all the subparagraphs relating to late-night talks and who-gets-the-last-cookie moments. But I was sure as hell happier than Disa, who looked like she'd just bitten into a rotten tomato.

The other vamps reacted more like I'd expected. Niall came forward to congratulate us. Sibley's jaw gaped even wider than her neckline. Admes stared at Vayl as if he'd never seen him before. Marcon bowed his head respectfully and said, "I believe you can release Rastus now." As if Vayl had him in a headlock. And the scariest thing? I could quickly get used to the total disregard the Vampere seemed to have for bloodletting. Considering I'd come into this mission thinking *they* were whacked, what did that say about *me*?

Vayl yanked out his sword, stepping aside so the spurt of blood missed him and instead sprayed a fanlike arc on the ground. It stopped almost immediately. And not just because Rastus had covered the wound with his hand. He was already healing.

Genti huddled with his crew, making a big show of supporting Rastus with his shoulder, though the vamp could clearly stand on his own. He threw a couple of annoyed looks back at Vayl as my boss turned to Disa, his long leather coat billowing out behind him in a sudden breeze that brought with it the smell of rain.

Despite the fact that he was surrounded, Vayl gave no sense of being intimidated. Part of it was his stance, patient as a hunting panther in his black knit shirt and light gray slacks, his new boots shining like onyx daggers. Part was the way he cleaned his sword on his handkerchief and sheathed it. Deliberate. Dangerous. Death on a short, frayed leash.

He said, "We are willing to continue the contract. If you choose to honor the voice of your former *Deyrar*, we could even be persuaded to forgive the insult brought upon us by these two." He pointed the reconstructed cane first at Rastus, then at the remains of Alan Binns.

Wow, that takes some nuts. We attack them and then force them to ask our forgiveness. For the most part our hosts seemed to feel the same. But I saw respect on a few faces.

"We can take care of ourselves," snarled the female vamp from Genti's group. I spent some time studying her because, to be honest,

I'd never seen a frumpy one before. It was nothing a good bra and some time in front of the makeup mirror wouldn't cure. But her look seemed to be full-immersion.

"You know my name," I reminded her. "What should I call you?" I asked.

"Koren," she said, spitting the word at me like it might land somewhere close to the corner of my mouth and drip off, sending me into dry heaves.

"Well, Koren, I'm going to have to differ with you there," I drawled. "Because if you *could* take care of yourselves, you wouldn't have a power-hungry madman trying to gobble up your Trust like it was made of goat cheese. And really, if you were any good at self-preservation, don't you imagine Eryx would've called the florists, or the caterers, instead of a couple of American assassins? Gosh, if you had any skills maybe he'd even be alive right now. Or do you have him tied up in a dungeon somewhere?" Vayl threw me a look that said, *Hey, I told you to act like the alpha, not to actually screw the pooch.*

I shoulda listened. But I wanted to see how hard I could push Disa's buttons. I didn't realize somebody'd already goosed Koren's. She got this wild look on her face that told me she was close with Eryx. Maybe even his *avhar.* And anything I said about him would be used against me. Now.

She screamed, *"Bitch!"* and *launched,* all fangs, nails, and unplucked eyebrows. Before I had time to react, she stopped suddenly, her eyes round and shocked as they lowered slowly to her abdomen. A neon green crossbow bolt as big as my middle finger protruded from her gut, still quivering from the impact.

"Did you really think we'd walk in here without some sort of backup?" I asked, glad for the first time that we'd been forced to bring the man who lurked out of sight, just at the edge of the trees. "Now, we don't have a whole lot of time to talk, because the little red pill attached to the pointy end of this missile is due to dissolve in the next minute or so, at which time it will set off a reaction in your system kinda like an internal sunburn. Can you say blister, peel, poof?"

Koren gaped at me as I continued. "Sorry I can't give you a closer timeline estimate." I shrugged. "But it's not an exact science." I held up my hand as she grasped the bolt and tried to pull it free. "It doesn't work that way. Only I can pull it out without leaving the pill inside you to do its dirty deed." Unless Bergman had fouled up this small revision of his original invention. Which was entirely possible. His prototypes hardly ever followed the playbook. But I wasn't going to advertise the fact.

Vayl locked eyes with Disa. She hadn't moved since the bolt had impaled her vamp. None of them had. Humans would've run screaming. Or collapsed into sobbing heaps. These *others* just became more still, further entranced. As if the smoking of Dinns, the stabbing of Rastus, and the shooting of Koren entertained them at the highest possible level. "So what will it be?" he demanded. "Are we on the team or not?"

The *Vitem* gathered around Disa for a whispered conversation.

At the same time the human from Genti's crew ran forward with a wide, teak chair and helped Koren sink down into it. As with the costumes and the aid to Bomber boy, it struck me as more theatrical than necessary.

I watched the *Vitem* converse with their leader, paying special attention to Sibley and Marcon. Hard to tell without audio if they were just spouting lines or if, like Niall, their actions stemmed from genuine opinions. Ten seconds later Disa emerged from the pack. "We will abide by Hamon Eryx's contract," she said.

"Excellent," said Vayl as I moved toward Koren.

"You need to back off now," I told the human who stood with her.

"Why?" she demanded, a you-don't-boss-me pout lining her face. Her pose told me right away she'd come from old money. The kind that sends their kids to camp all summer until they're old enough to drive, at which time the allowance kicks in, giving them the means to stay out of the house and in trouble well into their thirties.

I said, "Because my guy in the shadows has orders to keep me safe at any cost. And if he decides you're too close to me, you're going down."

When she still hesitated, Koren said, "Do as she says, Meryl." The woman finally backed away as I grasped the head of the bolt.

"Hold still," I said. I held it steady with one hand while I gently depressed the head with the other. Koren moaned dramatically as I accidentally wiggled the shaft. "Oh, for shit's sake, are you really that much of a candyass?"

"How dare you speak to me that way?" Koren demanded, a note of hysteria in her voice.

"You're the fool who attacked an assassin. Most people who do that don't end up chatting with me on their patios afterward." The button on the head popped out, bringing with it the metal wire that ran down its center.

"We do not have *patios* in Patras. Where on earth did Hamon find you? You are a complete savage!"

I glanced at Vayl, thinking, *I have to take this crap from the Mistress of Grunge?* But his eyes practically sparkled at her statement.

"Indeed she is," he said. "And you will survive a great deal longer if you remember that fact."

I pulled the wire free along with the vamp-killing pill at its tip that Bergman had created on one of our previous missions. Because he hadn't perfected it yet, I'd hesitated to make it a permanent part of my arsenal. But for this application — ideal.

I broke the pill free of its wax coating and showed it to Koren. "Lucky you that Disa decided to play ball."

She gestured to the shaft of the bolt, still sticking out of her gut. "What about this?" she cried.

"Keep it," I said. "A little souvenir to remind you not to mess with skinny redheads from America."

Chapter Three

At a prearranged hand signal from me, our third dropped from his perch in the tree he'd chosen for its panoramic view of the courtyard and emerged from the thick forest of fir, oak, and chestnut south of the lane leading up to the villa. He wore the uniform unique to his military position — green and black camo over full-length body armor, matching bucket hat, and equipment out the wazoo. This included a field knife, night-vision goggles, first-aid kit, and sat phone. He'd left his urban assault weapon at home, but his Beretta M9 currently rode a shoulder holster similar to mine under his jacket. We'd provided the crossbow.

Biting my lip to suppress the worry that twisted my gut whenever I recalled why SOCOM had, once again, partnered us with one of their best Special Ops commanders, I turned to Disa. She, alone, remained in the courtyard, having dismissed the rest of the Trust. They'd seemed eager to get back to whatever festivities we'd interrupted.

"This is David," I told Disa as our backup joined us at the table beside the garage. I omitted his last name. Hoped she wouldn't smell the whiskey on his breath. Or notice the fact that we were twins. Someone less self-absorbed might have caught the resemblance. We share the same green eyes and stubborn chins. But Disa wasn't interested in a man she saw as our servant. She didn't acknowledge him as he came to stand at my shoulder. Probably wouldn't even have raised an eyebrow if I'd turned around and belted him one. And I was tempted. What the hell was he thinking? No time to ask now. Disa had launched into conversation.

"Did you ever think I'd come this far?" she asked Vayl.

He regarded her with eyes the icy blue of a mountain lake. "Hardly."

Her smile reminded me of a teenager who's gotten away with a huge kegger while her parents were out of town for the weekend. "And really, I have you to thank for it."

"You are welcome."

Now, why would that smooth answer irritate her? I wasn't sure, but she suddenly looked like she wanted to pick him up, swing him around her head a few times, and throw him into a crowd of stake-wielding priests. I darted a glance at my boss. To my surprise, he looked just as pissed, though only somebody who'd hung with him as long as I had would've been able to tell. A master at damming his emotions, Vayl leaked them with the smallest alterations of expression. Just now the minuscule lowering of his slanted brows accompanied by a tighter than usual grip on the blue jewel that topped his cane let me know he wouldn't mind if Disa went the way of Binns before we completed our mission.

She sat forward, steepling her hands before her catalog-model face, her crimson nails practically glowing against the paleness of her skin. "You know, left to my own devices, I never would have called you." Disa spoke directly to Vayl, as if Dave and I had gone boneless and oozed into the cracks beneath her heels. "I can take care of myself." She nodded to emphasize the point. "And the Trust," she added, almost as an afterthought.

"I know," said Vayl, after a hesitation that lasted long enough to make me think he'd meant to say something else.

"I never meant to ally with Samos. Hamon was right in that point at least." Her tone said he'd screwed up royally in plenty of other areas. "At any rate, negotiations begin tomorrow, two hours after sunset." She jumped up from her seat, startling Dave enough that he'd trained his crossbow on her chest before her chair stopped moving. "Would you put that thing down?" she snapped.

"Perhaps it would be better if you stopped making sudden moves," Vayl murmured. Before she could retort, he added, "As for our contract, and the part we intend to play in the negotiations, maybe it would be wise to discuss those issues now?"

She brushed us off with a limp-fingered wave that let us know such conversations fell outside her job description. "I will send the *Vitem* to discuss those details with you after the *Sonrhain*."

The what? But nobody thought to translate and Disa had barreled on. "That was always your problem, Vayl," she said, leaning over to pat his hand almost merrily, her breasts pressing so hard against the material of her bodice it creaked in protest. "You never learned how to delegate. Now, we have really missed enough fun for one evening. Follow me."

Vayl shuttered his expression so tightly, no matter how high I arched my eyebrows, I couldn't get a response to my *What the hell?* and *Are we dealing with a lunatic?* looks. Which meant I followed my boss into the freak show without any warning at all.

Chapter Four

Apparently *Sonrhain* is the Vampere word for "gross out the human guests." Dave and I took one look at each other as we entered the Olympic pool–sized dining room and walked back out. "Who can I kill?" Dave asked, reaching inside his jacket. I put my hand on his arm, unsure whether he'd come out holding his Beretta or a fifth of Jack. Sucky plan either way.

"You know the rules. From now on, nobody dies who doesn't threaten us directly," I said.

"You're shitting me, right? You want me to stand in there, watch that . . . and what, applaud?"

I shook my head, feeling as nauseated as he looked. "Just keep your eyes open and avoid the sauce."

His eyes snapped to mine. "Is that what General Kyle told you? That I needed a sponsor to make sure I stayed dry?"

"No," I hissed. "What he said was that you're an excellent fighter who's been through hell. He basically asked me to give you something constructive to do before you throw a grenade under the same helmet you've stuffed your career inside." Okay, he'd said a few more things. Like my brother had turned into a walking volcano since our last mission. That he'd hit the bottle hard, along with a couple of fellow officers who, thank God, had respected him enough not to press charges. And if I didn't help him get his head on straight, and fast, he could kiss the military goodbye.

I reached into Dave's jacket, my hand sliding into the correct pocket first try. It emerged holding a half-empty bottle of whiskey. "That was just to keep me warm while I waited for you two to get your business finished," he told me.

I stared into eyes so like my own the similarity sometimes still startled me. And I felt my heart break a little. After all he'd been through, I figured he deserved better than this. But I wasn't here to pinch his cheeks and fluff his pillows. I put steel into my voice as I said, "Don't fuck with me, Dave."

I tucked the bottle in my own jacket, waiting for him to decide. After a long pause he said, "I don't wanna go in there."

"Me neither."

So we walked through the double doors together.

Funny how you equate time with mood. Even after working the night shift for nine solid months, at almost ten thirty p.m. I felt like we should've hit unwind. *I* could sure go for a cocktail at one of the ritzy hotels down by the ocean. But as Dave and I met Vayl on the other side of the blank, dark gateways to the Trust's party plaza, it seemed like we'd slipped on the double-barreled six-shooters of high noon.

The room shouldn't have made me shudder. Ceiling-to-floor drapes in red satin hung on the walls to my right and left. They were drawn back to reveal murals cleverly painted to look like windows into the countryside. One was a view of the Gulf of Patras with ships at the harbor and a ferry just heading off toward Italy. The other showed a wooded landscape with a couple of waterfalls tucked into the background. It was almost inviting. Except for the rivulets of blood that ran down the "panes."

You can get through this, I told myself. *Just don't let it touch you.* I could almost feel another layer grow around my core. A thick, pearl-like shell that I could wash all the gore from later on. I turned away from the art as Vayl touched my arm, pointing me toward my seat. It was only two down from Disa. She'd already taken her place at the head table, which was covered in black silk and formed a horseshoe with several others around the raised ring in the center of the room. Which, I decided, I'd better give a long, hard look before I lost all the kickass points I'd gained in the courtyard.

A silver fence hung from the ceiling, surrounding the ring, giving it an Ultimate Fighter feel. I pressed my lips together so I wouldn't drop the F-bomb again, though it lingered there, trying to jump out of my mouth every few seconds as I took in more details of the Main Event.

In the center of the ring two Weres ripped at each other, growling ferociously as they grappled with teeth and claws. The wolf made me glad something solid and steel stood between it and my tender flesh. The size of a Bengal tiger, it made the room seem to shrink every time it moved. Its ear hung by one stringy chunk. Its left eye had closed completely, though I couldn't tell if it had been gouged out or just injured so badly it would no longer open.

It battled a brown bear, which, in Were form, wasn't nearly as cute as its zoo cousin. Think leaner, with longer fangs, claws like machetes, and jaguar speed, and you begin to get the idea. It was missing huge mounds of fur and its throat looked like something you'd find in the garbage can at a butcher's shop. Blood covered both of the Weres' faces, their hides, and so much of the floor that they slipped and rammed each other just trying to stay upright.

I stood motionless, trying not to gag from the smell. Was it worse that the Weres hadn't been allowed to transform completely? That someone in this perverse little Trust had the power to force them to stop changing midway so that parts of their torsos, arms, and legs still maintained a semblance of humanity and therefore a horrible vulnerability to animal attack? Was I more revolted by the members' loud cheering of their chosen fighters along with the exchange of euro notes when side bets were won or lost? Or was I the most disgusted that, facing some real wicked shit, my mind still focused on maintaining the illusion of overwhelming strength we'd begun to create outside, realizing that I'd be utterly humiliated if I puked, or worse, fainted?

Genti and Koren distracted me from my internal mayhem, their jubilant screams jerking my head to the right, where they stood on their seats, cheering the werewolf to victory. Rastus stood beside them, saving the sliver of voice that had returned to him. Just as juiced, he demonstrated his support by slamming his fist against the table so that all the plates and silver jumped like frightened servants. Even as I noted their positions, Meryl slipped into the room behind me and took a chair next to Rastus, closest to the table's head. That surprised me. I'd have thought, socially speaking, she'd be required to sit farthest from Disa. But maybe Genti wanted as many bodies as he could get between himself and the *Deyrar*, just in case she completely flipped out. I also wondered about the significance of the empty spaces next to Genti, enough to seat four or five more. That open expanse of tablecloth struck me as odd.

"Rip his throat out, Wolfie!" Genti screamed, tearing a chunk out of his enormous turkey leg, as if to demonstrate. He'd set his hat down in front of his red glass plate, revealing a bald head that shone with excited perspiration as he pounded the air with his free fist, shouting exultantly as the wolf sank its fangs into the bear's shoulder.

Across the ring, Niall and Admes were talking so intensely it almost looked like a fight. Only the way Niall would occasionally touch Admes on the back of the hand to emphasize a point or Admes's tendency to rub Niall's shoulder hinted at civil conversation. Their human companion roared with approval as the bear shook the wolf off and followed with a belt to the head that sent a couple of teeth flying. The guard jumped up to gather a winning bet from Marcon, who shook his silver ponytail with admiration, then sat back down near the head of their table, which also had room for several more at its base. What was the deal with that? Or was it anything at all? Maybe I was just trying to avoid thinking about the senseless bloodshed going on almost within arm's reach.

I tore my gaze from the fight cage and looked at Vayl, trying to make my face a mirror of his since I could feel calculating eyes on me, including Disa's. "So this is the *Sonrhain*?" I asked between lips that tingled from pressing them together hard enough to clog my gag reflex.

"Indeed," Vayl said, his voice devoid of expression. "And Disa has honored us with a place at her side."

I pulled out my Lucille Robinson persona. She never wants to slam people against the wall and ask them how *they* like being the weak link in the food chain. "Seats with a view. How nice." I flashed Disa Lucille's brilliant smile, which has performed small miracles for me in the past.

She'd been smiling as well, one of those semi-vicious grins you get from people who are setting you up. Now she banged her teeth together so hard her fangs sank into her bottom lip. She licked off the resulting droplets of blood, swallowed whatever words she meant to say, and motioned to the chairs Vayl had pointed out earlier.

"Where's the third?" I asked.

"What do you mean?"

I nodded to Dave. "My guy here needs a place to sit."

She looked at him as if he'd just appeared, maybe stepping out of one of her personal guard's stomach folds. "I assumed he would stand," she said, throwing a glance over her shoulder at the men who flanked the doorway like a couple of Buddha statues. "Well, I suppose we could—"

"Don't bother," said Dave shortly. "I see an open spot down there." He nodded to the right end of the horseshoe and, before I could object, headed off alone. I nearly went after him. But I couldn't think of a good excuse to drag him back. He'd have a great view of the whole room from there, so he could provide a proper defense should we need one. Plus, I'd look like such a coward chasing him down. As if I was afraid to sit with the big bad vamps all by my lonesome.

We settled by Disa, Vayl next to her with me to his right. Sibley sat to her left. Disa leaned forward so she could converse with me. "You are so fortunate to catch us during our celebration. So rarely does a new *Deyrar* rise that we have few excuses to fight the Weres."

I nodded and faked a smile. "Ha. Well, Vayl and I are just lucky ducks today then, aren't we?" I didn't clench my teeth as a new round of roars filled the room, coming both from the ring and the audience surrounding it. But it was close. I ran my hand down the side of my pants, tracing the outline of the knife I kept sheathed inside my right pocket. A memento of an ancestor's World War I days, it practically buzzed, tempting me to pull it. Take off Disa's head and turn the we-got-a-new-leader bash into a wake.

To distract myself from my fantasies, I said, "Vayl has given you our hostess gift, I see."

"Yes, Vayl's kindness is even as I remembered it," she said as she turned her eyes to his. In her cleavage hung a silver chain from which dangled a pendant in the shape of a Hydra—the Trust's symbol. We'd meant to give it to Hamon, but Vayl had decided Disa wouldn't mind its masculine overtones. And he'd been right. What she didn't know was that my buddy Bergman had embedded a minuscule camera in the Hydra's oversized chest, one that would send images to the three palm-sized computers he'd provided for Vayl, Dave, and me as part of the bundle. Additionally, he'd implanted tiny doodads he called remote sensors in each of the Hydra's nine heads. While he wouldn't thoroughly explain their function, he would say that if the villa had a decent security system (and he figured, as paranoid as Hamon had been when Vayl had known him, it had to) it would be the latest in high-tech, wireless, camera-rich packages. Which meant the sensors could easily detect and latch on to the Trust's camera feeds, allowing us to download the images for our own use. It had more aggressive applications as well, which we might, or might not, put into use as the situation warranted.

As I watched Disa run her fingertips across the Hydra's serpentine body, I reminded myself to erase anything related to this particular scene that might appear on my Monise, which was Bergman's moniker for our minicomputers. If Vayl wanted a copy for posterity, let him record it.

He rested his arm across the back of my chair, not touching me, but making a statement all the same. "My *avhar* and I look forward to continued cooperation with you and your Trust, Disa."

I couldn't help it. The smug just leaped up in me like a fat wad of chewing gum demanding to be bubbled. Now I knew why Cole was addicted to the stuff. Since I couldn't quite keep the smile from my face, I turned to my neighbor. "Lucille Robinson," I said, introducing myself again. Normally I wouldn't, but this group seemed overwhelmingly self-centered and unlikely to remember anyone else's name for long.

"Charmed," she said, sounding anything but. She didn't bother reintroducing herself.

"You're Meryl, right?" Indifferent nod. "Nice to meet you." *Not really.* "Are you going to be part of the negotiating team?" I asked.

She shook her head. "Only the *Vitem* will do that. And, of

course, Koren will go." She jerked her head toward the makeover show candidate stomping her rotting canvas flats on the seat of her chair. Good God, she hadn't even taken the time to change out of her blood-stained shirt!

"Why her?"

"She was Hamon's *avhar*. That gives her the right to participate in events he arranged before his death."

Hmm, so Eryx *was* permanently out of the picture. That made Koren something like a widow. What I would be if Vayl ever . . . *Nope, don't go there, Jaz. Vayl will never . . . You'll probably go before he does. Yeah, that's the most likely scenario.* I glanced at him, taking in his stern profile, that long Roman nose, those luscious lips.

The last time they'd touched mine had been during our previous mission. A world-spinning kiss that still danced through my dreams, teasing me with its sugary deliciousness. A big part of me felt like a hound at the end of its chain, straining, slavering. *Woof, woof, ya big hunka man flesh!* But we'd left our relationship in limbo. Floating on a raft that couldn't ground itself until he found a way to put the memories of his centuries-dead sons to some sort of rest.

He'd waited a long time for me to sort through my horrors. And it could be I still wasn't done. You don't love a man like Matt Stae and then watch him die without taking some major hits. Although I'd said my goodbyes, I still woke up some mornings pressing my hands against my chest because my heart ached so badly just to see him again. Five minutes. Sometimes that was my greatest wish. Just to talk to him, know he was okay and that he missed me too. See, the trail for Vayl and me had never been easy. He'd been patient with me. I figured I owed him that and more.

I looked down at my plate, pulling myself back to reality, understanding part of what I'd just done was an attempt to escape. To step out of this crazed scene with its snarling, half-human

Weres and screaming bloodsuckers grooving on the carnage. I took a deep breath. *Okay, Jaz. Do something. Say something. Anything to block the noise.*

I turned back to Meryl. Not that I expected her to know anything. But talking to her was better than sitting silent while the wolf and bear destroyed each other. "So, had Eryx talked to Genti about how he wanted to handle negotiations?"

Meryl tossed her head, attempting to cow me with her superior beauty and fashion sense the way she must have once subdued the nerds at her high school. "He never told anyone anything, including the fact that he'd invited the *Tolic* and his *avhar* into the Trust."

Though Vayl seemed to be chatting it up with the *Deyrar*, when Meryl called him the *Tolic*, he stiffened so abruptly I thought for a second Disa had shoved a dagger through his heart.

I twisted in my seat, noted both of her hands wrapped around her goblet, and met her haughty gaze. The insult was clear. Vayl had left the Trust. Something only one other vamp had done that I'd heard of — ever. He'd explained to me that many, if not all, of the members would consider his departure the worst kind of betrayal. Some would even call it treason.

I turned back to Meryl. "I'd be careful what words I used to describe my boss," I warned her, slipping my hand inside my jacket to emphasize my displeasure.

She raised her hands and sat back. "I'm just repeating what I've heard him called since I came here ten years ago."

Sibley leaned forward. "Many among us still feel the sting of Vayl's departure. He, almost like Hamon himself, was part of the foundation of our Trust."

"Well, I am here to build a new foundation," Disa announced.

"Of course. I did not mean to imply anything to the contrary," Sibley said quickly.

Disa's tone made my teeth clench. And her hold over these vamps, whose powers lapped at me like lions' tongues, put me on edge. Why was she so adamant about her position? It just made me want to annoy her more. "How did Eryx die?" I asked, barely managing not to jump as the wolf squealed in agony and blood spurted onto the floor in front of me.

"He was in an automobile wreck," she said, her voice suddenly lacking as much inflection as Vayl's. I recognized her game right away, mainly because I'd seen him pull it so often. She was crushing her emotion, stuffing it into a tiny lockbox.

"Wow, that's so . . . normal. How did he not survive?"

Meryl answered me. "According to Genti, who was driving behind him, he pulled out in front of a fast-moving delivery truck. The impact took off his head."

Yeah, that would do it. "Was anyone else in the car with him?"

"You walk outside the Trust," snapped Disa. "Do not presume to meddle in our private matters."

"Sorry," I said easily. "You know how we cop types are. Very detail-oriented." But behind the Lucille mask, my eyes narrowed. It seemed like anywhere Edward Samos went, people ended up dead. So why not do a little Q & A to see if Eryx's recent passing sounded fishy, or if it really was just a coincidence? So I'd dug in, knowing Rule Number One regarding tragedies — people love giving you all the gory details. Unless they're criminally involved.

So. Had Disa killed Eryx? Maybe. She clearly thought his leadership skills stank, and some of the *Vitem* might even back her up on that count. But her timing? Well, maybe she figured Eryx would foul up the negotiations and they'd end up wriggling in Samos's net unless she did something extreme. Or maybe she hadn't even known about Samos's offer.

It was all theoretical BS right now, but I wondered if Vayl was sharing similar thoughts when he said, "I am missing several members of the Trust whom I expected to see here." He motioned to the empty spots at the tables that I'd noticed earlier. "Where are Aine, Fielding, and Blas, as well as my old friends Camelie and Panos? Did they also die with Eryx?"

The room didn't exactly go silent. The animals fought on, persistently savage, mad to kill each other and accomplishing the job, if very slowly. But the vampires all turned to their *Deyrar* to see how she'd react to Vayl's question.

"You have been gone, how long now, Vayl?" Disa asked.

"Nearly one hundred years," he said.

"A great deal can happen in that time." She seemed to be talking about more than the vampires he'd mentioned.

"Like what?" I asked.

"Change," she said, almost dreamily. "Evolution. The rise of new, exciting times, when Trusts can be more than stale, enclosed conclaves. When they can become—"

Two echoing booms silenced her, brought me out of my chair. I drew Grief and released the safety as I raked the room for the shooter. When I saw him standing in the corner, his Beretta still pointed at the fallen Weres, I finally realized how close to the edge my brother had come.

CHAPTER FIVE

The room swirled with the kind of silence that falls just before riots break out. Dave's voice thundered in the empty air, so painfully loud a couple of vamps covered their ears. "They're free!" he shouted. His wild stare burned into every pair of eyes in the room. "And as soon as I find out which one of you leeches trapped the poor sons of bitches, I'll make sure you go the same way!"

Holy freaking crap! Dave's gone ballistic!

Part of me wanted to pick him up and shake him till his teeth fell out. The rest couldn't blame him. Because he'd recently been the victim of a necromancer called the Wizard. This terror broker had killed and then reanimated him, only in such a way that his soul had remained trapped inside his body, slave to the Wizard's whim. We'd rescued him, only to have him die for real. Which was where my Spirit Guide had stepped in.

Raoul recruits people like Dave and me to fight the extra-creepies. Those others regular humans can't quite perceive and don't have the power to combat. We have the edge because we've died at least once already. And having been brought back by Raoul, we've developed special abilities that give us a leg up. Unfortunately, the hell we go through afterward also has a tendency to tear through our sanity like a California wildfire. I should've known Dave would identify with anything that had been forced into service against its will. But I never would've guessed he'd resort to mercy killings to fix what was broken.

Before anyone had time to react, Vayl lunged to his feet, his chair flying back into the wall as he rose. "Nobody move!" he snapped, his power billowing through the room like the fog from dry ice. Though I could hear the hypnotic command in his voice, I was surprised the vamps in the room obeyed. "This entertainment has voided our contract!"

I stood beside him, making sure my presence and the fact that I'd pulled Grief let everyone know they should think carefully before they reacted.

Disa's lips stretched so far back her snarl might actually leave wrinkles. The *Vitem* looked equally annoyed. Genti jumped up on the table. "Fine with me!" he shouted. He pointed a long-nailed finger at Dave. "That bastard has spoiled our *Sonrhain*. Kill him!"

Niall and Admes stood as one. "Genti, no!" they yelled in concert. Almost in harmony. If I hadn't been so worried, I'd have suggested they try out for their local talent show.

Genti, who'd kicked his furry hat onto the floor in his rush to kill my brother, bared his fangs. But he did hop down.

"What did you mean by that statement, Vayl?" asked Niall.

"Precisely what I said. Lucille and I are agents of the United States government. We would not work with Hamon unless he agreed to curtail all illegal activities while we sheltered in the Trust."

"Funny time to bring up that detail," snapped Disa.

Vayl's look could've frozen lava. "I did *just* suggest a review of the contract. However, you required me to attend the *Sonrhain*. As your guest, I could hardly refuse." And, as her outnumbered guest, he couldn't object to the horror show. Until Dave had done it for him, and then he'd had to take it to the finish.

An agonized whimper from the middle of the room caught everyone's attention. "They're not dead," I whispered.

"David's gun is not loaded with silver?" asked Vayl.

"He wasn't expecting to battle Weres on this mission." We stared at the fallen beasts, who'd both taken full animal form. I'd heard they healed better that way. But I didn't much care for sharing the same space with them, unchained and wounded as they were. "Do you suppose they're still enspelled?" I asked.

"I doubt it," Vayl answered. "Ending the fight should have effectively canceled the charm."

"Which means?"

"It is hard to say. They are already struggling to stand, and as soon as they are able, they will no doubt attack. They may choose one another, as before. Or they may go for easier game."

"But . . . the fence." I looked up at the ceiling, as if to command the hooks it hung from to hold.

"It is more to keep them from stumbling into the audience than to provide true protection. The power that half changed them was what prevented them from leaving the ring to begin with."

God*dammit!* "Dave! Get over here!" He looked my way without really seeing me. Still stuck in his own nightmare.

The wolf got to its feet first, stood unsteadily, and glared around the room. Was it looking for the weapon that had taken it down? Or the vamp whose influence had forced it into battle?

"Get those Weres out of here!" shouted Disa.

"Would it not be smarter to get *us* out and secure the room until they transform?" suggested Vayl. I'd begun nodding before he even finished his sentence. Sounded like a solid plan to me.

But Disa stuck out her jaw. "*I* am the *Deyrar!*" she yelled, her eyes bleeding to black as the rage took hold.

I opened my mouth to tell her she was also the Idiot, but Vayl put a hand on my arm. *No time.* He slanted his gaze toward the ring. The bear had risen as well. And he was headed for my brother.

"Dave!" I yelled. He didn't respond, though he was looking straight at me. "You're about to get eaten by a bear, ya dumbass!" I shouted.

That got his attention. As he turned to face the coming threat, I jumped on the table, figuring darting around all the pushed-out chairs and potentially uncooperative Trustees would cause fatal delays. I raced toward my brother as the bear attacked, charging at him with eye-popping speed.

The old Dave would've emptied his clip into the beast. But now, having freed it from bondage, the last thing he wanted to do was put it down again. Even temporarily.

I didn't have that problem.

I shot the bear at least five times before it reached Dave, and still I was too late. Its momentum tore the fencing from the ceiling as if it was a shower curtain. Beneath a cloud of dust and tile it surged forward, the sweep of its giant claws nearly taking his head off as it swung its massive forearm at him.

Somehow, probably aided by his Sensitivity, Dave managed to backpedal fast enough that the bear only got one hit on him before it fell. But it was a skull bender. A claw across the forehead that released a four-inch flap of skin and a gush of blood that instantly blinded him.

It's like vamps, I reassured my jittering heart as I reached Dave and grabbed him by the arm. *He can't become a werebear unless the sucker damn near kills him first.*

I jerked him away from the monster, whose wounds were already beginning to heal, and tried to lead him toward the door. But our way was blocked by Genti and his crew, who'd decided the best way to remove the bear was to roll it up in the tablecloth and drag it out. Rastus, Koren, and Meryl were hastily removing all the delicate and, no doubt, highly expensive tableware to chairs while Genti urged them on to greater speeds without lifting a single finger to help.

Are you kidding *me?*

I slammed Dave against the wall. "Don't move!" I yelled, as he tried to clear the blood from his eyes.

I grabbed the edge of the nearest tablecloth and jerked.

You know that trick you see on TV, where the material slides out from beneath all the plates and glasses, leaving everything unmoved and perfectly intact? Too bad I can't do that one.

China, hand-blown glass, silver, and bowl after tureen after platter of food crashed to the floor as Genti, Rastus, Koren, and Meryl gaped at me like the owners of an antiques store that's just been rolled.

"Here!" I threw the cover at them. "Now *move* your asses!"

"How dare you!" cried Genti.

"Genti Luan!" Disa yelled. She hadn't moved from her spot. She might not like getting her hands dirty, but she sure loved to throw her weight around. He responded instantly.

"Yes, *Deyrar.*"

"Wrap up that bear!"

While the Four Stooges got busy, I pulled Dave farther from danger. His shirt stuck to his chest, it was so soaked with blood. Too much of it, every damn where.

"You going to be okay?" I asked as I hustled him toward Vayl.

"Of course." He would say that. If the creature had chewed off his arm he'd have wrapped a tourniquet around the stub and laughed it off as a flesh wound. My brother. The original Black Knight.

Shouting from the other side of the room distracted me. Niall, Admes, and their human guardian had surrounded the wolf. Or so it seemed. The human carried a small-caliber handgun, hard to see what kind from my angle. Admes held a sword. *No way,* my mind whispered. But I couldn't mistake the nearly two-foot-long pointed blade with its ivory hilt. I'd seen the same model on display in the American Museum of Natural History the last time I'd hit New York. *That's a gladius. Admes is fighting with a sword that's twice as old as Cassandra.*

Dave's new flame, whose psychic gifts had helped us out of a jam before the two had even met, had let slip that she'd been globe trotting for a thousand years. If Admes was as old as his blade, we must all seem like irritating little rugrats to him.

For all his age, the broad-shouldered vamp hadn't lost any of his fighting skills. And the wolf seemed to recognize a worthy foe when it saw one. Or two, actually, because Niall was stirring powers that raised every hair on the back of my neck. The wolf must've felt them, too. Because, after hesitating for a few moments, it picked out the lone human and attacked.

I'll give him this, the man Niall trusted to guard his sleep didn't panic. He stood his ground, obviously meaning to empty his gun into the wolf, thinking he had plenty of time to take it down. But he'd underestimated how much the animal had healed and the speed at which it could move. It exploded into him, knocking him back into the wall, cracking his skull so hard I heard the impact from across the room. Before Niall and Admes could pull the Were off, it had ripped the man's throat out, spewing arterial blood in ever-weakening bursts that marked the last beats of his heart.

For a second that was all I could see. Blood on the floor, the walls, my brother's face, his shirt. And then a face swam out of that thick, dark fluid. One equipped with fangs that dripped so steadily it was as if they carried their own supply.

Its mouth twisted into an agonized grin. The eyes squeezed shut, fat tears trailing down the pitted cheeks of a man who looked like he'd survived slow torture only to find himself drowning in a pool of someone else's life source. "Dearling girl, I knew you would come," he gasped.

I hadn't had a nightmare in weeks. Now I knew why. My demons had been saving up, pooling their freakies for one big *BOO!* that would instantly transport me to the horrors of my past. The ones I'd survived but hadn't stomached — the deaths of Matt, Dave's wife, Jessie, and our crew of Helsingers. This face didn't resemble any of theirs. And the sickest part? I almost wished it had.

I shoved my left hand into my pocket. Clutched the engagement ring Matt had given me fourteen days before our last moment together. I kept it there as a sort of talisman against exactly this kind of event. I shut my eyes. Tight. When I opened them the face was gone. But I'd activated the special lenses I always wore. The ones Bergman had engineered that allowed me to see in the dark. For a second everything glowed green with that extra edge of dark yellow and maroon that my Sensitivity had added to the mix after Vayl had taken my blood when his regular supply had been tainted.

I didn't need better vision, dammit! In fact, I wanted some kind of reverse Lasik. *Yeah. Less graphic input, that's the ticket. Because it's getting to me just like that song "Doctor My Eyes" by Jackson Browne,* I thought. *I've left them open for too long.*

Chapter Six

I stood by the shuttered and shaded window of the suite Disa's boy toy, Tarasios, had led us to, watching Vayl stitch Dave's head back together. But my mind was on the Weres.

Which I hadn't hallucinated one single bit, thank you very much. Wait, I wasn't happy about that either. But at least it was real, dammit! The Weres had been rounded up and locked away where they could heal before returning to their regular lives. This was according to Tarasios, whose IQ continued to drop in my estimation the longer I knew him. So I'd questioned him closely on the details as he'd led us away from the blood-drenched dining room and the mutilated body of Niall's dead guard.

"Where will they be kept?" I'd asked, looking over my shoulder at the muzzled wolf being carried by Niall and Admes with the help of a curtain rod they'd run between its tied legs.

"The wolf goes in the garage," said Tarasios. "I had to back the cars out myself, because they might get scratched otherwise. And the bear goes in the wagon house. I don't know why it's called that because we don't have any wagons. But that's its name, so that's where he went."

I looked at his perfect face, serenely perched above his magnificent physique and thought, *God is a practical joker.* "Is the wagon house that big building at the end of the front-door path?"

He nodded. "I guess it's a guesthouse now," he said, snickering like a kindergartener at his own pathetic humor.

In order to get us to our temporary digs, Tarasios had to lead us past the villa's front entrance. Even if my Spirit Eye hadn't practically rolled back in its socket from the power I felt in that spot, I'd have had to stop. We stood in the second-floor hallway at a railing that overlooked the massive arched doorway, the handles of which were life-sized carvings of skeletons made to look as if the door was another dimension from which they were just emerging. I could imagine that when you let a guest through, it almost felt like you were pulling the skeletons into your reality as well.

Just inside the threshold stood the rough-hewn statue of a god. Though it had no face, I could tell it was divine. Nothing human could walk upright with a wang that size. The fact that it also had Pamela Anderson breasts just kinda made you go, *Huh.*

A chandelier the size of a big-screen TV hung from the ceiling, its brass base elaborately woven to resemble a face. I looked closely, my skin going cold as I peered, wondering if . . . no. It wasn't the same as in the vision I'd had. But it definitely read vampire, its eyes, ears, and fangs dripping ruby-colored crystals, its hair a mass of tiny white bulbs.

On the burgundy tiled floor lay a rug that looked to have been woven from human hair. The umbrella stand beside the stairs might once have served as a man's wooden leg. But those weren't the most interesting items in the room. That honor definitely fell to the masks.

They hung from the wall that lined the staircase leading up to our landing. Made of metal, ivory, glass, and wood. Carved with lasers and pocketknives. Ranging in size from yeah-that'll-fit-your-hamster to a whopping let's-see-how-many-college-students-will-fit-into-this, these were the source of the power that made my teeth try to sink back into my gums.

"That's quite a collection," I said, waving to the wall and then sticking my hand in my pocket before Tarasios could see the shaking. What the hell was the Trust *doing* with all that *alakazam*?

"That's just supposed to be like the spokes of the wheel," said Tarasios enthusiastically. "Disa says somewhere there's a——" He stopped, covering his mouth like a kid who's about to reveal the location of his mom's Christmas presents.

"A what?" I asked.

"Nothing. We'd better go." Tarasios hurried on, leaving Vayl and me to exchange curious glances over Dave's hanging head.

The more twists and turns we took inside that maze of a mansion, the freakier the decor got. Naw, I was cool with the black carpeted halls hung with red and gold flocked wallpaper. What shook me was the little zap of power I detected when we passed a glass case full of skulls whose teeth had all been removed and lined up neatly in front of them. Or the shelf full of ancient clay bowls whose internal stains, I sensed, had not been caused by clothing dye. I was just plain startled by a large frame that looked blank until you'd almost passed, and then you realized it contained a pair of holographic eyes.

Dave saw them too, the suddenness of their appearance causing him to stumble, making me want to put a hand under his arm to steady him. By now his coloring had shaded from its usual wind-burned brown to a sickly celery. But if I offered help he might never speak to me again. Plus Vayl, walking on his other side, was quick enough to catch him before he fell. So I tapped Tarasios on the shoulder.

"We're almost there," he said, picking up the pace even more.

Okay, he really doesn't want to talk about the masks. Or probably anything else that's tweaked my freak-detector tonight. So let's try something else. "Aren't you worried about the police finding out about the Weres?" I asked Tarasios. "I know they're not protected any better than vamps. But you still need a good reason to have one trapped in your garage. Unless he's just mangled your family and you're waiting for the local executioner, I'd say you're in a legal shithole here."

"Well, Hamon's——" He blushed prettily, looking over one shoulder as if afraid Disa would suddenly jump from behind the statue we were currently passing. It was a rather gruesome depiction of Athena emerging from Zeus's head, which, while scary enough in itself, might even give me the screaming jeebies if she leaped out and yelled, "I am the *Deyrar*!"

"Go ahead," I said gently. "We won't tell her what you said about Hamon. Right, Vayl?"

"I doubt we would tell Disa if her own hair were on fire," Vayl muttered.

When Tarasios gave him a hurt look, I waved my hand around in front of him to get his attention. "He's such a kidder. Go on."

Tarasios shrugged, cocked his head to one side, as if slightly embarrassed. "I was just going to say Hamon's apartments should be empty. But we've been prevented—that is—we haven't been able to pack up his things, so there's no room for a Were there." He turned to Vayl in delight. "Did you hear that? Were there. I made a rhyme!"

"You're a poet and you don't know it," Dave muttered. "Now, where the hell are we staying?"

While Tarasios led us to our door, Vayl and I traded interested glances. What would keep a bunch of determined vampires from clearing out their dead leader's drawers? *Given Hamon's tragic end, I think I smell a death-spell. One designed to keep bad-wishers out of your goodies if you happen to kick it unnaturally soon.*

I wanted a look inside those apartments. But first I had to experience ours.

The suite consisted of two rooms. The first, which had been

painted forest green, couldn't decide what it wanted to be. A table that looked like it might've been rescued from a library fire had been shoved against the wall to the left of the main entry. Two straight-backed chairs were pushed so far beneath it they actually tipped backward slightly. A bookshelf made of some dark wood, maybe black walnut, ran the length of the back wall. Knickknacks like the broken pieces of pottery you might expect to pull from an archaeological dig, and figurines of naked women and small round men with enormous genitals ran rampant across shelves that held only a few samples of actual reading material, all of which were written in Vampere.

The middle of the room held a fountain featuring a nude woman holding an urn on her head. Six brown wicker chairs with flowered cushions snuggled up to it. Given my surroundings, I couldn't decide if I was supposed to study for my final or host a tea. Neither might prove to be the healthiest choice. Because the walls smelled vaguely of mold. Brown water flowed down naked-stone-lady's body. And I was certain, given the right chemicals, I'd discover the stains scarring the wooden floor at the adjoining room's threshold were blood.

Its open door invited exploration. But I figured Dave might appreciate some moral support, given that he looked like he'd just been bitch slapped by a gangbanger wearing steel gloves. So I stood by the covered window as he sat in one of the wickers, his nostrils flaring when Vayl shoved the needle too deep. To give him credit, my *sverhamin* worked with surprising care for one who'd seen, and done, so much violence. I don't know what I'd expected. Something more along the lines of an old Western maybe. *Here, chew on this stick while I dig around inside you and see if I can hammer every nerve ending in the immediate vicinity of my oversized, blunt-ended, outmoded instrument of torture — um, I mean modern medicine.* But it looked like Vayl had plenty of experience stitching up slash wounds.

Come to think of it, putting members of my family back together seemed to be becoming a habit with him. My mind tracked back to the first night we'd returned home from our mission to Iran. When I'd traced him to his doorstep.

I'd stood in front of the redbrick Victorian with its wraparound front porch and Rapunzel-let-down-yer-hair turret and tried to square it with my mental image of Vayl. Who'd never seemed that attached to home. I'd expected to find him in a place similar to mine. Small. Nondescript. Hospital cold. But Vayl had a blue gazing ball beside his front steps. And flowers. Which didn't calm me one bit. Because I was already pretty far gone. Not panicked, but getting close, which is maybe why I couldn't stop once I started pounding on his sturdy oak door.

"Jasmine?" He'd thrown it open so fast my fists connected with his chest before I could stop myself. He caught my hands in his and held them still. "What is wrong?"

"I—" I gritted my teeth, trying to keep the words simple in my brain so they'd come out straight. "I can't seem to stop sh-shaking."

I felt him lift me, heard the door close. I curled into his feverish warmth, knowing it meant he'd just emptied the packaged blood he kept in his fridge. I wasn't cold, but my teeth clicked like fingernails on a keyboard as I buried my face in his white silk shirt. I breathed in his scent. And still the shivers rocked me, as if I'd spent the past ten hours stuck in the back of a milk truck.

He sat down, holding me like a child on his lap. I got the impression of a room paneled in squares of rich brown wood, a couple of tall, ivory-shaded lamps, and a coffee table stacked with books. "Tell me," he demanded.

"I don't know—"

"When did it begin?"

"When I was unpacking. I was putting stuff in a pile to wash. Everything was okay. But then I opened my weapons case. And I got out the knives. The knife. To clean it. Because it still had Dave's blood on it. From when I had to cut him, to get the Wizard's ohm out of his throat. That—the thing the Wizard used to control him with when he was a zombie." Vayl knew all this. I was babbling. But I couldn't seem to stop. "Do you remember?" I said. "It contained part of his finger bone—"

"Of course."

"Th-that's when I s-started to sh-shake." It had gotten worse. Just talking about it sent me into such spasms that Vayl had to fold his arms around me and hold me tight to keep me from juking off the long leather couch we shared.

After a minute or so I calmed down enough to say, "What the hell is *up* with me?"

While Vayl held me around the waist with one arm, he slid his free hand into my hair. As he slowly and repeatedly ran his fingers through my curls, he leaned forward until his forehead touched mine. Every move he made seemed gauged to relax and, bit by bit, I did feel myself begin to unwind.

"Jasmine, correct me if I am wrong. But in the past three months you have been murdered by a Kyron and brought back to life by Raoul. Spent weeks in hospital. Become an aunt. Endured killer nightmares. Come to terms with the loss of your fiancé. Saved the world at least twice. Freed your brother from a cursed existence only to see him die. Rescued your niece from otherworldly soul stealers. Sighed with relief when David did come back to this life, but then lost that relief because the next minute you found your father was the target of a murderer."

Nodding didn't seem to be among my current skill set, so I jerked my head a couple of times. "That about s-sums it up," I said. Then I shut my mouth before I could accidentally bite my tongue.

"Darling, your body is telling you to give it some peace or it is going to shake you right into a mental institution."

I was torn. Should I be delighted that he'd called me darling? Or terrified that my boss had brought up the idea of dumping me into the nuthouse? My feet, which were dangling over the side of the sofa, began tap dancing. Not a pretty sight.

I tried to get up. "I'm fine," I said. "I'll be fine. I shouldn't have come. I shouldn't have b-b-bothered you."

"Jasmine, look at me." For once my Sensitivity failed me. That hypnotic tone in his voice demanded and my eyes glued to his. They were amber. Glowing. He leaned in and kissed me, oh so softly, once on each cheek. "You will be fine. You simply need time and rest. Go to sleep. That is where the healing will begin."

As usual he'd been right about me. I just wished Dave could've come home with us. Partaken of Vayl's wisdom. Maybe then he wouldn't be here now, torn up inside and out.

The cell phone in my back pocket vibrated, signaling the arrival of another text message. *Oh yeah, as if I didn't have enough guys to worry about. Then there's him.*

I pulled it out and checked the screen. Yup, it was from Cole. Now working his first solo mission, he'd become a real pain in my ass. And not just because every time my phone buzzed against my right butt cheek I knew his sweet, funny message would send me into a spiral of confusion and worry about how badly I was going to break his heart when I finally said, "No, Cole, I can't see me married to you."

Since I'd helped with his training, I also didn't appreciate the spike of fear that jammed itself into my spine when I thought of everything that could possibly go wrong with him out there on his own. Which was the main reason I tolerated his ridiculous texts instead of putting him in his place. At least this way I could be sure he was still kicking.

I read quickly, happy that Cole spelled most things out, saving me the labor of code breaking.

Bored as a gay guy at Hooters. Cold, too. Mark is late. Rude of him, yes? Dreaming of you in ski boots and fur hat—nothing else! Tell Vayl he sux. Luv, C.

Uh-oh. Cole sitting around waiting for his target to show makes me wonder who's going to get the banana up the muffler first. I immediately texted him back to behave himself and stowed the phone for later study. If I could figure out what part of the world Cole had been assigned to I might be able to give him better, more specific advice on how to stay out of trouble.

"I'm sorry, Jaz," Dave said.

"Yeah?"

"I know you're mad as hell right now."

"Really? How can you tell?"

"You're staring at my shirt. Which means you're not meeting my eyes. Therefore you're trying pretty hard not to punch me."

Oh. Ha, ha, ha, not at all. I was just hoping that bizarre, bloody face wouldn't reappear before we burn that rag you're wearing. And then, yeah, come to think of it, I may have to beat the crap out of you.

Before I could say anything, Vayl stepped in. "Tact does not run in your family, does it?"

Dave and I shared a wry smile. Together we said, "No."

Since that seemed to be the last word, Vayl leaned into his final stitches and I wandered into the bedroom. Just to the left of the door sat a canopy bed with a scrolled headboard. It was dressed in enough white lace for three brides, which made the arch-lidded trunk at its base seem like a shipwreck survivor. Beside it sat a table whose finish was flaking like hickory bark. It held a lamp and an empty wooden bowl big enough to hold an entire birthday cake. On the other side of the table sat an armchair in dire need of reupholstering, but once fit for royalty if the velvety blue and green fabric gave any clue.

Two white armoires that needed repainting covered the wall adjoining the bed. I was betting they blocked a window as well. The bathroom was just to the right, a mildewed, water-stained closet that I'd have to attack with a case of bleach before I'd feel comfortable using it. As in the sitting room, the floor had been left in its original wide-planked, wooden state.

I was getting ready to claim the bed and let the guys fight for floor space when I took a closer look at the painting mounted on the wall opposite the door. The bed's occupant would view this picture every night before closing her eyes. If she could manage sleep, that is, after subjecting herself to its bold, slashing images. It showed a vampire feast. Without actual food. Yeah, screaming victims, their blood running like red tar in a backdrop of a blazing city. Chicago, maybe, back when everything was flammable, including the sidewalks.

I thought about it a second. Would it be better to snooze in the sitting room next to the rusty water and the fungus-covered walls? Nope, I still wanted the bed. But the picture had to go.

A tap at the outer door brought me back to the sitting room. "Were we expecting somebody?" I asked Vayl.

"Always," he replied gravely.

I drew Grief, triggered the magic button, and sank into the chair nearest to Dave, holding the crossbow comfortably in my lap. All that my Sensitivity told me was that the creature on the other side of the door scented vampire. At least I had that. Before I'd died the first time, I'd been stuck in the five-sense box with everybody else I knew. I still hadn't figured out if these extra-specials had been worth the price. But at the moment—any advantage they gave me got a definite *hell yeah!* As soon as I nodded to Vayl he said, "Come in."

Marcon stepped inside and stopped, his eyes darting nervously from Vayl to Grief and back again. He winked, which I found odd, until he did it again and I realized he'd developed a twitch.

Which meant something had changed. He'd been nervous before. Now he seemed überstressed. "Disa and Sibley wish to discuss Hamon's contract with you," he said.

"It's a little late now," I replied roughly.

"Ah, my apologies." His bow, so courtly, took me to another age. I suddenly felt underdressed and ill-mannered. "Our sense of timing never seems to be in step with that of the outside world," he said.

Despite my obvious redneck ancestry, I soldiered on. "What is there to discuss? You people are in breach. You've allowed injury to my guy, here. Plus, you don't seem to be able to tell your asses from a hole in the ground. What guarantee do we have that you won't pull some idiotic stunt during negotiations that will blow our chance to eliminate Samos, or worse, get us killed?"

Marcon's eyelid fluttered so wildly he put a finger to it and rubbed. "Sibley requested that I extend to all of you the *Vitem*'s deepest apologies, and ask if you would consider rejoining the contract. If so, we would like to confirm the details you and Hamon agreed to, as well as any new deals you might like to make."

"What did Disa say she would do to you if you came back with a negative reply, Marcon?" Vayl asked gently.

He shuddered. "N-nothing."

"But if I walked in the Trust once more, you would tell me . . ."

Marcon stared at him miserably, then shook his head. "You should never have left."

"I was little more than a killer when I was here."

"Yes, but you were *ours*."

Vayl shrugged. "Now I am the CIA's. And" — his eyes strayed to mine — "I am more."

Marcon's sigh could almost have been a sob. "What shall I tell the *Vitem*?"

Vayl tied off the last stitch and cut the thread with the scissors Dave handed him. "I will tell them myself."

"Do you want me to come?" I asked.

"Not this time," he said. Before I could argue, he was crouched in front of me, his fingertips warm on my face.

"I should be there to guard your back," I whispered as his eyes lightened to the green I equated with long, breathless kisses.

"That is David's job," he said.

But he's injured! Plus, the danger around us is so electric it's practically sparking. If we're separated here, where everyone's against us, will we ever come back together?

Small nod of Vayl's head. "Perhaps you could bring our bags in and get us settled. I believe that vehicle you wanted to take off-road is now parked in the garage. At least" — he lifted an eyebrow — "I am fairly sure Tarasios said that is what he did with it."

It took me longer than it should have to get his drift. First I had to get past the *I'm-not-your-goddamn-maid!* reaction before I could decipher his real message. Tarasios had pulled all their cars out of the garage. Ours wasn't even on Trust property. Which meant Vayl was giving me an excuse to go outside. Why?

Because Disa would never allow those Weres to live.

They were too hard to kill in their present form, so she'd probably just wait until they turned and then have one of her lackeys do them from a distance. It would be bad news for the Trust if the wolf got back to his pack and told his story. And the bear — well, he'd have his own loose-knit league who'd be enraged at his tale. Wars had started over less.

My job wasn't to prevent the conflict. That problem was for people higher up the political chain than me. I only had to save a couple of lives. For once. Which meant . . . *one more round with the injured, pissed-off Weres. Thanks a lot, boss.*

But I smiled inside. I so liked this part of him. Even a lot of humans I knew wouldn't have given a second thought to the welfare of those wounded moon-changers. But he'd made it part of our mission to ensure their survival.

"Will you be okay?" I asked Dave, knowing the question would piss him off. As expected, he launched out of his chair and grabbed his crossbow. "Aw, for chrissake, it's just a scratch! I'll be fine!"

I smirked. It had been a mean move. But I was sick of seeing him mope. Better to have him hurt and yelling than feeling crappy and keeping mum.

As Dave went to the bathroom to wash up, Vayl took me aside. "When I return, we need to talk."

Though he kept his voice low, I was sure Marcon could overhear us. So it seemed strange that he'd even bring up a private conversation for the Trust vamp to get curious about. "Yeah?" I said.

"I did not realize Disa was alive, much less living here still. Otherwise I would have told you of our history much sooner."

"Ah." Suddenly that word, "history," meant so much more than boring stories involving stuffy wig-wearing lawyer types.

"I am sure it is nothing to be concerned about, now that I have you, my *avhar.*" Vayl's eyes searched my face, almost like he was memorizing it.

But I couldn't stifle the creeping sense of dread I felt as we went our separate ways. Marcon gave me directions that I didn't need and led the guys away. I kept looking over my shoulder until they were out of sight. And then, realizing a divided focus could be the death of me, I shoved my concern to one corner of my mind and put all my effort into the job at hand.

I went back out to the courtyard. But I didn't try the vine-framed door; despite the villa's covered windows, I still suspected someone might see me from the inside. Instead I left through the open gate. Rather than hiking up the hill to where our SUV was parked, I followed the wall that circled the villa to the back. It stopped at the garage, which hadn't even existed in Vayl's time. When he'd drawn the layout of the place for us to memorize, he'd left it out completely, instead penciling in a one-room stone building he called the Gardener's Hut. He'd told us in his time it had been used as a sort of halfway house for newly recruited vampires.

"You had to keep them at such a distance?" Dave had asked incredulously. "What, were you afraid they were going to rise a half hour before everybody else, steal all the silver, and run off with the kitchen help?"

Vayl's chuckle, which usually sounded more like a guy choking on his porterhouse, flew round and full from his upturned lips. "You keep forgetting what a suspicious old wretch Hamon Eryx is. While he knows the Trust must grow if it is to survive, he still believes every other Trust is trying to infiltrate him and learn all his secrets, thereby stealing everything he has worked so hard to build."

"So why doesn't he just turn people?" Dave asked. When I gaped at him, he raised his hands. "Not that I'm advocating the practice. God knows—" He shook his head at me. "No, I'd never be okay with that, Jaz."

My heart, which had twisted painfully at his question, relaxed. His wife had been turned before showing up at my back door, begging entry, planning violence. I'd ended Jessie's undeath, because I'd made her that promise long before either of us dreamed our fates could actually unwind that way. I nodded at Dave, grateful his forgiveness still held true.

He went on. "All I'm saying is, looking at it from Eryx's perspective, he'd have to think he'd get a more loyal brand of member that way."

"A valid view," Vayl replied. "But no one in the Trust is allowed to turn another. In fact, it is an offense punishable by execution."

That conversation seemed even more significant as I scoped out the back of the garage. I whispered to myself, "They kill their vamps for turning humans. Wonder what they do to humans for turning Weres loose?" I pulled Grief. "What do you say we don't find out?"

Outside the garage, on a wide concrete pad that stretched from the building to the lane, sat the vehicles Tarasios had moved. A BMW 523i that made my mouth water. A Porsche Boxster two seater that caused me to think things my Corvette would've considered adulterous. And a blue Fiat Scudo minibus that I could only assume the Trust used for field trips. It seated nine and looked like it had one of those tootie-toot horns that warn you all the passengers carry disposable cameras and close their shoes with Velcro straps.

The garage was windowless and the only other entrances were the shut and locked bay doors. So far the only close presence I'd detected was that of the werewolf inside. Since the locks were somewhat intricate, requiring time and possibly noise to defeat, I decided to check out the wagon house first. If I could free the bear more easily, so much the better for all of us.

The wagon house, surrounded on three sides by a confused mass of herbage that included chestnut trees and wild primroses, was a square, tile-roofed echo of the villa. To my relief, it held no vampires. All I felt was the prickling at the base of my brain that told me whatever lurked behind its extra-wide, barnlike door had a two-edged psyche, one of which was a beast.

This is just stupid, I told myself as I holstered Grief and pulled my coral necklace out from beneath my shirt. *That damn bear is probably waiting right inside, licking his chops at the thought of a little grain-fed American for his midnight snack.*

The shark's tooth at the necklace's center fit perfectly into the padlock that held the sliding door shut. I could almost see the tooth melding to the form of the key the lock required. *You know, Bergman may be too good. Sometimes it would be nice if I couldn't get into places. Like this one.*

The padlock clicked open. A voice sounding oddly like *South Park*'s Cartman echoed through my quivering brain. *Goddammit!*

Grief came back to my hand as if attached by a spring. I switched to crossbow mode for silence. Keeping my shoulder to the outer wall, I braced my foot against the door's edge and shoved. It slid a couple of feet to the left, opening a twenty-foot-tall crack that felt like a hole in the universe.

Nothing happened.

Is he in there waiting for me? Or is he unconscious? Why doesn't Vayl ever give me the easy jobs? I swear, if one of us was ever forced to get a massage, or watch the whole first season of Futurama *for Uncle Sam's sake—he'd assign that one to himself!*

"Would you get the hell home already?" I snapped. "I don't have all night!"

"Okay, okay, sorry if I thought maybe you'd come to kill me." I'm not sure which of us was more surprised when the werebear, now fully transformed to a towering hulk of humanity, came shuffling out of the barn with his hands raised. Well, one hand. The other was covering his manly parts, since the vamps hadn't seen fit to throw his clothes into captivity with him.

Though thick hair covered his chest, the pink puckered marks where Dave and I had wounded him practically glowed. And he'd been bitten so many times on the neck he looked like he was wearing a red chain.

"Do you remember anything that happened before you were brought here?" I asked.

He shook his head, his long brown curls bouncing like fishing pole bobbers as he moved. "Not much. I was flirting with a girl in the bar at the Hotel Patra. And then . . . nothing."

"What did the girl look like?"

"Lovely, clear skin with eyes like honey. Petite. Sweet. I didn't like her hair so well. But"—he shrugged—"it was worth all the rest."

"What was wrong with it?"

"She had the, what do you call them?" He scrunched his free hand into his own tresses until a hunk of it fit tight into his fist.

"Dreadlocks?" I asked.

"Yes."

Aha! So Meryl had been a key player in the Were-trapping scheme. "Okay," I said. "Now get going. I don't know how long they'll be busy, but someone's coming out here soon and it won't be to hand you a pair of jeans."

"But I must thank you. And to know your name, for the prayers of blessing."

"You're welcome. My name is Jasmine Parks." I did mean to say Lucille Robinson. But she's plenty blessed.

"Thank you, Jasmine Parks. My name is Kozma. And may Rhiaak bless you."

A sudden, loud boom from the vicinity of the garage made us both jump.

"Shit! The wolf!"

"We must save him!"

I put my hand on Kozma's chest as he tried to rush past me. Even from here I could tell. "He's dead. And soon the vamp who shot him will be coming after you. Can you run?"

"Not far. I am still weak from the wounds."

"O-kay. Follow me." The walk from the wagon house to the lane only took half a minute. But it was all uphill, and Kozma was sucking air after the first five steps.

I whispered, "He's coming. I can feel him. Too far away to hear us. Too close to dodge. Hide in the trees." I handed Kozma the keys to the Range Rover as I described where it was parked. "It's unlocked, and you'll find a change of clothes in the back. When you see it's clear, get your ass to town."

"How can I ever repay you?" he asked as he took the chain and looped it around his finger.

"Make sure the rental agency sends the vehicle back tomorrow. And look, I know your league is going to be pissed when you tell them what happened. Just keep them away from this Trust for at least a week, okay? By then our business with them will be finished and you can do anything you like with them."

From the light in his eye I figured whatever he had in mind wouldn't be pleasant. But, remembering the shot we'd just heard and the sudden absence of the wolf's imprint, I didn't really care. "Fair enough," he said.

I met Rastus halfway down the hill. He didn't even bother to hide the Makarov he held, which told me two things. The son of a bitch could pick his handguns. And I'd just hopped on a thin, shaky wire. Was it a bad thing that the head-banging, mosh-pit groupie in me craved a showdown? Maybe. It's not such a big deal when your only weapon is an emery board and your greatest skill is accessorizing. But given time and a little luck I could take out a small village if I freed that wild child inside me. And the fact that I could feel her clawing so close to the surface? Not a good sign.

On my back I carried the black bag holding my miniature armory plus Dave's pack. My left hand gripped the handle to my ratty old traveling trunk; my right held Vayl's suitcase minus an outfit for Kozma. I tightened my fists until it hurt. Maybe the pain would help me think straight.

"What's all this?" asked Rastus, waving his gun at me as if he thought I might be concealing several more Special Ops types in

Vayl's Samsonite. His voice had roughened since its encounter with my *sverhamin*'s sword. And I knew, from the look in his eye, he'd love to use me for payback. I hoped I wasn't about to give him an excuse.

I shoved my trunk at him so hard he either had to grab it or be trampled. "What's it look like?" I demanded. "Disa said you were coming twenty minutes ago. Where've you been?"

"I . . ." He gestured back toward the garage, realized that was a story he shouldn't tell. His eyes strayed toward the wagon house. "I have some—"

"Here." I unloaded Dave's pack, hung it over that waving arm, making it sag enough that if the Makarov went off it would take a chunk of my thigh with it. "You know where our suite is, right?"

"I'm kind of busy . . ."

I dumped Vayl's suitcase at Rastus's feet. Then I got in his face, started poking him in the chest. "You vamps think you're so special, don't you? Think you're better than everyone else on the planet! Too good to do dishes or take out the trash or carry luggage for mere humans!" I gave him a push that nearly toppled him over. "Well, you and your Trust can go fuck yourselves for all I care!"

I stomped into the courtyard, deposited myself in a chair, and ignored him as he spent thirty seconds trying to figure out what to do with his gun, finally decided it would be okay in the pocket of his coat, and then spent another minute trying to load up the stuff I'd dumped on him.

I waited for him to disappear inside the villa, then I checked out the keys I'd lifted from his jacket pocket. Hey, it wasn't in my nature to leave myself without wheels.

While I listened to the music of the Range Rover rolling Kozma away from imminent danger, I noted that one set of keys belonged to the minibus I'd seen parked just outside the garage. A couple looked like house keys. One might've been to a lockbox or safe.

And also hanging from the chain was a remote opener for the garage door.

Looking back to make sure Rastus had committed himself to his delivery job, I went out the gate and thumbed the remote just enough to allow myself room to crouch down and get a good view of the floor.

Like Kozma, the wolf had changed. He sprawled in a pool of his own blood as if he meant to swim in it. His lips were still drawn back in a snarl, his fighter's eyes wide and angry.

Wait a second. Shouldn't they be empty? Is this sucker still alive? Can't be. I don't feel a presence . . . do I?

I ducked under the door, closed it, and moved to his side. While I hunted for a pulse I reached out with that extra sense Vayl had been nurturing since day one. There it was, the smell of werewolf, so faint it barely penetrated the vampire din coming from the mansion. And the pulse — also hardly existent.

"Aw, geez. *Now* what am I gonna do with you?" I whispered.

I knew enough about Weres to kill them, and that was about it. So the bullet Rastus had used must've been silver. Even if it had gone completely through his body, it had probably left enough residue to cause a fatal poisoning. But Rastus had played it lazy with that single shot. If you want to make sure a Were is dead, you have to cut off his head. Because he's capable of sending himself into a trance while he tries like hell to heal. Which is what this guy seemed to have done. I supposed that meant he had a chance. If we had a place to stow him. If we could find somebody to draw out the silver and pump in a buttload of antidote.

I stared around the garage, searching for inspiration.

A workbench stretched across the far wall. Shelves full of paint, oil, fertilizer, and whatnot filled both sides of the place. A garbage can full of shovels and rakes took up one corner. Other than that — only blood.

"He must've lost half his supply already," I whispered hopelessly. I was so bummed the Were was going to die I didn't even blink when a face, *that* face, appeared again, swimming in his blood. "Great. Just when I think I'm pulling myself out of that pit of blackouts and nightmares that came after—after the Loss. I finally start pulling myself out of that hell and what happens? I go stark raving mad."

"I love the mad," said the face with an anguished smile. "They are so much more interesting than the sane."

"Jesus Christ, could you at least not talk to me while I'm losing my mind?"

The face twisted. "That name is anathema to me. And I am already in enough pain. Can we at least agree that you will abstain from holy references and I will treat you as if you were stable until after we have saved the Were?"

"Only if you tell me your name."

"But I do not know. Every day it seems as if I lose more of myself. Soon there will be nothing left."

I could've told him he was already little more than narrowed eyes, pitted cheeks, and long drippy fangs protruding from a mass of spilled heart-fluid. But we didn't have that kind of time. And I wanted the conversation to get saner, not weirder.

"Okay. I have maybe five minutes until Rastus comes to dispose of this almost-corpse. So. Considering that he's damn near dead, do you have any idea how to reverse that?"

"Fresh blood."

"I'm not putting anything of mine near his mouth."

A breath of annoyance. "As if he could swallow it. No, woman, be direct. I can feel your powers from here. Just a few drops in the wound will begin the process. You should know what to do next."

With no time to stall, I did anyway. "How's my blood going to help? He's so far gone."

"It will act as a stimulant. Much as doctors administer adrenaline to patients who are severely allergic to bee stings."

While my hallucination had been talking I'd finally decided to get busy. I'd pulled the bolo out of my right pocket. *Talk about overkill*, I thought as I made a quick, horizontal incision about four inches above my wrist. One of my throwing knives would've worked better. But I hadn't strapped them to my wrist since returning from Iran.

Holding the cut above the Were's bullet wound, I squeezed my arm, forcing as much of my blood to drip into him as I could manage on short notice.

Nothing happened.

It won't be long now, I told myself. *Then I'll leave. After the mission I'll contact his pack and let them know what happened. Maybe try to help them locate the body.* My eyes strayed to the shovels in the corner. We'd probably never find it.

I was so sure the Were was going to die that when he grabbed my arm with both hands I jumped a couple of inches off the floor. "What the hell?"

He muttered something I didn't understand. It sounded like Greek. He surged upward in a half sit-up, using my arm as a brace. We froze in that position, our eyes meeting in a moment of perfect comprehension. I felt my vision expand, as if my contact lenses had suddenly become telescopic. More than that. My Spirit Eye, which usually allowed me to sense *others*, track them, mark their vulnerabilities, and take them down, turned inward. And I Saw that I could wrap my vision around him. That I could use it to reach inside him, blast the blood I'd donated across his internal wasteland, and make it work like rain in the desert.

So I did.

What I didn't expect was the return. This must've been what Vayl had meant when he'd first taken my blood. That, despite appearances, it wasn't a donation. It was an exchange. For a moment that felt somehow eternal, the Were and I existed inside each other. No lies. No bullshit. I *knew* him. Not details, like a name and address. The big picture. Intentions, beliefs, hopes, regrets. They all swirled among my own, stirring, sparking, but never judging. And, just like that, I loved him. Not like I had Matt. Not like I could love Vayl. More like how I'd cared for my vamp-slaying crew in that once upon a time when I'd believed they'd live forever.

As soon as I felt his vitality rise, I closed my Spirit Eye. I realized I was covered in sweat, suffering from a pounding headache, a crushing desire for chocolate chip cookies, and a cramp in my right foot from sitting at the wrong angle.

"Holy *shit*, let's not do that anymore, all right?" I muttered. "That's just too . . . extreme. Plus, it makes you talk to yourself afterward." I pulled the Were to his feet. He said something else in Greek. "Sorry, buddy. My universal translator is still in the aw-please-you-gotta-build-this stage."

"Where are we going?" he asked in perfect English.

"To hide you. What's your name?"

"Trayton."

Come on, pal, please stop looking at me like your mind's blown too. Let's pretend we're normal for a little while longer.

"You can call me Lucille. Listen, I happen to know there's a secret tunnel leading from the wagon house into the mansion. You're going to have to walk about two hundred yards, naked, in sixty-degree weather. Can you handle that?"

"I can do anything you ask." Trayton gazed at me with copper-colored eyes that seared themselves into my heart. The other reason I never wanted to repeat what I'd just done. Because, at least in this moment, with no one in my head but me, I could admit it hurt too much to care. In fact, it scared the shit out of me.

As a result, every act of kindness or (gulp) outright affection required a response from me that simulated a charge up a heavily fortified enemy hill. I didn't need more friends, dammit.

I hid my wince in my sleeve as I wiped it across my mouth. "Okay. Let's get the hell out of here before Rastus shows up and spoils all our fun."

CHAPTER SEVEN

I don't relish hanging out in guys' bedrooms. Especially ones that see lots of use. In this one, half-burned candles stood in groups of four or five on every flat surface — the claw-footed table beside the king-sized sleigh bed, the highboy, the tea table flanked by two armchairs covered in faded red fabric with gold diamonds. The bed hadn't been made, its rumpled blue sheets inviting its last occupants to resume where they'd left off ASAP. I apologized to them as I dumped Trayton in their midst, noting from their feel how expensive they must be.

"Don't get comfortable," I told him. "We're going to have to move again." *As soon as I figure out where we are.*

I moved quickly to shut the secret door, which disappeared behind an old grandfather clock that informed us we'd made it back inside just after midnight. The Were had survived into a new day. I decided to take that as a good omen.

The room had two obvious entries. The first led to a section of hallway I didn't recognize. But I immediately knew which way to turn to get back to the suite. I have an innate sense of direction, something that rose in me as part of my Sensitivity. I don't always appreciate it. Like when Vayl gets pissed and ditches me in the middle of Tehran, knowing full well I can find my way back to base. But that's another story. Now my pathfinder told me we'd come to the central base-block of the villa.

The second door required a key to unlock. But I could hear something when I put my ear to the smooth, dark wood. Music. Something slow and mournful coming from what sounded like a piano. Also, someone murmuring. Maybe even singing along.

A moan from the bed brought me back to the Were's side. His eyes fluttered open.

"Trayton? How're you hanging in there?"

"Hurts," he muttered.

"I know." I almost felt it myself. Could nearly see the poison, like a pus-colored pall, floating over his body.

"Do you remember anything about the person who ensnared you? What happened?"

"Smell."

"You smelled something?"

He winced. Blinked his thick black lashes. "Grapes."

Now why did that ring a bell?

Think of it later. Now, just get the wolf to safer ground.

I put my hand on his shoulder. "Sorry, buddy. We gotta move again. One more time, that's all. Then—" What? I might have pulled him from the brink, but he was still far from well.

One thing at a time, Jaz. Get him dressed. Find the suite without being intercepted. If he's still alive after that, then we'll talk cure.

I went to the highboy and started yanking out drawers until I found clothes for him. I grabbed the arm-length sword I discovered in the third drawer as well.

"These should fit you," I said as I laid the clothes and the weapon beside him. "Do you need help?"

"No," he said, giving me a grateful look. "I can manage."

He did get the clothes on, but I had to help him off the bed. Once he was up, he brought my hand to his lips. And licked it.

"Dude! What the hell!" I had one arm around his back. The other, clasped in his, badly wanted to wipe itself down the creamy white shirt that hung on him like a tent. That, more than any-thing, told me this room belonged to Admes. I hadn't caught his scent earlier. But now it would always be intertwined with the memory of the hurt in Trayton's eyes as he moved away from me and I caught a whiff of dead leaves. "Sorry," I said quickly. "I'm sorry. I keep forgetting you're part wolf. I just—I don't know a helluva lot about how you guys operate."

"Growling usually means get away," he said, his voice shaking enough that I looked at him again. And realized I'd never given myself the chance to *see* him until now. With him kissing the hem of Death's robes, why would I want to imprint the memory of a kid barely out of his teens with a mane of raven hair that kept flop-ping into his eyes? A face that had just found the sharp angles and planes of manhood. And that by-God-I-*will* expression that as-sured me he'd do his part when it came time to get well.

Now that face would forever be tied with what I'd learned of him during my donation. That he'd rather run than eat. He hated the taste of beer but would never admit it to his friends. And he'd promised himself to a Were named Phoebe, but kept putting off the final ceremony because, deep down, he feared she'd be a bad mother.

"Sorry about that," I said. "It's kind of a hereditary thing. My dad's a growler. Although *he* sounds more like a garbage disposal trying to process a set of flatware."

Quirk of the lips, so reminiscent of Vayl that I wished hard for my *sverhamin* to join us. Lift this boy in his arms. Make him *his* burden. "Your father sounds frightening," Trayton said.

"He once made a general cry."

"No."

"I shit you not. The guy had to retire after that. I mean, really, who's going to follow your orders after some damn colonel's re-duced you to tears?"

He shook his head, which is how people typically react to Albert stories. But the tightness around his eyes had relaxed. I checked the hallway. "It's clear."

We began our slow march to the suite. Trayton insisted on holding the sword, though he leaned pretty heavily on me. "I don't sense any vamps nearby," I whispered as we half walked, half staggered down a flight of stairs. "But if we happen to run into some, we need a plausible excuse for your presence. Unless they've all seen your human face?"

"No. Only the one with the gun and the one who smelled of grapes."

"So let's come up with a reason for you to be here with me."

"We could say I got lost while I was hiking and you found me outside."

"That sounds reasonable." He gasped as we reached the bottom step. We didn't have far to go, but then it looked as if he didn't either. I went on. "Of course, your story's a huge snore. We *could* say you're my escort. And I've, you know, worn you out." When he looked over at me, I wiggled my eyebrows suggestively. He grinned.

"As if you could," he whispered. Gad. Guys are guys the world over. Even when they're nearly dead!

I acknowledged his machismo with a smile. "Not that I'm suggesting anything," I went on. "I'm sort of spoken for. But it would make me look such the formidable opponent."

"So you're not with these vampires?"

"Just visiting," I confirmed. I felt his shoulders loosen. And before I knew it, his nose, nuzzling into my hair. I stiffened.

"Doesn't anyone ever touch you?" Trayton asked.

"Uh, no. That is, until just recently." I thought about it. Felt a surge of frustration. "And still, not much."

"Relax. It's not sexual, okay? Think wolf. I can feel your blood working in me. You're part of me now; you always will be. And

I'm yours. So let me learn you." Irritation in his tone, like I should be old enough to know this by now. As if I was keeping him from something that was his by right.

Okay, well, maybe it was that easy. I tried to lighten up. Then I saw myself, leading this post-adolescent down the hall while he sniffed my neck, up into my scalp. And I couldn't help it. Suddenly I was imagining a supermodel standing twenty paces downwind, holding a bottle of Head & Shoulders, saying, "Even werewolves can't tell the difference!" I started to giggle.

"What?"

"It tickles," I said. He took another deep breath. "Now it feels like you're blowing loogies into my roots."

I stopped, mainly because we'd finally reached the right door. But also because he'd laid his chin on my shoulder. "You know what I think?" he asked.

I glanced at him sideways, not quite willing to meet his gaze. "What?"

"You need a comrade."

"I have friends."

He shook his head, his hair waving across his face so I could barely see the shine of his eyes. "I've been inside your head, remember?"

"Could we not talk about that?"

He rubbed his cheek against my arm. Already his closeness seemed less threatening. "You keep the circle small and give only the affection you think you can bear. But, in doing this, you harm yourself the most." He nodded, as if deciding. "I can be what you need."

"I don't *need* anything from you. Except for you to heal up so I can get you back to your pack. The worst thing that could happen is for them to declare war on this Trust right now." I wrenched open the door, scooted him inside, and closed it. As soon as I had him settled in the bed it was like he decided he could stop faking. All the color drained from his face and he admitted to serious nausea. I brought the wastebasket over to the bed in case he couldn't make it to the bathroom.

"You must find the one who smelled of grapes," Trayton said. "He trapped me and forced me to turn. He can draw out the silver."

No problem. I'll just run around sniffing butts till I figure out which one of these egotistical maniacs smells like—wait a minute! Grapes! I know this one! From the courtyard! Nobody stood out in the crowd. Except Disa, who made me want to gag. And the grape guy—Niall! "I'll be back!" I said. But Trayton didn't hear. He'd already fallen asleep.

Chapter Eight

I found Niall back at the site of the *Sonrhain,* mopping up. Literally.

With Genti and his crew also involved in cleanup, I couldn't just walk over to where Niall stood in the ring and demand help with the Were. I wandered toward him, noting that the fence had already been rehung and he was transferring blood from the floor to a big blue bucket with the help of a bedraggled long-handled squeegee.

On their side of the room, Koren and Meryl swept up broken glass while Genti and Rastus piled the unmarred dishes into plastic bins. "Came to help out, did you?" Genti asked sharply.

"I kept the bear from taking off your head, didn't I?" I replied. I turned to Niall. "Sorry to bother you," I said. "But since Disa and Vayl are tied up with contract talks, they sent a note out that I'm supposed to get you so we can drive to town for champagne to celebrate the new agreement. I'd go alone, but I don't know the area."

My only warning that Genti had moved on me was the blur I saw out of the corner of my eye and the breeze that stirred the curls off my shoulders. I whirled, triggering the syringe of holy water.

"Genti Luan, stop!" I yelled. Knowing his name. That's what saved me. As soon as he heard it he froze, his fangs centimeters from my neck. I'd already plunged the needle into his chest. He looked down. "Holy water," I told him, my thumb firm on the plunger. I realized I was panting and made myself breathe deeper.

Niall had raised the mop in both hands like a spear. "Enough, Genti," he said sternly. "We need these people if we are to defeat Samos."

"Admes might not agree with you."

"Admes is patrolling, just as the *Deyrar* ordered him to do. Therefore she is happy with *him*. But think how she would react if she found *you* had killed her lead negotiator's *avhar*."

Genti's puffy lips began to tremble. "Remove the needle," he snarled.

My thumb hovered. So tempting. I yanked it out. "You're lucky I love my job. Because that's all that kept you from floating off into the air ducts just now." I reseated the syringe and stalked out of the room, assuming Niall would follow. He did.

"I need to talk to you," I growled, realized how that would sound to Trayton, and cleared my throat. "Uh" — I looked over my shoulder — "I noticed you weren't really into the Were-fighting while it was going on."

Niall allowed some distance to grow between us and the dining room before he answered. "I feel the same for my Trust as you do for your job. I imagine we have both done things we prefer not to in order to preserve our place in the order of things."

A-fricking-men. "You understand our contract?"

"I believe so."

"Okay, well, under its terms you're required to help us do everything we can to bring Samos down."

Niall looked amused, as if I'd begun to tickle him under the chin and talk like a baby. "I would hope so."

"In a roundabout way, this next favor I'm about to ask of you fits under that provision. Because if you don't help, your Trust could be in big trouble, which would weaken it to the point where

Samos might be able to do you from a distance. And if he doesn't have to show for a face-to-face, we're screwed."

"I have no idea what you mean."

We'd reached the suite by now. I took him inside, sat him on one of the library chairs, and put myself between him and the bedroom doorway. "Vayl and I couldn't allow the Weres to be killed."

"Of course not."

"Excuse me?"

"I was planning to speak to them later tonight."

"Niall, I know you helped trap them."

He dropped his head. "When the *Deyrar* orders . . . you obey. She knew I wished to deny her. But she'd called Admes to stand beside her at the time. Within reach of those razor-sharp—" He looked up, as if realizing he'd almost let a state secret slip. "I promised myself I would find a way to make it right afterward."

"Well, you waited too long. She sent Rastus to cap them."

"Cap?" He shook his head. "I don't—"

"Kill." *You goddamn old fart!* "I helped Kozma, the werebear, escape in time. But the wolf was shot." I grabbed Niall's hand and pulled him out of the chair. "He says you can help him."

"He *knows* me?"

"Your scent anyway. He's full of silver," I said as I led Niall toward the bedroom. "Do you know how to extract it?"

"Of course. My power centers around the moon-changers." As soon as we crossed the threshold to the bedroom he stopped so suddenly he jerked me back into him.

He took maybe three seconds to process the sight of Trayton resting on my brown pima cotton sheets with their gold chalice border. Then he closed the door so hard it actually shook, setting his shoulders against it, as if an army was about to take a battering ram to the other side.

"I thought we were coming in here for a jacket and car keys. So you could take me to where you were hiding him—in the woods perhaps. But he's here. In. The. Trust. Are you insane?" Niall demanded in a stage whisper.

I started to laugh. And couldn't stop. It became the most hilarious question anyone had ever asked me. Niall didn't get it, of course. As I held my aching stomach and tears rolled down my face, he went to Trayton and studied his wound, which I'd bandaged with a handful of Armor All wipes and some electrician's tape I'd found in the garage. Hey, somebody else could worry about infection. My job was to figure out how to keep the guy from leaving a trail for his would-be killers to follow.

"Trayton's my—" I stopped. "Just fix him, Niall. Otherwise the contract is void and Vayl and I will get Samos on our own."

He stared at the armoires, seeing beyond the wood and the walls behind them, struggling with the fears that skittered across his face like the bugs that frequent cesspools and murder scenes.

"All right," he said finally, his shoulders slumping wearily. "I'll do what I can." He bent over the Were, his power rising as he moved. The Vampere called this central ability a *cantrantia*. And I felt it like a shifting inside my bones. It grew out from him, a primal force that made me check to make sure I had a wall at my back.

I watched him pour that power into Trayton, who jumped as if he'd been shocked. Immediately his wound began to bubble, first red, then silver, as the toxins from the bullet bled out of him. He clutched at the mattress and bit his bottom lip as the pain rocked him.

Shit! I wrapped my hands around my stomach, which didn't like this show any more than my noodly knees did. How had I allowed this to happen? The last guy who'd tried to lick my hand had ended up dead on the floor of an abandoned warehouse thirty seconds later. Of course, he'd been a psychotic mail bomber who'd worked his way up the federal employee ladder to the secretary of state before we'd finally nailed him. But still.

Niall looked up to find me watching him. "We need something to wipe this off. Tissues. A towel. Quickly," he urged. "This will burn back into his skin if I don't remove it at once."

I dove into the cabinet under the bathroom sink, hiking supplies at Niall like the center for the Cleveland Browns. Finally he said, "That will do."

"So, you must enjoy a *cantrantia* that allows you to control Weres, huh?" I said as I came back into the room. "You've probably thought about starting your own little slave colony with that kind of power. Or at least a booming betting ring."

Not fair, snapped Granny May from her bridge table at the front of my brain. For this game she'd partnered with Running Bull against Doctor Who and Darwin. While Darwin nodded in agreement she continued, *He's helping and you pull out the smartass on him?*

She doesn't want to face the truth, replied my Inner Bitch from her favorite bar stool. *Every time she gets close to someone, she starts a fight. Then she doesn't have to.*

Can we stop the ego gossip, please? I begged. *This is not about me. This is about . . . well, shit, now I've forgotten. Let's hope the vamp remembers.*

Niall took his time cleaning Trayton's wound before he said, "The Weres are not, have never been mine to destroy. Not until . . ."

"Until Disa showed up?"

"Oh, she's been here since the mid-1800s. But she was just someone to be pitied back then. She kept her ambitions, and her powers, hidden until quite recently. By then it was too late for us to stop her. Though we did try."

Trayton moaned and Niall put a hand on his forehead. He quieted immediately.

"So why didn't she just off the Weres when they went wild in the dining room?"

"I suppose she didn't move against them because you were there," he said. "You'd already made it clear that Hamon had bound us to lawfulness during the negotiations. And she couldn't endanger the Trust."

"Maybe she thought you should be able to control them."

"I did try. But once the original hold is broken, it's difficult to weave a new one, especially when the Were is infuriated and hurt. And so we did nothing." He winced. "Which meant we had to sacrifice one of our own. Disa felt it was worth it. After all, he was one of the Trust's least important members." Niall sounded like he was trying to convince himself.

Trying to maintain that loyalty to something bigger. I guess I can see that. But to the point where you're rationalizing deaths and subverting your cantrantia? *I gotta know more about this little woman who always gets her way.* "How did Disa become part of the Trust?" I asked.

"You mean you don't know?"

I shrugged. "Why should I?"

Niall snorted. "Because Vayl is the one who brought her here."

Chapter Nine

I 'm not psychic, but sometimes I get these feelings. Like once the phone rang and I knew I'd be happier if I didn't answer it. But I did anyway. It was my Granny May, calling to tell me my mother, *her* daughter, had just died of a massive heart attack. Granny May didn't last long after that, proving once again that parents should never outlive their children.

Now I realized I should let the details of Disa's arrival into the Trust remain in the Blissful Ignorance drawer of my life file. It would have no bearing on the mission. Might even make it tougher to pull off. But I had to ask. "Vayl was here before Disa?"

Niall avoided looking at me. But, oh, I could feel the eagerness radiating off him. Like an old lip-wagger who's trying to figure out if spreading her juicy morsel during the church service will count against her in the afterlife. "Long before."

"Why did he bring her in?"

Niall looked around the suite, went to the hall door to make sure it was locked, and came back to sit on the bed beside Trayton. I drew the chair up beside it.

"Has Vayl told you about his sons?" he asked after we'd settled in.

"Yeah." Hanzi and Badu had been the only surviving children of his eighteenth-century marriage to his fellow Roma Liliana. The boys' murders had sparked their parents' turning, Vayl's revenge on the farmer who did the killing, and his endless search for their reincarnated souls.

Niall said, "In 1857, right around this time of year in fact, Vayl heard of a Seer who had gained great renown among the literati of Athens. He wouldn't rest until he'd met with her and asked if she could feel the presence of his sons' souls, either in the netherworld or here, on earth."

"I imagine he was pretty excited."

Niall leaned forward, got rid of a small bubble of silver. They'd slowed to a dribble, leaving Trayton to rest easier, though he'd gone as pale as his vampire nurse. "He was practically babbling with glee. Some of us thought he'd taken some bad blood he was so changed from his usual quiet demeanor." Which would have been worse in April, the anniversary of the deaths of his sons.

"So he went to Athens?" I asked.

"Often. Every week for half a year. And all the time his behavior became more and more erratic. Great highs when he would laugh and dance and demand huge parties. Intense lows when he'd hunt the streets alone, endangering himself and the entire Trust."

"What was he hunting?" I asked through lips that had suddenly gone dry.

"We eat to live," Niall said flatly. "But even then we preferred willing donors. It is better to coexist than merely survive, yes?"

I might have nodded, but I wasn't feeling quite connected to my head anymore, so I couldn't be absolutely sure. "So Vayl went hunting for unwilling donors?"

"Precisely. People who would not be missed. Those whom other humans would prefer to be rid of. He would take on entire gangs of street thugs, come back bloodied and beaten, but still be triumphant. Then he would return to Athens."

"What happened in the end?"

"He began to suspect Disa had not the second Sight she

claimed. He asked me to come along with him to help discover the truth."

"Wait a second. So Disa was this famous Seer—and she was human at the time?"

"Yes."

"Okay . . . so you two met her, where, at her shop?"

Niall shook his head. "She was the daughter of a wealthy merchant who kept her well provided for in a home near the center of town. That was where she gave her readings."

"Did she ask for money for her services?"

"No. But people seemed to enjoy giving her expensive gifts. Even Vayl had given her a diamond necklace and a pair of matching earrings in gratitude for her efforts." *Wow, she sounds like some kind of slick talker. Maybe I underestimated her.*

Niall went on. "At any rate, we went to visit her on a cool October evening, Vayl had just been through an episode of abject misery during which he had not left his apartments for perhaps three or four days. Now all he could talk about was seeing Disa, getting a good reading, finally uncovering some real details. He became so eager and excited to hear about Hanzi and Badu that he forgot why he had invited me along in the first place."

"You will be polite?" he asked me as we tied our horses to the rail in front of Disa's house that night.

"Only until she raises the shade of my dead grandfather, and then all bets are off," I joked. He didn't laugh.

We used a massive boar's head knocker to signal our presence at the entrance of a three-story town house that rose straight from the street with no architecture or garden to relieve its simple, white plainness. Its brown-painted windowsills were recessed, and without benefit of a light closer than the one halfway down the block, they seemed even to my vision like hollow eye sockets staring from the pale face of a dying man.

Disa came to the door after a prolonged bout of knocking. She had thrown a thin, white robe over her chemise. I didn't think this boded well for my companion. How could the Seer not have foretold his visit? But this detail escaped him. He grasped both of her hands in his. "Tell me about my sons," he demanded. "I cannot wait another moment. When will I meet them and where?"

I expected her eyes to go blank, her mouth to slacken as the truly Gifted's will when the Sight is upon them. Disa just snatched her hands back and drawled, "Vayl, if it were that easy, don't you think you'd have found them long before now?"

He looked at me then, and I could tell he remembered why I was there. "May we come in?" I asked.

She clearly wanted to refuse us. But then Vayl would know for certain. So she said, "Of course."

She gestured for us to enter, and we followed her into a small room dominated by a round table covered with a floor-length black cloth and surrounded by ladder-backed chairs. Five black candles formed the table's centerpiece. She lit these and then asked us to sit, one on either side of her.

I had a moment to register the long black curtains drawn across the two windows, the fireplace—its mantel empty, its hearth bare though it had been an extremely cool fall—and the white, floor-to-ceiling shelves containing all manner of mismatched bric-a-brac, from china teacups to pottery urns to a vase full of wilted flowers. And then I turned my attentions to Disa. She had made a new plan for her client.

She leaned toward Vayl, her robe gaping open to reveal a distracting view of her neckline. "Since I, and in fact all of your Seers, have had such a difficult time deciphering the whereabouts of your sons, may I suggest a different tack?"

Such was Vayl's obsession that his eyes never wavered from her face. "What is it?" he asked.

"Let me try to contact your father. I believe he could tell us what we need to know."

Vayl sat back. "My . . . father?"

"His name was" —she closed her eyes and rested her hand atop Vayl's— "Nelu, was it not?"

"Yes," he whispered.

"I can feel him," she said without opening her eyes. "Let me reach out, Vayl. Let me see if he has spoken to Hanzi and Badu."

"Yes," he said again, tears springing to the corners of his eyes.

I was not so taken in. Charlatans aren't stupid. They're simply not smart enough to follow the law. So I watched closely as Disa "fell" into her trance. As she "contacted" Nelu, who had, miraculously, just spoken to Hanzi and Badu that very morning. They had not been reincarnated as Vayl's last Seer had intimated, but still wandered in the Spirit World, waiting for their time to return. Which meant Vayl could talk to them anytime he wished. Through Disa.

"Now," Vayl croaked, his voice so cloaked in tears he sounded like an entirely different man. "Please, let me speak to them now."

Suddenly, though no logs stood to receive it, a fire lit in the hearth. A teacup flew across the room and smashed against the wall. And Disa spoke in a voice not her own. A young man's that said, "Papa?"

Vayl cried, "Hanzi?" as both windows flew open. The curtains billowed. Another item flew off the shelf and rolled to the floor. When I looked, I realized it was the vase, and the flowers had somehow revived to their former splendor. I glanced back at Disa and thought, My, but you have talented feet. And is that an accomplice whose excitement I sense just beyond the boundaries of this room?

I rose as the candles guttered out. I upended the table, allowing Vayl to see the pedals at Disa's feet and the levers on the table legs at her hands' level, all of which had been hidden by the tablecloth. I yanked a lever and one of the windows closed. Another caused the fire to go out *and the room descended into darkness. I could feel the fury and fear of the accomplice. His indecision would not last long.*

"We must leave, Vayl," I said. "Someone else knows what we have discovered, and they will not suffer the knowledge to spread."

For a moment I was not sure Vayl heard me. He stood as still as a man who has just prophesied his own doom.

"This will not stand," he whispered, so softly even I barely heard him.

"Vayl, really, we have to go now. Later. Later we can —"

"No."

"But —"

"No!" he bellowed. He strode to Disa, who had backed almost to the fireplace. He grabbed her hand just as she raised it to the mantel, pulling her away from the spot even as the fireplace — mantel, wall, and all — began to pivot. It revealed a hidden doorway and, stepping from it, a broad-shouldered, bearded man with wide, fear-filled eyes. He was armed with a large crossbow.

With barely even a glance in his direction Vayl backhanded the man, sending him and the crossbow flying into the back of the fireplace so violently that I suspected he was dead. Disa gave a little scream, which eroded to a whimper when Vayl slapped her across the face and snarled, "No more from you, woman. Not a word. Not a sound."

I followed him out of the house, feeling like a stranger in my own skin having seen such behavior from him. He'd never even been rude to a woman before this night. And yet now I'd seen him hit one even as the bloody tears from his supposed reunion with his beloved sons still stood upon his face.

He hitched Disa's carriage to her team, threw her into the back, and ordered me to drive. Though I didn't see what happened next, I heard it. Vayl said, "You heartless bitch. Six months you played me. And meant to for how long? Another six or eight before you disap-

peared? With as much of my fortune as you could get your hands on, I suppose. And I, pitiful wretch that I am, fell right into your grasping hands. We both deserve this."

"And then," Niall said, "he ripped her."

I grabbed the arms of my chair. Felt my nails dig through the tattered material to the cushioning underneath. "Did you say . . . ripped?"

"Yes."

Huge sigh of relief. I think. "What is that?"

Niall had finished pulling the silver from Trayton's body. He set the towel he'd been using aside and rubbed both hands across his eyes, as if he didn't want to visualize what he'd witnessed that night. "Humans believe you must choose to become a vampire. Most of the time that is the case. However, very occasionally, a person is ripped, or forced, into vampirism. The risk of permanent death for both parties involved in such a turning is so extreme it's almost never attempted. However, sometimes, as in this case, the vampire feels justified in the attempt."

"I don't . . . Are you saying he tore away her chance at eternity in heaven by forcing her to spend forever here on earth?"

"I suppose you could see it that way. But that was never his intent. Because he didn't plan for her to live beyond the next dawn. Already maddened by the desire to see his sons again, he allowed the pain and humiliation Disa caused to destroy the remainder of his self-control. He did in five minutes what a purposeful vampire would have taken a year to accomplish. He took her to the brink of death. Then he brought her back. After which he left her tied to a tree to watch the sun rise."

Here it was. The thing I knew I'd have to face about Vayl. He'd hinted at his shadowed past. Had even told me I wouldn't have wanted to know him back when. So how did it feel to be romantically involved with a reformed ripper?

No clue.

My insides were so jumbled I couldn't have made sense of them if I'd been a professional code breaker. "So." I cleared my throat of whatever had suddenly become lodged there. "She's obviously still kicking. Did you go back for her?"

Niall laughed without a trace of humor. "And invite Vayl's wrath? Do I *look* suicidal? No, indeed, Vayl himself returned. He heard her weeping, even from miles away. That is how strongly the turning connects you. In the end he couldn't leave her to die. So he brought her into the Trust." Niall's eyebrows arched. "An enormous risk in itself, since turning was, and still is, forbidden. But, as you may have noticed, Vayl is a survivor. A skill he passed on to Disa. It is amazing to me, the Gifts that are transmitted between Maker and mate. But then, that still was not enough to make him forgive her, not even when she begged him to on the day he left."

"Excuse me," I said, Lucille's polite smile frozen on my face. "Just now. Did you say Maker and mate?"

"Yes."

I laughed. Because I was getting real stressed, real fast, and that's my funky way of showing it. "Ha, ha-ha-ha. My understanding was that Makers kind of guide their, um, makees. Like teachers. Maker and *student*," I said, loud enough that Trayton opened his eyes.

"I understand that is the case in North American nests and many of those found in New Zealand and Australia. But Trusts view the relationship much more seriously. They grant those who are turned the power to bind their Makers to them for a specific length of time, which is why we call them mates. When Hamon decided to allow Disa to stay, he did as much for her."

"Why?" I clenched my fists, realizing if Niall didn't answer I'd willingly resort to violence for the information I needed.

He must've sensed my intent, because he answered quickly. "It assures the survival of our young, as some Makers have been known to abandon their—Excuse me. Are you going to be sick?" He reached out.

Don't. Touch me. "Are they . . . were Vayl and Disa bonded? Bound?"

Oddly, Niall glanced at his watch. "Actually, yes. About thirty minutes ago."

"WHAT?"

He shrugged. "It makes no sense to me either. She sent the news to us through one of her guards. That was why we were trying to put the dining room to rights so quickly. She wants to have another feast tomorrow to celebrate her invocation of the binding."

"Invocation. Binding." The words seemed to sear themselves into the air as I released them. "What exactly does that mean?"

"Vayl has no choice. Despite the fact that he left the Trust, he is still her Maker. And so, for the length of time she requires, they are tied to one another. Like a married couple."

"Like a married couple," I parroted. My lips had gone numb.

Niall nodded. "Except without the option of divorce."

I felt like I was speaking from behind my eyeballs and seeing from the top of my head. I recognized the tactic. Had used it before almost every hit of my career. "And how long . . . ?"

"Fifty years."

I looked down to make sure I hadn't floated out of the chair. Nope, still sitting there, still breathing, even though I felt like I'd just been stabbed to death. Why is it that the deepest wounds never show?

"Oh." I stood. Glanced at my knees, slightly surprised they were holding me up. "Oh," I said again. I looked at Niall. "Will you excuse me, please?"

I went out the hallway door. Checked my bearings. Raised

Cirilai to eye level. Since the ruby and diamond ring Vayl had given me connected us in all kinds of ways, one of which would bring him running if he sensed I was in danger, I blasted that message now as I strode away from our quarters. Soon I could sense them coming. Not just him. The whole bunch of them, just as I'd expected. Because if you were smart, you didn't give the *Tolic* free rein of his old stomping grounds.

Rounding a corner I found them, Vayl in the lead, eyes narrowed, lips tight, the way they get when he's worried. Dave followed close behind. And at their heels, Disa, Sibley, Marcon, and the sumo guards, unhappily stuck in the back because they were too big, the hallway too narrow for them to flank anyone. Brushing past Vayl, I walked up to Disa, raised the crossbow I held in my right hand, pressed it against her chest, and . . .

In that split second, when everything slows down before a killing, I saw and heard everything.

The fancy wallpaper, yellowed and peeling.

Dave, his bloodshot eyes bulging with shock, yelling, "What the hell are you doing?"

Vayl reaching out to grab me, bellowing, "Stop!"

Marcon's eyes widening as he saw the advantages of a dead Disa in his Trust.

Sibley's screech of dismay as her hands flew to cover her own chest.

The sumos' desperate efforts to plow through the unmoving vamps in front of them.

Disa's moment of paralysis, stemming from the conviction that, of all people, Vayl's wimpy little *avhar* would never attempt such a thing.

I pulled the trigger.

Nothing happened. I hadn't released the safety after I'd left the bedroom. Never thought to do it in the hallway, because I'd assumed it was already done. And that mistake saved my life.

"What the fuck do you think you're *doing?*" Disa demanded, her voice so close to high C my eardrums shivered. Part of me noticed something strange going on at her throat that even repeated swallowing couldn't explain. But that observation got filed away with the rest under *Who gives a shit?*

"Vayl is my *sverhamin*," I said, standing my ground despite the fact that the guards had made excellent headway and could almost reach me now. "He's also my boss, my partner, and my . . ." I let that one drop. Too hard to speak from that point. "If I'd been there when the Wizard enslaved my brother I'd have shot the bastard right between the eyes. I wasn't. But I'm here now. Nobody traps anybody who belongs to me. Not now. Not ever."

When your gun fails, words can make for powerful mojo. But not as bad as a Vampere bond. I turned my back before Disa could see I knew that.

Chapter Ten

I stalked away from the shocked and gaping group. Within minutes I'd returned to the suite. I dropped onto the bed and lay there for a full thirty seconds before I realized it should've been full of werewolf. I bolted upright. "What the hell?" A rushed search of the room followed. Why I looked under the pillows and behind the painting I have no idea. My guess — too many hours spent watching *Abbott & Costello* marathons. I finally found the note where it had fallen on the floor beside the door.

Jasmine,
Trayton will be safer in my room. I have access to the outside in case we need a quick getaway. He says you'll be worried, so please stop by soonest. I'm two doors down from Admes. You'll know it by the warhorse carving.
Niall

I wadded up the note and fell back onto the bed. Trayton. The ultimate annoyance. Not so much because his move had scared the crap out of me. But because he'd known it would.

Suddenly the room smelled too much of him. I strode into the sitting area and slumped into a chair. Studied the floor. Interesting pattern in the growth of the wood that had gone into its making.

Lovely lines and whorls all combining to form a nice hard place to rest my feet. Which were tapping like mini machine guns. *That would be a satisfying way to take Disa out. Just shoot her in the head until it disintegrates.* I jumped up and began to pace.

Each step seemed to click off the names of the people thrashing through my mind. Disa. Vayl. Dave. Trayton. Samos. Images of me pulling that trigger. Vayl, running his fingers through his hair, his eyes dark and fathomless. Dave looking horrified and slightly hungover. The blood vision. Trayton's trusting gaze. Over and over again my mind ran that loop until I clenched my teeth, pissed that my brain had fallen right back into the torturous track it had built sixteen months before when I'd lost my love — my friends — and yeah, maybe a little bit of my sanity.

My phone rang. I looked at it. Not Vayl. Or Dave. Okay, I could talk to anyone else. "Yeah?"

"Jasmine." Cassandra's soft, low voice made me stop. One of the few Trayton had sensed on the inside of my heart, Cassandra had wanted to accompany me on this mission just like she had on the last two. But I'd reminded her and Bergman both that they had businesses to run and they'd better, by damn, pay some attention to *them* for a while. Thank God they'd listened to me. To have them here in the middle of all this — unbearable.

"What?" I asked.

"You're barking."

Instant guilt. Goddamn that Were. "I'm sorry, I just — you wouldn't believe what I just did." I paused. "Actually, you probably would."

"I wonder if it was related to the vision I just had?"

"What did you See?"

"This is a pivotal time for you. If you kill *anyone* for the wrong reason, someone close to you will die as well. I didn't see his face. Just yours, covered in tears, dark with despair."

"Well, that's pretty straightforward. Any more great advice before I pack Grief in mothballs?"

She ignored my sarcasm. "Only this. The woman I Saw must not die by your hand, or you will never be joined to Vayl."

"I don't . . . That is, Vayl and I . . ." *Okay, why am I trying to BS a psychic?* "What's she look like?"

Cassandra described Disa in minute detail. *Shit. Of course, we can still take her out. Maybe when Cole gets finished . . .*

"Stop, Jasmine. Think what you're plotting."

I realized I'd walked all the way to the door. I bowed my head against it. *Son of a bitch. Fifty years? What the hell did she think* — and then it hit me. I turned around.

"Cassandra, I have just tried to kill the one person who can lead us to Edward Samos. Because of Vayl. And because I'm so torn up about Dave. You should see him; he's never been this close to the edge. Which is making me absolutely crazy. But that's beside the point. No, that *is* the point. This fucking Trust is turning us all into something we're not."

"Jasmine, I am so worried about you," Cassandra said. "I can hear the strain in your voice from all these thousands of miles away."

I looked up at the ceiling, and suddenly the cracks seemed to converge into a form. One so gigantic my brain could only capture it for a millisecond. "It's like this entire villa is at our throats, sucking out the logic, the sense. Holy Christ, it's like the Trust itself is a vampire. And as long as we stay under its roof, we're going to be locked in some sort of battle with it."

I began to pace the room as realizations hit me, one after another. "Everything. Dave shooting the Weres. The binding. Me trying to kill Disa. They were all symptoms of the fact that we were under attack."

"What does that mean?"

"I'm not sure. Vayl warned me about the power of this place. But at the moment, all I really know is that I've totally jeopardized the mission. And my job." I locked eyes with the fountain statue, who stared back at me without pity as I whispered, "So what am I gonna do now?"

CHAPTER ELEVEN

I lay back on the bed, trying to ignore the freaky painting, pouring my poker chips from one hand to another. One of Dave's men had given them to me when we'd worked together on our last mission. I could've used that guy's help right now. Cam's scars, a combination of killer acne and a close escape from a grenade, were visible proof of how good he was at surviving sticky situations.

"Obviously my perspective is trashed. Maybe . . . Should I quit?" I asked the round clay tiles clacking their soothing music against my fingers. I imagined writing out a letter of resignation. Watching that paper flutter onto Pete's desk with the same death knell they used to toll the loss of sailors at sea.

Gut churning. But not as bad as letting Samos walk. I really have to consider this. But not lying down. I jumped up. *Sitting around here is driving me crazy. Plus, I'm so not ready to talk to Vayl and Dave. What would I tell them? The big bad house made me do it? Yeah, that'll go over like a lead balloon. Especially considering the Trust is in their heads too.* And *they're pissed at me.*

Maybe if I had some proof. Hamon's room. That's it! Try to find something from his stash to back up my theory.

I left a note for Dave to call Cassandra, her last request before we'd broken our connection, and headed out the door. Moving toward the apartments that had once housed the king of these vampires, I tried to imagine what Vayl and the rest of the group were discussing right now. Spaz Jaz, the renegade assassin, no doubt. Was Vayl trying to talk Disa out of flaying me alive? Had Dave told any embarrassing stories of my high school flip-outs? Forget that — was Vayl trying to extricate himself from her fifty-year trap? No. Niall had said it was permanent.

Just the thought made me feel so wild I actually punched the wall, bringing a rain of dust down on my shoulders before I even considered the consequences.

I pondered my bloody knuckles and said to myself, *It's the Trust screwing with you again. Plus, you did just donate your blood and, maybe, part of your soul to a young werewolf. That'll mess you up any day of the week. Won't it? Answer me!*

I stopped next to a painting of a lady vamp with an upturned nose and ruby red eyes. "What do you do when even thinking hurts?" I asked her. "And by the way, how the hell do I get myself into these situations?" She had no answer beyond her eternally hungry stare. I drew my knuckles down the painting's face. And when I pulled them away she was crying for me, bloody tears that ran down the canvas like slow, thick rain.

"Work," I whispered. "Go to work, Jaz. Before you lose it altogether."

I reached for my watch, a Bergman special, which, when its band was flipped, emitted a shield that allowed me to move even more quietly than usual. I figured that could be handy in a mansion full of creatures that could hear better than elephants. But as I moved away from our suite and deeper into the villa, I realized my watch was just the techie portion of a bigger, badder silence that had suddenly become available to me through my exchange with Trayton.

Sliding past full suits of armor, creeping beneath a twenty-foot section of ceiling-hung blue crystals, skulking down carpeted avenues that couldn't capture even a hint of my footsteps, I felt like I could walk up right behind a vamp, flick him on the back of the ear, and disappear before he ever even turned around. I liked it.

And I hated it.

Because I couldn't tell anymore what fit me and what had been slapped on like a pair of gigantic clown shoes. I felt like I needed my own *Antiques Roadshow* expert who could, with only a brief glance, say, "As you can see by the red curls marked by one white streak, this is a genuine Jaz Parks. The Sensitivity and its various accoutrements, while interesting in themselves, do nothing to detract from the value of the piece, which should be insured for ten billion dollars." *Hey, if you're going to price yourself, I say go high.*

I jerked my head around as my senses raised the alert. Two vamps at least, coming my way. Talking loud and angry. Probably freaking about my latest move. And I *so* didn't want to be on the receiving end of the wrath I felt pounding down the hall.

I rushed to the nearest door, ducked behind it, and nearly split my skull on an iron pole before I realized I'd stepped into a coat closet. My semi-claustrophobia let out a yelp, which caused me to whisper, "Holy crap, that was close!"

"It'll be even closer if you back up another step."

"Shit!" I whipped around, nearly braining myself again as I confronted the creature curled up in the corner, his face hidden behind a line of leather and furs. "Don't move," I hissed. "Don't even think about giving my position away."

"Do I look like I want to be found?"

Good point. I held the syringe of holy water tight in my right hand, where I'd triggered it the moment I'd realized I was sharing space with a vamp, and left the mystery of why I hadn't sensed him, and still barely did, until later. Bigger, scarier boys were coming. Genti and Rastus to be specific, and Genti at least seemed to have an awful lot to say. Unfortunately, it was all in Vampere.

I set my ear against the door, straining to hear the few words I understood. But I doubted their heated discussion would include the phrases "I come in peace," or "No, thanks, I prefer water." Then I heard a word I did recognize. "Werewolf."

Ahh. Rastus has had to admit he's lost a dead wolf and a living bear. And Genti sounds überpissed! I would so buy tickets to that ass-kicking.

The next word I recognized sent me diving to the other corner of the closet. Genti had said "outside," as he'd paused by the door. Problem was, the unnamed vamp had decided my corner provided a lot more privacy too. Though we moved at the same time, he was faster and I ended up pressed against what I hoped was his shoulder.

I tried to relax, since some vamps, like Vayl and Niall, can sense strong human emotion. But it's hard to chill when you're teetering on the edge to start with, and the two jerks who want you gone the worst are inches from outing you.

The door opened.

I stopped breathing. Quit thinking even.

Still yapping like a sergeant who's found contraband in his private's footlocker, Genti reached into the closet and whipped his fur-collared coat off the rack. Since Rastus still wore his bomber jacket, within seconds the door slammed shut again and they'd moved on. Even so, I waited to the count of two hundred before I let my breath out in a sigh of relief. At which point my companion said, "Is your butt buzzing?"

Cole, you have the worst *timing!* I jerked upright, trying to pull my phone out of my pocket and managing instead to bang my elbow against the wall. "Ow! Oh, shit, that hurts! You know, the guy who decided it should be called the funny bone was just a freaking masochist. Or is it a sadist? I always get those mixed up."

"Sadist," the vamp replied gravely.

"Oh." By now I'd reached the other end of the closet, where I leaned against the back wall, nursing my bruises and looking over to where my savior still crouched, the upper half of his face hidden by a slick black raincoat.

"Listen, I appreciate your help," I said. "However, I should warn you I'm holding a syringe of holy water. So if you're hungry, don't be looking for appetizers in this corner."

"I would never dream of hurting you."

"Wow. That lie stinks worse than my dad's farts on Super Bowl Sunday."

Soft laughter. "All right, perhaps a dream of pain, but one mixed with intense pleasure. And only a dream." Like a bomb from a B52, the amusement dropped out of his voice. "My reality has become such a nightmare I have sworn to let no one take part in the journey."

"Well, as long as you're hanging out in closets, I don't see that being a problem."

"You were hiding from them as well."

"Yeah, so?"

"The great American comeback."

"Okay then, let's make a deal."

"The great American game show."

"You *are* old."

"You have no idea." I recognized the same droll humor in his voice that I often heard in Vayl's when he referred to the difference in our ages. But only a pinch. Mostly what I heard was despair. The kind you understand because you've fallen into a bottomless well of it yourself.

"Obviously you're no fan of Genti and Rastus either. So why don't you tell me what they were saying?" *I've just gotta know how bad Rastus was getting his ass reamed. Holy geez, wait till I give Trayton the details. He'll be rolling!* "If you give me a down-and-dirty translation I can—"

"What will you do for me?" the vamp asked, his voice suddenly bitter. "Will you restore me to my place in the *Vitem?* No?" he demanded when I didn't answer. "Well, perhaps something easier. In return for your jewel of information"—he leaned forward—"will you give me back my face?"

CHAPTER TWELVE

I slept with a night-light till I was six. In high school, when I came home after a date, my skin would practically jump off my bones until I'd flipped on the light switch. Because I knew exactly what could be lurking in the shadows if I didn't crush them right away, and it scared the crap out of me. I just never thought my childhood fears would chase me into my twenties.

When the vamp moved into my line of vision, the sight of him rammed my head back into the wall and caused my heart to stop for three full seconds before it boomed in my chest, like it wanted to pull the rest of me through the plaster and lathe back into the hallway, out the front door, and *screw* this place!

Then what? asked Granny May, who had a hand full of hearts and was trying to give Sitting Bull the high sign without the others catching on to her cheat. *Seriously, Jasmine, what are you going to accomplish, running from the monster in the closet?*

Won't have to look at him anymore, I thought mulishly.

I'll give you that, Granny admitted.

You sure as hell better. And while you're at it, tell me what on earth is capable of eating a vampire's face to the point that it won't heal back right again.

He had no eyes. No sockets even. His nose and right cheek were also just . . . gone. And in their place, the stuff you're never supposed to see. The mass of tissue behind a face. But not clean and excised. This was twisted and scarred, especially just above his upper jaw and at his left cheek.

"Some things you are not meant to survive," he said, and now that we didn't have to speak in whispers, the odd twang of his voice struck me, its resonance lost along with his nostrils.

"What did this to you?" I asked.

"I believe you mean who."

"Not a Were, then?"

He shook his head. I really wished he hadn't. "Disa," he whispered.

I slid down the wall until my butt met my heels. "I knew something was wrong about her the second we met. Something just smelled off." *And now she's bound herself to Vayl.* I rammed my elbow into the wall, realized it was the one I'd hurt earlier, and gritted my teeth as twitchy pains zoomed from shoulder to fingertips.

He cocked his head at me and I wished I could drape a towel or something equally opaque over his mutilated face. I could hardly bear to witness the damage Disa had done anymore.

Okay, you know what, quit being a goddamn wimp! Your career may have hit the shitter. And your position as Vayl's . . . whatever . . . may be as shaky as a Parkinson's patient. But while you're in the CIA, at least suck it up and act like a pro.

"What do you mean?" he asked. "Disa smelled strange? Are you a Sensitive?"

I took a deep breath. "Yes, I am. And yeah, she did," I said. "Like a psychic diaper fire. Now you. Tell me what you can."

He slumped into himself, raising his hands over his head as if to shield his ravaged face from even the memory of the attack. "I don't even know you."

"I would've thought sharing a space the size of an ironing board had taken us beyond etiquette, but okay. My name's Lucille Robinson. I came with Vayl to help negotiate with Edward Samos."

His chin came up. "Vayl has returned?"

"Eryx invited him. We didn't know he'd been killed until we arrived tonight."

"If only we'd known Vayl was coming," the vampire murmured. "The outcome might have been so different."

"What do you mean?"

His sigh made me shiver, it sounded so alien. "My name is Blas. I was part of a group in the Trust who did not believe Hamon Eryx died by accident, and who wouldn't accept Disa as *Deyrar*."

I remembered Vayl asking Disa about the missing vamps, one of whom had been this creature. "What happened?" I asked.

"It . . . it is difficult to recall. We were all gathered in the dining hall for the Mourning." Blas sighed. "I won't bore you with succession of power in a Trust. Suffice it to say that the Articles of Transformation were not scheduled to be read until the next evening."

Blas paused to listen, as if he'd heard someone coming outside our stifling little elevator to nowhere. I reached out with my own senses and felt nothing except a strengthening desire to LEAVE. I began feeling around for a secret door. I know, I know. But the hope that there was one kept me in that hole, listening to his tragic story when I would have much preferred running straight back to America, my feet pumping so fast I wouldn't even need a ship to get me across the ocean. Nothing behind me. But to my left my fingers managed to budge a section of wall big enough for me to feel from shoulder to hip. I relaxed by a factor of ten.

Blas continued. "Camelie had just finished reciting 'McNaight's Refrain' when Disa stepped into the Speaker's circle. It wasn't her place to talk. Until then she had been but a *knaer*, tolerated at first because Vayl asked it, and then because she showed some aptitude for recruiting willing donors."

"I claim the chalice!" she cried, pointing dramatically at Hamon's personal guards, two enormous, mute humans who held the chest con-

taining the golden cup that the new Deyrar *would drink from after
we had all given of our blood to fill it.*

"Be silent!" Aine snapped. She had been Hamon's Second, and
the one we all supposed would succeed him. *"If you can observe the
traditions of our Mourning, perhaps tomorrow we will allow you to
speak in support of a qualified member."*

"The slap was clear," Blas said. "No one even acknowledged
Disa's pronouncement. In hindsight, of course, I can say we should
never have underestimated her ambition or her brutality. But I am
surprised none of us realized what she managed to achieve without
revealing her plan to anyone. Arrogance is always the stair that
trips you."

I said, "It doesn't sound like Disa had any trouble negotiating
her stairs."

"No. She had planned for her moment so thoroughly I don't
suppose even *she* could get in her own way. She strode up to Aine,
the long tails of her sleeves trailing her like pet snakes. Though
Aine was at least six inches taller, Disa seemed to tower over her.

*"I don't think you understand me!" she screamed as she grabbed
Aine by the throat. "I am your new Deyrar!"*

*"Get off of me!" Aine choked out the words as she spun her arms
under and up to break Disa's hold. It should have sent the lesser vamp
flying. But before the break could occur, Disa's neck bulged horribly.
As if she'd turned bullfrog, a low croak spilled from her lips as the skin
of her throat thinned and split. A beaklike appendage shoved through
the opening like a blood-covered fist. It flew open to reveal dozens of
fleshy pink tendrils that looked quite harmless. In a movement so swift
even my eyes could not follow, the tendrils shot at Aine's head. They
caught her just where her hairline began, wrapped around to her chin,
and"* — Blas paused, took a ragged breath — *"and sliced off her face."*

I crossed my hands over my chest, as if that could stop the stut-
ter it had begun when it realized the truth. "So Disa's a Vera?"

"What is that?"

"It's a CIA term, taken from the name of the first *other* who somehow managed to move beyond the typical boundaries of her biology. Veras learn how to trip a transformational trigger that should take thousands of years. But it's not a permanent deal. They can swing back and forth between representations. That must be what she meant by evolution. But how'd she do it?"

Blas shook his head, making my blasted ticker pause to flip-flop before it stumbled on its way again. At this rate I'd need a pacemaker before my next birthday. He said, "We have no idea. But vampires are terrible snobs about such impurities. The fact that she had accepted, no, sought a change so radical spoke volumes about the role she had played in the Trust since Vayl brought her in, and how firmly she intended it to change."

"Yeah, but . . . poor Aine."

Blas clutched his hands together at the memories. "She tried to scream, but there was nothing left of her to make sounds. The blood gushed from her wounds as she fell to the floor. Not dead. No, never dead."

"What happened after that?" I asked.

"We rushed Disa. But she had already enlisted Hamon's guards, as well as Genti and his bunch. The guards took Fielding and Panos with crossbows. Camelie fought Genti and Rastus like a tigress, but in the end they overcame her, taking her head. That left me alone to fight Disa."

"Wait a second. Where were Niall and Admes? And their guard would've still been alive then. I mean, I don't know the guys. But they don't seem the types to take something like that sitting down."

"She had even thought of that. Niall and Admes are, without doubt, the best fighters among us. But when a *Deyrar* dies, the shields that protect Trust lands weaken. As a result, during the

Mourning our fiercest warriors must guard our borders. All three were outside the walls, patrolling the edges of our property. Too far to be of any use in the battle. I, alone, was left to destroy the threat."

His hands, which had been resting on his thighs, balled into fists. "But you can see how that ended. Though I slashed at her with my *cantrantia*, which can liquefy small pockets of flesh and bone, she managed to protect herself quite well. The wounds I caused healed instantly. In return she sent those razor-sharp tentacles slashing at my face."

"I wonder why . . ." I stopped. This was not an anatomy class. I couldn't just . . . well, could I? Hard to know if he'd be receptive with no expression to read. I decided I had to know worse than he needed me to protect his feelings. Maybe it would help in the long run. "I've seen vampires survive wounds that would've been catastrophic to anyone else and wake up the next nightfall completely healed. Was the damage just too extreme or . . ."

He shook his head. "Those tentacles. I could feel the sizzle when they hit me, as if they had released a sort of acid that ate into my flesh. After I went down, Sibley and Marcon carried me to my rooms. When I woke, it was to this monstrous facade." He pressed his palms against his temples, as if by sheer will he could put everything back like it had been. "I was never a handsome man," he whispered. "But I keep remembering how once, long ago, my mother told me I had the eyes of an angel." He dropped his forehead to his knees. "Oh, how I miss my eyes!"

"They've been doing face transplants," I blurted, feeling idiotic for saying so because, really, what did I know about this guy? He'd been in the Trust when Vayl left. So, despite his mother's opinion, he was no angel. Still, I felt sorry for him. So I continued. "I've seen the headlines. Not that there's a huge demand for them, but . . . well . . . I'm just saying . . ." I trailed off because Blas was making funny sounds, which I feared might have something to do with sobbing. And I so didn't want to be stuck in a closet with a crying vampire.

"Do you think it possible?" he asked, snuffling a little between words.

"I have no clue. But, you know, it's something to think about."

"Yes, perhaps . . . Excuse me, is your rear end buzzing again?"

I dug out my phone. "How did you know? It's not like I was leaning up against you this time."

Blas shrugged. "I felt the vibration through the wall."

"Yeah," I said. "There's this guy who thinks he wants to marry me. He doesn't understand how miserable we'd be together, so he keeps texting me."

"In other words, you have not told him no?"

"I haven't figured out how. I don't want to give him that tired old line about how I want to be *his* buddy and someone *else*'s lover. My impression is that's the best way never to see a guy again. But then, I don't want to lead him on, either. So I've been walking a line so thin I think my feet are starting to cramp from the pressure."

I checked the last two messages. When I started chuckling, Blas asked, "What does he say?"

I considered telling him it was none of his business. But he was such a pathetic little bundle there in the corner. Plus, it was nice to finally have someone I could talk to. A guy who literally couldn't nail me with a look of disdain because I'd allowed my life to become such a tangled mess. "The first one says: 'If I have to sit still for one more hour, my ass is going to look like a manhole cover. Hey, wait a minute!'"

Blas laughed softly. "And the second?" he asked, the eager note in his voice making me wonder how long it had been since he'd spoken to anyone. Did he spend all his waking hours in this coffin of a room?

"He says: 'Great, now I have to pee. Maybe I shouldn't have drunk that eighth cup of coffee. Plus, I've got the caffeine jitters. Do you think anyone would notice if I wrote my name in the snow and then break-danced around it?'"

Blas let out a delighted sigh. "Your friend sounds amusing."

"Yeah."

"*You* sound wistful."

"He's been a better pal to me than I've been to him. I miss him. Especially now when—" *when everything is falling apart.*

I'll admit it. For about three seconds I considered staking out the corner of the closet Blas hadn't laid claim to. I wouldn't take up much room curled into the fetal position. The rocking and sobbing might irritate him some, but it would pass in a few hours. After which we'd probably get along fine. I'd pace the length of the closet, bouncing off the walls every third step like a Roomba doing the vacuum tango. He'd enjoy all the stories I'd tell of my exploits. Yeah, that's what we'd call them. Exploits. But then, eventually, he'd get hungry and sink his fangs into me. At which point I'd have to smoke him. *You know what? Never mind.*

"Why do you miss him particularly now?" Blas asked.

"Because, despite his feelings, he'd help me find the third alternative I'm looking for," I answered. "Then he'd say or do something that I'd find absolutely hilarious." I sighed. "But at the same time, I'd be wishing he was far, far away from me." Blas tipped his head sideways, as if he didn't quite understand where I was going. Which he wasn't supposed to. "Never mind," I said. "I've gotta get back." I couldn't tell him that Cirilai had begun sending me signals. Ones that made me think I should save the evidence search for a time when I actually had a clue how to get past the death-spell locking Hamon's door. Right now I needed to hustle my ass back to Vayl's side before the ring burned off my finger. Dammit. "I'll be here for the negotiations with Samos and then I'm leaving. If you're interested in that plastic surgery option, let me know. I'll make sure you're on the plane with me when I go. Deal?"

"Deal."

Chapter Thirteen

Vayl and Dave sat beside the fountain, staring at the rust-colored water as it flowed down the statue's perfect breasts. I guess it said something about their states of mind that their eyes were on the H_2O rather than the knockers, but my own was so fouled I hardly noticed.

The silence in the room ran so deep that when I closed the door it sounded like I'd just pulled up a drawbridge. I leaned my back against it, not wanting to enter any farther than necessary, making sure I had a clear means of escape if I needed one in the near future.

Finally Vayl looked up at me and said, "Have you gone stark raving mad? If I had not done some extremely fast talking, your ridiculous stunt would have ruined our entire mission! What were you thinking? Have you no self-control?"

I glanced at Dave, who had the sense to respond to my dawning anger with an expression of absolute neutrality. I sent my gaze back to Vayl, feeling the blood begin to pound in my head as I found myself spotlighted by his accusing gaze. Part of me noted that his eyes had remained brown throughout. When he's mad they usually go black. Sometimes they even get little red sparks, like laser sights that all point straight to that spot between my eyes.

I said, "I had a talk with Niall. He told me you ripped Disa. And that she bound you. For fifty years."

He at least had the grace to wince when I said the word "ripped." "I had every intention of telling you. But I supposed she was dead, and that gave me the chance to reveal it to you at a time of my choosing. Once we got here, everything moved so quickly—"

"Yeah, about that. You're a big, strong vampire. How is it that the little tramp cornered you? Or is it that you *wanted* to be bound? Couldn't wait to be rid of the loud-mouthed American with all the hang-ups so you could snuggle with your old honey, could you?" I glared at him, the fury crushing my brain, making it hard to think straight. *This isn't right!* cried Granny May, clutching the arms of her chair. *Stop and look at what's happening to you!* But I was sick of listening to the old bat. Since when had she uttered a word that had helped me?

He jerked to his feet. "That must have been it," he sneered. "Seeing Disa brought back so many fond memories that I could not wait to be shed of you. At least now I can acquaint myself with someone who considers the consequences before she acts." His voice was hard and sharp as the sword he always carried. Which I didn't see right now, but that hardly mattered. I could still feel myself bleeding inside.

I yanked Cirilai off my hand, ignoring the wrenching pain that nearly doubled me over when I lost the connection it gave me to Vayl. "Here!" I slammed it down onto the seat of the nearest chair. I looked into his eyes, still the warm brown typical of his most relaxed state, and wanted to slug him. He'd drawn his lips past his fangs. I'd never seen the expression on his face, so I didn't recognize the emotions behind it. But I really didn't give a shit. It was like the rage had rolled me up in an icy ball and we were tearing down some snowcapped peak, gathering speed and momentum, trampling everything in our path.

I said, "I felt so bad about what I did, I was going to quit my job. Can you believe that? I was actually going to throw away the career that saved my freaking sanity! But now I see the real problem is you and me, Vampire. I'll finish this mission, because I'm a pro. But as soon as we hit Ohio, you can find yourself somebody who doesn't care that all you really want is a puppet to jerk around at the end of that ring!"

I was about to make my grand exit, spin on my heel, stomp to the bedroom, slam the door so hard that the nightmare picture fell right off the wall, when we heard the shriek of a smoke alarm. Moments later Sibley burst through the hallway door. "Everybody out!" she ordered. "The villa is on fire!"

We'd returned to our suite within thirty minutes. Apparently part drama queen, Sibley had evacuated us without real cause, since the three fires that had erupted on different parts of the property never truly threatened us. The mystery was what had started them in the first place. One had begun in the garage, another in the dining room, and the third in the wagon house. All three had been caught by detectors in the ceilings and walls and quickly extinguished.

Dave was fascinated by the possibilities. He paced the length of the sitting room, throwing out ideas, while Vayl occupied the edge of the table. I stood by the bedroom door, wishing I had anything better to do. What I felt was the distance between Vayl and me, a universe squeezed into twenty feet of air space. Cirilai now hung from the chain around his neck, where he'd worn it for centuries before giving it to me. I ignored the ache that thought caused and forced myself to focus on my twin.

"Maybe it's the werebear's people, taking their revenge on the Trust for what they did to him."

"I don't think so," I said. "He promised me he wouldn't do anything until after we wrapped up our mission."

"And you think he's going to keep his word?" Dave asked, raising a cynical brow.

"Yeah, I . . ." I glanced at Vayl. "You know what, maybe not. It turns out I'm not the best judge of character."

Vayl rose to his feet, his brows banging together like thunderheads. "You are so—"

"What?" I demanded.

He stopped. Took a breath. "Never mind." I couldn't read the look he gave me. Decided I didn't want to. Facts are facts, folks. He was connected to Disa supernaturally. Every moment I was with him now, knowing that, it felt like she was in the room too. And it made me want to kick something.

Dave looked from him to me and back again. He patted down his pockets, found them empty, and dropped his hands. "Maybe I'll go check out the rooms where the fires started," he said. "See what they have in common." Under his breath I heard him add, "Like being away from you two," as he exited the room, leaving Vayl and me to share a long, cold silence.

After a few tense moments Vayl fixed his eyes on mine and said, "If your bolt had flown, you would have destroyed me tonight." He brushed some dust off the knee of his slacks, giving me time to compute. Nope, it just wouldn't key in. I had to hear it again.

"What?"

"The bonds that tie Maker and mate stretch beyond contractual obligation. For the next fifty years, if one of us dies, so will the other."

I realized I was shaking my head. Denial. The story of my life. I dropped my gaze to the floor. "Vayl, I never wanted—" I stopped, because suddenly he stood in front of me, close as a shadow. When

I looked into his eyes I realized they'd finally changed — to the dark purple of a new bruise.

"Tell me, Jasmine," he demanded, his voice as hoarse as Rastus's had been after having been pierced by a blade. "Why is it that after sticking Grief in Disa's gut and pulling the trigger, you are no longer willing to fight for us?"

The wall behind my back felt like it was rippling, but I knew it was my own dizzy desire to throw myself into Vayl's arms. Which made no sense. Wasn't I still pissed at him? "Niall made the situation sound hopeless," I told him. "So did you, for that matter."

His hand came to my face, brushed my cheek and down to my neck. I fought the urge to reach out, sink my fingers into his flesh. He said, "Yes. It seemed that way at first. And then I looked into your eyes and remembered that you and I have never failed anything we set out to accomplish together."

"*Your* eyes just turned. They've been brown up to now. Do you think *that* means something?"

He cocked his head thoughtfully. "Indeed."

I dropped my gaze to his lips. Too tempting. Down to the V of his open shirt. Nope, too sexy. I closed my eyes. "I can't think straight, dammit. There was something I wanted to tell you before. About this house. In fact, the entire Trust. The masks. The masks were throbbing."

I opened my eyes when his hands dropped to his sides. "Some sort of spell," he muttered.

"What?"

"That must be it. I can feel it working on me even as we speak. Like an itch, but not as strong now that I have identified it. Disa has been plotting, just like the old days. Of course. *That* is why she bound me! The underhanded little shrew!"

I nodded. "Yeah. Yes, that was *it!* Remember you told me before we came that we'd have to be careful? Well, you were right.

This place is fucking with us, Vayl, I'm sure of it." Before the thoughts could skitter out of my mind again I told him what I'd realized about the power of the Trust. "That fight we just had, I'll bet that was part of it too. It's messing with our heads. Divide and conquer, you know?"

Vayl had begun pacing back and forth in front of the fountain, tapping his fingers against his thigh. He didn't demand proof, thank goodness. That gut wrencher we'd just been through must've been enough to convince him. "We are being manipulated, no doubt about it. Disa wants me to rejoin the Trust, that is clear. But as to the reason — I have no idea."

"You mean beside the fact that she's in love with you?"

Vayl's jaw dropped. He looked so comical that I couldn't help but smile. "No." He shook his head. Adamantly. Like a guy who can't believe Congress has raised taxes again.

"Yeah, I think so." My hands ached to reach up to that face, smooth out the creases of consternation. I dropped them. *Why do I do that?* I suddenly wondered. *What's wrong with comforting someone you care for?*

My inner bitch put down the mai tai she'd been glugging and winked at the bartender before pointing a wavering finger in my general direction. *It's not that part you're worried about, ya' idiot. It's the caring. 'Cause they always end up dead on the floor — or in Studly's case, poof — before you even have a chance to give them their Christmas presents.*

Why should I listen to you? I demanded. *What kind of character leads a person in the right direction even as she adjusts her thong and tries to remember if the condoms are in her purse or the glove box of her Corvette?*

Why are you asking me? she demanded. *You're the one who's fucked up!*

No argument there.

"So. What next?" My mouth felt dry. As I wished for a beer, I realized Dave had probably gone somewhere to snitch a bottle of booze. Which meant, as soon as I confiscated it from him, I'd have something to wet my whistle with. Unless . . . nope, this round was definitely *not* going down the drain.

Vayl gazed down at me. "The ball is in your court, as they say."

"It is?"

His eyes darkened. Oops. Even when I wasn't trying, I pissed him off. Well, damn, it would help if he'd stop emitting that bone-melting, come-jump-me vibe. How was I supposed to concentrate with the Trust hammering at one side of my brain while a wild woman panted for Vayl on the other, stomping and screaming like the tipsy maid of honor at a Chippendales show?

As I stood there, fighting for balance, gazing at the ring I'd abandoned as it nestled against Vayl's chest, Dave walked in. I made myself inhale. Concentrated on my lungs filling with clean, clear air. Or the closest I was going to get considering my less-than-antiseptic surroundings.

Okay, just concentrate on the mission. It's really important you get this right. Think of the lives you could save if you nail Samos. If you keep that in the front of your head, everything else will somehow fall into line. Won't it? Yeah. Maybe. As long as you don't panic. I shoved my hand in my pocket, felt Matt's ring slip around my pinky, quickly followed by a sense of peace. I hadn't lost that token. And some of him still remained, forever part of me, undiminished by time and distance. I felt myself straighten, realized my chin had lifted as I stared Vayl straight in the eye.

I'll do whatever it takes to win, I told him silently.

His nod, a barely perceptible bob of the head, gave me his answer. *That is what I wanted to hear.*

I watched Dave edge into the room, looking from Vayl's face to mine as he tried to gauge our moods. When I managed a smile he visibly relaxed.

"I didn't make it far," Dave said. "Only got to look around the garage long enough to figure out the fire started right in the middle of a huge pool of blood before Tarasios intercepted me and demanded to know what I was doing snooping around outside."

I considered checking Dave's breath to see if he'd been sampling the schnapps before he got here. "That makes no sense. How could a fire start in liquid?"

"No clue," Dave replied. "But that's where it was."

"Weird." A spidery sense of unease navigated my stomach. The fire's location reminded me of the drippy face, which I still wanted badly to suppress. Could *it* have had something to do with the blaze?

Dave went on. "Tarasios was really pissed, and I got the feeling it wasn't just because I was checking out the fire damage. He kept muttering about being taken for granted and just giving and giving and see what he gets?"

"I think he's just been dumped," I said as evenly as I could.

"Well, that would explain it."

Vayl dropped into one of the wicker chairs, making it creak like an arthritic old man. "This is ridiculous."

"Disa's crush on you, or the fact that she's trying to trap you?" I asked.

"Both!"

Dave's grin doesn't surface often, but when it appears, the entire room pretty much dances. My own mood lightened by several shades as he said, "Hey, Vayl, if she asks you to prom, I know a great limo service you can use."

Vayl's slumped shoulders and crossed arms made him so resemble a honked-off teen that Dave laughed. "This is serious!" Vayl declared.

"Of course it is," Dave said soothingly. "That's why I am *not* signing her yearbook."

Vayl shot out of his chair. "You are incorrigible!"

Dave held up his hands. "Whoa, calm down, buddy, I'm just teasing. Plus, I don't even know what that means." He glanced at me. "Do I?"

"Constipated?" I guessed.

Dave shrugged. "I would've said it had something to do with my top-notch spitting skills." He hawked and blew a wad of jaw-juice right into the fountain. "Did you see that?" he demanded. "Nothing but net."

"I'd point out how disgusting that was, but considering the state of the water, you've probably just dramatically improved the pH. Speaking of which, you're in a good mood."

"I finally got a hold of Cassandra." He gave me a significant look. "She doesn't hate me yet. Plus"—he gestured to his black T-shirt—"I finally got time to change."

"Good deal." I looked at Vayl. "You know, Disa not hating *you* could be a point of strength for us. If you'd care to use it to your advantage."

Vayl had gone to the bookshelf, where he was alternately picking up and putting down doodads. "I want nothing to do with her!" he said, setting one of the little statues down so hard that it broke. "Now see what you made me do?"

"Actually, I felt something when that happened," I told him. I went over and picked up another figurine, a fat naked chick with gigantic mammaries. My hands tingled as I held the piece. It oozed power. They all did. Even the books. Just like the masks I'd seen in the villa's entryway, only not enough for me to sense until one had broken and sparked a response in the others. When I told the guys about it, they tried to feel what I meant. But neither of them reacted as I had.

"Okay, so you can't perceive the power directly," I said to Vayl. "But this is more proof of what we've been talking about. It could even be the source of that itch. What if the binding Disa set on you is powered by the objects in this villa?"

"What are you suggesting?" asked Dave. "That if we smash everything in this mansion we break the Mating bond?"

I sighed. "No. I don't know. I'm just saying."

Vayl nodded. "This is good," he said. "We might be able to do something with this." He considered the broken pieces with a look so piercing I almost expected them to disintegrate. He nodded. "Excellent work, Jasmine."

Before I could stop myself, I put my hand on his arm, let my fingers wrap around the smooth curve of his biceps. His eyes tracked to mine, their icy blue interest making me blink, as if I'd just walked out into a blizzard. "Thanks. You . . . you hardly ever compliment me. And I like it when you do." I dropped my hand. *Holy crap, was that ever hard. I think I'd rather chase a murderer through a ghetto full of gangbangers!*

The corners of his lips rose. "Then I will be sure to do it more often."

Dave clapped his hands together, making me jump. Vayl just looked at him inquiringly. "Now that we all know what an ace assistant Jaz is, can we review the plan? I've got places to go. People to see." He patted his pockets again and checked his watch. He figured we'd think he was joking. But I could tell he still wanted to snag himself some liquid Valium. My first reaction? Kick him, hard, in the shins.

Instead I said, "I'm free."

Dave took a seat by the fountain, where we joined him. He gestured to Vayl. "It's your baby. You start."

Vayl bowed his head slightly as he said, "Unwisely, Hamon allowed Samos to dictate the details of their first meeting. It is set for one hour after dusk, to occur in a place called the Odeum. Hamon must have felt safe in agreeing to the spot, since it is somewhat in his territory, but Disa tells me it is an ancient amphitheater. I do not need to tell you how vulnerable we would be once Samos had us sitting on that pit of a stage with a stone backdrop on one side and seating marching up a steep hilltop on the others."

"You act like we're really going to negotiate with this guy," Dave said.

"Not at all," Vayl replied. "But we have to be able to terminate him in such a way that everyone in the Trust can escape unscathed."

There it was again, one of those words that reminded me that Vayl had never quite moved beyond his past. I admitted to myself that I partied a little every time I recalled that fact. Because he'd held on to a lot of the good stuff. And some of the bad. But now, watching him work, I felt something vital was missing that had been a part of his long march through history.

Vayl went on. "Because eliminating him at the Odeum would be too dangerous, we must force Samos to a different location. One that we can control. Once we have accomplished that, our mission should run smoothly."

"And that's where the dog comes in," Dave put in.

"Indeed," Vayl agreed. "We must gain possession of it well before tomorrow night's meeting. And when I say we . . ."

"You mean Jasmine and me," Dave finished.

Vayl nodded. "We did agree the wisest time to take Samos's malamute would be when its master and his strongest people are at rest, leaving only his human guardians to contend with."

"And here's where you lose me," Dave said. "Because I just don't get why a guy as villainous as you say Samos is would risk his power play to get a *dog* back."

I leaned forward, resting my elbows on my knees, clasping my hands together as my mind went back to the vision I'd had of our target. The one that had led us to this assignment and this moment. "Do you remember when I told you about the time Raoul took me to hell?" I asked my brother.

His sharp nod told me the less I said about that discussion the better. Because it had involved the fact that I'd met our mother there. "I had a vision of Samos during that trip," I said. "He was trying to make a pact with a demon called the Magistrate. But in order for it to work, he had to give up something incredibly precious to him. His dog. In the end, he refused to do it."

"But how do you know the dog really means that much to him?"

"The Magistrate knew. And look, *I* had to give something up in order to gain that vision. Something that meant the world to me." I stopped, mainly so I wouldn't start bawling. Dave wouldn't understand how much I missed my playing cards. How the whisper of the bridge, the slap of the shuffle, had worked on me like coke on a junkie. "I promise you, Samos loves that dog like our sister adores her baby girl. We get that malamute, we can play him like a drum."

"And Disa's fine with this plan?" he asked.

Vayl paused, as if trying to think of a tactful way to put his next few words. He shook his head. "She believes you and Jasmine will fail, in which case you will die, which is her ideal. With you two dead and me bound, she wins."

Chapter Fourteen

I thought about Disa getting her way like some spoiled brat who's managed to cruise through life on Mommy's looks and Daddy's Visa. And the more I considered, the hotter I got. *She thinks she's got us all right where she wants us, huh? It's too bad somebody didn't rip her face off when* — my thoughts halted as somewhere in the house an alarm went off.

STOP STARTING FIRES! The voice of my Spirit Guide, booming at me across the planes of our existences like a mountain with a megaphone, sounded disgusted. Like I was some kind of arsonist or something!

It's not me, Raoul!

YES, IT IS.

Even if I thought I was capable, which I don't, why would I be doing that?

YOU TELL ME.

I thought about how I'd been feeling before the alarms went off. And about my overall mood lately. *Well, I suppose I have been a little . . . wound up . . . recently. I've got a stressful job, don't I? And now that I don't have cards as an outlet. Or sex. Or drinking, drugs, gambling . . . You know what? How about you just leave me the hell alone? If I could set stuff on fire with my mind, I should be allowed to burn down the whole damn villa if I feel like it!*

Amusement in his tone now. *YOU DON'T MEAN THAT.*

Why was it that everybody knew me better than I knew my-self? Un-freaking-fair.

Okay, maybe not. Inner sigh. *So what are you saying? I've developed some sort of mental Aim 'n' Flame? And it just goes off arbitrarily?*

NOTHING RANDOM ABOUT YOUR TINDER.

I recalled that both times the fires had started I'd been mad as hell. But apparently instead of steam coming out my ears, I'd caused flames to pop up in my least favorite stomping grounds.

What am I supposed to do? I asked Raoul in utter frustration.

CONTROL YOURSELF.

That was easy for him to say. If he didn't have to fight creeping evil every time he turned around, he'd probably be a saint by now. However, since he could probably fry my brain just by clearing his throat, I decided to cooperate. Self-control would be a cinch if Disa was dead, so I tried to calm myself with an imaginary montage starring both of us. Wouldn't it be awesome if we could do a little Cartoon Network scene where I blew her up with TNT, dropped her off a mountain, ran her over with a steamroller, and catapulted her into the side of Rockefeller Center, after which she would get up, stumble around groggily for a few seconds, shake it off, and *then* impale herself on my lance-sized stake? Ahh, if life was only like television. *I'd* certainly feel better. In fact, just fantasizing about it elevated my mood.

THAT'S BETTER, said Raoul. REMEMBER YOUR POKER FIXATION AS WELL.

His voice had such finality to it that I felt a surge of panic. *No, wait, don't leave yet! I'll practice shifting the chips, I promise. But I have to know what to do about the firebug trait I've suddenly developed. And, in case you haven't noticed, I'm in a major predicament with this Disa mess. Couldn't you —*

ON THE FIRST ISSUE — PRACTICE. I'M OUT ON THE SECOND.

Why?

NOT MY FIELD OF EXPERTISE. I wished we had video to go along with the words in my head. Because I was sure it would've confirmed the deceit I heard in his voice. It wasn't that he couldn't help. He simply wouldn't. Which was when I realized my Spirit Guide didn't approve of my *sverhamin*. I wasn't overly surprised. On paper they seemed to fall on opposite philosophic poles. But we were all working toward the same goal here. Which made me feel like Raoul was being somewhat narrow-minded. I wondered if it was a personal deal, or if he was acting on orders from Above.

Either way, we were SOL. Judging by the stubborn set of Vayl's jaw, he wouldn't have accepted outside help on this anyway. He spoke to Dave since I obviously had nothing useful to say. "I wonder if perhaps Disa is still smarting from the humiliation I brought down on her when she was still human. She hates to lose. Perhaps she has found a way to exact her revenge upon me after all these years."

"I could drop a boulder on her head," I murmured.

"Excuse me?" said Vayl.

I looked at my watch. "Wow, three a.m. Where has the time gone? Are we squared away on the dognapping?"

Dave nodded. "Just what I was going to ask. I understand our cover. But not how we're supposed to get this mutt's attention."

"Bergman has provided us with the tools we need," said Vayl. He turned to me. "Jasmine?"

Since I'd packed the goodies, it came to me to run into the bedroom and unearth the plain silver aerosol cans that contained Bergman's invention. Barely resisting the urge to cover my brother in doggy-sniff mist, I tossed him one can and gave the other to Vayl. As I resumed my seat I said, "When I told Bergman we needed to take temporary custody of a large canine, he sent me these. He said to treat them like bug spray."

"You mean, they're a repellent?" asked Dave.

"Just the opposite. As soon as he gets a whiff of us, he'll want to be friends for life. He'll go anywhere with us, no problem. By the way, the dog's name is Ziel."

"What're we going to smell like to him?" Dave asked. "Steak?"

"That's what I asked. No, Bergman says he won't think we're dinner. It's more a let's-play kind of scent. Like we're just a couple of other malamutes."

"Is this a prototype?"

"Nope. He invented it about five years ago. Tried and true."

"So we are set," Vayl pronounced. "You two will use Bergman's spray to aid in your mission tomorrow. Samos is staying at a hotel called the Olympia. David already has the address because he is going to place cameras outside the entrances at his earliest convenience." He rubbed his hands together like he was about to dig into a big old piece of apple pie. But I knew better. He just didn't know what else to do with them. Which was when I realized what had been missing from the overall picture.

"What happened to your cane?" I asked.

He opened his empty hands, stared at them as if he'd just seen them for the first time today. When his eyes rose to meet mine, they were nearly black with fury. "I cannot remember. But I can imagine."

"Disa," we both said at the same time. We looked at Dave.

"Exactly what happened in that meeting?" I demanded. "Describe everything. Any detail could make the difference."

"What are you saying?" asked Dave. "What's the cane got to do with the meeting?"

"Maybe nothing," I told him, shooting Vayl a comforting look. "Maybe you just left it under your chair when it was time to go."

"But I have never forgotten it," Vayl said, rubbing the heel of his hand across his forehead. "It has been my constant companion for over two hundred years."

I nodded. "Which means it's become a part of you. Objects like that can be dangerous when they fall into the wrong hands. So" — I turned back to my brother — "details."

Dave scratched his cheeks, the sandpaper scrape of his nails against the new growth of his beard the only sound in the room. "We went to Disa's private quarters. There's a stone balcony built off her bedroom with a wall that curves out and a stairway that leads to the ground floor. That's where the talk happened. There weren't many chairs, so most of us stood. In fact, I think the only people who sat were Vayl and Disa."

"Who else was there?"

"Sibley and Marcon. Those two gigantic guards were there too."

"What happened when you came onto the balcony?"

"Sibley handed us copies of the contract. I remember being surprised she'd found it so easily after all that bullshit about not even knowing we were coming." Dave glanced at Vayl. "What did you think about that?"

My boss had gone stiff and wary, as if he suspected an imminent ambush. "I . . ." His hand went to his forehead, triggering an overall tightening of his facial muscles that aged him by at least a decade. "Something distracted me almost from the moment the meeting began. I found it hard to concentrate. I kept looking at the guards, thinking they were being rude speaking so loudly during an important meeting. But they were not talking at all."

"Did you have your cane when you stepped onto Disa's balcony?" I asked.

He nodded. "Of that I am sure."

"What else?" I directed the question to Dave.

He shrugged. "Pretty straightforward stuff until the end. They went over the details while the guards and I made sure everybody behaved."

"But in the end Disa didn't toe the line. In fact, she drew an entirely new one." I tried, really I did, but I couldn't keep the accusation out of my tone. Dave faced it squarely, as he'd been trained to, though the toll must've made his shoulders creak, considering the load he was already carrying. "I'm sorry," I said immediately. "Your job is just to watch Vayl's back. And you did exactly that. She didn't stab him. She trapped him. There's no way you could've prevented that."

"Maybe if I'd have known what to look for," Dave said with a regretful shrug. "But after the contract discussion was over, all she did was lean sideways, pick this two-handled cup off the floor, and say, 'With this blood I bind you for the next half century.' Then she poured the contents over his hand."

As Vayl studied his pale, empty fingers, I said, "Wait a second. You didn't mention a cup before. Was it big?"

What's the difference? said Dave's gesture. "It stood about twelve inches high. Gold. Reminded me of the Ryder Cup trophy with the golfer hacked off the top."

"That's a pretty showy item to have missed when you first came onto the balcony," I said. "Neither of you noticed it at all?" The men shook their heads. "And, Vayl? You just sat there and let her pour blood all over your digits? No avoidance? No protest?"

"At the time I felt she had the right." He shook his head. "It is as we have realized. The power of this place. It worms its way into your pores, and before you realize it, you are behaving as if everything the *Deyrar* says and does is correct and natural." He clenched his fists. "So she bound me. That still does not explain what happened to my cane. Or why she needs it."

"Did you have it when she poured the blood over your hand?" I asked.

"Yes. I remember thinking that I needed to clean it off of the wood before it stained. So I went into her bathroom and washed my hand. But before I got to the cane, I decided to leave it. In her bathroom."

"Why?" I asked.

He put his fingers to his temples. "I had the oddest feeling I should give her a gift since we had become bound. I tried to resist the urge. Part of me understood the best course of action would be to find you and get out, despite the fact that it would end our mission. But my hand began to burn with such heat I had to hold it under the cold-water tap. After I had stood there for another minute, I decided to leave the cane after all. So I did. And I promptly forgot it."

Dave sat forward. "Let's go get it. I haven't kicked ass in so long, the steel toes of my boots are getting rusty." When Vayl hesitated he pressed. "You know Disa can't be up to any good with it."

"I agree," I said. "You and I both understand what trouble people can get into when they lose something they value as much as you do that cane. She might try to control you through it."

"Or she may use it as a *pwen*," Vayl countered.

Crap, he might have hit the mark there.

"What's a *pwen*?" asked Dave.

"An object used in self-defense," I explained. "Considering what Disa's done to Vayl, and what she might be planning, she could be thinking he'd be tempted to move against her. Especially since he's already shown an ability to resist the Trust in the past. In that case, she'd have stolen the cane to use as a shield against Vayl's powers if he becomes violent. Since he's had it so long, it's absorbed a lot of his energies, so it's the ideal item for the job."

"But she's already manipulated him," Dave argued. "He couldn't even remember leaving it in her possession. Now that she has it, I'm betting she's using it to tighten the screws." The stare he sent Vayl was more bitter than day-old coffee. "It's just like the ohm. Only it's not stuck inside his neck."

I put my hand on my brother's knee. "The Wizard's dead, Dave. You won."

He shrugged. Gave me his *whatever* look.

I studied him as he turned back to argue with Vayl. Spoiling for a fight, Dave gave it his best shot while my boss debated for the wait-and-see side. As they talked, I tried to open another eye. It wasn't easy. I'd been alone for eight months before partnering with Vayl. You tend to develop cataracts working that way. Makes the killing easier. Dams the nightmares. But eventually you go blind. Vayl had taught me new ways of working, unique avenues of thinking. It didn't mean I'd gotten tons better at stepping out of my own head. But for Dave's sake, I tried.

What would it be like to be at another person's mercy? Trapped by a power more adept and much more willing to do evil than you? Especially when you were accustomed to leading a force of elite troops trained to operate independently and tasked with only the most nut-cracking assignments the military could dredge up?

That's a vulnerable situation to be in. With your soul straining to fly while some badass necromancer binds it with magic and bone. And then my spine straightened, the answer I needed flying up from the seat of my pants to encase it in iron. That was Dave's real problem. He'd been like a hostage. A prisoner of war. All the crap he'd heaped on top of that original victimization he could probably deal with if only he got his head past the conviction that he should have fought in a situation when he couldn't possibly have done anything different.

I suddenly felt the gap in my training. I knew how to be a prisoner. Like my twin, I could survive the incarceration no matter what it entailed. But the aftermath? I had no idea how to slog through that, much less help somebody else deal. He needed professional assistance. But I might as well suggest he dress in drag and sing "Girls Just Want to Have Fun."

Then I realized I had a pro right at my fingertips. But before I could make the call, I needed to discuss one more item. And I thought I might have calmed down enough to do that without setting off any more alarms.

I waited for a pause in the discussion. "I ran into Blas before."

Vayl sat even straighter. "You did? But Disa said he was—" I waited while Vayl recalled their conversation about the lost vampires, during which Disa had not told him what happened to a single one. "Where did you find him? Why did he stay inside when the rest came out to confront us?"

"I imagine that would have something to do with the fact that he couldn't have found his way without a guide. And he seems to be avoiding Disa like the plague since she's the reason he's"—I almost said blind, but that didn't go far enough—"maimed," I finished.

"What has she done?" he demanded, his features so taut you'd have thought I'd threatened to stake him in his sleep.

I didn't take any pleasure in telling him. I sensed he'd begun to feel personally responsible for Disa's horrors, like the father of a girl who opens fire on all her least-favorite classmates. Well, maybe he should. I'd terminated plenty of targets whose parents had been even more monstrous than them. Then again, as my Granny May used to say, some people are just born with the devil in them.

As I described my conversation with Blas, part of me wondered what it had been like for Vayl, living here. From bits of information he'd let slip during our time together, I figured he'd spent a little over a century in the Trust. A hundred years hunting, gambling, partying, fighting, eating, and yeah, most likely sleeping with these people. I thought of Sibley and the woman he'd called

Aine and quickly doused a spark of jealousy that might easily have set some papers aflame in a wastebasket somewhere.

As grief etched long lines in his cheeks, I blurted, "What were you like?"

He reared back, almost as if I'd slapped him. "What do you mean?"

"When you lived here before. What kind of man—" I shook my head. Why did my brain keep classifying him as human? "What kind of vampire were you?"

He gave Dave and me a long, considering look before he spoke. And then he shrugged. "After the split from Liliana I became a Rogue. It is not an easy life. Vampires are quite territorial. I spent nearly all my waking hours either fighting or moving on. It became tiresome trying to find a new safe spot to rest every morning before the sun rose. So when I met Niall while I was hunting one evening and he did not immediately try to rip my throat out, I began to think perhaps I had found a way to a better life."

I licked my lips. They'd dried out suddenly when he'd mentioned hunting so casually, like Albert and Dave had right before deer season started, when they'd begun to get their gear in order for opening day. But what he'd meant was that he'd hidden in dark alleyways and abandoned warehouses, waiting for drunken sailors and unsuspecting night owls to stroll by. At which point—

"Did you kill them?" I asked, unable, somehow, to find any tact now that I'd taken this line of questioning. "The people you hunted, I mean? Did they die after you . . ."

He shook his head. "Some vampires kill their prey, but it is only for the pleasure of it. Death is not necessary for sustenance. You know that, Jasmine." Rebuke in his voice. *How could you think that of me?* his eyes asked.

Don't try to bullshit me, I told him in a way he could read clearly on my face. *I know you're a natural-born killer.*

As are you, his expression said.

Just so we're clear.

He inclined his head. "I have destroyed many vampires and their human guardians in my time. More than I can count. While I was a Rogue, I did it to survive. Once I began to walk in the Trust, I killed the ones who threatened our territory. I even smoked a few within the Trust who, for one reason or another, threatened the stability of the group to such a degree that they could not be allowed to continue." He jerked his head up, almost defensively, as if he could feel me judging him. "I found no joy in it." He leaned forward. "But it is one of the things I do best."

"Have you turned anyone besides Disa?" I asked.

"No."

Dave piped up. "And you can't think of any way to break this binding?"

"Not as yet. Every Trust is wound with the power of its members. This creates something more that is unique to each community — that power Jasmine has discovered that pulls at me even now. And it builds over generations, so that a century ago the villa I escaped might be compared to a fort. Today it is a citadel. Impassable, yes? This is what Disa used to bind me."

We nodded. Maybe we'd been naive to think all that *shazam* would just sit there, pulsing, and not try to manipulate us once it had us in its grasp. Or that the *Deyrar* wouldn't use it to further the Trust's agenda. But that's what happens in this line of work. Sometimes you don't have all the background you need before you go in and the risk factor spikes to holy-crap-where'd-we-stash-the-hazmat-suits? Which is why they pay us the big bucks.

"You make the Trust sound impregnable," I said. "But we got inside."

"Hamon had opened the way for us. A path Disa had apparently failed to block."

"Or one she left open," Dave said. When we turned his way, he added, "I'm sticking with the puppy love theory. It's just too cute to drop."

Vayl rolled his eyes. "At any rate, I believe our best hope is to find the true source of her power. Remember what Tarasios said about the masks being spokes of a wheel? Jasmine, with your observations of the power in the Trust's objects, you have at least given us a place to begin."

"That could take years, which we *mortals* don't have," said Dave. "Why can't we just take Disa out?" His casual tone chilled me. It seemed slightly hypocritical, since terminating bad guys was my gig after all. I decided it bothered me because I didn't *want* him to be like me. Married people might talk about their better halves. But Dave really was mine. Seeing him go down my road made me all the more determined to detour him. Where was an exhausted, pissed-off construction crew when you needed them?

Vayl said, "Beyond the fact that her life, and death, are now inextricably linked with mine, the *Deyrar* exists at the center of the Trust, its strong heart. As such, she wields her own power, the Trust's, and everyone else's as well. She cannot be denied."

"You got out," I said. "That implies that the *Deyrar* isn't omnipotent."

Vayl shrugged. "It took me decades to build the strength. And in the end, it was what Hamon and I both wanted."

Dave said, "That seems pretty convenient. Care to elaborate?"

Vayl spent some time studying the fountain. "I had begun to realize I was trading safety for freedom, and the price was the erosion of what remained of my—" He glanced up. Tightened his lips. It reminded me so strongly of Bergman's nunya-bizness look that I smiled. Vayl said, "I realized I did not want to fit into Hamon's world anymore. But many in the Trust felt my new leanings would serve them better. When I expressed a desire to leave, they asked me to challenge him instead."

The way Vayl said the word "challenge" let us know he wasn't referring to a chess match.

Though we all knew the ultimate outcome, none of us mocked Dave when he asked intently, "So what did you do?"

"I had found a new Seer. A Sister of the Second Sight, like Cassandra. She had told me I would meet my sons in America. It was 1921. I had spent one hundred and nine years in the Trust. More time than I had lived anywhere else in all my life. But the possibility of seeing my boys again began to obsess me as it had not in over thirty years. So I went to Hamon with an ultimatum." Vayl looked at his empty hands, rubbed his fingers together as if he missed the feel of his cane. I realized with a sense of awe that he'd probably held that very item in his hands the night he'd confronted Hamon with his choices. "I told him either he had to let me go. Or I would drape myself with the powers of my supporters and tear him from the center of the Trust like a cancerous tumor."

"What did he say to that?" Dave prodded.

"He sat back in his throne of a chair, steepled his hands like the mathematics professor he had once been, and said, 'Dearling boy, I see no need for us to be at odds. Of course you may go.'"

That word "dearling" caught my attention, but before I could figure out where I'd heard it before, Vayl had gone on with his story. "So I packed my bags and took the first ship I could find for New York. Of course Hamon sent hunters after me. It could do his reputation harm if word leaked that one of his own had deserted the Trust."

"But you killed them," Dave said, trading a knowing look with me.

"You might call it my introduction to my new career," Vayl said with a slight nod, his gesture taking in the room but referring to every mission he'd had since signing on with the CIA in 1927. "Of course, it took the government some time to organize a department that could use my particular talents. But when it finally evolved, I became its first staff member."

I hadn't known the department Pete now supervised was created around his longest-living and most legendary staff member. But when you thought about it, it made perfect sense.

"That was a pretty slick escape," said Dave, rubbing his neck as he once had when the Wizard was in charge of him. I could tell by the tone in his voice that he wondered why he hadn't been able to pull off something similar. Well, hell, if he'd had forty years to plan, maybe he'd have figured something out as well!

Deciding now was the time to make my own exit, I said, "'Scuse me," as I headed toward the bathroom. When I was safe behind the locked door, thumbing through my short list of numbers, I realized Cole hadn't contacted me in a while. Did that mean his mission was going well? One could only hope.

My father answered the phone with his usual grumble. "*Judge Judy's* on. Make it quick."

"It's good to hear your voice too, Albert. How's Shelby?"

Shelby is Albert's nurse, and the main reason the old man still has all his fingers and toes. Though why any diabetic needs another human being to explain the dangers of donuts and hot chocolate to him on a daily basis I still have no clue. "He's fine. He's the only person I know who can make a salad that fills me up. Explain that, will ya?"

"I imagine he's injecting the lettuce with steak and potatoes."

"That's what I thought too, but I couldn't find a trace of either one in there." He sounded so sincere I nearly laughed. Then I went ahead and let 'er rip. Because only a few weeks before I'd thought I might never hear his voice again.

While I'd been working in Iran, Albert had been hit by a

woman driving a minivan as he toured his neighborhood on his new motorcycle. During the time he'd been stuck in Chicago West with tubes sprouting from every orifice, he'd become convinced the woman had hit him on purpose. Especially when she skipped bail. But by the time he and Shelby had driven to my sister's house in Indy to help us celebrate Easter, his whole thought process had changed. Mine hadn't.

"Any sign of that driver?" I asked.

"Naw. The cops are baffled. They say it's like she never existed. Dumbasses."

"Any more phone calls from nowhere? Ghostly guests?"

"I told you what I saw was probably a morphine hallucination."

I thought the grinning skull that had taken the place of his ICU nurse's face to warn him of future visitations had probably been as real as the phone in my hand. But when my family doesn't want to stomach a reality, they do a damn good job of denying it. I didn't have time to talk sense into him, and nothing had happened since to convince him otherwise, so I decided to go along with the pretense for a while longer. At the moment, Dave's problem pressed harder.

"Look, I've got a situation here." I explained my theory about Dave. "You've been in the military forever. Even if you don't have firsthand experience, surely you know somebody who has an idea how to get him through this. Someone who's dealt with guys who've been taken hostage or spent time as prisoners of war?"

We sat in silence for so long I began to wonder if I'd lost the signal. "Hello?"

"Goddammit, I'm sorry, Jazzy. So sorry to have brought you and your brother to this spot."

I was so shocked I plopped down on the toilet. Thank God its last user had dropped the lid or I'd have sunk to the bottom. Thing was, Albert didn't know the half of it. If he had, he'd probably be on his knees blubbering. Yuck. "We're grown-ups, Dad. If we'd wanted to do anything different, we would've."

He took a breath. I could almost hear him pulling himself together. Old guys pop like bubble wrap. Especially marines. "Yeah, you know what, there are a couple of people I could call." There, that assured tone in his voice that had gone missing after his forced retirement. It kept me calling him, asking for small favors that others could have done for me. Well, I had to admit, he'd pulled a few strings lately that had helped my missions skip right along.

That's what I told myself. But there was still a little girl inside me, her swing set virtually hidden behind a tall, green hedge. Usually I could only see the tips of her white shoes and the matching bow in her hair as she pumped her swing high enough to top the shrubbery and shriek a message that might, or might not, be heard over the heavy droning of my heart and its various connections. Just now I actually saw a red curl flutter in the breeze of her whoosh upward as she called out, "Maybe he loves you after all."

Chapter Fifteen

When I returned to the sitting room the men had stopped talking. It felt like they'd been waiting for me.

"What?" I asked.

"I would like to speak to Blas," said Vayl. "Can you take me to the place where you found him?"

I shrugged. "Sure. But I doubt he's still there. I got the feeling he was hiding from them as much as I was."

"Perhaps, then, you could follow his scent?"

"I can try." I wasn't holding out much hope though. With camouflage like his, I'd be more likely to pick up a physical clue.

As we walked toward the door I realized Dave wasn't with us. "You're staying?" I asked over my shoulder.

"Yeah." That was it. No other explanation. I swallowed the surge of panic that wanted to jump out and start screaming, "Don't go searching for liquor! You don't need to get blasted! Help's on the way!"

I said, "Okay." I turned to go. And then it hit me. One of those evil thoughts siblings get because, well, that's what we do. Looking over my shoulder I said, "You know, since you have some free time, maybe you could . . . never mind."

"What?"

"Well, it's just that, all those extra calories you've been drink — I mean — not burning off have kind of settled on your gut. I didn't want to mention anything," I said as Dave's hand stole to his mid-section. "But the general pointed out that you'd lost a few steps training-wise." I laughed and waved my hand. "I'm sure it's nothing switching to light beer won't cure."

"I am sure Jasmine is right," Vayl said from behind me. "Cassandra told me once she likes her men pudgy. Something about more to love?"

We left Dave trying to pinch an inch off his battle-hardened frame. As soon as we were out of earshot I said, "So, do you want to give me odds?"

"On which side are you betting?" asked Vayl.

"I'm putting two bucks on the Special Ops commander to do push-ups and squat thrusts the whole time we're gone."

Vayl's lips quirked. "You are a devious woman."

"Whatever it takes."

I led Vayl to the closet, which, as I'd expected, was empty. He crouched by the open door. "Blas was just sitting here when you walked in?"

"Yeah. But I'm not sure he came through the same door. There's another opening." I showed him the one I'd found during my claustrophobic search. It looked crude, the sides curvy, the edges uneven. Definitely not a planned part of the architecture.

"So did he exit by it?" Vayl asked.

I spent some time in the doorway before crawling into the closet, closing my eyes to better focus my extra sense. "Yeah, I think so."

Vayl dropped to his knees beside me. "Then let us go after him."

Vayl's shoulders would fit comfortably on a linebacker. Or a Brahma bull. No way could we share that space without rubbing up against each other in ways that felt uncomfortably intimate. Suddenly the closet shrank like tight jeans in a hot wash.

I leaned back, trying to get some air, but it didn't help. It just gave me a better view of his broad back tapering down to a lovely, firm — I cleared my throat. "Is it hot in here? Are you hot? I think their heating system is definitely on the fritz."

Vayl smirked at me. "I will go first, shall I?" He reached forward, pushed the door until it came free and fell into the next room, giving him the space he needed to crawl through the opening it left. While I, well, all I really did was ogle until his legs were through. I only snapped out of it when he said, "Jasmine, get in here," with a sense of urgency that forced me to roll up my tongue and scramble after him.

Vayl had flipped the light switch, activating the wall sconces, but still my feeling was of emerging into a cavern that smelled of must and cobwebs. Since I was trained to find exits upon entering a new area, that's where my eyes traveled. But no traditional doors or windows broke the lines of plastered walls that had cracked and yellowed with age and dirt.

A layer of gray dust shaded the dark blue carpet, which showed footprints that meandered around the stone sarcophagus that dominated the room. Okay, so this was where Blas slept during the day. I could tell by the scent he'd left, even though it was so faint it read like he hadn't snoozed there in weeks. I turned to ask Vayl what had concerned him when he put one finger to his lips and pointed to the back of the room.

I squeezed my eyes shut. Rarely did I have to activate the contact lenses Bergman had made me anymore, since my Sensitivity had honed itself to the point where I could almost see in the dark. But still, they gave me that extra little oomph I sometimes needed to make out — *What the hell is that!*

My mind flipped through its normal files first. Scarecrow? Suit of armor with its arms outstretched?

Think again, Jaz.

Don't wanna.

Go ahead. Step closer. Take a hard look. Yep, that's it. I obeyed the voice in my head because it was the one that spoke to me when I pulled the trigger. Something soothing about the clipped rhythm, that icy tone. No fear in a voice that spent so much time straddling the grave.

I shivered. I wasn't sure what scared me more—myself, or the moment. "It's a body," I whispered.

"I think it has been hung from the ceiling. Like a marionette. Look at all the wires," Vayl replied, his voice as muted as my own.

I pulled Grief, pressing the magic button as I felt Vayl raise his powers. We approached the body from either side of the sarcophagus, moving deliberately, our eyes sweeping the room every few seconds for surprises.

"What's on its head?" I whispered. I wanted to reach across Blas's stone bed, grab Vayl's hand, and hang on until he assured me we were having a mutual nightmare.

"Hat?" he guessed.

"That's a funky-shaped—" Then I stopped talking. Because the hat unrolled its legs and perched them on the body's shoulders. It made a horrible sucking sound.

No hat, my mind shrilled. *No hat, because no head for it to sit on. It's a—what the fuck is that?* The creature scuttled down the neck and perched on the chest like an enormous throbbing tie tack.

"Shit!" I jumped up onto the sarcophagus in a single bound. Superman would've been proud. Of course he probably wouldn't have missed when he squeezed off a bolt, but then he always was too perfect for my taste.

"Forget the crossbow!" Vayl yelled as he filled the room with frost. "That is a *grall*. Bullets, Jasmine, and now!"

I reversed my Walther's load as I reviewed what I knew about the *grall*, all of it book-learned because this was the first one I'd met up close and personal. Adults the size of a volleyball, and where you saw one, since they were hermaphroditic, you usually had at least a dozen young infesting the place too. They moved like lightning on six hair-covered legs the color of cranberry sauce. A light shell covered most of their crab-shaped bodies, but in the middle, multiple portions stuck through the carapace like thick, fleshy antennae. Though these were vulnerable areas, they also allowed the *grall* to attach themselves through a set of dagger-sharp teeth to any living creature. And here was the funky part. They didn't just suck out blood. They took secrets. And if you gave the *grall* the right kind of offering later on, you could get those secrets for yourself.

I took aim. The creature had frozen to its victim's chest, like an opossum that thought playing dead might buy it an escape. Holding my breath, I fired. At the last second the *grall* dodged, its squeal of pain letting me know I'd hit it, but probably not fatally. Most of the bullet seemed to have lodged in the corpse.

Vayl kicked something that bounced off the wall with a high-pitched squeal. "There are young!"

"Get up here!" I yelled. "I'm less likely to hit you that way."

He leaped up beside me. "What I would give for my cane right now!"

"Grab my bolo!" His hand slid into my right pocket. My body responded with a *wow-baby!* thrill that I did my best to ignore as I blasted a couple of the offspring into meat chunks. Vayl's chilling of the room had slowed them more than it had the parent, which had taken refuge on the wall behind the body.

As Vayl released the knife from my pocket sheath, I scanned the floor and walls for movement. Nothing. I turned to Vayl, preparing to ask if he'd ever heard of such a small litter, when something fell past my face, slashing my cheek as it went. As I looked up I felt a weight hit me in the middle of the back. "Vayl, they're on the ceiling!"

He stabbed upward, impaling one on his knife.

"Check my back! My back!" I yelled, turning so he could see.

"Hold still!" I heard the air scream past the blade as he slashed at the creature trying to chew its way through the leather of my jacket. As soon as I heard the piece plop to the stone at my feet I gave Grief free rein. Only when I paused to reload did I hear Vayl grunt in pain.

I looked over. He was surrounded by *grall* corpses. But one had dropped on him while he was busy with the others and dug in just behind his right ear. Before I could react, he ripped it off his head, throwing it against the wall so hard it splatted like a bug on a windshield. Blood ran down the back of his neck, making the four remaining young shriek with hunger.

These were smarter than their brothers/sisters. They'd realized the ceiling offered no protection and had taken cover behind the two glass lamps that provided light for the room. I'd thought we'd have to get up close and personal to pick them off. But Vayl's scent had drawn them out.

I took a second to glance at the body. Nope. The parent knew better than to leave its hidey-hole. *Okay, fine. We'll take out your disgusting little juniors first.*

They came at us in a rush. I took out one before the rest were on us. Vayl stabbed another as it hit the stone between his feet. The remaining two leaped at his throat, squealing as they closed on their goal. Since Vayl was too close to risk a shot, I threw a jump kick that nailed one of the beasts square in the back, sending it flying into the ceiling. When it flopped to the ground I shot it twice. I'd have gotten it clean on the first try, but part of my focus switched to Vayl, who caught the last one on the end of the knife, impaling it like a spitted pig.

We gave each other a satisfied nod and turned to the hanging corpse. "Whose remains do you think?" I asked.

Vayl touched his neck gingerly, grimaced at the sticky on his hands, and replied, "I cannot be certain, of course. But the ring on his pinky is quite unique. I would guess it is Hamon's."

"What? No! Hamon lost his head. Which means the rest of him would've gone bye-bye. That's how it works with you guys."

"That is how it *usually* works," Vayl contradicted. "One exception would be if you had a *grall* attached to your body at the time you were decapitated. In which case it would not dissipate."

"The *grall* has that kind of power?"

"Yes. Because some secrets could still be drawn from your blood, your organs, even your bones."

I eyed the corpse, its ruffled cravat and rust-colored suit coat stained with the blood of the head that had once completed it. "Bullshit."

"What do you call forensic pathology?" asked Vayl.

"That's different!"

"So speaks the woman with a Spirit Eye, a Spirit *Guide*, and a tendency to rise from the dead."

Smartass. "Say I buy your explanation." *Which I think I'm going to have to, dammit.* "Does that mean I can't kill the adult? I mean, if Blas set it on Hamon to suck out his secrets, do you need to know what they are now?"

"I think we can surmise what Blas needed to know without risking our lives any further."

"Really?"

"Certainly. Blas obviously lied to you. He was the one who wanted Hamon's authority. Or perhaps he and Disa both wanted it. But it is a powerful position, and ascendance requires secret knowledge to which only Hamon had access. If I had challenged and beaten him, he would have been forced to hand that knowledge over to me. Blas and Disa obviously found another route. But something went wrong, either before or during the coup, and she turned on him."

"So I can shoot the creepy crawler?"

"Be my guest."

Finally, good news. Should we celebrate? If I backed up a step Vayl would be pressed against me like a winter coat. Maybe, if I killed the *grall*, he'd even be in the mood to forgive me for returning Cirilai. Which I was beginning to think I wanted back. I gave myself a mental shake. *This is why you shouldn't hook up with your boss, Jaz. So distracting when you're trying to concentrate on the job.*

I considered the situation for a moment. If the adult hadn't moved at the prospect of fresh, vulnerable food, it obviously meant to stay put until we left. Or forced it into action. "Somebody's going to have to get that body jiggling."

This is going to be so gross. The stuff of nightmares, actually.

"I will do it." He stepped forward.

"Don't!" I realized I'd laid my hand on his chest and he was looking down at me, his lips inches from my own. "I . . . it's just, the *grall*'s so fast. Speedy enough to take a vamp like Hamon off guard, right?"

"Why, Jasmine, you act as if you care."

"I . . ." *Aaargh!*

"Never mind. I have another plan. Give me your belt." I did as he asked, watched him connect mine to his and then loop one end of the resulting rope around the hilt of the knife. "Ready?" he asked.

I steadied myself and raised Grief. "Yeah."

Walking to the edge of the sarcophagus, he held one end of the belt rope in his left hand while he balanced the blade of my knife in the other. His throw, strong and true, buried it in the corpse's thigh. Using careful side-to-side movements, Vayl got the corpse to move. Unfortunately the wire it hung from had some give in it, so it also began to bounce.

"Vayl, this is not a pleasant moment for me," I confessed.

"No?"

"Locked in a windowless, doorless room with a dancing, headless corpse and a secret sucker that can move fast enough to tear us both a new one if I miss?"

Vayl took a second to ponder. "Think of the body as what Pinocchio would have looked like if he had lied to the Mob."

"That's so not funny."

"Then why are you chuckling?"

"God, we are so warped. And the *grall?*"

"An amoral gossip that must be silenced before it can spread the word that Santa subcontracts much of his work out to the Chinese."

"I love Santa."

"Then take the shot."

I narrowed my eyes. There it was. Crouched behind the body's left hip, appearing every third jiggle and bounce, its antennae waving like wrinkled fingers as it tried to figure out what the hell its cover was up to now.

I raised the gun. Took my time. Made the rhythm part of my breathing. One, two, three. One, two, three. One, two, three — *bam!*

The grall dropped to the floor. As it began to writhe I shot it again. And again.

"Jasmine?"

"Yeah?"

"I believe it is dead now."

I looked up at Vayl. "That's what you get when you malign Santa."

He nodded gravely. "Indeed."

CHAPTER SIXTEEN

V ayl and I had just emerged from the closet when Sibley appeared at the far end of the hall.

"Did you hear something?" she asked as she rushed up to us. "A popping sound?"

We exchanged puzzled looks. Vayl shook his head. "Nothing from this area," he said. "Have you had another fire?"

"We're not sure. Marcon is checking to see if the alarms are all working."

"I was just telling Vayl it felt kind of warm in here," I said. "Maybe your furnace is malfunctioning."

She threw up her hands in frustration. "Hamon may have had his faults, but at least he maintained the place. All Disa does is sit in that library reading histories of the Trust and snapping at anyone who disturbs her." She bit her lip, looking over her shoulder, as if afraid her new *Deyrar* had taken a break just to spy on her. Then she shrugged, shook her head, and moved on.

"Now, why would Disa need to fill herself in on the Trust's background?" I asked.

"I would imagine for the same reason Blas needed the *grall,*" Vayl answered. "Hamon always intimated that there was more to running this Trust than simply stomping your foot and insisting you were in charge every twenty minutes or so."

"So let's go find out the real story about how the little ladder climber came to power," I suggested.

"You forget how close-mouthed the Trust members can be," said Vayl.

"Oh, I don't know. Niall might be convinced to share a story or two."

"What makes you believe that?"

I told Vayl about Kozma and Trayton and my confrontation with the vamp who had trapped them both. It only took him a couple of minutes to jump onboard. Which worked out well for me, since I'd already decided to stop at Niall's room whether Vayl accompanied me or not.

Trayton, how did you get under my skin so fast? You're like a freaking virus! Still, I felt a spurt of anticipation as I led the way to my Were buddy's hideout and knocked on the walnut door with its bas-relief etching of an armored mare galloping across a field.

"Who is it?" came Niall's voice from inside.

"Lucille and Vayl," I said to the sound of three locks being disengaged in quick succession. I shouldered through the door as soon as Niall opened it wide enough to admit me. "Trayton!" The relief I felt when I saw him sitting up in the brass bed, the cluttered tray on the chair next to it giving evidence that he'd eaten, was like seeing the sun after two straight weeks of rain.

As Vayl and Niall conferred, I leaned over to check the Were's wound, now little more than a bright red welt marring the smooth skin of his chest. "You look a helluva lot better than you did the last time I saw you."

He smiled, revealing teeth that crossed at the front just slightly and elongated canines that were twice as thick as a vamp's. "I *feel* better," he said, brushing his hair out of his eyes so I could see them sparkle. "It was worth almost dying to share blood with an Eldhayr."

I looked at him blankly, stunned that he even knew the word my Spirit Guide had used to describe himself once during a rare moment of revelation. Raoul had been an earthly soldier who'd continued his fight after death against even stouter foes than those he'd faced in life. I'd never given much thought to what I'd become after he'd brought me back. For sanity's sake, I figured it was better not to go there. Better, in fact, to just continue as Jaz. Even with my Sensitivity blooming like spring roses and my Spirit Eye making me wish for shades, it was easier to think of them more as extra abilities than of myself as someone different. Something no longer human.

No, look, you're still mostly human, I assured myself. *If you weren't, well, surely you wouldn't be so pissed off at Dave or so confused about Vayl right now, huh? And you definitely wouldn't want to pinch Disa's head in a vise and then attach her body to a tire rotator.*

That's how you judge? asked Granny May. She'd moved to a new spot in my mind, one where I'd spent lots of time waiting for her in life. The beauty shop was old-school, with massive hair dryers that came down over your head like astronaut helmets and hair spray so thick in the air your eyelashes would stick together just walking to the waiting area. She flipped to a new page of her *Better Homes and Gardens* and gave me a sniff. *You're human because of all your negative emotions? Give me a break. Even demons feel rage.*

How would you know? I demanded.

Don't try to change the subject.

Fine, then. I . . . I'm human because . . . I floundered around, getting a little more panicked with each passing second. Then I knew. *Because I choose to be, dammit!*

Bingo! shouted my granny as the Were spoke up.

"Lucille." His smirk told me he'd call me that if I wanted, but we both knew I was full of crap. "You smell of ferocity and distress. Are you all right?"

"That's my perfume," I said caustically. "Eau de oxymoron. By the way, this is my boss, Vayl."

Vayl waved from where he stood with Niall by a second locked door, which exactly resembled the one we'd seen in Admes's room. He seemed intent on getting the real story of Blas and Disa from his former ally, so I let him continue with his conversation while I took care of my new pal.

I asked, "Can I get you anything? Are you bored? Maybe I can find you some magazines or books or something."

"I'm good," he said. He nodded to a TV sitting across from the bed on a small entertainment center. "Niall is an Xbox 360 fanatic. So I'm set for as long as I have to stay." Any other guy his age would've been content with the forced rest as long as he could play all day. But I could tell something was digging at him. He held the sheets wadded in his fists like only they could keep his hands from the items his longing eyes kept resting on: the spare clothes folded in Niall's massive dresser, the door standing unlocked at my back. Freedom.

I put my hand over his knuckles and he grabbed on to me like I meant to pull him back from the edge of a precipice. I said, "We should get you out of here as soon as possible. I'm planning on going into town in the morning. Do you think you'll be up to leaving by then?"

"I'll manage," he said. Though his voice was low, almost sarcastic, his longing for the outdoors pierced so deeply I nearly staggered.

No windows in this room, his suffering stare told me.

The ones in mine are all covered, I silently replied.

"What are you two communing about?" Vayl asked sharply.

When I turned my head to look at him I felt like I was moving in slow motion. Trayton's pain overwhelmed me, making it hard to breathe. It wasn't just that, of course. It never is. Everything builds on the blocks that are already in place until they all threaten to tumble down around you. Like this monstrous villa, my issues couldn't be contained in any sensible sort of structure anymore. Which meant I didn't even know how to tackle them. I gazed at Vayl. I don't think I spoke out loud. Being his *avhar*, I didn't have to.

He strode to me, reached up as if to take me by the arms. "I am getting you out of here."

I stepped back. If he touched me I'd lose it completely. Holding up my hands, I said, "I'll be okay. It's just . . . been a long day." My eyes went to my empty ring finger. I clenched my hands into fists and hid them behind me. Vayl, his eyes suddenly lighting to amber, stepped even closer.

"Jasmine—"

Both Trayton and I suddenly looked at the hall door at the same time and breathed, "Vampire."

Niall hesitated. "No time to access the secret exit," he whispered. "Here."

He produced a set of keys from his front pocket and unlocked the door to the adjoining room. Vayl picked Trayton up off the bed, covers and all, and the three of us rushed out of the bedroom. As soon as we were clear, Niall shoved the door closed and called out, "Come in!"

I recognized Rastus speaking, his tone ragged, frustrated. But I couldn't make out the words. Then my focus turned to the woman who sat in the center of the room we'd entered, playing softly at the shining black grand piano. It matched her hair, which swung forward to hide her face as she rocked into the keys, as if she could somehow dive into the song.

Did she play any of the other instruments that surrounded her? One corner held a harp. It made such a bold statement with its elegant shape and fine, golden frame that it worked simply as sculpture. A couple of violins, a viola, and a cello stood on stands against one darkly paneled wall, as if any minute now a string quartet planned to swing by and start practicing.

More modern instruments had been added to the mix as well. A drum set. A Clavinova digital piano. Enough brass to satisfy a blues band. All of it lovingly preserved.

Without looking up, even as she continued playing, the woman whispered, "Why are you here?"

Vayl froze, holding Trayton against him like a sick child. I stepped forward, but stopped when she held up a long-nailed hand that commanded me to. In the lowest voice I could manage I said, "Niall didn't want his visitors to know he was harboring a healing werewolf and a couple of unwanted guests."

"Which are you?" she asked.

"My name's Lucille. The werewolf, Trayton, is by the door, being held by Vayl. If you've been here any length of time you probably—"

"Yes, I remember my old friend," she said, finally looking up from the keyboard.

"Holy shit!" I breathed, desperate not to be heard by the vampires on the other side of the door, in dire need of a scream.

It had hit me again. Like in the closet, only worse this time. Because the woman had no face. None at all. *It's Aine,* said the prim little librarian in my head, who seemed to be shocked by nothing because she felt sure it could all be cataloged. *Remember Blas describing the fight—*

Of course I do! I was there, wasn't I? Shut the hell up!

Vayl staggered forward, ramming against me, knocking us both off balance so that we did a little whoops-are-we-gonna-fall dance before regaining our centers. I heard Trayton whimper softly as he beheld the empty cavity that should've held eyes, nose, and mouth.

I think I'm going to be sick, and that's so impolite. It's not her fault,

I thought as I backed up. I didn't stop until my shoulders brushed the door. Since I'd wrapped both hands around Vayl's right arm, I pulled him and Trayton with me. Vayl dropped the Were to his feet between us, and we stood there for a second like a group of coeds about to be shredded by a serial killer.

Luckily my curiosity is a ravenous and unsleeping monster. So I had to know before I repeated my closet collapse, "How is it that you can talk to us?"

She'd never stopped playing. Now the melody changed. "I speak through the song. It was once my *cantrantia* to bend humans to my will through the quiver of a piano wire, or the pluck of a harp string. But once I lost the ability to speak with my own tongue, the music filled the empty spaces."

I couldn't look at her anymore. Any other injury, no problem. Take off her arm, her leg, rip a chunk out of her side, I could deal. But Jesus, this injury hit me like stories of the Holocaust. The horror I felt when I looked on her nonface was so overwhelming I was almost paralyzed by it.

"Listen," I said, staring down at the hardwood floor. I'd made this offer to Blas, not realizing he probably deserved his fate. Well, maybe Aine was no different. I hadn't heard Niall's version of events to know for sure. Still. "We might be able to find you a plastic surgeon. I don't know if there's any chance to help. It's probably never been tried on vamps. But —"

"No."

"No?"

"I am simply waiting for the moment."

"The . . . what?"

"I cannot just walk into the sun. Not after what she has done to me. I can't leave my Trust under her heel." The music had become harsh, dissonant even. Suddenly it softened. "Niall tells me you have come to vanquish our enemy, Edward Samos."

"That's our job."

"You have witnessed what Disa is capable of."

I nodded, realized she couldn't see me, and said, "Yes, I have."

"Surely it is enough to give you reason to kill her as well?"

I glanced up at Vayl. The wish in both our eyes was so strong I half expected it to leap into life between us, a wooden stake that would fly straight into the *Deyrar*'s heart. "Oh, I have plenty of reason. But she's bound Vayl. So unless we can figure out how to release him, it's not going to happen. I'm sorry, Aine," I said, in response to the dirgelike turn of the music. "At this point, even if Vayl was free, I believe that if I killed her it would be outright murder." *And I've already tried that once.* I felt chilled as I remembered that moment. How close I'd come to ending my career. Losing my freedom. Most probably my life. And how none of that would've meant anything if Vayl had turned to mist before my eyes.

We felt the door budge behind us and moved aside so Niall could come into the room.

"Rastus is wildly upset that the Weres have escaped. He is afraid Disa will take off his head if he doesn't recover them before they can cause us terrible trouble. And this is the only reason he has not killed you outright." He raised an eyebrow at me. "Apparently someone freed the bear, which allowed him to escape in your vehicle. Of course, Rastus thinks that someone was you, since he encountered you outside around that time."

"No kidding?" I said blandly.

"I reminded him that you were under the protection of the *Deyrar*'s contract, but that may not stop him if he catches you alone. So I suggest you avoid him at all costs."

"Understood," I said.

Niall crossed his arms. "Rastus also says he has detected a pack moving in the area. Knowing my affinity for them, he has asked me to help him track them. He is hoping if he can kill one or two, matters will go better for him when he finally tells Disa what happened. I have agreed to meet him beside the wagon house in ten minutes."

I felt Trayton stiffen beside me. Putting my hand on his shoulder to keep him from blurting out something Niall didn't need to hear, I said, "Be careful."

Niall nodded sharply. "Lock up after yourselves," he said. Moments later he was gone.

"My pack," Trayton murmured.

"I'm worried about them too," I said. "War between your people and the vampires would be more devastating than you can imagine right now."

He nodded. "Especially with me forced to sit on the sidelines and watch." He took my hand, held it up against his cheek. "You have to go to them. Tell them I'm fine. That you're bringing me out in the morning and they shouldn't make a move until then."

"Will they listen to me?" He opened my hand and licked the inside of my wrist before grinning at me in that way that made me shake my head. "You do get how gross that is, don't you?"

"It's just like in kindergarten, Lucille. Or whatever you want to be called. We're blood brothers. BFFs. I've made you an honorary wolf, so deal with it. I know my pack will."

"I don't like being friends with you."

"You'll change your mind after we go to a movie together." He looked over my head at Vayl. "We always drink a six-pack of Heineken first and then have a competition to see who can hold their pee the longest."

"Oh, you are a laugh a minute, I can see that already."

"But you're smiling!"

"That's only because you're too sick to punch. Now, it's after four in the morning and you have to be up early. Go to bed."

As Trayton moved back into the sleeping area, Vayl and I faced Aine. "We have to be leaving now," Vayl said.

"Of course. You have your work to do," the keys sang.

"I am sorry about Disa."

But she'd risen from the piano and turned her back to both of us. We eased out of the room, locking the door behind us.

We lingered with Trayton just long enough to get the name of his alpha and his promise to catch a nap before locking him in as well.

"Have you noticed this place is like the poster child for dead bolts?" I asked as we followed Niall's trail to the front entrance. Though our Monises confirmed nobody was even close, I still felt the need to whisper. "The masks. Do you feel it?"

"Only that the compulsion to walk in the Trust is stronger here." Vayl's jaw tightened. "Damn this place. I should not have brought you."

"You're worried about *me?*"

His glance showed the blue of a stormy ocean. Yup, he was vexed. "Humans do not tend to die of natural causes here." His eyes had gone almost black now.

"What are you saying?"

He put his hand under my elbow. Began to lead me down the stairs. "I am thinking how fine it would be to turn you. To make you mine forever. To bring you into the Trust as if I were a full member." His head jerked up, his gaze darting over the leering eyes and sneering mouths of hundreds of masks. "Can you hear the voices?"

"No."

"Outside," Vayl said, his voice strained.

As soon as we reached the door I wrenched it open, stepping back just in case the damn skeleton did jump off the handle. But all that flew in was a whoosh of cool spring air. When Vayl hesitated, I said, "Come on, let's go."

We both stepped onto the worn brick of the small entryway at the same time. I practically slammed the front door closed. But it was too late. Vayl pulled me into his arms, holding me so tight I could hardly breathe.

"You," he said, his growl reverberating against my neck. "Just the scent of you drives me half mad. Do you realize that?"

"You're into Ivory soap?"

He chuckled. Traced his lips up to my cheek. Gave me a soft, brief kiss. "What were we doing?"

"Going to talk to Trayton's pack."

The relief I felt when he dropped his arms wasn't nearly as great as I'd anticipated. *Okay, Jaz, admit at least to yourself that you really like the hugging. In fact, you'd sacrifice a couple of meals a day for more of the touchy-feely. And eternity with this wonder by your side doesn't sound half bad. Could you be honest about that? Then at least the people in your head wouldn't think you were such a damn hypocrite.* Chorus of *hell yeah*s from the crowd.

But I didn't say anything as I followed Vayl across the lawn and into the woods. Because wanting somebody, even loving them, didn't make you right for them.

Chapter Seventeen

The forest that crowded the base of Mount Panachaikon felt a lot like the national parks Albert had marched us through when we were kids. Lots of pines mixed with oak, chestnut, and white poplar left only minor undergrowth to wade through. A recent rain had left the leaves limp underfoot and smelling of decay. But not the Trust kind that made you want to gargle and spit.

"Are you going to be able to track these wolves?" asked Vayl. He strode beside me, so close that we could've held hands if we'd wanted to. I did. *Goddammit, would you grow up?*

What's wrong with a little hand holding in the woods? Especially when you're with a devastatingly handsome vampire who makes you feel slightly tipsy every time you look at him despite the fact that you haven't imbibed in weeks?

It's not professional, that's what! Plus, it makes you look wimpy. And you can't draw your gun if your hand is busy somewhere else. Any more questions, ya big squishy?

Just one.

What?

Do you want to be alone forever?

"Jasmine?"

"Huh?"

"I was expecting a response." Don't-ignore-me sharpness in his tone.

I sighed. "No, I can't really track them. I mean, I get this general sense that they're out here, but that's about it. Maybe if there was just one whose scent I knew . . ."

"So what are we to do?"

"How the hell should I know? You're the boss here. You decide!" I plopped down on a fallen log, ignoring the fact that dampness immediately began to seep through the seat of my jeans.

He strode up to the log, dug his boot into it, and leaned over me. "What is your problem now?"

I looked up into those dark, confused eyes, such an accurate reflection of my own feelings, and finally decided to tell the truth. "I want the ring back."

He dropped to his haunches, his legs flanking mine so that I felt oddly embraced. "Why?"

"We need each other." It was that simple.

As a leonine smile dawned on his face he pulled the necklace out from under his shirt and unclipped the ring. Instead of handing it to me as he had the first time, he slipped it on my finger. We shared a shocked look as we both realized it now sat on my left hand. Like a promise.

As Cirilai gave me its own form of Swedish-massage welcome, Vayl leaned forward. The message practically sang in his eyes — a kiss to make the moment eternal. I pressed my palm against his chest, feeling the abnormally slow whump of his heartbeat as I shook my head. "No," I whispered. "You're taken."

When he tried to protest, I shook my head harder.

"She may have pulled a fast one, but the fact is that you turned her. You're connected now. And until that's broken, I can't . . . I'm sorry. I just can't. Plus, we already discussed this. About your boys. You still haven't—"

"I understand," he murmured in that velvet baritone that caressed my skin like hot oil. "Time. Perhaps now it will favor me as never before." He took my hand in his, kept his eyes on mine as he lifted Cirilai to his lips. He smiled. And if he looked as dangerous as he seemed hopeful, well, that was all part of the package.

İt turned out that wandering aimlessly wasn't the best way to find a pack of werewolves. But stopping and sharing a quiet moment worked like chum in an ocean full of great whites. Vayl and I had just risen and I was pausing to wipe the bark off my fanny when a mocking feminine voice from behind me said, "Aw, Krios, wasn't that touching? Now can I rip them apart?"

I jumped about three feet, turning as I did so, which would've made me fall in a tangled heap if not for Vayl, whose quick reflexes saved us both from utter embarrassment.

"Watch your temper, Phoebe," said a tall, gray-haired man who looked like he should've been shelving books at the local library. He stood with his hands in the pockets of his brown slacks, one shoulder supported by an enormous oak. The young woman he'd just spoken to crouched comfortably at his knee. That we'd neither seen nor heard them advance to those positions said a great deal for their abilities. And just how wrapped up we could become in one another.

Phoebe viewed me with wide, irate eyes framed by spectacularly long lashes. *Those can't be real,* I decided, especially considering the shocking amount of blue eye shadow backing them up. She pursed her lips, generously glossed in candy-apple red, and for a second I thought we were going to be witness to a string of expletives, delivered with the same barely contained zeal as her first pronouncement. Normally I would've wondered what chemical carpet she was riding as I watched her busy hands, tipped with blue-and-red-striped nails, fiddle with the pockets and buttons of her ancient army jacket. But she wasn't sweating and her eyes seemed clear. Phoebe just had to move.

"You must be Trayton's pack," I said. Trayton had said Krios was his alpha. But he'd left out the part about his buds looking like they could bench-press a tour bus. As I looked around, maybe a dozen more people dressed for hiking had stepped into view. They ranged in age from sixteen to maybe fifty-five. And damn, were they fit.

"Why is it that you smell of him?" asked Krios. He made the question sound casual, but I could see the tension in his upper body. The unspoken messages flying from him to the surrounding wolves oozed barely contained violence.

"Well, he licked my hand a couple of times." It sounded ridiculous put so baldly. I wished I had Cassandra's portable library. The Enkyklios could've replayed the entire drama in Technicolor and surround sound.

"Trayton is mine!" growled Phoebe.

Krios put his hand on her head as I said, "Sure, fine. We're just friends."

Krios walked up to me, and now the bland old man facade dropped away and I realized why he'd come to power within this group. Immense strength in that gaze backed by the will to put it to use. "Why is it that though we tracked him to this villa, we can't sense his spirit moving anywhere within it?" He took a deep breath, and when his brows drew together and his black eyes glittered dangerously I remembered clearly why I never let relationships grow beyond a certain point. Eventually the people you attached to, or their alphas, were bound to turn around and rip your heart out. "And tell me, woman, how is it that while I smell him *on* you, I also scent him *within* you?" He grabbed me by the collar and yanked me toward him. I took him by the wrists, more to keep my balance than to respond with violence. At least not yet. Especially not when he said, "Have you dared to eat my son?"

CHAPTER EIGHTEEN

I laughed. Actually, it started as more of a giggle that grew. Because my mind went straight to the gutter. And I always crack up at the worst possible moments. I'm the only person I know who tee-hees during eulogies. Can't help it, my mind always comes up with the oddest images.

Krios must've started to feel stupid manhandling a hysterically cackling female, because he let me go. Which caused Vayl to abruptly bank the powers he'd pulled up the second Krios began to threaten me.

"Trayton's okay," I finally managed. "He's inside, healing up. That's why you smell him on me. In me. Whatever. I gave him some blood after one of the vamps shot him." Whoops, wrong choice of words. The pack didn't quite growl, and humans can barely pull off bristling. But, yeah, my words had just stirred up a whole pot of what-the-fuck? I stopped laughing. Hell, I practically stopped breathing. Suddenly I just wanted to bring the world to a screeching halt so I could put all the pieces back where they belonged.

I spoke slowly, so maybe I wouldn't screw anything else up today. And because I was suddenly exhausted. "I think you can't sense him because that villa is wrapped with Vampere power. But Trayton has made me a member of this pack. So I'd appreciate it if you'd at least stop treating me and my *sverhamin* like you want to bite our heads off."

Krios gave Vayl the once-over, decided all he deserved at this point was a nod, and went on with the third degree. "Why is he in there?"

My shoulders dropped. Realizing my brain would not spit out a decent lie until I'd had some real rest, I told the truth. "They lured him there to fight a werebear. He was nearly killed, but I found him an ally inside who's nursing him back to health."

"We want him back," said Krios.

"And then we're going to kill those sons of bitches!" yelled one of his pack, a brawny dockworker type whose shoulders were almost as wide as he was tall. His pronouncement was followed by a roar of approval from the rest of the Weres, one Krios did nothing to discourage.

"You don't have the strength," I said, hoping it was true. "The vamps would never have had the *Sonrhain* if they'd thought it would really threaten the Trust." I let the mutters of outrage and denial die down before I went on. "Listen, this whole mess is because of their new *Deyrar*, Disa. You can bet your asses the werebears aren't any happier than you are. But they've promised not to move on the Trust until at least next week."

"Why?" Dockworker demanded.

"Ask them," I said.

"I can do that!" Phoebe volunteered.

"First things first," said Krios. "We want Trayton back."

"No problem," I said, wondering if I was setting myself up for disaster by uttering those karma-tempting words. "I'll bring him out to you in the morning, when the vampires have gone down for the day."

"I don't trust her!" yelled Dockworker.

"Then you're a fool!" I shouted right back. "I picked your buddy up off the floor after giving him my own blood." *And letting him make me into a* friend. *Like I need friends. Which I* don't!

"Just so you understand, he's mine," insisted Phoebe.

"You got a glitch, there, Pheebes?" I asked her. "Because I'm pretty sure we've been over this."

"Wolves mate for life," she informed me. "It's important for you to understand that he's already chosen his mate."

I looked up at Vayl, who'd remained silent through this whole exchange. "Did you hear that, boss? Wolves mate for life."

"And Trayton has made you an honorary wolf."

"Huh." I looked at Krios. "Am I in this pack, or not?"

He spent some time silently communing with his people. More time while each of them came up to sniff me. Damned unnerving considering how easily they could tear me apart. Force another change on me that I honestly didn't know if I could stand. "You are pack. But bottom tier," he warned me. "No power. No vote."

"Fine." I looked up at Vayl and smiled, my face actually hurting from using muscles I hadn't worked out in too long. "Are you thinking what I'm thinking?"

"This is so bizarre."

"You're telling me!"

"However . . ."

"It's worth a try." I turned to Krios. "Listen, you guys need to get out of here. A couple of the Trust vamps are out looking for you right now. And even though one of them is trying his best to avoid you, they still might stumble on to you. Where do you want me to drop Trayton off?"

We agreed to meet at a cemetery located in the oldest part of town around ten the following morning. As soon as the last of them disappeared into the trees, Vayl and I hurried back to Niall's room to ask Trayton how werewolves worked out the mating ceremony. On the face of it, you wouldn't think it would cancel out a Vampere binding. But, then, we weren't discussing a math problem. Our idea was so strange, it just might work.

Chapter Nineteen

"No way!" said Trayton. He didn't even look away from the TV screen. His thumbs flew. Guns blared. Crap blew up. He was having the ultimate recuperation experience. And I wanted to strangle him.

"Why not?" I demanded as I sat on the chair beside him. I glanced over my shoulder at Vayl, who'd elected to stay by the door and play watchman. He shrugged. *Let us go,* he mouthed. I shook my head.

Trayton paused the game and dropped the controller onto his lap. Finally, his full attention came to me. Weird that he looked almost as pissed as I felt. "You can't take something like this lightly!" he fumed.

"Am I laughing? Look, Vayl's in a helluva spot, here. Disa's got something malevolent planned and she's put my boss front and center. You've been the victim of her plots. Would you want that to happen to anyone else?"

"That's not the point! We don't mate outside the pack. Okay, maybe sometimes, and actually Krios is one of the few alphas who would go for it. But mating is for life, and even *I* can tell the two of you aren't ready."

Suddenly Vayl was towering over the both of us. "What do you mean by that?" he demanded.

"You're not *partners.*"

"What the hell?" I asked. "We've been working together forever."

Trayton snorted. "See, you don't even get it."

In the silence I could almost hear the semi-farting sound of our ego balloons deflating. Vayl found his voice first. He spoke with the careful control of a man who's trying hard not to rip off anyone's head. "Explain yourself, boy."

Trayton blew his hair out of his eyes. "It's obvious. There's plenty of hot going on between you two; even a rabbit with a cold could smell that. But there's not nearly enough warmth for it to last. And you can't have a lifelong love without a solid partnership to shore it up. Geez, how old *are* you?"

Vayl jerked his head at me so I'd follow him back to the door. "There is a word for children like him," he hissed.

"Smart-ass?" I asked.

"Aha!" He shook a finger in my face. "As if someone like him, a mere *boy*, could tell me anything I do not already know!" He slapped himself on the chest to emphasize his point. Which made me laugh. "What!"

"You kinda reminded me of a gorilla just now with the pectoral poundage. You sure you're not offended because maybe he's figured something out in less than twenty-two years that you still hadn't realized in nearly three hundred?"

His black glare made me wish I had something bulletproof and Jaz-sized to roll between us. "Why do you think I have not given you more than a single caress? Taken more than one kiss? When everything in me demands that I make you mine, what do I do instead? I talk. I listen. I wait."

"For what?"

Uh-oh. The look again. The one that said I wouldn't be so ignorant if I'd just pay attention. "I wait for you to believe I will not die like Matt did. To trust that I will always care for you, no matter what you do or say. To relax enough to swear, and cry, and share your innermost thoughts with me." He shrugged. "For your friendship. You are, perhaps, right about me. I do need to put my old griefs to rest so that I can move forward to new joys. But even after that happens, I will still be marking time until you find a way to let me past that enormous steel door you keep closed against your heart."

"Oh." Suddenly I didn't know what to do with my hands. I shoved them in my pockets. But they were full. I ran them through my hair. Wrapped them around my ribs. And tried not to think how humiliating it was to be the biggest idiot in the room.

"Trayton, we have to go," I said, without looking at him.

"Okay. See you in a few."

"Yeah."

"Lucille?"

I turned to him.

"I'm sorry if I hurt your feelings." He really did look apologetic. "If there's another way to break this hold Disa's got on Vayl, and I can do anything to help, believe me, I'll be there."

"Okay. Thanks. Get some damn sleep, wouldja?" I made sure the door was locked behind us and joined Vayl as he walked back toward our suite. Since I wasn't ready to talk about our relationship and how much I sucked at it, I said, "What did Niall tell you about Disa and Blas?"

"It was much as we had thought," Vayl replied. "Blas planned the coup, with Disa as his cohort. They took out the majority of the Trust's fighters together, and then she turned on him. Niall thought he was dead."

"What a great liar he turned out to be," I said. "He sure had me going."

"I agree. So if you see him again, shoot to kill."

"Will do. And, about the other matter . . ." He waited, not blowing it off like I'd hoped, making me hunt for the right words.

I can honestly say, when my phone rang, I was never so relieved to answer it despite the fact that my father was at the other end of the line.

"Jaz, can you talk?"

"Yeah."

"I'm in trouble."

"I thought you said—"

"Naw, things are still calm on that front. It's your sister."

"Evie called? How's she doing?"

"Fine. Except she wants me to come down next month for a family portrait. Tim's parents will be in town, so she's made an appointment with this big-wig photographer. I thought this Grandpa crap was supposed to be fun!"

"It's all in how you see it."

"Give me an excuse to stay home."

"Albert, you need to be in the picture. Literally. Evie will cry if you don't come. On the phone. To me. So go, and find a way to have fun."

"Well, it might be okay if Shelby and I can sneak E.J. off to the park for a couple of hours. Old gals love the babies."

"There you go. Use your granddaughter to pick up women. That'll get you points in heaven."

"It's better than sitting around the house with Lemon Lips and Pencil Head!" Tim's mom and dad were *way* uptight compared to our clan. His mother, Alice, kept her lips puckered in a permanent expression of disapproval. She was always saying, "Bless your heart," but somehow you knew it meant, "You're going straight to hell." And her hubby, Reverend Lester, really did look like you could turn him upside down and use his round, bald dome as an eraser. They'd probably been a couple of firebrands in their younger days. But they'd had Tim late in life, and evidently raising him had worn them out.

"Okay, sounds like a plan to me."

Moment of silence. Why were they always so uncomfortable lately? I waited until Albert said, "So. About your brother."

"Yeah?"

"Opinions vary."

"They would."

"Some say you should help him relive the event in a safe way, where he has control. So he can see how it really was."

"I don't see how I can do that from our present location."

"I thought you might say that."

"Any other ideas?"

"Lots of talk. Now. When he goes back to work. In the years to come. Also, there's a program I've signed him into. He won't be happy about it, but it'll keep him in the service and on his team."

"So what should I do?"

"You're the one who has to get him started. You know, with the blabbing."

After another long pause he said, "Jazzy? You still there?"

"Oh, that's going to be a cinch! Why don't you just ask me to fly to Mars and get you a few ice cubes for your tea?"

"Hey, you're the one who called me! So quit your bitching and get on it!" *What. An. Asshole!* "Well?"

"Oh, all *right!* God! Were you always such a prick or was it something you had to practice for an hour every day?"

To my surprise, he laughed. "Talk to you later," he said, and then he hung up. As I stared at the phone I realized I had another message from Cole. In an effort to put off my coming conversation with Vayl even longer, I pulled it up.

Mark's long overdue. (Sigh.) I've named my steering wheel Lucretia. Don't be jealous. She's just a fling.

Oh, Cole, what am I going to do with you?

We'd made it back to the suite by now. Vayl opened the door for me. Feeling like a condemned woman trudging to the gallows, I walked through. And jumped about a foot off the ground when I felt a pinch on the butt as I passed.

"Aah!" I spun around. "Did you just—?" Vayl put both hands up like I'd just attempted to mug him. "Stop smirking!" I demanded. "There's nobody here but you!"

"What is a small tweak between partners?"

"Are we? I mean, we *are*, but can we be? I don't . . . Vayl, my life's been in the crapper so long, I'm honestly not sure I remember how. I thought I'd torn myself free of that safe house where it all went down. But it's still got me by the ankles."

"Yes, well, perhaps I was too harsh with you before. It seems to me that your heart may be leading you to a new dwelling."

"Yeah?"

He tugged at a curl as he walked past me. "You seem to have taken to Trayton. Bergman and Cassandra are fond of you. And that idiot, Cole."

I shut the door. Not quite a slam, but almost. "Would you knock it off about him? He's harmless!"

"Do you see what I mean? You leap to his defense in what I would call a loyal gesture. Something a friend would do."

I threw up my hands and strode away from him, at a loss to see how I could make him understand. The fountain stared impassively at me until I wanted to knock her head off. Instead I crossed my eyes at her. I also considered flipping her off, but thought better of it since Vayl would probably catch the gesture and how would I explain the crazy out of that? I turned around. "I care to a point," I acknowledged, "and then I stop."

Vayl came toward me slowly, as if he thought I might feel threatened by his approach. My throat did kind of close once he hit the three-foot mark. And when he murmured, "Sit," I plopped into the chair like my knees had turned to tapioca.

He sat opposite me, pulling his seat so close that our legs brushed against each other as he leaned forward. "What?" I asked as his eyes stared into mine and I could no longer bear the silence.

"You have been through a great deal in such a short time. More than any one person should have to bear." He opened his hands and the relief I felt when I slid mine into his was like coming up for air after diving into a deep, dark pool. "You are not alone anymore. *I* will never leave you. All you have to do is pick up the phone to be surrounded by people who care for you. Friends."

"Like you?"

He nodded. "If you would allow me to take the first step."

"Which is what? A pinch on the butt?"

He shrugged, the dimple on his cheek making a rare appearance. "Was I out of line, then?"

"Hell, yeah. Nobody pinches my ass until they first buy me a waffle cone full of cookie dough ice cream."

"I had no idea you enjoyed that flavor."

"Well, there's a lot you don't know about me. And vice versa."

"We do have a great deal to learn."

I looked down at our intertwined fingers. "This isn't always going to be easy for me. I'm . . . sort of queasy about the idea of being close to people again."

Vayl leaned in until his cheek brushed mine and his breath tickled my earlobe. "Then I will have to work to make sure that is your only desire."

The hall door slammed open, causing Vayl to rear back so fast that his chair's front legs left the floor and he nearly toppled backward. Our fingers tightened on one another and together we pulled him upright. But we didn't have time to congratulate each other on the save. Because I had hit my feet and lunged for the entrance.

Prevented only from throttling my brother by Vayl's arm snaking quickly around my waist and his whisper in my ear. "Give him a chance to explain." Just as quickly he let me go, giving me the freedom to decide.

I stood still, squeezing my fists so tightly that my hands cramped. Dave came toward me, staggering slightly as he tripped on an untied bootlace, spilling some of the liquid from his open bottle of tequila. As he came toward me, I glanced at the bedroom door and kicked myself in the pants for assuming he'd decided to get some shut-eye before our dognapping mission in the morning.

"Get me outta this place," he demanded, grabbing me by the shoulders, slopping some of his booze down the arm of my jacket.

I tried to shove him aside. "You smell like a roach-infested cantina."

"You can't imagine what I've seen."

"How much have you had to drink?" I pushed him into the chair I'd just left.

"Nothing. I wasn't even planning to. You had me so worked up about losing all that training time that I was in here doing push-ups and sit-ups until I realized what I really needed was a run. So I decided to do a few miles down the lane." He took one longing look at the tequila, shook his head, and drained it into the fountain.

"What happened?"

Dave touched the gauze at his forehead, the only way he'd ever reveal the fact that his injury was bothering him. "I went. I ran. On the way back in I checked my Monise to see if it was safe to come in. It wasn't."

"Why not?"

"The room I wanted to enter by was being used." His tone told me to *quit asking stupid questions and listen, goddammit.*

"All right," I said, sitting beside him. "Give me the rundown."

"This was the room we passed the first time we came inside,

after Disa decided to play ball, remember? Big sitting area with brown sectional couches, thick red throw rugs, and a couple of primitive-looking shields on the wall. And near the door, a pretty well-stocked bar. I think they were going for a comfortable look, but still the ceiling and walls were stained everywhere, like they'd had a bad leak and didn't have the money to make repairs."

I nodded.

"Disa and Tarasios were sitting on the couch with a human between them. Admes stood at the entrance to the place like he was on guard. He was almost out of camera range. In fact, all I could really see was part of his leg and that kickass sword of his."

"Had you seen the human before?"

"Nope."

"Where do you think he came from?"

"Can I just tell the story my way?"

"All right, all right, you don't have to snap."

"Yeah I do. Because I'm —" He held up his hand, showing Vayl and me his fingers spread about an inch apart. "Seriously, I'm this close to staking a couple of these sons of bitches. And I don't think you two want that."

Well . . . "Go on."

"So Disa and her gigolo look like they've just settled down with the new man between them. It's a guy in his early twenties wearing a T-shirt, jeans, and sandals. Looks to me like they just hauled him out of a bar somewhere. He's shivering a little. I can tell because his scruffy little beard is shaking and every once in a while a crumb or something falls out of it."

"So he was unwilling?" *Come on, say yes. That's grounds for termination right there.*

"I thought so at first. Then Disa kissed him and I changed my mind."

Crap.

Dave went on. "Pretty soon she's moved on to his neck, and now she's really dug in. Tarasios is watching with this eager look on his face, which I can't quite figure out. Then she pauses to bite her own arm, which Tarasios then begins to suck at like it's a Popsicle. I'm telling you, it was all I could do not to gag."

"She must be turning him," I murmured. "He still scents human, so it's probably just begun." We both looked at Vayl.

"I would tend to agree," he said. "Perhaps that is another reason she has been perusing the library materials. Simply to make sure she turns him correctly."

Dave grimaced. "Well, he was about as grateful as a kitten with a bowl of milk. I think when she bound you, Tarasios must've thought she was going to desert him."

"Yeah," I said, my heart clenching as it did every time I thought of the two of them ceremonially linked. *There's got to be a way to break this. Think!*

"—listening to me?" Dave demanded.

"Yeah, yeah," I said. "Go on."

"So Disa and Tarasios are both feasting and this other dude is damn excited about the whole situation. If it's turning into an orgy, I definitely want to make sure my Monise is in record mode. Especially if that Sibley shows up. I'm thinking I'll send some stills off to the guys and just settle in to being their all-time hero."

"What's Admes doing all this time?" I asked.

"Just standing by the door like somebody might show up and need to borrow his keys or something. It was bee-zarre."

"Okay, so Disa's bleeding this guy . . ."

"Yeah and he's getting pale quick, so I can't decide. If he needs help, do I jump into the room and pull on them? I only have my M9, so all it's gonna do is slow them down. Which gives me time to grab the dude and run—where? I'm still debating when I see things start crawling out of Disa's throat."

He had to take a second, pull himself together. We were brushing painful territory now. Dave rubbed his forefinger against the scar, which still glared an angry red, just an inch or so below his Adam's apple. Seeing Disa's appendages emerge from the very spot that tormented him with daily reminders of his former bondage must've made him want to do major violence.

At last he went on. "The guy's eyes were closed, or sure to God he'd have started screaming. But he didn't see that beak slide out from between the oozing folds of her neck skin. It opened and tentacles like a storm of jellyfish legs slid down the front of his shirt, lifted it up, and nestled against his bare skin. He jumped a little when they attached. I thought sure he'd figure out the score then. Disa and Tarasios rolled their eyes up to watch his face, not even pausing in their snacking to take a decent look. But he sighed and moaned, like somebody had just given him a great back rub, and then he slipped his hand down Disa's top."

"So what did you do?"

"What do you think? I took a picture."

"Show me."

"Jaz, that's just gross. Now, if you weren't my sister—"

"Show me, dammit." He fished out his Monise and displayed the photo. Yup, there was a pretty good shot of Disa with all her extra specials hanging out. *Gross.*

I glanced up at Vayl. "Have you seen anything like this before?"

He shook his head. "Never." His lips tightened. "We need to send this to Pete. Perhaps he or someone else in the department will recognize it."

I told Dave how to send the shot, along with a research request, back to Ohio. Then I mentioned meeting Aine. He shook his head. "I agree it would be nice to know if there was a way to fight Disa up close and personal without risking your entire identity. But isn't this where I'm supposed to remind you that you guys didn't come here to overthrow the leadership of this Trust?"

I glanced at Vayl. "That's true. But what about the Weres they might drag back to the cage? Not to mention . . . Okay, I've got nothing else. But the Weres. That was enough to make you go ballistic!"

Dave dropped his head into his hands. "Yeah, please, remind me again how I totally lost it tonight."

"Sorry, that wasn't fair. I know the Trust was yanking your chain. You're right about terminating her — we have no just cause. But if she comes after us, we need to know how to defend ourselves." And that was enough to justify at least the study.

Dave took a second to ponder, then he looked up, propping his chin with his palms as he said, "There was one more thing. I was thinking maybe we should look into it. And, considering where your thoughts are headed, maybe you will to."

"What's that?"

"After all the bloodsucking was done and Disa had tucked her nasties back inside her skin, Tarasios asked her if she'd found the entrance to the Preserve yet, because he'd be happy to take their new friend to meet Octavia if she had. He said, 'She's got to be pretty hungry by now.' From the look on Disa's face, I got the feeling it was another one of his stupid, shouldn't-have-asked questions."

We both looked at Vayl, whose eyebrows shot up.

"The Preserve? It wasn't on your map, was it?" I asked.

"No," he confirmed.

"Have you ever heard of Octavia?"

He shook his head.

Dave said, "Well, Disa thought she was important. She waved

her hands at the dingy room like it was a personal insult when she said, 'Hamon should never have kept so many secrets. How am I supposed to keep this Trust from crumbling when I can't even find his mate?' And then the blood donor sort of woke up, so she stopped talking and Tarasios took the guy away."

"I wondered what had happened to the villa since I left," Vayl said. "It has been so long, I just assumed all this . . . decay . . . had come naturally. But it sounds as if the problem is related to Hamon's unplanned passing and the mysterious Octavia."

"Do you think she's in the Preserve, whatever that is?" I asked, turning so I could see his face better.

He nodded thoughtfully. "And I believe I know how to find them both."

Dave and I spoke at the same time. "You do?"

Vayl wandered over to the shelves, thought about picking up a book, changed his mind. He looked at me. "We should get rid of these objects. They keep giving me"—he cleared his throat—"ideas."

"I'll move them out as soon as possible," I said.

"Good." He clasped his hands behind his back. "We know both Blas and Disa have been trying to gain secret information that was privy only to Hamon. We also know, due to his untimely death, that Hamon's quarters have become sealed from the other members of the Trust. I believe we may find the answers they are seeking, including the location of the Preserve and the identity of Octavia, in those rooms."

"But how are *we* supposed to get in there?"

Vayl looked at the covered window. "I have an idea. But since it is nearly dawn, you will have to attempt the entry without me. Only *after* you get the dog. That"—he gave us both significant stares—"is the priority."

Dave and I shared a shrug. I said, "Okay, fine. What's your plan?"

CHAPTER TWENTY

I murmured a swift apology to sun-drenched Patras. *Someday I'll come back when I have time to savor your spectacular scenery, your ancient landmarks, your charming restaurants. But right now —* "Jesus, Dave, could you hit another bump, please? I'm sure Vayl won't mind coming out of this trip with a double concussion."

Why the hell didn't I drive? I'm so much better at it than this dumbf—

Because your brother needs to feel useful! Granny May snapped. *Now quit complaining and act your damn age!*

Why are all the voices in my head so annoying? Couldn't I, just once, channel someone nice?

Mr. Rogers is booked through the millennium, growled Granny May. Inward sigh.

"How're you doing, Vayl?" I glanced into the back of the minibus we'd stolen from the Trust. Vayl's light-impermeable tent took up the space where we'd lowered the backseat. "I am fine," came his muffled voice.

My twin and I traded looks, still slightly dazed from our initial discovery. It takes a while to get used to the fact that your vampire boss has not gone down for the day and, as a result, must be watched like an escaped convict.

At just after eight in the morning we'd outfitted ourselves for the trip to town and decided a couple of small fires would be the ideal distraction for the Trust's human occupants. Something to keep them occupied while we joined up with Trayton. I was working up a smoking rage when Vayl opened the bedroom door. Like a couple of executives whose lackey has just walked in late, Dave and I checked our watches.

"Well, stop staring at me as if I had just grown a tail," Vayl said irritably. "I cannot seem to sleep."

"But . . . dawn was over an hour ago," I said.

"Do you think I am not aware of that?"

Dave walked up to Vayl and began studying him like he was a rare specimen just flown in from the Salk Institute. He said, "Bergman is going to be so pissed he wasn't here for this." He glanced at me and sobered instantly. "Of course it's bad. Vampires have to sleep during the day. The ones I've heard about who were forced to stay awake have committed some of the worst atrocities known to the species."

"All of them?" I demanded.

"Well, the ones who escaped."

"Who has been experimenting on vampires?" Vayl demanded, the threat clear in his voice.

Dave shrugged. "Mostly other vamps. You people have some weird-science guys in your ranks, you know that? One of our units came across a mad tester called Frilam in the sixties who found a way to 'deny the day-death,' as he called it. But when he did, the vamps wigged out. Usually in a rip-the-skin-from-the-skeleton kind of way."

I went to Vayl. Smiled up into his stormy blue eyes. "Hey, if you decide to tear up the town, you can always use the leftover bread from my breakfast in place of your cane. I'm pretty sure it's hard enough to bust heads."

To my relief his lips quirked. "You seem unconcerned, considering your own potential for danger. Given the situation, I mean."

"What situation? So you're awake. Big whoop. If you get grumpy we'll sic the dog on you."

Vayl lowered his voice. "I can feel the Trust's power, Jasmine. Disa is squeezing it into and through me. That is why I walk when I should sleep. I am holding on to my control, but I can feel its edge now."

I gulped. "Would it help, uh, if I gave you some of my blood?"

Vayl's eyes changed to red so suddenly I felt dizzy. *"Yes."* He licked his lips. "However, I fear I would not be able to stop myself in time."

"Have you eaten today?"

"Yes."

Whew. "Most vamps, I wouldn't give them a chance in a hurricane to get through this," I whispered. "But I believe in you."

He pulled back. Straightened as his eyes bled to brown. "Then I will endeavor not to disappoint."

Now, as Dave hit another bump, I decided Vayl's brain damage may have started before the trip. Possibly around the time he ripped Disa. But my brother's driving wasn't improving his chances at recovery. "Seriously, are you trying to lobotomize the undead guy?" I demanded.

"I am fine," Vayl called.

My neck was beginning to ache from craning to see. "Are *you* okay?" I asked Trayton, who lay on the seat behind me.

"I've been better," he said.

"Did you hear that, Dave?" I snapped. "The werewolf's been better. Have a heart, will ya?"

"Well, it's tough to concentrate with somebody yapping in my ear!"

"I'm not a poodle, you inconsiderate jerk! Did you remember the camera?"

"Of course—do I look like a fool to you? Lean forward, like, an inch. Now look at me. It's hanging from a strap around my frigging neck, ya doink!"

"Well, I couldn't tell. Your jacket's in the way!" At least it wasn't camouflage. He'd chosen a button-down brown suede over a navy blue mock turtleneck and faded jeans. But no way in hell was I gonna tell him how great he looked, especially when he said, "Boy, they really sharpen your observation skills in the CIA, Sis. So impressed with your trainers, lemme tell you. Speaking of which, what the hell is with this piece of crap equipment? Nobody with a clue about photography is going to buy my cover if they get a close enough look at this camera."

"You know what, next time we'll risk turning your thousand-dollar Nikon into a really heavy necklace if our plan unravels and somebody puts a bullet through it."

"At least we'd get some good shots before it all went to shit!"

"That doesn't even make sense!"

Trayton said, "I'll bet they fought like this growing up."

"All the time," Vayl confirmed.

"How would *you* know?" I demanded.

"Okay, everybody just shut up so I can hear the directions to Samos's place!" Dave roared.

We lapsed into silence, resentful on my part because I hated having to whisper so the *car* could be heard. But, as the navigational system's smooth anchorwoman voice rapped out left and right turns, taking us ever closer to Samos's hotel, I had to admit it was better than the bad-old days, sitting in the back of the smelly station wagon between Evie and Dave, trying to pretend I cared about Barbie and Ken's latest fling while I read Dave's *X-Men* comic over his shoulder and Albert and Stella fought over the enormous map she had unfolded across her lap.

It always seemed miraculous to me that we ever got where we wanted to go, considering that she could never find the highway we were on, and he tended to navigate by sound. That is, he'd say, "Chippewa Falls, that sounds interesting, let's go." And he'd squeal those retreads across four lanes of traffic to get us to a trickle of water running down a rust-colored rock face beside a diner full of truckers and prostitutes. They always had great pumpkin pie though.

"What do you think of my city?" asked Trayton.

"It's nice," I said.

He leaned forward, poking me in the shoulder so I'd turn around. "Have you even looked?"

"Not really," I confessed. "I've been kind of distracted."

Grasping both front seats with his hands, he slowly pulled himself into a sitting position. "Come on, take a peek. You and I are going to have to party before you leave, and I want you to have some idea what the place looks like before I get you so hammered you can't even see straight." He began to grin. "Had you there for a second, didn't I?"

I let my hands fall into my lap. Did he realize how close I'd come to shaking him for even suggesting such a stupid idea when he could barely move? "Do you even know what hammered means?" I asked.

"Something to do with drinking your American beer out of a hole in the side of the can?"

Dave reached back and slapped him on the shin. "Close enough."

"Shut up," I told my brother. Turning back to Trayton I said, "So you've lived in Patras all your life?"

"Yes. We natives call it Patra."

"Oh." I looked out the window.

"So . . . what is your impression?"

"It's a huge city, yeah? Lots of multistory apartment buildings, flat roofs, balconies everywhere, most of them covered in plants.

You guys must really have the gardening bug. And always there on the horizon that beautiful blue ocean. Makes the buildings seem like they're only squished together temporarily, like a big crowd waiting for the beach to open."

"Traffic sucks," Dave volunteered. "It's like the signs are more suggestions than actual rules."

Trayton laughed. "That's how we get where we want to go so quickly."

We drove past a wide plaza marked by an enormous stone arch so ancient it was easy to imagine curtain-draped Grecians lounging around beneath it, trading the latest god gossip while their slaves pulled off the major chores at market. But now, at nearly nine in the morning, it shaded only a few businesswomen headed to work in dark, tailored coats and high heels.

As the minibus announced, "Hotel Olympia," Trayton practically stood on his head in his effort to see between the front seats and over the dashboard.

The hotel, a twenty-floor high-rise built recently enough to still shine in the sun, shared the block with an ivy-drenched coffeehouse and a nightclub called Dio's, its darkened neon sign making it look as hungover as its previous night's patrons probably felt.

"Is this where we're meeting the pack?" asked Trayton.

I said, "Nope. That's at some old cemetery. I take it we can be more easily overwhelmed there if we decide to double cross them."

"Why would you do that?"

"Ask them."

"Krios is such a paranoid old gnawbones."

"Which is probably why he's still the alpha."

"So why're we here?"

"We're helping the Trust with some negotiations here later this evening," I lied. "We just wanted to take a look at the place before we get to business. Never hurts to be prepared."

Dave pulled into a vacant space across the street as Trayton snorted in disbelief. "If you're negotiators, I'm a pussycat," he drawled. "I can smell the oil on your guns from here. Plus, we predators have a way of recognizing fellow hunters."

I sighed dramatically. "I believe your near-death experience may have temporarily affected your senses."

"Come on, Lucille. Whatever you're up to, let me help. I owe you"—he raised his hands, trying to express the capacity with his outstretched fingers—"well, everything."

"Vayl?" I asked.

"I will let you decide this one," he said after a moment's thought. "Only you can determine who deserves your trust."

Suddenly I felt like I was about to take a big final. And I hadn't studied. Plus my alarm hadn't gone off, so I'd missed the first hour. *Dammit!*

I twisted in my seat so I could fully face the werewolf who'd wormed his way past my defenses. And, that easy, I knew. This creature, who'd barely left boyhood, was someone I could lean my life on. "Honestly, it's not that big a deal. We just need to borrow a guy's dog for a while." I cleared my throat. "Without his permission. But then we're giving it back." *What, after you kill him? Has this mission totally separated you from reality? If you intend to off Samos you're going to have to find Ziel a new owner. One who's not a complete tool. You know that, right? Right?*

Suddenly Trayton was all business. "I can help with that. For instance, I can keep him calm after you take him. Because wolves and dogs can communicate."

"At what level?" I asked, thinking so fast my tongue could barely keep up with my brain. "Could you, say, give him commands? Like, don't bite the nice redheaded lady? Or could you—oh, this would be ideal! Could you direct him to a certain location?"

"Not in so many words. I could call him, though. And if he's running without a pack, he'd be likely to come."

"He's alone. That is, he has a master, but that guy's down for the day. So there's only a human handler. No other dogs." I began to get excited. "And he's big. Like, a hundred and forty pounds. So he could pretty much insist on going anywhere he pleased, and I don't think his handler would deny him. Samos would be too pissed if he found out the dog had been mistreated. Like, killer pissed. Yeah, this just might have a chance."

I spoke to the rest of my team. "What do you think, guys? Should we try the plan now?"

Dave checked me out. I already wore the white sundress with red trim and matching jacket we'd decided would be best for this gig. Grief remained hidden in its shoulder holster and my .38 was strapped to my thigh, but I shouldn't need them. Today my weapons would be the aerosol cans in the black bag at my feet and the lacy red parasol lying across my lap. He said, "I'm ready if you are."

I nodded. "Vayl?"

"Go ahead."

I pulled my phone out of the bag and called the hotel desk. "Hello, this is Angelina from the Patra chapter of PETA. Yes, that *is* the People for the Ethical Treatment of Animals. You catch on fast. We understand one of your guests has a malamute that has not been walked properly since they checked in. If that animal is not exercised, and we mean at least twice daily, we will have to take very public, loud, and obnoxious action. Am I understood? Very well." I hung up. "Now we wait."

"How can you be sure they haven't already walked the dog?" asked Trayton.

"Dave came down and put cameras on the hotel last night. We have a way of monitoring them from anywhere we happen to be.

Nobody's left that suite since dawn." I glanced at Trayton. "How much distance can you make your sound carry?"

"A couple of blocks."

"Good. Dave, as soon as you see them —"

"I know the drill."

"Fine. Then you can repeat it back to me."

He blew an impatient breath through his teeth. But he said, "I pull out. Stay ahead of them. Lead them to the fortress. Kastro. Whatever the hell these people call that massive ruin on the hill. Where we move into the second stage of our dastardly plan. Do you need to know every little detail of that too, or have you committed it to memory?"

"I'm clear."

While we waited, I decided to check my messages. As I'd suspected, another one had come from Cole.

Mark's travel plans delayed him until tomorrow. But guess who showed instead? Cam! Small world, yes? After I catch some z's we're hitting the town. Wonder if we should warn the mayor.

I looked quickly at Dave, but he was watching the entrance. And I didn't want to get into it with him again by asking what his strong right arm was doing globe-trotting when he should be working. So I sent back a message.

Don't destroy anything you can't afford to replace. Also tell Cam Dave needs to talk. A lot. Start draining the Wizard out of his system. So if he wants to lend an ear when they're back together, great.

We only had to wait a few more minutes, then out the front door trotted an enormous dog. If I hadn't already known, I never would've guessed this tail-wagging, ear-twitching monstrosity was Samos's one vulnerability. Ziel had a white face, chest, underbelly, and legs. Otherwise his coat was gray. He wore a studded harness, which kinda made him look like he was into doggy S and M, and his tongue practically dragged the ground. Honest to God, it looked like he was grinning. His black, intelligent eyes regarded the just-waking city, with its charming antique lampposts, enormous palms, and urns of flowing red bougainvillea, as if he had a master plan and everything was going according to it.

He was towing a guy with hair so blond I had to strain to be sure he had eyebrows. Not a happy camper, but cooperating with the dog's wishes so far.

Dave started the minibus and rolled down the window. He said, "Go ahead, Trayton."

"I am."

"I can't hear you."

"Quit talking to him," I said. "He's doing something." Exactly what, I couldn't be sure. The Were's Adam's apple bobbed up and down, his throat tightening as if he was emitting noises. But if anything escaped his lips and flew out the window, it certainly didn't register in my ears. Ziel felt different. He leaped forward, yanking at the leash so hard he made his handler stumble.

Dave took his cue and pulled into traffic. We had, maybe, a mile to drive to get to the Byzantine fortress used for the defense of Patras from the sixth century right up to World War II. That meant a big commitment on the parts of Trayton and Ziel. But loyalty seemed bred into their bones.

Dave drove up steep streets lined with flower-bedecked pastry shops and small cafés whose raven-haired owners were just opening the umbrellas on their outdoor tables, to a spot where the sun-bleached ramparts and towers of the Kastro rose above the well-tended lawns, shrubs, and palms that surrounded it. Traffic was thick enough that our pace didn't annoy anyone. And within fifteen minutes we were parking in the lot provided for tourists and local history buffs.

I handed my twin one of the aerosol cans, took the other for myself, and opened the door. As Trayton began to follow me out, I held up my hand to stop him. "There's no room in this plan for a recovering werewolf. You've done your part. Now stay in here where it's relatively safe. If you get hurt again there's no way I'll be able to explain before Krios bites my head off." Literally. *Ouch. What a nasty way to go.*

Though he looked disappointed, Trayton had the grace to sink back into his spot. "I understand."

Dave and I paused by the car to spray each other.

"Ugh! This stuff stinks!" I declared. "It's like how those African buffalo must smell. You know, the ones on *National Geographic* specials that have poop all over their butts and spend half their day snorting bugs out their noses?"

"What the hell did Bergman put *in* this stuff?" Dave wondered.

"We can ask, but you know he'll just shrug. No way is he going to give up his favorite chocolate cake recipe, much less the ingredients to his unleash-the-mongrel spray."

"Point taken."

We walked around the Kastro, feeling it loom over our shoulders like a sleeping dragon as we sought the approach Ziel and his walker would take as pedestrians. There it was. A steep concrete stair with a stone railing on one side and a series of fancy cement banisters on the other looked intimidating enough that older folks might decide to take the route Dave and I had chosen instead. A couple of fiftyish, black-mustached men wearing flat gray caps loitered near the bottom, breakfasting from Styrofoam cups before beginning their day's work. Beyond them the buildings and streets stretched out in a sensible grid right to the gulf, where we could see a ferry chugging off toward Corfu.

Dave began taking pictures of me, with the Kastro providing a stellar background, which was why I'd dressed up in the first place. To an outsider we looked like a photographer and a model, trying to get in some quality shots before we lost the light. We'd thought we'd have to wait until much later for this. Drop Trayton off and then stake out the hotel until Ziel decided he needed to pee. At which point we'd place ourselves downwind of his route and let him come running. This method was so much better though. It made me wonder if taking similar risks with my heart might pay off in the same immensely satisfying way.

Less than five minutes later the dog arrived, still leading Samos's man so strongly that if the guy had been on Rollerblades he wouldn't have had to put any effort into his progress at all. As they began to mount the steps, we moved our poses to the same area, working ourselves into position well before they reached the top.

My back was to the steps, the parasol leaning prettily on my shoulder, so Dave gave me a play-by-play. "I think Ziel has smelled us," he whispered. "Blondie's having a hard time controlling him. The dog's trying to take the steps ten at a time. Can you hear the guy yelling at him?"

"Yeah. What language is that?"

"Sounds like German. They're almost to the top. Are you ready?"

"Yeah."

I closed the umbrella, pulling it tight until the catch that readied the dart inside its tip clicked. When I turned, Blondie was concentrating fully on controlling his muscle-bound bundle of inertia, who seemed eager to greet me.

Ziel began barking. Not the typical deep-throated *ruff* of a big dog. No, this sounded like Chewbacca at Han Solo's bachelor party. "Woo, woo, where's the strippers? I don't wanna miss all the fun. Woo, woo!"

I aimed the parasol at Blondie and fired, triggering the tranquilizer I'd loaded it with earlier by depressing a small button at the base of its handle. Dave and I turned and moved swiftly back toward the parking lot. According to Bergman, once he was released, Ziel would follow us. Judging by the dog's current behavior, I figured he hadn't exaggerated. Still, I took a quick look over my shoulder.

Blondie had sunk to his knees. Though he tried to the last to hold on to the dog, Ziel badly wanted to go bye-bye. One last lunge and he'd broken free. He raced toward us like a big, furry missile.

"Dave, he's not slowing down!"

Dave glanced back. "He doesn't look like he wants to eat us." He snapped another picture of the fortress.

"But that's not let's-play-fetch speed either."

"You could tackle him." *Click. Click.*

"That dog weighs more than *I* do! Now quit trying to set up money shots and help me think, dammit!"

"Fine. You stand behind me and I'll try to catch him."

I didn't argue. Dave turned around, muttering about how he'd never get a picture on the cover of *Time* magazine without some damn cooperation. For once, I let him rant. Because, despite the fact that Ziel's tail was wagging like the starting flag at the Milwaukee Mile, I could see every one of his teeth. And they looked *sharp.* I ran behind Dave, bracing him the best I could by pressing my shoulder against his back. He shoved his forearm out, as if he expected Ziel to pull a police dog leap and latch on just like they do on TV. Not this canine. He dodged to Dave's left, came around his flank, and jumped on me.

"Oh my God, would you get *down!*" I yelled, trying to peel back his enormous paws. They pressed deep into my right shoulder. Though the jacket provided some protection, I still expected them to leave bloody imprints, both from their sheer weight and the fact that it felt like his nails had never been trimmed.

I looked down into his face and, I swear, he was sticking that wide pink tongue to one side to make it easier for him to laugh. I said, "You need a Mentos. Ugh, I'm not kidding. The second I'm free, we're brushing your teeth. Now get down, you monster! Dave, why are you *laughing!*"

"He's ha-ha-humping you! Now I know what was in Bergman's spray cans! No, no, stand still, I've got to get a shot of this!"

"Aw, for the love of—get *off*, you perve!" I shoved a hand into Ziel's chest and lowered him to all fours before Dave could record my humiliation for all history. "Do I need to remind you we're working?" I snarled as Dave worked the zoom on his camera.

"Hold that bitchy face. It's classic Jaz," he replied.

"Would you please grab the leash?" I demanded. "We need to get the hell out of here!"

"Fine, fine." He let the electronics dangle and took hold of Ziel's lead, allowing us to hustle to the parking lot. Well, we tried. "Goddammit, Dave, can you at least keep this mutt from nose-goosing me every four steps? I can't think with my underwear stuck up my crack. I know it's a weakness, but it's just one of those things." As Dave practically doubled over with laughter, I kept myself from boxing his ears by saying, "I don't get why he's not trying to get up close and personal with you. You sprayed too."

"I used the stuff in the other can. Maybe it's got different chemicals. Here, we're at the minibus, you can call Bergman and ask."

"Before or after I kill him?" More howling from my brother, who at least had the presence of mind to pull the dog off me and shove him in the vehicle for Trayton to hold.

Okay, Jaz, I told myself as I belted in and grabbed my phone out of the bag, *don't yell. Remember how Vayl gets results? He talks in a reasonable tone. And people listen. And then* — I pressed the last button of Bergman's number and yelled, "Fuck your protocols, Bergman! Answer this phone right the hell now!"

"Jasmine?" Dammit, his voice wasn't even quivering. It would've been nice if he was still the shaky-quaky I'd roomed with in college. But he'd grown a backbone recently and was a lot harder to intimidate as a result. Still, I tried.

"What the hell, Miles? This dog — no, this miniature *grizzly* — thinks I'm his one and only!"

"Well, I didn't know if he was neutered or not. So I put sex pheromones to attract an unneutered animal in one can, and the chemicals necessary to get a neutered animal's attention in the other."

"Well, I'm covered with love potion and he's about to yank the arms off the guy who's trying to hold on to him. What do I do now?"

"Are you wearing a jacket?"

He'd know I typically did in order to hide the gun he'd made for me. "Yeah."

"Maybe if you lost it," he suggested.

Which meant I'd also have to take off my shoulder holster. At this point I was willing to make the sacrifice if it meant getting that cold, wet nose out of my personals. I slipped the jacket off and threw it toward the back of the bus. Only I was so frustrated I hefted it farther than I meant to. It flew through the gap between Vayl's tent and the side of the bus. Trayton wisely let go of Ziel, which meant he wasn't injured when the dog tore after it. I wasn't sure we'd be able to say the same for my boss.

"Vayl, brace yourself!" I cried.

"Why would, oof, *ow!*" Vayl responded as Ziel galloped over his tent, trampling it and various parts of the vampire's anatomy in his effort to reach his new love. Finally he snagged the jacket at the back of the bus, where . . . well, I just couldn't watch. It had once been a piece of my clothing. Now it was a dog's sex toy.

Pete, you have no idea what sacrifices I make for this job, do you?

"Gross," I said. I began to turn around. Then something about Trayton's body language caught my eye. "Dude? Are you okay?" His pupils had doubled in size and he kept licking his lips as he looked at me, unblinking, his focus becoming a little creepy as it continued without even a glance in another direction.

He spoke in a hoarse, barely controlled monotone. "The spray seems to have an effect on werewolves too."

This day just keeps getting better and better. "Dave! Get us to the cemetery. Quick!" I pulled my .38 just as Trayton made a move on me. "Don't even," I warned him.

"But you smell so—"

"It's not *me*, ya sex-crazed wolfman! It's spray-on fake-out juice. Dude, tell me you're smart enough to know the difference!"

Finally, a reaction, even if it was just a couple of blinks. "Of course. But you, that is, I . . ." He sat back, his nose twitching, a look of confusion warring with the one of desire that now sat on his face.

"Plus, Phoebe told me you guys mate for life. Is that right?"

"Yes."

I said, "Well, I'm not that girl. I'll bet you can smell that too, if you just let yourself."

"Can I have your dress when you're done with it?"

"NO!"

He sat all the way back as I muttered, "Dave, where's that can of your stuff? I'm drenching myself in it." From then on, the only sounds that accompanied us to the cemetery were the *whish* of aerosol covering me in yet more pheromones and my own mumbling. Which went something like, "I don't give a crap if this outfit is tax deductible, it still cost me seventy-five bucks, and that was on sale! Bergman, this stuff had better not stain. And thanks a helluva lot for explaining what was going to happen. Next time I take you on a mission, how 'bout I leave out the part where you have to give a six-hundred-pound man a sponge bath? I smell so disgusting I don't even think they'd let me onto an episode of *Dirty Jobs*. And I've seen that guy clean up pig shit! I swear to God I'm about to bust a couple of canines right upside the head!"

Bergman's apologies finally sounded sincere enough that I let him off the hook, especially after he promised to invent me something extra special to make up for it.

After we hung up I lapsed into one of those steaming silences where you can actually feel the heat coming off your own skin, but there's really nothing left to say. Except, "Shit. Trayton, here's my phone. Call the fire department. I think I just set that Dumpster ablaze."

Dave glanced at me. "You mean, you're the one—"

"Yup. At least, according to Raoul I am." I leaned my head against the window.

"Jaz, that's—"

"I don't want to talk about it," I said. In fact, I wanted to pull the plug on all my senses. Then I wouldn't be able to feel Vayl's powers, despite the fact that they were at low ebb, washing up against me like cool waves on fevered skin. And I could easily block the sound of Ziel in the back, sweet-talking my jacket in Wookie. It sounded like, "Woo-woo, I love you. This poly-cotton blend is so soft on the yoo-hoo."

Behind me I heard Vayl stifle a chuckle. Then Trayton snorted, and when I looked over at Dave he was grinning so big the sides of his lips may have actually touched his earlobes. And suddenly I was laughing out loud, cackling like a mother hen, holding my gut, the tears streaming down my face because, really, how often can you say a huge dog chased you down, humped you, and then confiscated your outerwear? See if you can find a Precious Moments figurine to commemorate that one.

Chapter Twenty-One

ombstones and werewolves crowded Patras Cemetery, which had been terraced out of the side of a hill. The stones smacked you right in the face. The Weres I could only sense as Dave pulled into the street just north of the area. The three of us got out because we never could've driven through like we might have at home. The plots had been placed too close together, and they all consisted of raised marble rectangles big enough to contain at least four bodies. Burial must be a group gig in this part of the world.

For a moment Dave and I stared at the layout, random as a fast-growing city, sprouting wildflowers and cypress trees, large crosses, arched stones, and a couple of shed-sized monuments that proved some monied mourners hadn't realized you can't take it with you.

Krios and Phoebe emerged from behind a miniature Parthenon, and when they saw how slowly Trayton was moving, met us near the entrance. Phoebe, wearing orange eye shadow and a matching hair band to celebrate Trayton's return, threw her arms around him and whispered something in his ear that made him clutch her so close that she squealed.

Now that we'd put some distance between ourselves and the Trust, the pack stood out clearer for me, as if my Sight had gained focus. Krios had brought them all and distributed them behind some of the larger monuments, among the shrubs and stoic angel statues that gave the area the feeling of a chronically depressed park.

"I'm so glad you're back," Phoebe told Trayton. She sniffed. "Though you do smell kind of funny."

"Actually," I said, "that would be me."

He buried his nose in her hair. "I missed you." Then he kissed her. Which meant that when he came up for air he was also wearing a layer of glossy orange lipstick. None of us said anything while Phoebe wiped it off with the hem of her denim jacket. Then Krios put his hand out. I shook it first.

"Thank you for everything," he said, a sincere smile on his face, though I could tell he badly wanted to pucker from my odor.

"You're welcome," I said as he and Dave shook. "We've got to be going though. Lots to do."

Krios reached into the pocket of his corduroy blazer. "If there's ever anything you need from me . . ." He showed me a stiff white card. Which said he was, in fact, a librarian at the local university. Can I call 'em, or what? "I would give it to you, but considering your current residence, I would prefer it if you would just program the number into your phone." He smiled wryly. "Safer for my pack that way."

I gave him the same line I'd handed the werebear. If they could all just hold off until we left, I didn't care if they started a sure-as-Shootin' Southern-style feud and ended up blowing each other's heads off with their twelve-gauges. "Other than that, I think we're square."

"Please," he said. "You never know when a friend on the *outside* could be helpful."

"I guess that's true," I said as I plugged his number in.

"One of the certainties of life," he said gravely as he and Phoebe led Trayton to their waiting sedan.

I felt the pack following them as a lessening of the tension in my shoulders and at the back of my neck. They'd done a good job blending in. I hadn't seen a single one of them. Which made this an excellent location for hiding. I turned to Dave. "We should check this place out. I know we were going to use the Kastro, but this spot may be an even better one to lure Samos back to later to-night."

He gave the layout his military stare. "I'll buy that. But, re-member, he's going to have some vampires with him, not to men-tion Blondie and his buds. How are the two of you going to deal with all that muscle given that the only help you brought was a washed-out soldier?"

"First of all, you're not washed out. You've just been beaten against the stones until your threads are starting to strain." I hesi-tated. Dammit, there was never any good time to discuss this, was there? You just kind of had to jump and hope he didn't smack you in the teeth on your way in.

I cleared my throat. "Speaking of which, I just wanted to say I've been trying to imagine what it was like for you. Living under the Wizard's spell. All I can really come up with is how much it must've sucked. Like growing up with Mom and Dad, only with-out the possibility of turning eighteen."

I looked at him from under my lashes. Noted him chewing the inside of his cheek, the way he did when deeply stressed.

Finally he said, "You know, when I was in that place, it wasn't all bad. I found out I liked not having to think or be responsible. Not caring." Dave stole a look at me, his face paling, as if he'd just confessed to murdering his best friend. "And when I came back. When you saved me, my pain-in-the-ass life sort of crashed on me, avalanche style. But I knew I shouldn't feel that way. Not for a sec-ond. And at the same time I was shit-eating humiliated that I'd basically become a terrorist's slave. Me, Dave Parks, American stud. Special Ops commander. Hero to men. Red-hot lover to women.

At least," he said, before I could make some snide remark, "that's how I liked to think of myself."

We stood there in silence for maybe a minute before I said, "Wow, you are fucked up."

He punched me, soft enough to let me know he got it, his half grin backing up the gesture. "Thanks for the support."

I shrugged. "Nobody's ever survived what you've been through. *Ever.* So who's to say what you're feeling is wrong? Or even abnormal? The fact that you're still fighting is enough for me. Just, you know, don't try to do it alone anymore. I've driven that route. It's a dead end with straitjackets and little cups full of pills waiting to snag you on the turnaround. Okay?"

He nodded. "Duly noted."

"And since we're talking about fighting, what do you say we figure out a way to even up the odds between ourselves and Samos's crew?"

"Only if you promise to shower first."

"That's a given."

Chapter Twenty-Two

I took half an hour to scrape off the skank I'd sprayed on myself while the guys discussed strategies and Ziel raced around the suite sniffing everything like it smelled of dog chow. My sundress had found new life as a doggy bed, so I didn't even bother slipping it into a plastic bag after my shower. I just left it on the floor beside the door and dressed in a much comfier outfit. A pair of hunter green jeans and a moss-colored sweater that didn't feel clingy until Vayl gave me a look that made me double-check to assure myself his hands were safe in his lap and not roving my curves like it suddenly felt they were. I turned back to the bedroom. "I think I'm going to change," I said.

"No!" the men replied in unison. Dave's tone made it clear he was sick of waiting. Vayl—well, when my brother gave him the thumbs-up for voting with the team, he must've finally realized what was up. Because he stared at my boss, then he looked back at me until I started playing with my hair. At which point he said, "Dad's gonna kick your ass."

To which I replied brilliantly, "Nuh-uh."

"What, you're not going to tell him you're romancing a vampire?"

"To be fair, it has largely been the other way around," Vayl said.

"We're just friends," I said, sounding as defensive as a nun who's been caught flirting with the neighborhood rabbi. I held my hands up to fend off Vayl's glare. "Okay, hardly that. And a lot more than that. Like many things in my life lately, I've come at this whole relationship backward. We're trying to be friends so we can be a really great couple that Albert doesn't have to know anything about yet. Please?" I asked them both. Okay — begged.

Dave and Vayl spent some time in silent conversation. It was a guy thing, so I had no idea what flew back and forth between them, though my nerves were strung so tight they could've played a twangy sort of clang-ring-bang accompaniment to the communion. Finally both men nodded and looked back at me.

"Okay," said Dave. "I won't tell. But since I probably won't be there for the big reveal, you have to tape it for me."

"How am I supposed . . ." He just smiled, which was when I realized he meant for me to make the full confession to Cassandra so she could record it into her Enkyklios. Holy Jam on a Crapcracker, this blowup was going to be fodder for all of freaking history to chew on! I thought about backing out. But the idea of unleashing Albert's fury any sooner than necessary made me shudder. Not that he scared me much anymore. But I so didn't want to spend one more second pissed off, depressed, or contemplating patricide than I absolutely had to. I sighed. "Okay. Although how it took you this long to figure out Vayl and I —"

"Hey, I've been busy! Former zombie turned semi-alcoholic nutjob, remember?"

"Oh, that."

"But I'm getting better."

I smiled. "I noticed."

"Come and see what else your brother has achieved," Vayl said as he motioned to the tableau they'd arranged on the library table between them.

"Vayl helped," Dave protested.

As the two of them explained their tightening of our execute-Samos plan, it began to resemble something out of a military manual. A thing of beauty that belonged on some strategist's chalkboard. Only Dave had gone one better. He'd picked the lock of one of the display cases upstairs and stolen a couple of handfuls of teeth. Once you got past the yuck factor, they worked great as miniature tombstones. He'd set them up across the table just as we'd mapped them.

As I sat down at the table with them Dave said, "You'll come in from the south, between this line of molars. So I'll set up behind this bicuspid. Remember the raised plot with two slabs marked by an angel standing with her wings spread? That's the one I'm talking about."

"Where's Vayl—" I began, but Ziel distracted me. He'd gone to the hall door and begun scratching at it.

"Does he need to go out?" Vayl asked.

I looked at my watch. "We got back at, what, ten forty-five? That was about an hour ago, and he went before we came inside," I said.

"Enough to keep an army of dung beetles busy for a week," Dave added. He shook his head. "I bet it costs a fortune to keep that dog stocked with Iams and chew bones."

Ziel kept scratching at the door, so I went over to him. But as soon as I crouched down, he bolted into the bedroom. *What the hell?*

The door crashed open, throwing me into the wall like one of those sticky toys kids get for a buck at Wal-Mart. I reached for Grief, but the blow to my head had thrown off my dexterity and I ended up with a handful of boob. I looked down. *Goddammit!* I commanded my hand to rise to the butt of my gun, watched it grip.

At the same time Vayl and Dave had risen from their chairs.

Dave's hand was on his holster. Vayl's powers had spiked, raising a chill breeze in the room. I scrambled to my feet.

"Stop!" commanded Blondie. His hair stood out on one side like he'd gotten too close to an überstrong fan. I could see grass stains on his powder blue suit.

Beside him, lined up in a semicircle of intimidating guy-flesh, were three of the largest men I'd ever laid eyes on. Which explained why I hadn't sensed them outside the door. Oh, I can pick up on strong human emotions, but these guys weren't emitting anything, except possibly an invisible steroid fog that would make them all wonder why their kids couldn't divide simple numbers sooner or later. They, too, were dressed as if to attend a back-to-the-seventies charity event, each of them sporting suit coats in varying shades of pastel, two days' growth of beards, and way cool shades. I know, we were inside, but apparently their pupils couldn't adjust.

In addition to Blondie, we had to contend with a balding dude whose overbite was so pronounced it left his lower lip in perpetual shade. He stood to Blondie's left, blocking the exit. Beside him, flexing his hands as if preparing to reach forward and strangle one of us, stood a black guy with a sparkling Mohawk. While I wondered what kind of product he used, I also decided the last goon had aged out of this game at least a decade ago and nobody had bothered to tell him. He hunched his enormous shoulders inside his lemon-drop coat and frowned at me, as if pissed that I'd pulled him away from his daily rendezvous with a mug of Boost fiber drink and the latest issue of *Sports Illustrated*. Overbite and the Old-Timer both held silenced Baikal IJ-70s at their sides, letting us know it could get nasty but they'd rather it didn't.

A lot of stuff flew through my mind in the five seconds we stood there, closer than football foes, sizing each other up. Some of it made no sense. Thoughts like, *Damn, I think I forgot to pay my water bill!* And, *I'll be so mad if I die before I've done the Indy Racing Experience.* And, *I'm glad I don't have to pee right now.* Like a tornado, it all whirled around a quiet eye, which clicked off the relevant thoughts rapidly, calmly, and without regard to the cows, minivans, and occasional tourists who flew past, trying to distract it from its vital business.

They've come to take back the dog. But they shouldn't even know Ziel's here. We snuck him in through Admes's tunnel. And the Monise showed us all the humans were in the kitchen when we brought him to the room. Or were they? Does Samos have an insider here we haven't even met yet?

I lowered my hands to my sides. That way, when it all went to crap, I could grab the bolo from my right pocket. And, with a twist of my left wrist, I could put Bergman's latest invention to use.

It was actually a new take on an old gadget he'd never quite perfected. The application fit my purposes nicely, however. So, hiding beneath my sleeve was a device that shot tiny rockets. Well, that's what they looked like, though they didn't burn when they released, and Bergman wouldn't explain the technology that made them fly. He just said they somehow targeted what you were looking at, hit it, and then burrowed in. Once under the skin they released hundreds of miniature robots that went straight to the brain. At which point they exploded.

Bergman noted that his original plan was to use the robots as tumor eaters. But apparently that required a lot more finesse than his little guys were capable of. Thus, the kaboom. Lucky for him, we in the CIA love the kaboom.

"Who let you in?" I asked. "And does Samos force you to dress like the Lollipop Guild, or is it just instinct?"

Ignoring my jibe, Blondie said, "We have people in *all* the major Trusts in Europe. Soon they will begin falling like dominos." He looked at the ceiling, as if we'd stowed the mutt in the crawl space, and snapped, "Ziel, come." No sound from the bedroom. I imagined the malamute crouching inside the tub, trying to figure out if there was a way for a four-legged dude with a hard head and a strong will to barricade the door.

"Bring him to us," said Blondie, "or we start carving up your friends." He nodded to Mohawk, who pulled a bowie knife from a sheath at his belt as he strode forward to grab Dave.

I didn't even have to look at Vayl. Some things you just know. Like that he'll always give you the last bite of his brownie. And he'll never fail to defend the people you love.

I fired my rocket at Blondie even as I charged their line. My idea was to surround myself with bad guys who would, no doubt, pummel me senseless within a matter of seconds. But at least they couldn't shoot me. Not without hitting each other.

Blondie dove to the floor. At the same time he yanked Overbite toward him, using him as a shield. The slug hit him in the shoulder, flipping him ninety degrees, at which point he smacked into the wall.

I shot another missile at Old-Timer, who'd had the experience and presence of mind to stand still and target me. It hit him in the chest, throwing off his aim just enough that I heard the bullet split the air above my head. He sat down hard, pulling it out like some badass cowboy. The rip it left revealed the bulletproof vest he was wearing. *Shit!*

Dave had disarmed Mohawk, whose right wrist dangled at such an odd angle I was sure it wouldn't be working correctly for some weeks to come. They were fighting hand-to-hand. And it wasn't pretty, like you see on TV. Mostly grunting and a few choice blows that landed with a sickening, flat sound that lets you know something underneath the skin is either broken or bleeding.

Vayl filled the air with winter, making Samos's gang groan, slowing their reflexes as they faced two people who were pretty much immune to vamp powers. But my boss didn't move into the melee as I'd expected. Instead he disappeared into the bedroom.

I didn't have time to wonder about his plan. Because the hint of a blur out of the corner of my eye told me to duck. I heard the whir of a blade slice off a hunk of hair as Blondie followed through with a kick that caught me in the kidneys, knocking me into Old-Timer. Though my lower back felt like it had caved in, I made the move count, isolating his gun arm so I could grab, twist, and break. He doubled over with a grunt of pain that he soon repeated when I followed up with a knee to the jaw.

By the time I stood, I'd drawn my great-granddad's bolo and loaded up another missile. I met Blondie's blade with a clash of my own, just managing to transform a major stab wound into a minor slice of the upper arm. At the same time I aimed the rocket at Overbite, who was just regaining his feet. It fired just as Blondie threw a punch that hit me under the collarbone. Suddenly struggling to breathe, I fell. The missile launched and flew upward, digging into the ceiling, where it released its robots into the intricate white tiles above, making them tremble and bulge. And still, no explosions.

If I'd had a second to spare, I'd have used it to curse Bergman and his goddamn prototypes.

I began to rise, planning an attack that would leave Blondie at least lame and, at most, dead. Which was when I felt the round, cold metal of a gun barrel pressed against my temple.

Chapter Twenty-Three

G et up real slow," said Old-Timer.

I couldn't have moved any other way. In fact, Blondie's blows to my kidneys and lungs made me think it would be nice if an elderly lady would appear beside me with her walker, which I could then attempt to summit. I did consider grabbing the wall for support as I tried to rise. But they'd like that too much. So I just let my mind scream, *Ow! Ow, ow-ow-ow!* as I made it first to my knees and then to my feet.

At which point I realized Overbite had Dave covered as well.

"Have a seat," ordered Old-Timer, pointing his gun at the fountain-bound wicker, his other arm hanging useless at his side.

Overbite shook his barrel at Dave. We both began walking.

I don't know how many steps I'd taken, enough to feel like I was going to make it to the chair before they killed me, when pain lanced through my back. I spun, barely stifling a scream as I realized I'd been cut; that huge droplets of blood had splashed onto the seat cushions and into the fountain behind me. Blondie stood before me, his dagger red and dripping, his smile wide and lustful.

Screw getting shot. I'm going to kick your pretty teeth in, I thought wildly. With Old-Timer standing to my left, and Overbite to my right, the latter holding his gun to my chest, it wasn't going to be a long, drawn-out revenge. But I thought I might at least get to wipe that disgusting look off his face before I died.

Mohawk beat me to it. He shouted from the doorway, where he stood watching, holding his damaged wrist with his good hand. "These are proven warriors! They have earned an honorable death!"

"Who are you to decide?" Blondie demanded. "I am Samos's field commander."

"Not after he learns you lost his dog."

Blondie flinched, his eyes going just round enough to make me wonder what kind of punishment Samos would mete out to an underling who'd screwed up as badly as he had.

Mohawk went on. "In fact, I think your only way clear of slow torture is to have died in battle retrieving Ziel. Which will, of course, leave Samos free to consider a new commander." He nodded to Overbite and Old-Timer, who each nailed Blondie with a single shot. *Blam, blam.*

The crack of both guns going off simultaneously, even though they carried silencers, still sent a doomed whip of sound snapping through the room.

The impact, hard as double sledgehammers slamming into his skull, threw Blondie backward. He died before he hit the floor, his last expression one of mild surprise. Blood pooled beneath him, filling the cracks in the floorboards, running toward my boots as if to lick them in belated apology.

Old-Timer turned to speak to Mohawk, but before he could get the words out he was interrupted. By singing. Loud, raucous, off-key belting in the deep voice of a man who's had way too much to drink, coming closer by the second.

"Well, it's a girls' night out. Honey, there ain't no doubt. Hey!" Tarasios appeared, grinning happily in the doorway, his head practically on Mohawk's shoulder. "Well, if it isn't the exterminators. Did you find the cockroaches okay?" He glanced down. "Aw, look, a dead man!"

Crowding Mohawk aside by virtue of a drunken stumble combined with a sigh that had to smell strongly of the bottle of ouzo he held, Tarasios half knelt beside, half fell on Blondie.

"I know how you feel, buddy. I'm a"—pause for monster belch here—"a smidge under the weather myself. Love stinks, didja know that? Well"—he nodded wisely—"I'm here to tell ya. It stinks like . . ." He paused to think about it, took a whiff of his own armpits, and nodded his head. "Yup, that would be me." His eyes wandered over to us. "How you doing?" he asked. "Enjoying your stay at the Heartbreak Hotel?" He suddenly launched into an amazing imitation of Elvis. "It's down at the end of Lonely Street at Heartbreak Hotel."

Overbite and the Old-Timer looked at each other, shrugged, and pointed their guns at Tarasios.

"Everybody freeze!" We did. Mostly out of surprise because the command came from the forgotten vampire who now stood in the bedroom doorway, hair standing on end, shirttails hanging, scratches running down his cheek, and a large malamute tucked under his left arm. Ziel's head drooped and every few seconds he licked at his nose, which I suspected had taken a thump sometime during his struggle not to be caught by the dude who currently dangled him like a naughty child.

"Here is what we are going to do," Vayl said. He stared down Samos's men, one by one. The certainty in his voice a concrete barrier, he went on. "You are going to pull your men out of this room. You have until the count of three, after which I will crush this animal like a beer can."

Overbite's face went red. I got excited. Maybe that was the sign that Bergman's little robots had finally done their job. But no. The explosions going off inside his brain had nothing to do with my sci-guy's technology.

Vayl said, "One."

The Old-Timer raised his eyebrows at Mohawk. "I've seen bluffing. That's not it." Actually it was, but only I knew Vayl well enough to tell.

"Two."

Mohawk gave his cohorts a curt nod. "All right, we're leaving," he said.

"*All* of your men," Vayl insisted.

They paused to grab Blondie's corpse by its arms and legs, which meant they had to holster their weapons. The second I saw those Baikals stored I pulled my own gun. I didn't intend to shoot. We were at stalemate. I understood that. So did Mohawk, who'd pulled a Glock 37 from behind his back the second Vayl showed his hand.

"When do we get the dog back?" Mohawk demanded.

"We've got your number," I told him. "We'll call at dusk to let you know."

Mohawk wanted to linger, do more negotiating, but shouting from a lower floor told him he was out of time. "Dusk," he said firmly, trying to make it an order. They took off. I went to the door, but by the time I got there the hall held only a dusty gold chandelier and a framed print of a bunch of Christians being eaten by lions.

I turned to compliment Vayl on his quick thinking. But Dave stood in my way. "The cut on your back—I think it looks more spectacular than it actually is." He winced and touched his fingertips to his jaw as his own injuries pained him. "You probably won't even need—" But I didn't hear the rest. A face, that face, had emerged from the pool of Blondie's blood. I knew it was real because Ziel perked up his ears, looked straight at it, and then decided he wanted to bury his face in the gap between Vayl's shirt buttons.

As my *sverhamin* dealt with the dog, the face blinked a couple of times, rolled its red eyes as if trying to get its bearings. And then it rose into the air.

"That's new," I murmured.

"What did you say?" asked Dave.

"I said that's a new deal for me. Not needing stitches."

"And not dying," he added. I glanced up at him. Were we reverting to weird jokes? Already? I looked back at the face, hovering over the floor like a huge red mask. *Nope, I'm not laughing yet. In fact, I'm trying pretty hard not to scream.*

Because the face was staring in my direction, and once again he was horribly happy to see me.

Dave said something about leaving his first-aid kit in the bedroom when he'd changed clothes. As he went to retrieve it I wished he could've dabbed a little Neosporin and stretched some gauze across my damaged cerebrum. Vayl seemed pretty intent on Ziel, who'd gone slightly batty once he'd been set down, demanding lavish praise and repeated apologies for how he'd been threatened just now. Tarasios, still sitting in the spot where he'd collapsed earlier, seemed fascinated by the ceiling bots, so I decided it was as safe as it was ever going to be to confront my vision.

"What do you want now?" I hissed to the face.

"She is nearly finished with me!"

"Who?"

"The Destroyer."

"This riddle shit is really pissing me off. Who is she?"

"You must stop her! Before she kills me!"

"You're alive?"

A look of confusion twisted the face so severely that for a second it became an indecipherable blob. When I could make out features again, it blinked at me with such despair I actually felt a flash of sympathy. "It seems, for me, the answer is not so simple. But you and your *sverhamin* are essential. Only you can save the Trust."

"The Trust?" I whispered. "Or you?"

"We are interchangeable."

"Why?"

"Because . . ." The face drooped in defeat. "I cannot remember."

Tarasios began to sing again. Not Elvis this time. Ed Cobb's "Tainted Love."

"Yes!" The face raised his bloody brows in triumph, shouting so loudly that I slapped my hand to my forehead. "Her mangled notions of love have brought me to this. You must undo the coil. You must save me. Save me and you save the *sverhamin*."

"But you just said my *sverhamin* was supposed to save the Trust."

"We are all One!"

"You are really bonkers, you know that?" I wasn't exactly sure I was addressing the face.

"It is *her* you must kill," he insisted. "The Destroyer. Kill her!"

"Her who?"

"I cannot capture her name in my mind. The . . . the *Deyrar*." Oh. Her.

I cleared my throat. "Dude, you've dialed the wrong number. I'm just here for Samos. That's it."

His sigh ended almost in a sob. "Then all is truly lost."

Chapter Twenty-Four

It would've been great to spend the rest of the day flat on my stomach recuperating. Sleeping. Dreaming of a world minus one highly annoying *Deyrar* who everybody wanted dead, including me. In that world Vayl and I would never stop at one kiss. The brush of a hand would lead to a night full of caresses. Yeah, I pretty much wanted to spend the next nine hours in Fantasyland.

Dave wouldn't allow it. As he worked over my back he whispered, "Tarasios may know a way to get Vayl out of this mess."

I looked over at him from where I sat the wrong way around in a library chair. He'd passed out on the floor right next to the pool of blood. "The guy has the IQ of a cornstalk," I said. "I doubt he knows why Disa goes night-night when the sun rises, much less how to break the binding."

"He may have seen something though," Dave insisted. "They were getting along fine last time I saw him. And now he's turned lush." He paused, came around the chair to confront me. "Tell me I was never in as bad a shape as him."

I took some more time to look over Disa's reject. "I don't know. What kind of condition were you in when you punched those officers?" I gazed up at Dave, working to keep an expression of mild inquiry on my face.

His face went blank. Pale. For a second I wondered if he'd had a stroke. Then his nose scrunched, followed closely by his top lip.

Anybody who'd followed his sports career through high school and college would've recognized that snarl. It had won more football games, wrestling matches, and track meets than any other expression in his arsenal. "I'm done being that guy," he growled.

"Good," I said. "Because I don't think he'd be nearly as successful at weaseling info out of Tarasios as you."

Dave nodded so sharply it reminded me of a salute. "As soon as he wakes up I'm going to become his very good buddy. See what I can find out. In the meantime, you and Vayl should check out Hamon's room. Remember he said he had some idea how to get in? We've got to find out who this Octavia bimbo is and why Disa thinks she needs to be fed."

"What about the mutt?" I asked. Ziel had finally calmed beneath Vayl's gentle hands and soft murmurs and, after giving him a couple of final sniffs, trotted off to check out the blood and the unconscious guy next to it.

"I'll watch him," Dave said. "We've still got that steak we stole from the kitchen when we brought him in, so maybe I'll give him some of that. He looks like he could use a snack."

That took care of my excuses. Which made me wonder why I kept looking for more. Did Hamon's secrets worry me that much?

Or was it the idea of being alone with a vampire I had no clue how to befriend?

"What do you say, Vayl?" I asked. "Wanna do some breaking and entering?"

The dimple in his cheek told me I might've just made a good start.

Hamon Eryx's room stood at the end of a wide hall lined with six glass cases, each of which held a single item.

"What are these?" I asked Vayl as we passed a black glove, a brown leather shoe, a tan fedora, a dangly pearl earring, a pair of round-lensed sunglasses, and a white lace corset.

"Artifacts from former *Deyrars*."

"Whatever happened to presidential portraits?"

Vayl's eyebrows rose just enough to let me know he saw the humor. He glanced at the cameras that covered the area. The slight narrowing of his eyes told me what he wanted. I reached for my gun.

Overkill, he mouthed.

Party pooper, I replied in the same manner. Instead I pulled my phone out of my back pocket. Bergman had programmed the Monises to obey simple commands sent from them, including those that would shut down cameras within a twenty-foot radius. You never know when you're not going to want an audience. But in the CIA, you're always pretty sure the time will come.

I could've done the same job directly from the Monise as well. But this way, whoever was monitoring us would think I was just pulling a typical American stunt that involved my cell. Especially when I provided audio to go along with it.

"Cole's been sending me text messages," I said as I activated the code. "This hat reminded me of one I just got." I held the phone up for Vayl to see and he nodded with interest as we both watched the screen until it blinked the words we were waiting for: *Video Feed Deactivated*.

I returned the phone to my pocket as Vayl swept his hand across one of the artifact containers. "Can you feel their power?" he asked.

"Nope."

"As I suspected, the glass is as much for containment as it is for protection." He looked the boxes over. "No discernible locks." He slammed his fist into the glass. It shivered, but didn't break.

"Wow, vamp-proof. I'm impressed," I said.

The corners of Vayl's mouth turned up even farther. "Wait until you see this."

He positioned his hands on either side of the box and raised his power so swiftly that even I shivered in the rush of its increase. Clouds appeared inside the glass. Which turned into sparkles of ice. And then suddenly the bottom popped out of the case. I lunged forward to catch it, barely snagging it before it hit the floor.

"Geez! You could've warned me!"

He shrugged. "I thought the top would come off." I picked up the glove. "Put it on," he said. "It obviously belonged to a woman."

I didn't want to. With its powers unmasked, the glove felt like a beating heart to me, something alive that had no business being anywhere near my skin. But my boss had given me an order, so I obeyed, sliding the black silk over my tingling palm. It was too long, its tips hanging nearly an inch from where my fingers stopped.

He pulled the same stunt with the other five boxes. By the time we were finished, he wore the shoe, sunglasses, and fedora, which made him resemble a muscular Johnny Depp cast as a gangster for his next big film.

I'd clipped on the earring and Vayl had tied the corset over my sweater.

"You look incredible in this," he murmured as he stood back to admire his handiwork.

I peeked down. "You mean my rack looks great, don't you?" Frankly, I had to agree. I'd never thought there was much you could do with average. But, by golly, someone had hunkered down and come up with a pretty spectacular idea.

When I looked up it was to meet sparkling green eyes, twin jewels in a face taut with desire. "Jasmine." The way he said my name, drawing out the syllables so it sounded like Yaz-meena, made me shiver. I ran my tongue across my lips, drawing his gaze.

"We, uh, didn't we have a plan? You know, for you to settle your past and for us to learn to be friends? Because I suck at that?"

"Do friends ever kiss?"

"Um."

He took it as a yes, pulling me to him so quickly that my hands slapped against his shoulders as our bodies met. "Just one," he murmured, more to himself than to me. "Just a taste to help me through the rest of this interminable day." And then his lips came down on mine.

Sometime later he whispered, "How can it be that your kisses sustain me?"

"Dunno." Honest, I just wasn't capable of any reply more intelligent than that. Also, I'd forgotten how to inhale by that time, so I'd probably experienced some level of brain damage.

He took a deep breath. Not because he needed to. Maybe to clear his head. "I usually have better restraint than this. Perhaps it is the power of the artifacts combined with Disa's binding pulsing through me. Or the feeling of the sun shining bright outside these walls. I truly meant to give us more time. I *will*." He dropped his arms, his lips tightening with remorse.

"Don't you dare feel bad about stealing a smooch here and there. I haven't studied the friends-to-lovers credo lately, but I'm sure it's allowable under certain conditions, including the ones we have right here." Plus, if he stopped, I'd probably end up doing something unladylike. Several examples came immediately to mind. As usual, my top picks were taking an African hunting trip wherein I got to kill all the poachers I could locate, and eating an entire chocolate cream pie while drinking brandy-laced coffee and watching every Jason Bourne movie ever made.

Vayl was smiling now. "So you like it when I kiss you?"

"I'm panting, aren't I?"

"But you agree we should get to know each other better."

"We have a pretty thorough professional knowledge of each other. But, yeah, I guess personally there are a few [*huge!*] gaps."

"Which we never seem to have the time to fill." He glanced at Hamon's door, which was blocked by a second, iron-barred gate. "For instance, we have already used precious minutes that should have been spent trying to enter this place. Someone could come past at any moment and ruin our plan."

"Yeah, although according to my Monise they're sticking pretty close to their chosen vamps' rooms. Maybe because Disa's pissed us off so much she's afraid we're going to come hunting her while she sleeps." I stopped, gave myself a second to fantasize. "You're right though. Let's get inside if we can. I guess we'll just have to keep stealing moments for ourselves until—"

"Until you agree to visit my diamond mines with me." He'd turned away, so he didn't see my jaw drop. But maybe he sensed it, because he chuckled. "No, I have not forgotten your promise. And I know you have vacation time coming. A month at least." He slanted a look over his shoulder. Sly, brilliant vampire. "If we kill Samos, perhaps then—"

"You never know." I tried for cheerful and ended up sounding like a nervous little virgin instead. *Geez! Would you relax? Every time you even smell the potential for something terrific, you do not have to lay a damn egg!*

Vayl went to the door. He motioned for me to come stand in front of him and then pulled me tight against him, his arm warm around my waist.

"Put your hand over your heart and tuck your hair back so the earring is visible," he whispered. I did as I was told, noting that he slid his left leg forward beside mine so the shoe showed clearly to whoever—or whatever—was watching. "I am going to whisper words in your ear. Then we must repeat them together."

"What are they?" I asked.

"You said that when Hamon died Camelie recited 'McNaight's Refrain.'"

"That's what Blas told me."

"It was Hamon's favorite poem, one he often quoted. I am sure Disa tried using it to get into his room. But not with the relics. I believe they are significant because some are meant for a man, and some for a woman. Are you ready?"

"Yeah."

He whispered the first line into my ear, and together we said, "As separate souls we met in the moon-bathed glade."

With pauses for prompting, we continued to the end.

"And if our eyes locked, they are the bluer for it.
Never should we have tarried, not a sigh, nor a touch,
For now we mix and cannot blend our hearts, our minds, ah
These bodies serve to curb our love,
We two,
We ultimate duet.
In the end, we sing alone,
Our voices rent by fate."

The door began to weep. At least it seemed that way. Black flecks fell from the bars like tears for the next several seconds. And then we heard a click.

"I think the sucky poem worked," I whispered.

"You did not like it?"

"Hell no!"

"Which part?"

I looked over my shoulder and rolled my eyes, though Vayl's were hard to see, hidden behind the specs like they were. "*You* know. That bullshit about being alone in the end. Once you've loved for real, you're never alone. Lonely, maybe." I stuck my hand in my left pocket. Gave my old engagement ring an affectionate squeeze. "But never truly alone."

Vayl cocked his head to one side. "I like that." He motioned to the door. "Shall we?"

I pulled on the bars and they moved easily. Behind them stood your standard *Deyrar*-style door. Ceiling-high oak engraved with the image of a Hydra. A simple twist of the knob revealed a sumptuous bedroom that had not, like the rest of the house, fallen prey to any sort of rot, mold, or mildew. Hamon had hung wallpaper in thick blue and white stripes that made me feel like I was standing inside a circus tent. Ornate white woodwork lined the paper top and bottom. A plump-mattressed bed framed by black iron scrollwork took up one wall. Another held a bachelor chest and a brown leather wing chair. A full-length mirror flanked by wall shelves that supported busts of Einstein and Newton filled a third.

"Just one room?" I said. "That doesn't seem right for the head of a highfalutin Trust like this one. Or at least, like it used to be."

"No, not at all," Vayl agreed. "Nearly everyone had a secret place where they kept their crypt. So if we search along the walls, perhaps we will find the entrance to another room."

"Like the one Blas had?"

"Precisely. Or, perhaps, the one referred to as the Preserve."

As we searched on opposite walls I spent some time trying to convince myself Vayl's former sleeping arrangements were none of my business. Then I decided this was exactly the kind of thing a friend would ask. "Um, Vayl?"

"Yes."

"Did you, ah, have a stone, that is, a coffin-type thingy when you lived here?"

Long pause. I counted to ten. Gave up. Then he answered. "No. I could never bear the feeling, the thought—"

"I so get that," I said. "When I was a little kid one of my greatest fears was of being buried alive. I don't even know where I got the idea it could happen. Some show, probably, about scratch marks on the inside of coffin lids and people who could fall into comas so deep that doctors thought they were truly dead."

Sigh. "Yes," he said. "You understand. Also there was the real possibility that an enemy would discover the crypt and seal me inside."

"Did you have many enemies?"

"Several." Another pause. "Did I ever tell you why I am so bothered by snakes?"

"No." Although he had let me know he didn't appreciate them. To the point where I'd had to dispose of one for him during a previous mission.

"When I was a child we were traveling from one camp to another and we had to cross a river. My dog had been traveling on the wagon, but he loved water, so as soon as he could, he jumped in. About halfway across he squealed and began to struggle, as if he had been caught by a fast-moving limb. I cried for my father to come to his aid, but when he pulled him out by the scruff of his neck, his entire underbelly was covered, crawling with water snakes."

"Oh my God."

"My father threw him back in. It was a miracle neither he nor the horse was bitten as well. But still, the vision haunts me."

"Stuff that happens to you when you're little, it just sticks, doesn't it?"

"Some of it, yes. And some memories I cannot grasp though I experienced them fully at the time." I moved to the next wall, looked over to see him shaking his head. "Ah, but it has been a while, as you say."

"Hey, I think I found it!" I'd made my way to the mirror. Framed in pewter, it had lots of scrollwork, but at the top and bottom were smooth, round expanses of metal inscribed with Vampere phrases.

"What's it say?" I asked as Vayl joined me.

"It is a famous quote from one of our first Council members, Sereth, who passed perhaps a century ago. *Reality is but a reflection of humanity's manipulation of itself.*"

We began pressing and prodding the mirror, pushing the round sections, trying to shove it in different directions. Vayl looked around the room. "This has to be it," he said, resting his hands on his hips in frustration.

"Wait a second. That word, 'manipulation.' See how it's in a different font?" I said.

"Yes!" Vayl pressed his forefingers onto the word and pushed. It sank into the surrounding metal. Moments later, with the whispering whoosh I associated with hydraulics, the mirrored section, along with the geniuses Eryx had idolized, swung inward.

We grinned at each other in delight. Vayl felt inside and found a light switch. When he flipped it we saw a hallway covered with a mural the artist had called *The Daemon Wars*. The setting looked fairly recent. Times Square full of cars I dated to the fifties. Humans carried on with their business, oblivious to the vampires and hell spawn battling in alleyways, sewers, and on rooftops, just out of their sight.

"Were you around for this?" I asked, shoving a thumb at the painting.

"Of course."

"How come I've never heard of it?"

He darted a glance at me that looked almost — amused. "Our department was only involved peripherally. And other than us, the government stayed out completely."

I stared at the painting another minute. One of the fighters had caught my eye. A woman with honey-colored hair pulled back into a braid. I could only see her profile, but it looked oddly familiar. I shook my head. *Couldn't be. Evie's twenty-four, for God's sake.*

I pulled Grief and nodded as Vayl led me into a red-painted, gold-carpeted room full of open shelves, glass cases, and carefully arranged displays.

"This must be the Preserve," he said.

"Wow" was my brilliant reply. Vayl had said Hamon was a math professor, but given how the items we passed were posed, lit, and grouped, it looked to me like his secret passion had been museum curation.

Enormous statues of long-nosed faces stood on their own waist-high pedestals. Original paintings, all depicting scenes of war or martyrdom, filled the walls. Skeletons of dinosaurs posed as if in full chase of the recomposed bones of their mammalian prey. Two gigantic round tablets containing ancient writings stood on their ends, propped by intricately detailed Ionic columns. They filled one entire end of the room.

"Don't these people ever throw anything away?" I asked.

"Why would they? This is the stuff of legend!" Vayl fingered a full-scale costume made of dried yellow grasses that reminded me of Dorothy's Scarecrow minus the suit that made him charming. The mask that topped it looked like the contraptions people wear after they've broken their necks, except colorful tufted feathers stuck out of the band that ran around the forehead. To one side of it stood a six-foot-long spear draped in hemp-braided beads.

We explored the whole area, discovering priceless relics neither of us had ever seen before and antiques my grandparents' folks would've used when they were kids. We knew we'd found Eryx's prize possession when we reached the center of the exhibit. Sitting on a velvet-covered dais was a mask the size of a pro basketball player. When worn it would cover the entire body, front and back, except for maybe the ankles. The carved wood shone as if it were polished daily. And a wreath of silk laurel leaves circled the forehead.

Though some of the other masks we'd seen in the Preserve had worn the faces of animals and fiends, this one clearly symbolized a human. It looked like a Master's hand had done the carving of lips, nose, ears, cheeks, and forehead. The most amazing parts of the whole piece were the eyes, painted so artfully that they looked real, and you had to look hard to see where the empty space had been left in the pupils for the wearer to see through.

Vayl said, "I do not care for the whiskers. It detracts from the artistry of the rest of the piece."

It did seem odd that the crafter had carved lines that radiated out from the face to the edges of the mask. "It's probably some magically symbolic thing like those words at the bottom," I guessed. I'd been taking pictures with my Monise all along. Now I got a close-up of the phrase, which wasn't in a language either one of us recognized.

"Do you suppose *this* is symbolic?" he asked, pointing to a small door that had been built into the front of it, about a foot below the face. It was square, with a round, black knob. As soon as he touched the door, an image appeared to the left of the dais. It was a vampire wearing a brown suit with a ruffled white shirt underneath. He'd clasped his hands in front of his hips to speak, making it easy for me to recognize the ring on his pinky finger. The same one I'd seen on the dangling corpse in Blas's room.

"It's Hamon, isn't it?" I asked as Vayl stepped back from the hologram.

"Yes."

For a few seconds we watched the former *Deyrar* stare thoughtfully over our heads. Finally he spoke. "I will not welcome you," he said, in a voice I found hauntingly familiar. "Not yet at least. By solving the puzzle of my death-spell and the riddle of unlocking the Preserve's doors, you have proved yourself clever. But that does not necessarily make you a fitting *Deyrar*, dearling. Especially if you are the one who killed me, since my sudden demise is the only way this recording could be activated."

He swallowed several times, struggling with emotions he didn't care to share. "I have given *everything* to assure the continuance of this Trust. You could have had all my secrets willingly if you had just waited until I was prepared to step down. But now — no, I will not reveal it all. Only this. If I am gone, my mate, Octavia, will follow me quite soon. We ruled over the Trust together, partners, as has been the case for *Deyrars* since the first pair powered this Trust. If you wish to keep this community alive, you must also find a partner. Ideally a mate. Give her to the mask. Let Octavia decide if your choice is appropriate. But do it quickly. If Octavia dies without initiating a renewal within the mask, the Trust will die with her."

Hamon's image flickered and faded away.

"Dearling! That's where I've heard that word before!" I exclaimed. When Vayl sent me a startled look, I said, "Every time we're in a room full of blood this face appears to me. The first time it showed up, it said 'dearling.' I think it's Hamon, or what's left of him, still hanging around trying to save the Trust."

Vayl shook his head. "He was certainly devoted."

"I guess you could use that word. I'd go for something a little more extreme myself. Like obsessed. Or, oh, I don't know . . . bonkers?"

Vayl ignored me as he regarded the mask with even more interest than he'd shown it before. "What do you think he meant by equating Octavia with the mask?"

"Maybe it belongs to her."

"Or maybe . . ." Vayl reached forward and pulled the small square door open. Behind it, moving on its own as if animated by some outside force, sat a beating heart.

We must've stared at that organ for five solid minutes.

"Octavia?" I asked.

Vayl closed the door, his cheekbones looking more prominent than usual because he'd locked his jaws so tight. He walked around to the back of the mask. "Take a look at this," he said grimly. When I joined him, he pointed out a line of chocolate-turtle-sized protrusions running down the center of the piece.

"Looks like a spinal column," I said.

"Do you feel any power coming from it?" Vayl asked.

"Like an all-over skin crawl. And I'll bet my savings there are actual vertebrae hidden behind those bumps."

"I believe you would win," said Vayl.

"So where's the rest of her?"

"I have no idea."

Aw, hell. He reached around to take my hand. His was cold, and oh, so strong.

"Vayl." I squeezed his hand as hard as I could. Which, to him, probably felt like a mouse jumping on a trampoline. "I'd like to point out how much this sucks."

"Agreed." He moved back to the front of the mask, studying the face so closely that my urge to pull him away nearly got the better of me. "I believe she must be sleeping."

"Well." I gulped. "It is daytime. If she's still a vampire, that would be a logical conclusion."

"We must return tonight."

"Do you think she'll know how to break you free of Disa?"

"It is difficult to say. But given the fact that she is dying, I would suspect whatever information she has to offer will be genuine."

"Okay." I stifled the urge to kick the mask over and stomp it into kindling. Destroying the Trust could free Vayl from Disa. But he might see it as slightly extreme given that he still had some friends here.

I followed Vayl back to the Hydra-covered door, which we once again secured with the barred gate. The artifacts went back where we'd found them and Vayl resealed the cases. After unblocking the cameras we returned to our suite.

Dave was still at the library table when we came in, studying the cemetery layout as if he could somehow make the whole plan work just by staring at its visual design. He readily switched interest to the photos we'd taken. "Are you telling me this mask is somehow alive?" he asked.

I looked to Vayl. *Are we sure about this?* His nod gave my answer confidence. "Yeah. We don't know how, but it's packed with power."

He took a closer look at the picture. "What are these symbols in the base?"

Vayl said, "It is not Vampere."

"Cassandra's really good at ancient languages," I hinted. "And if she can't translate, maybe the Enkyklios has a clue." It often gave her a leg up in the research department when her own knowledge came up short.

Dave looked at his watch. "It's just after twelve thirty p.m. here, which means it's, what, eight or nine thirty where she's at?"

"Something like that," I agreed.

"Okay, I'll give her a call. Maybe she can come up with something." He dug out his phone.

I looked around the room, finally noticing the blood had been cleaned up, though Tarasios was still passed out on the floor. "Where's the dog?" I asked.

"In the bedroom," said Dave as he waited for his call to go through. "He's sprawled out on that dress of yours like it's made of ermine or something. Which reminds me. He snores."

"Thanks for the warning. I'll grab my earplugs before I try to get some shut-eye," I said. "Anybody have any objections?"

Dave shook his head and walked away as Cassandra answered her phone and he began to talk, hesitantly at first, but more eagerly as the conversation went on. I glanced at Vayl. "You okay with me catching a nap?" I asked.

"Of course." He smiled. "With Disa clear of the library, perhaps I can spend some time in there. Among all those old tomes there must be one recommendation as to how a Maker can force his nestling to fly."

I realized I'd clasped my hands together like a little girl who's just been promised a dolly for her birthday. "You think there might be some info in there about breaking the binding?"

"Absolutely." For a couple of seconds I believed it. Because I wanted to. But I could tell he didn't hold out much hope for rescue. Which was when I finally got fed up. *I'm killing that bitch. Not just for Vayl. But for Aine. And Niall and Admes. For the werebears and my honorary pack. And that bloody face that makes me go ewww.*

Suddenly the question was no longer how to break the bond between my *sverhamin* and the woman he'd ripped, but how to keep him alive once I'd smoked her.

Chapter Twenty-Five

As soon as I hit the bedroom I sent the word out through Pete, Albert, and Cole. *Contact your experts. Let me know if there's a way to kill a bound vampire without also destroying its Maker.*

The answers came back depressingly soon. *There is no way. When they're magically entwined, the vultures die with the nestlings. Always have. Always will.*

"Goddammit!" The cursing woke up Ziel, who came over to check on me. "Go away. I'm pissed off," I grumbled.

He laid his head on the bed. When I refused to pet him, he jumped up, clearing me and landing on the other side, where he turned around three times before settling in beside me. "Okay, you can stay, but don't get used to this. I'm only allowing it because I'm so bummed and for some reason you don't smell like dog."

I turned my back to him and instantly fell asleep.

When I opened my eyes they landed on Vayl, standing at the end of the bed, a shadowy figure in the dimness of the room.

I sat up. Slowly. Why is it that you never really feel the effects of a fight until after you stop moving? I groaned, silently cursing Samos's men as I glanced at the dog they'd tried to retrieve. Ziel lay at my side, gnawing on a bone I hoped hadn't once been some guy's leg.

"How long did I sleep?" I asked.

"Hours. Dusk has fallen."

"Time to call Samos?"

"Nearly so." Vayl cocked his head to one side. "Pete called while you were asleep. He wanted to know why you were trying to spare vampires. When I did not know what he was talking about, he had to explain."

I crossed my legs in front of me and swallowed a gasp as I reached for the poker chips that stood like a tower of happy thoughts on the bedside table. When I still didn't say anything, Vayl went on. "You cannot kill Disa."

"So I've been told." *Click. Clack. Click.*

"Even if her death were to have no effect on me, you should still not be pondering this course of action."

"Okay."

"That does not sound convincing."

Clack, click, clackety, clack. "I could swear on my mother's grave if you want."

"What good would that do when she is in hell?"

I shrugged. *Ow, dammit!* He came and sat down in front of me. "Do not cross the line, Jasmine. Not for me. Do the mission, do it well, and go home."

I met his eyes. "The mission's changed."

"According to whom?"

"Me. And you, if you're thinking straight. Look, Pete can't call this one. Neither can any of the candidates vying for a seat on the department's oversight committee. They're not here. They don't *know.*"

"But if they were, their feelings for me would not cloud their decisions."

"You forget what a valuable asset they see you as. If Disa ties you up for the next fifty years, they're pretty much screwed, aren't they?"

His brows arched. "What are you saying?"

"I have a good case, if it comes to that. But I don't think it will. I think Pete will back me a hundred percent. So the second I figure out how to keep you alive—I'm taking Disa down."

Actually my biggest concern was Cassandra's warning about what would happen to Vayl and me if I pulled this off. But I'd detoured her prophecies before. I glanced up from the poker chips. Gave myself just a second to imagine what it would be like to spend the rest of my life with him.

"You cannot look at me that way," Vayl said.

"Why?"

"Because suddenly it becomes impossible to keep my hands off you." He reached up and cupped my face in his palms, his fingertips sending spirals of excitement down my neck into my heaving chest. Suddenly nothing hurt at all. Anywhere. As Vayl said, "And then I find I must kiss you," his lips lowered to mine. Just a brush, a touch of flesh and then the alarm went off again.

I jumped, banging my nose against Vayl's cheek. "Ow!"

Dave ran into the room, yelling, "Jaz, can't you control your temper for one—oh."

Tarasios came stumbling in behind him, holding his hands to his head, mumbling, "Stop the sirens. Please, stop the sirens." He kept moving straight toward the bathroom, tripping over the doggy-dress-bed by the door. He landed on all fours and crawled toward his target, making it just in time to leave his mess where at least nobody would have to mop it up.

"I'm going to go find out what's going on," Dave said. "You two—get your own damn room. God knows what I'm going to walk in on next," he muttered as he left.

"So, Tarasios," I called. "Did Dave get a chance to ask you any questions?"

No answer but the sounds of his misery. Ziel took great interest in the entire process. He'd jumped off the bed when the alarm sounded and, after running around tracking everyone's movements, followed Tarasios into the bathroom. He kept looking from the puking man to us, as if trying to solve a mystery. By the end we were trying not to laugh. It was the sound, I think. Like a bullfrog that's just coming off a bad cold. Or maybe it was the mutt who decided it was a game, and began poking his nose in Tarasios's butt every time he ralfed, which made him jump and squeak a little too.

"Dogs are disgusting," I finally told Vayl.

"Yes, but high in entertainment value."

We heard the hall door open.

"It's not Dave," I whispered.

"Disa's lot?"

I nodded. "More than one, for sure." As we moved into the sitting room I said, "Nobody knocks anymore, Vayl. Have you noticed that?"

Vayl arched his eyebrow at me. "You know, they say the first sign of a community's downfall is when they scrap their good manners."

Disa, Sibley, Marcon, Rastus, and Niall had all crowded into the open space between the door and the fountain. "Vayl," Disa said, relief flitting across her face as she saw him, "come with us." When he stared at her impassively she added, "Please."

"Why?" I demanded.

She gave me a get-off-my-lawn-peasant stare. "It is none of your concern."

"I disagree." Vayl slipped his hand under mine, raised it so she could see Cirilai glittering on my ring finger. "My *avhar* is always welcome to join me."

Disa didn't seem to appreciate the reminder. She threw her head back and I saw her neck begin to bulge. *All right, if that's how you want it*, I thought. But I couldn't erase the chill that iced my blood when I thought of those tentacles leaping out to slash my face away. I'd never be fast enough. But I reached into my jacket anyway.

Niall stepped forward. "We are under attack. The wagon house is afire. Rastus believes the werewolves we sensed earlier have returned in force. Surely this is not the time for squabbles amongst ourselves?"

Disa snapped her eyes to him and Sibley swayed in his direction. It was like she wanted to jump in front of him but couldn't muster the courage. In the end there was no need. Disa acknowledged his argument's logic and backed off.

"I don't believe the Weres have the strength or the will to attack us, but someone has breached our defenses," she said. *You have no idea,* I thought, glancing at the spot on the floor where blood had been pooling only hours before. She looked into Vayl's eyes, her own a midnight blue. "We need you, Vayl."

Only because I was watching him closely did the slight arching of his eyebrows tell me he'd realized something key. He looked down at me. And we had one of our silent conversations.

All right, I shall play on her affections. Her vulnerability may lead us out of this mess after all.

Are you sure? She seems awful strong to me.

I sense desperation. We may be able to get the upper hand.

Okay. But I have my limits.

So I have seen. He gave me such a look of tenderness I nearly jumped him right there. Oh boy, this was not going to be easy. I lowered my eyes, where they came to rest on Ziel, who had somehow managed to open the armoire and pull out one of my favorite dress shoes. A black suede pump with a kitten heel, it was now covered in teeth marks and dog slobber.

"Do you have a death wish?" I asked the malamute, who gazed

up at me with the same look of innocence con men give their marks just before making off with their life's savings.

"All right," said Vayl, stepping forward to join them. "I will help if I can."

I started to follow them out the door. But Disa stopped. "What are you doing?" she demanded.

"Niall said you were under attack," I replied.

"You are not welcome."

"I wasn't asking permission." I tried to keep my voice level, but it began to tilt anyway. Ziel stuck his nose in my hand. I glanced down. He moved forward until his head slid under my fingertips.

What, after you've eaten my best shoe?

He wagged his tail. So I scratched his head and immediately felt the tightening in my chest loosen. Good thing too, or we'd have been hearing more alarms.

When Disa realized I didn't mean to back down she said, "Fine, you may join your man on the border. I sent him to patrol with Admes when I found him scampering through the halls like—"

And that's when I went temporarily deaf. My temper's kind of like dynamite with the fuse snipped to half. Considering that Disa had lit it the moment she'd breezed into my life, we were overdue for a really big bang. My first clue that the time had come? Heat like laser beams around my ears, lancing in toward my face until my entire head felt like I'd laid it under a broiler. "You *what?*"

Vayl might've said my name, but if he had the sound fell like a pebble into a canyon. I realized I'd raised my hands. Did I mean to strangle her? And was that really such a bad idea?

Disa saw something in my face that made her fold her arms across her chest, as if to shield herself. "Well, he wasn't doing me any good inside."

"He's not yours!" I roared. "He's ours! Where do you get off telling complete strangers to fight your battles for you?"

"I am the *Deyrar*!"

"You're a fucking loon!"

I suddenly became aware of several things. Disa's throat was starting to split and I had moved to within striking distance. Niall was having a hard time keeping a straight face. Sibley's eyes were round as saucers. Marcon looked like he wanted to applaud, and Rastus had raised a rusty sword, which he shook at me in a manner that he thought was menacing.

"Put that down before you poke somebody's eye out!" I snarled at him.

"Disa," Vayl said. "You have once again acted against the terms of our contract."

She turned to him, her hand flying to her throat as if to hide the changes trying to take place there. "How?" she asked, trying for an innocent expression and succeeding only in giving him the same old plastic stare.

"You have deliberately put my people in harm's way."

"*We* are your people."

I opened my mouth, one of my taunts just seconds from flying through the air to slap her frozen face, when Vayl made a small motion with his hand. *Wait*, that gesture said. *I have her right where I want her.*

"You have wronged me and mine," Vayl said in a soft, deadly voice. "We will speak of this again. But perhaps now is not the time? Not when the Trust is burning?"

Disa's hand dropped. The skin of her throat had mended. Her eyes faded to brown. "Of course. The Trust is what matters. Even you can see that. Come, we must see to the breach."

Vayl gave me a moment's glance. I nodded. We both knew what to do.

I gave them sixty seconds to go their way. Then I launched.

Chapter Twenty-Six

Most rescuers run right out the door. Which is why many of them die right along with the people they're trying to save. I dove into the armoire where I'd stowed my weapons bag.

"I heard," said Tarasios as I pocketed a couple of extra clips and slung my new crossbow over my shoulder.

"Huh." I dumped Bergman's faulty missiles and replaced them with my throwing knives, shuddering as the sheath bit into my skin. *Gonna have to find some other weapons for this arm,* I finally admitted to myself. *These suckers are going to haunt me forever.*

As I checked to make sure my syringe of holy water was full, Tarasios said, "I want to go with you." He'd come out of the bathroom to stand at the foot of the bed. The battered old trunk looked better prepared to face an invasion than he did.

"Do you know how to shoot?"

"I took a class once."

I checked the safety on my .38 before tucking it in the small of my back and then handed him the weapon I called No Frills. "This is a twelve-gauge shotgun," I told him. "The barrel has been sawed off, which means it sounds like a bomb and kicks like a cannon. Just point it at what you want to hit and you'll do fine."

"So," he mused as he turned the gun in his hands, "you're not going to argue with me?"

"Why should I? Gives them another target, which means my chances of survival skyrocket."

"Oh."

"Disa said Dave was with Admes, patrolling the border. Any idea where they'd be?"

"Probably as far from Niall as possible. She likes to keep them apart because they take such joy in being together."

"Isn't that kind of petty?"

"Well, Niall wanted Aine to be *Deyrar*."

"I'm saying."

Tarasios acted like he wanted to rush to Disa's defense. Then he remembered. "Yes."

"Okay. So if they're all headed toward the wagon house, we'll go in the opposite direction, to the woods southwest of the villa. Surely somewhere around there I'll be able to pick up Admes's scent."

I put Ziel on the short leash Blondie had brought him walking with. Then I glared at the dog. "You try to hump me one time and I swear I'm wrapping this sucker around a tree trunk and leaving you to the wolves. Got it?"

He stuck his tongue out, panted a couple of times, which I took to be an affirmative, and the three of us trotted through the dank, empty villa and out the back door.

"You going to be able to keep up?" I asked Tarasios as we quick-hiked through an olive grove whose canopy loomed over us with a menace I assured myself had more to do with him stumbling and gasping every few steps than any actual danger Dave might be facing up ahead. I glanced over my shoulder. Disa's former flame was breathing harder than necessary, looking pale and sick in the early-evening moonlight. I wasn't so much worried about him. But if he dropped No Frills I was going to be pissed.

"No problem," he said.

I wasn't so sure. Maybe if I kept him talking he'd be able to continue moving as well. "So why the dive into the ouzo bottle? Did you and Disa have a fight?"

"I told David already. You don't fight with Disa." Well, that certainly had been proven. "She just . . . dismissed me. Like some employee. She actually said, 'Your services are no longer necessary,' and shoved me out the bedroom door."

"Did she say why?"

"She didn't have to. I may be slow, but I'm not stupid."

"Uh-huh."

"It's your boss." Hard to ignore a theory that was gaining momentum. But I tried.

"Are you sure? He ripped her into vampirism, you know."

"Oh, I know." Tarasios rolled his eyes. "Haven't I heard that story a hundred times? How he took her hard and fast like a pirate captain. How he left her to die, only to return and save her, murmuring apologies into her ear until she wept with joy. Ugh."

Yeah, that version grossed me out too. It sounded like something she'd pulled from the pages of a bodice ripper. Had the reality warped in her mind over time? Or had she always loved him? Always wanted the eternity he could give her if she just played the right strategy?

"So Disa's in love with Vayl?"

"As much as someone like her can be."

Which led me to wonder if she'd manufactured this whole situation. Had she arranged for Samos to prey on the Trust, knowing that Hamon would call on the one vampire who could save it? And then had she killed Hamon and maimed Blas so she'd be in charge when Vayl arrived? Hmm, that seemed a little extreme. Plus, her job was to protect the Trust, not tear it apart. On the other hand, she *had* offed several of its members.

But she hadn't known the details of our contract. She hadn't been aware of it at all until Vayl mentioned it. Aw hell, it was all too confusing to straighten out while running uphill, dodging the shrubs that had grown up between the trees, trying to scent out werewolves, werebears, and whatever else the Trust had mortally offended. I had a feeling the list was lengthy.

I'd activated Bergman's lenses. Though nothing moved within my enhanced vision, I could sense *others* lurking just outside the border of the Trust's lands. Not Weres. Vampires. But it was so faint I imagined it was miles distant, maybe a group of hunters stalking prey in one of the dark alleyways of the city whose lights filled the coastline below us.

I reached out for Admes's scent and found it much closer. I began to run, no longer caring if Tarasios could keep up or not. Ziel galloped by my side, his tongue flopping like a big pink necktie. Thirty seconds later I found my quarry, walking the tree line carrying his gladius in one hand, an AK-47 in the other, a crossbow strapped to his back. After a space of about three feet, Dave followed.

"It's Jaz," I called in a low voice, hoping neither of them felt extra jumpy tonight. Admes nodded while Dave motioned me over. "Tarasios is with me," I said as the vampire and my brother turned to check out the injured-boar sounds coming from the darkness behind me. Somebody should just put that man out of his misery.

"Whose dog?" asked Admes.

"Uh, he's a loaner," I said. "We're letting everybody in the Trust have some face time with him to see if he grows on them. Do you like dogs?"

Dave came over and hissed in my ear, "What are you doing?"

"We got to find this ball of fur a new residence pretty soon. It would be highly convenient to leave him in the villa after we go if—"

"You're going to dump an innocent animal with *vampires?*"

"He's hardly pure. You should've seen what he did to my shoe!"

Tarasios caught up to us, interrupting the argument with a short bout of hawking and spitting. "Don't get any of that on No Frills," I said.

"Sorry. Just trying to get this taste out of my mouth."

This from a guy who's drunk Disa's blood?

"Let's keep moving," said Admes. He led Dave, Tarasios, and myself along the trail he'd been taking, though I didn't really see the point. All the action was at the wagon house. Where Vayl had no backup, except possibly Niall. And not even him if it came to a choice between my *sverhamin* and the Trust. Now that I knew Dave was safe, I couldn't help but think that's where I needed to be.

I stared into the darkness between the fir and beech trees that grew thickly on this edge of the property. I tried to reach out with my Spirit Eye to sense any threats to the Trust. But I couldn't make myself concentrate on the job at hand. Knowing Dave and I should be watching Vayl's back made me so jumpy I nearly shot Tarasios when he stepped on a stick, cracking it so loudly I thought we'd been attacked.

I went back to my obsessing. *We should leave. Admes and Tarasios can hike all night long if they want to. Disa wanted Dave here, which is enough in itself to insist we get the hell out.* I stopped just as Dave said, "I don't like this." Most people would've thought he meant our patrol in general. I knew different. Something about the layout of the land disturbed him.

We'd just begun to head down a hill. The forested edge of the property, which we'd kept to our left, banked around in front of us before straightening out again, enclosing the depression we were about to enter on two sides. The grapevines that filled the area hadn't leafed out yet. Between them the grass grew short. In most places it barely brushed our ankles. A couple of trees had gone down recently, their bare branches reaching into the path Admes meant to take between the vineyard and forest like the open jaws of sleeping sharks.

Would it be so bad if I grabbed the AK-47 out of the vamp's hands and sprayed the tree line until bark and pine needles flew like grenade fragments? I knew I'd feel better. Especially now that I'd look like a big wuss if I tried to get us off this crappy little detail.

I clutched Grief, solid and reassuring, in my right hand. The other held Ziel's leash so tightly it would leave red marks when I finally released it. As we trekked down the hill I wished we'd had time to break out our communications devices before Vayl left. Now the only way he and I could contact each other was through Cirilai. Maybe if my emotions tipped the *holy-shit!* scale he'd get the message. Were we there yet? I took inward stock. Almost.

Ziel backed up three or four steps, causing me to stop again. "Hang on," I said. "Something's wrong." Another faint whiff of vampires. I concentrated on it. Realized it was more familiar than it had first seemed. "Aw, no."

"What?" Dave asked.

"Vamps," I whispered. "A lot closer than I'd thought." Admes gasped and went to his knees, a bolt sticking through his left shoulder.

"Take cover!" Dave yelled. We hit the ground just as a bullet whined between me and Tarasios. Both had come from beyond the fallen trees ahead of us.

"I need them alive, you idiots!" came a slightly accented voice off to my left. I concentrated my fire in that direction. When I heard a body crash in the woods I paused to reload.

We'd hit a tough spot. Our cover consisted of the night, our ability to make like flatworms, and the trees most of our attackers seemed to be hiding on the other side of.

I saw Dave's blade flash and realized he was cutting the bolt that had hit Admes so he could lie comfortably while he fired. "Thanks," Admes whispered as he rolled to his stomach. He began shooting his AK in short bursts that forced our enemies to keep their heads down. Meanwhile Tarasios lay with both hands clasped over *his* head, moaning, "I don't want to die," over and over again, No Frills forgotten at his side.

"How did we not sense them?" Dave asked as he rolled to his back, Beretta in one hand, crossbow in the other, watching for maneuvers meant to surround us.

"Blas," I said bitterly. I pressed the magic button. Heard the whir of machinery that meant Grief was transforming. Though I could sense some humans feeling hugely pumped by their surprise attack on the other side of those gnarled branches, I figured Admes had them covered. The vamps were the ones Dave and I needed to worry about. And I was pretty sure they still lurked near the edge of the forest.

I went on. "He can camouflage his own psychic scent. Apparently he can do it for others too. He didn't claim it as his *cantrantia*, but as masterfully as he fooled me, I think that's his main ability. He's the cause of this mess."

"I thought he was dead," Admes said unbelievingly. "You're saying he invited this *attack*?"

"Oh yeah," I said. "I kind of admire his tenacity. You'd think losing half your face would quench pretty much any ambitions you had left. But he keeps on trucking. I suppose he figures Samos is his best bet to dethrone Disa."

"*I* should be *Deyrar*, not that mutation they've all bowed down to."

I was so startled by the voice of Blas, coming from every direction but seemingly disconnected from any physical form, that my entire body came off the ground. Ziel, who'd been lying quietly beside me, began to growl.

I baited the vampire, trying to make him reveal his position. "And here you had me thinking you were the poor, pitiful victim."

"*I* am the one who called the Raptor from the skies. Hamon's leadership had already begun to crumble. Beneath Samos's attack it would have fallen, and Aine would have found no support for her succession, she was such a sycophant of his. The rule of the Trust would have fallen peacefully to me if Hamon hadn't phoned Vayl."

"What's he got to do with this?" I demanded, staring into the night, trying to track Blas by the sound of his omnipresent voice.

"I overheard them speaking of a contract. I could hardly let Hamon live once I knew Vayl was coming to shore up his position, now, could I? So I killed Hamon and made my play."

"But it didn't work out the way you'd planned, did it?"

"How were we to know about the Preserve?" he shrieked. "Hamon kept everything such a secret! Hoarding all his power like a damned . . . power hoarder!"

I almost had him pinpointed now. Out of Grief's range. But Dave should be able to reach him. I whispered, "He's standing between your ten and twelve o'clock."

"Can you be a little more specific?" Dave replied quietly. "That still leaves a whole lot of black between the trees."

Admes traded another few rounds with our human ambushers. I waited for the firing to pause before I yelled, "We found the Preserve, Blas. Lovely little spot right off of Octavia's dressing room. You should see all the relics Hamon's collected in there. Oh wait. That's right. You can't."

His scream raised the hairs on the back of my neck. In the extremity of his emotion he allowed his guard to slip. I saw movement. And so did Ziel. He didn't bark. Just shot straight toward the faceless vampire like a furry torpedo, leaped, caught him just below the jaw, and tumbled him backward into the grass.

Blas squealed like a little girl as Ziel tightened his hold.

"Can't get a shot without hitting the dog," Dave said, so calmly he might've been discussing lunch plans as Admes fired off another burst and one of the humans screamed his death cry into the night.

"Leave him to me," I replied.

"Fine. I'll take care of the vamps at our six o'clock," Dave said. As he readjusted I realized there were at least two more heading our way. Easier to sense now that Blas was down, they must've left the woods after we'd passed them and snuck up behind us. Dave would have his hands full.

I snaked my way forward, pulling my knife as I moved. Ziel, making growly sounds deep in his chest, was chewing Blas up pretty good.

"Don't hurt the dog!" screamed Samos as he came charging out of the forest, both arms raised as if Blas could see him waving them in a desperate negative. But somewhere in his panic, Blas had realized he was stronger than the enormous canine and had managed not only to pry himself free but to throw him forcibly into one of the dead trees. Ziel hit it with a yelp that went straight through my gut. He landed on his feet, staggered a few steps, sat down, and shook his head as if to say, *That's going to smart in the morning.* At which point I realized he was the toughest four-legger on the face of the earth.

But my focus, every atom of my being, pointed toward the vampire I'd been sent to kill. I took careful aim.

"You imbecile!" Samos grabbed Blas at the precise spot where Ziel had let go and lifted him just as I pulled the trigger. The bolt that should've taken Samos down smoked Blas instead. One moment the Raptor was shaking him like a piñata. The next he held two fistfuls of air.

"God*dammit!*" I had a second to note the blotch of blood on

Samos's thigh while I waited for Grief to reload. So he *was* the one I'd hit with my blind shot into the woods earlier. Nice. Then Dave said, "A little help here," and I turned to find him barely holding his own against Samos's two assistants.

Dave's bolt had just missed the sweet spot and jutted from the gut of a tall, lanky woman who came at him with a pair of escrima sticks, wielding them with such speed they were a bone-breaking blur.

"Tarasios!" I yelled. "Get your head out of your ass and fight!" I shot at the second assistant, who was swinging some sort of net as if he was a Roman gladiator who'd lost his trident in a game of poker. The Gladiator pitched forward, only temporarily sidelined. But it gave Dave the breathing room he needed to roll out of Stick Lady's path and empty his Beretta into her chest.

Tarasios's scream brought my attention back to Samos, who'd advanced so far that his bright brown eyes shone like the headlights of a train on whose tracks our vehicle had stalled. I recognized his expression. Crazed, baby. So far past reason, in fact, that the crossbow in my hand counted as nothing to him. I brought my right hand up to steady it. Nothing was going to screw this up for me. Not this time.

"You stole my dog," Samos growled. "You killed my *avhar*. I would tear you into tiny pieces and make you watch me eat them if I could. But the witches say if I am to gain the power I need to overtake this Trust I need a burning — the more bodies the better. I was going to wait until I had the *Vitem* together in the Odeum. But you forced my hand taking Ziel as you did. Of course, listening to your screams for mercy will be so much more satisfying."

"I don't think we're up for any more fires, Eddie," I said as I sighted him in. One shot, that's all I was going to get. I had to hit the sweet spot the first time. "Although, for what it's worth, I didn't smoke Shunyuan Fa. I just thought he was a colossal pain in the ass."

Samos's *avhar* had been killed as he tried to protect the last vampire I'd been assigned to terminate, an ancient Chinese dragon named Chien-Lung. Hell, I hadn't even been on the yacht when Shunyuan Fa lost his head. But Samos would never believe that one.

I took a breath and held it. My finger crooked. I swear, I was so close to that final triumph I was actually grinning. And then Cirilai shot me. Pain lanced up my arm straight to my heart. Suddenly I couldn't breathe. Couldn't move. Couldn't see.

Vayl?

Yeah, said another part of my mind. *Where is he? He would've been here by now if it had been at all possible.*

Cirilai struck again. My left arm curled into my body, cramping so badly I couldn't have stretched it out to save myself from drowning. My eyes were open, but all I could see were black dots flying in a red haze.

I heard Tarasios scream again, couldn't make myself care. Vayl was in more trouble than I could imagine. The kind that meant I might never see him again.

"Jasmine!" Dave yelled. I identified the ripped-air sound of those escrima sticks right before something smashed into my head and everything that mattered faded to black.

Chapter Twenty-Seven

I woke with the taste of puke in my mouth and the swaying sense of vertigo accompanied by stretched muscles that told me I was being carried hand and foot.

"Are you sure she'll be awake for this?" I heard Samos ask. "I want her to be conscious when she burns. I don't care about the others. But she must be aware of the pain."

"Absolutely," someone assured him. It took me a second to identify the voice as Mohawk's. "Listen, she's moaning again."

Well, I wouldn't sound so pathetic if you'd stop swinging me like a hammock in a hurricane! I could feel the bile rising and tried to turn my head, which made pretty lights go off behind my closed eyes. Too bad they were accompanied by thick shafts of shooting pain that buried themselves in my brain and then beat time with my pulse as they sent out little metal stingers to remind me that I, a trained assassin, had been bested by my target.

But Vayl!

Shut up. No excuses. And no panicking. You can't rescue him until you save yourself. Nimrod. You make me want to puke. Which I did. This time I leaned sideways as far as I could so that the next round of barf landed at least partially on somebody's shoes.

"Aw, would you... That's just disgusting!" Sounded like Overbite to me. Good. Served him right for walking around like nothing had happened when his head should've blown off hours ago. At least that meant Admes had taken out the Old-Timer during the battle.

I felt myself deposited on soft grass. *Mmm, nice.* No, wait, this wasn't the time to get comfy. Somebody was planning something nefarious. What a Vayl word. I liked it. So old-fashioned and descriptive. Nefarious. *Play it again, Sam. Nefarious, nefarious, ne —*

"Yes, that will do nicely." Samos sounded happy. Now, that couldn't be good. I felt a rough tongue lick my sore cheek. *Ouch! Freaking mutt!*

"Ziel! Get away from her!" Okay, now he was pissed. The dog had ticked him off. *Good for you, ya jacket-humper, you.* That's what I'd call him if he was my dog. Jacket-humper. Kinda had a ring to it. Although it seemed a little long for vet visits and intros to lady dogs. *Jack. Yeah, that's better.*

I felt my arms jerked behind me so painfully I moaned. And then the tying began. Ziel — *no, Jack —* barked. Only it didn't sound like *woo-hoo, let's party* this time. I'd put it more in the range of *you-fulla-doo-doo.* I was so touched, actual tears gathered inside my eyelids. I realized the blow to my skull might've caused some damage that had led to me thinking — and emoting — in spirals. Still, how cool was that Jacket-humper?

Should I open my eyes? Nope. That'll just make me puke again. Which'll hurt like hell and do nothing to clear my mind. I decided to study the inside of my eyelids instead. It struck me that this must be what Vayl saw every morning when he zipped himself inside his tent. And then died for the day. Which he might have done again — for good this time.

Shaft of pain. Not up my arm. More centralized, and so massive it would paralyze me if I let it. I knew how to do pain though. How to cordon it off like a nosy crowd at a murder scene and say, *Step back, you callous, cold-blooded gorgons, and let me get to work.*

Problem was, when I finally did open the old peepers, I realized it wasn't going to be that easy to finish the mission I'd started. Dave, Tarasios, and Admes had been arranged in a circle, which I closed, my head and feet to theirs. We were all trussed like pot roasts. And we lay inside a carefully arranged pentagon of wood that was already smoldering.

At each point of the star Samos and his men stood like the executioners they were, waiting for the fun to begin. He wore an ivory leisure suit and matching fedora, both slightly stained from the recent ruckus. His blue silk shirt and white tie gave him the air of a porn star going for the look of an international playboy. It wasn't a style I'd seen on him before, but that time he'd been in his office, doing a deal with the devil.

Mohawk held Jack tightly, otherwise the straining malamute would've jumped the smoking barrier and come to me. Overbite stood with his head in his hand, doing a continuous rubdown. Hey, maybe those robots were causing some damage after all.

Samos's vamp-groupies looked even more wrecked than his humans. Stick Lady slumped badly, the holes in her chest only now beginning to close. And the Gladiator kept alternately spitting blood and glaring at me, like burning alive was too good a punishment for someone who didn't mind shooting him in the back.

They were all chanting. At first my battered brain interpreted it as heckling. Then I imagined them doing a really lame rap, their black stiff-brimmed hats cocked to the side, their arrhythmic hips missing the beat as they droned, "We are da baddest, 'cause we kicked your assest."

"Assest?" I giggled. "That's not even a word."

Samos gave me a dirty look. Apparently the doomed weren't supposed to do any hallucinating as they fried. Then his phone rang. That did piss him off. But he answered it. "What do you mean Disa left? I can't finish this tonight if the *Deyrar* is absent! Where did she go?"

As he listened, he kept looking around, like he'd gladly punch somebody if they'd give him a reason. "Why should I ask the town psychic when *you're* already costing me so much, Koren?" His phone hand dropped as he stared at first Tarasios and then me. "Disa has absconded with your *sverhamin*. Where do you suppose they went?"

"Depends on what happened at the wagon house," I said.

He shrugged, like it didn't matter if I found out now. "A minor distraction that would keep them busy while I crossed their borders. Blas said they had been battling unexplained fires, so that seemed the most logical choice."

"If that's all it turned out to be, they probably went to town to celebrate. They're übertight, you know. Maker and mate. Even if you do burn us, it's going to be impossible to bring the Trust down now that they've been reunited."

When Samos's lips pinched I thought, *Take that, you sack of crap.* But my inner celebration quickly fizzled. *So Koren was Samos's inside guy. Girl. Meaning all that rage at my unintended insult to her former* sverhamin *was just overdone fakery. Shoulda seen through that, Jaz.*

Samos shoved the phone back to his ear. "You listen to me, you little bitch! I didn't put my blood to paper just to see this deal crumble because you can't figure out where some *puta* took the object of her obsession! Find them!" He snapped the phone closed, jammed it back in his pocket, and began chanting again. More logs flared, along with a new understanding that sent a shaft of pain spiking through my brain. Samos had made another deal with one of Satan's minions.

"What did you do, Edward?" I asked. Both because I wanted to know, and because interrupting him slowed the spell and the fire. "What did the devil make you give up to pull off this deal?"

"This was a special one," Samos said. "It had to be this Trust, because your sweetheart once dwelt here. And, as I well knew,

Trust roots grow deep. So he would come running if his old homestead was threatened. Which meant he would bring *you*." He spat at me, missing by a mile. But hell, if it got any hotter in this circle I'd be grateful for any form of liquid that came flying my way.

The hatred in Samos's eyes felt like sulfur in the air, maggots on the skin. Until I reminded myself why it was there. Because Vayl and I had beat him. Repeatedly. And I wasn't dead yet, dammit. Which meant—

"You didn't answer my question, Eddie. Demons demand more than blood for their dirty deals. What did you have to give up to get to me?"

Though he turned his face from Jack, Samos's eyes betrayed him. For just a moment they filled with anguish as they fell to the animal, still prancing restlessly at his henchman's feet.

Ahhh . . . now I understood why the dog had transferred its loyalty over the course of a few hours. What irony. I'd relinquished my precious cards in order to find out what Samos loved most. And now he'd sacrificed what he loved most, his beloved Ziel, in order to kill me. And it looked like we'd both succeeded. Already the interior of the pentagram had become unbearably hot. We were beginning to sweat and writhe.

"Gotta *do* something," said Dave. I wished I could see his face. No, on second thought, it was probably better that we lay back-to-back. It would make the end slightly easier to bear.

"Like what?" I asked as I struggled with my bonds. It was no good. They'd tied them too well for me to release myself before the fire did its work.

Tarasios began to cry. "I don't want to die like this."

"Should have thought of that when we were fighting," Admes growled.

Despite our situation, I had to smile. No wonder Niall loved him.

"Jaz!" Dave suddenly hissed in our language, the one we'd made up before we learned to speak English. "Get mad!"

"I already am! What, do you think I'm lying over here wishing I could bake these suckers a loaf of bread?"

"No!" Despite the fact that they couldn't understand us, he'd dropped his voice even more. I turned my head, digging my brow into the ground so one ear, at least, was directed toward him. "Remember what happens now when you get pissed? Sometimes alarms go off. And people have to, you know, come running."

I closed my eyes. He wanted me to start a fire? When we were about to burn? How would that . . . oh. Okay. Because wildfire fighters did that sometimes. They'd set a fire to stop the killer flames.

But he was asking me to control something I didn't understand. *Well, you'd better figure it out,* said Granny May. Now why, facing death as I was, would I imagine her and Jimmy Durante playing croquet? *Hush up and concentrate!* she snapped. *Because all of us imaginary characters in here don't relish the idea of roasting!* This comment was followed by a chorus of *hell yeah*s from the rest of the cast, who'd gathered in lawn chairs at the edge of the yard. They seemed to be slugging beers and vodka tonics in equal doses in preparation for the big finale.

Great. I can't even experience a moment of sanity at my death.

By now the four of us sacrificial lambs had scooted as close to the center of Samos's pentagram as we could. Our hands were touching, tearing at each other's bonds though so far our efforts had gotten us bupkes. Tarasios was crying so hard I could hear snot shoot in and out his nose. Admes had begun to swear between bouts of coughing. Only Dave was still talking.

"It came to you, when? What had you done before the fires started?"

"Gave my blood to the werewolf," I said.

"Which caused what?"

"I have this thing called the Spirit Eye. It's a Sensitivity to the supernatural, like yours only souped up. Your eye might be open just a slit. Mine is cracked pretty wide. Vayl's blood. The tears Asha Vasta gave me in Iran. *My* sharing of blood with the Were. They all revved me up, so to speak."

"So how have you worked those abilities before?"

"Concentration. Visualization. Yeah, it's pretty much a mental thing."

"Well, do it, Jazzy, because I think my shoes are smoking."

I closed my physical eyes and thought about opening that other awareness. Only this time I wasn't trying to trail killer vamps or locate soul-stealing reavers. Now I wanted fire, in a very specific ring, burning away from us. I realized instantly I needed a source, a spark, and then something to feed the flame. Rage, ready at my fingertips since nearly everyone I loved had died a year ago November, rose in me like a chronic disease. It laid its black, festering hands on the grass around us. And though it was still green from a recent rain, it didn't matter. My anger made it crackle like last year's threshings.

"Something's happening!" Dave whispered.

I encased us in a shield that I imagined as a water-cooled protective bubble. But outside that circle I seethed. It wasn't just this moment, having been caught, manhandled, and used as kindling for some madman's power-crazed scheme. It was failing my mission. Losing my life and my brother. Lying helpless while Disa led Vayl toward disaster. Missing my last chance at a love that had promised to be real, and right, and fine. And, yeah, not knowing how to lay my dead to rest.

"What's happening?" Samos yelled.

I could feel the fire now, a circle of rage and heat that I pushed out — *whoosh* — canceling his spell. When I opened my eyes, the logs had gone back to their smoky origins. But I'd done more than that. My flames had somehow reversed the abracadabra, made it reach out and grab on to the vampires and humans who stood at four points of the pentagram. Only Jack and Samos had been spared. The dog had torn free, run to a safe distance, and stopped to watch the proceedings. Samos, well, I had no idea why he wasn't burning. Whether it was because he'd interrupted his own chant, or because he'd backed away from the fifth point, I couldn't be sure.

He watched with a this-can't-be-happening look on his face as his people spun and ran and rolled on the ground, all of them screaming with agony as they burned. He backed away as Overbite came at him, both hands pressing against his head. But he couldn't stop the robots, who'd finally reached their limit. The explosion took off the top of his head, sending tiny, burning automatons flying in every direction. Hundreds of them landed on Samos, who instantly began yelling, trying to flick them off as if they were poisonous spiders.

And then the bots dug in. I couldn't quite believe it, figuring the initial shebang would've taken all the oomph right out of them. I watched closely, at some level understanding Bergman would quiz me later on. Tiny black holes appeared in Samos's face, neck, chest, arms. Everywhere you looked, more and more holes. It was like they had a secondary purpose. One even Bergman hadn't discovered.

"What the hell?" I murmured.

Samos went to his knees, clawing at his clothes, tearing off his jacket, his shirt. Even as we worked at each other's ropes we could see the miniature machines crawling toward him from where they'd landed. Hopping up onto him and burrowing under his skin. He began to twitch. To shake. Seconds later he was supporting himself with his hands, coughing up blood.

"I think they're eating his organs," I said.

"But why?" asked Dave.

"I don't know. Bergman said he originally made them to chow down on tumors."

"So, what, they think his entire internal system is a tumor?"

"He's a vampire. Their insides might work like ours, but that doesn't mean they're the same."

Samos looked at me with bleary eyes, blood dripping from his lips. "Make it stop," he begged.

"I don't know how," I told him.

"Please."

"You just tried to burn me and my guys to death. You're in no position to beg."

Jack came trotting up to him, gave him a sniff. He sent the dog a ghastly smile. "That's my good Ziel."

"He's not yours anymore." Finally I wriggled my hand free. Within seconds we were all loose. As I struggled to my feet, the dog came to stand by me. I patted him on the head. "He's mine now, Samos. And I'm naming him Jack."

The look on the vampire's face might've melted a softer heart. But mine had been encased in something harder than diamonds. And I would never forget the people he'd killed. Or the horrors he'd underwritten to advance his own, obscene agenda. So, despite my desperate need to be moving, I watched and waited while the bots ate their way closer and closer to his heart.

At the end he smiled, his teeth a sickening red, and peered up at me.

"Do you have any last words?" I asked.

He pulled up two handfuls of grass and dirt, spit on them, and peered up at me with a ghastly leer. "Are you certain you know my name?" He began to chant, words in the same language he'd used during the fire spell.

"Jaz, don't let him talk!" yelled Dave.

I threw a kick at his head, but at the moment it should've connected—nothing. The bots had done my job for me. The only bits that remained of Edward "the Raptor" Samos lay in a crumpled little pile at my feet.

Chapter Twenty-Eight

To an outsider we must've looked like shipwreck survivors, leaning on each other because we couldn't get our legs to work right and my head kept trying to spin off into the night like some demented fruit bat. Even Jack seemed bummed, as if watching his former master go poof had not figured into his evening's plans. He'd observed the smoke and steam that had been Edward Samos fade into the darkness, took a second to sniff the bits of ash, cloth, and bone that had remained, and then followed us with his tail drooping as we began the hike back to the villa.

Our first stop had been the pile of weapons and phones the vamps had left at the battle site. Once we were all properly equipped again we stood straighter and stopped looking around like we were surprised to be taking yet another breath in each other's company.

"Do you usually cut them that close?" asked Dave as he rebuttoned his jacket.

The night had turned cool, but I was still sweating from the close scrape with immolation. So I threw mine over my arm as I said, "Naw, I was just showing off for you." I bumped him with my hip. "But seriously. That idea of yours? Pulled our asses out of that jam in a truly stellar manner."

"Good thing I wasn't drunk, yeah?"

I wrapped my fingers in the leather, because I knew he'd reject the hand I wanted to reach out to him. "Swear to God, Dave. That thought never crossed my mind."

"It did mine. You know what else I realized?"

I looked at him sideways, afraid if I met his eyes square on he'd clam up and I'd never learn what went on behind that conflict-hardened face. "What's that?"

"Even though you freed me from the Wizard nearly a month ago, I've still been all tied up inside. Lying in that circle, trussed like a turkey, felt familiar in a way that truly honked me off."

"I can see that."

"I'm thinking maybe I should make some changes before I feel like I need to invest in a hemp farm. Starting with this." He reached into his pocket, pulled out a silver flask, and handed it to me.

Suddenly I knew how it felt to accept the Pulitzer. All I said as I slid the container into my hip pocket was "Good call."

"Damn, I feel better," Dave said. "I'm calling Cassandra." He dove into another pocket and within a minute he was trying to wake her up enough that she could process his good news.

While they were talking, I shoved my phone into Tarasios's hands. "Call your *Deyrar*," I told him. "Find out where she's gone." But his fingers were still shaking so hard he had to give me the number and let me do the work.

After a moment that seemed to stretch for ages, he said, "Disa? Is that you?" I nearly kicked him in the shins. What the hell kind of stupid question—never mind. I rolled my hands at him. *Come on, get to the point.* He nodded. "Are you still at the wagon house?"

He opened the phone so I could hear her end of the conversation if I didn't mind getting up close and personal. I moved in. Despite his spectacular good looks, it wasn't as wowsa as it sounds. We both smelled like ash, and after the way he'd conducted himself recently, I'd have chosen to cuddle up next to a whale carcass before picking him. But with Cirilai sending needles up my arm, I had no choice. I did snatch No Frills out of his free hand first. He'd lost the right to carry it the second he started blubbering.

"No, the wagon house is a total loss," Disa said, sounding more cheerful than I'd ever heard her. "We couldn't find any breach, or sign of the werewolves, so it was probably faulty wiring. Niall, Rastus, and the rest are making sure the fire stays out while Vayl and I take a little trip."

I whispered in Tarasios's ear, giving him the words to say. "Is this really the time to be traveling? I mean, you're supposed to be meeting with Samos tonight."

"Sibley is going to call and tell him tomorrow would be better," she said, in such an offhand tone I wondered if she truly understood what kind of danger she'd put her Trust in by delaying the negotiations. Not that they were an issue anymore. But she didn't know that.

"So where are you headed?" Tarasios asked so casually I gave him a thumbs-up.

"We're taking a flight north. Don't worry, we'll be back by tomorrow. And I'll have such a surprise for you all then!"

"Do you need a guard?" Tarasios asked quickly, before she could end the conversation.

"Not necessary. See you soon!" she sang.

Dave's conversation had ended by the time Tarasios handed back my phone. "Cassandra didn't See any of what just happened, since I was involved." He stopped. "That's probably a good thing. But she's been getting flashes of Vayl. And you. She says you shouldn't kill Disa."

That woman was becoming a broken record.

"She also says to trust Vayl."

"What?"

"I don't know. Just that he knows what he's doing."

Which meant whatever danger he was in, he'd welcomed. Typical. "Well, *I* know the two of us need to get our butts moving if we're going to catch up to them in time."

Admes tapped me on the shoulder. "Don't you mean the three of us?"

"Yeah, uh." I looked up at him. How do you say, *We're not sure we can trust you now,* without offending a guy you've just fought beside and nearly died with? I shrugged. "Our work here is essentially done now that Samos is dead. So it's really just a matter of collecting Vayl and then we'll be out of your hair."

"How old do you think I am?"

"Um—"

"I understand precisely what Cirilai means to Vayl. Did I not see it dangling from a chain around his neck every day he walked in the Trust? And then he left, something none of us ever managed, yet we all understood the ring was what allowed him to survive when the rest of us would have shriveled up and died."

"Admes—"

His raised hand cut me off. "He came to us with you on his arm and his ring on your finger. And, during the battle, I saw how it took you down. Vayl is in dire straits, is he not?"

I gulped. "I think so, yeah."

Admes put his hand on my shoulder. "Then I will help you save him."

"Why?"

"Because I hope it will mean Disa's fall. And that will be the best thing that has happened for Niall and me in decades."

He headed for the villa, and without the energy or numbers we needed to tackle the Trust's best warrior, we plodded after him.

After a few minutes Tarasios said, "Can I go too?"

"No."

"But—"

"What's Disa going to say when you show up after she's already told you to stay home?"

"Oh." His face fell. "I see your point."

"Tell you what you can do," I said. He actually looked more eager than Jack, whose tail had started wagging the second we began moving again. "Find Niall. Tell him Koren was working for Samos." I gave him my number and hoped he'd actually memorized it as we reached the villa's outer wall.

Since I still had the keys to the minibus, Dave, Admes, Jack, and I piled in, leaving Tarasios to trudge into the mansion and spread the word about Samos.

I'd never been so glad to slip onto the smooth, cool seats of some wheels that could speed me toward my goal. I gripped the door handle, leaning my forehead against the window as Dave took the wheel and Admes grabbed a rear seat. I was sick and sore and, from the way my shirt stuck to my back, pretty certain my cut had reopened. But none of that mattered. Trouble was, the pains Cirilai kept shooting up my arm at odd intervals made it hard to put my real problem into a perspective that didn't leave me utterly crazed.

Finding Vayl. Just make it a goal to press toward, not a quest that will destroy you if you fail. Don't think about what happens if the ring goes cold on your finger. If you never have another moment when he looks into your eyes and suddenly you feel happy, and whole, and alive.

Jack jumped into my lap. Which practically gave me whiplash as I heaved backward, trying to take all that weight without yelling. He shoved his face into mine.

"Okay, let's get one thing straight," I told him. "I know where that tongue has been. No, don't give me that innocent look. I've seen you giving the privates a good washing. So there will be no licking of my face, hands, or any other area of exposed skin. Got it?" He laid his head on my shoulder and blew something wet in my ear. "Gross," I said, "but acceptable." I rubbed the side of my face against his and whispered, "Thanks."

Dave had backed us onto the lane leading to the main road to Patras. As soon as he threw the van into drive, without warning, he slammed the accelerator. Admes swore as he dropped something metallic on the floor. I squeezed my eyes shut, hoping the next sound I heard wouldn't be an accidental burst of automatic-weapons fire.

Jack lost his balance and shoved a paw in my chest trying to get it back, which made my left breast hurt so much I looked down to make sure it hadn't caved in. Thinking about my two typical appendages led my mind on to Disa's multiple freaky ones. And I decided we'd given Pete more than enough time to research their various applications. With a major confrontation on the horizon, I needed to know how to defeat them. Now.

It took him nearly a minute to answer his phone.

"I still have an hour before I have to get up for the day," he griped.

"Then you shouldn't have given me your home number," I replied.

"Did you know you're the only one who ever calls me here?"

I bit my lip. It's never good to stand out in a crowd, especially one as sparse as the group that comprises our department. "It's important."

"Then get to the point." I decided the reluctant acceptance in his voice might spare me a lecture the next time we met, and launched into a brief review of the night's events.

"So Vayl and I got split up and now I'm going in to back him up. He's with the face-eater, so I could definitely use any info you guys have dug up, you know, before I go pick a fight with her?"

"Hang on." I heard the squeak of bedsprings as Pete moved his side of the conversation to a location that wouldn't give his long-suffering wife nightmares. "Listen, all we've got right now are a couple of radical theories. Nothing we're willing to let you risk your life, or your nose, on. So far all I can tell you for sure is she's not a true Vera."

"You mean this *isn't* something she's evolved into by using her own powers?"

"Exactly. She seems to have entered into a symbiotic relationship with a new species."

"And by new you mean one we don't yet know how to kill."

"Pretty much," he admitted. "Our researchers are working on it, but currently all they can tell me is if you terminate her, the thing that's connected to her should die as well."

"That's easy for them to say. They haven't seen the damage she can do!"

"True."

I sighed. It looked like I was still stuck in improvisational mode regarding Disa. And that couldn't include smoking her unless I figured out how to separate her from Vayl. Maybe if I managed to slow her down. Paralyze her even. *Huh. Now there's a thought.*

"Listen, Pete, I know Vayl has fed you information on Trusts in general. Has he told you anything about this one in particular that might help?"

"Hang on. Let me get my laptop."

I stared at the twinkling lights of Patras, growing larger in the window as we left the countryside and headed toward the docks. I realized I was petting Jack's head while I waited and feeling better because of it. Too bad my work kept me moving so much. It might've been nice to try life as a pet owner.

"Jaz?"

"Still here," I told him.

"Okay, I've brought up a copy of Vayl's report. There's not

much you don't already know. He says that the Trust demands absolute loyalty. That Hamon nearly killed him when he turned Disa, because that was one of the cardinal sins of the community."

"Somebody mentioned the rule, but I didn't realize Hamon reacted that strongly."

"Yup. Says here most other Trusts encourage turning. But Hamon insisted that nobody create a mate for him- or herself. It also says Vayl suspected the only reason Hamon spared him was because he despised Disa so much. When Hamon discovered Vayl wanted nothing to do with her, he calmed down considerably."

Aha! And there you have it, folks, the missing thread of holograph Hamon's tale. The only way you can step into his and Octavia's shoes is to be a Maker whose mate would wear the mask. Or vice versa. But, damn, who would willingly do that?

I put my hand to my reeling head. "Pete, Disa needs Vayl in that mask in order to keep the Trust from losing its power. I think if that happened worse things than Samos would show up to enslave them, so she's got to be pretty desperate. But I can't figure out why she'd take him away. The mask is in Patras."

"You'd better find out. And soon. Vayl's the strongest vamp I've ever come across, but even he can't resist all that Vampere magic forever."

"Got it." I hung up and tapped the phone against my head, as if it could send me the one signal I actually needed. "Where are you going, Vayl?"

Admes cleared his throat, said something unintelligible. I pushed Jack off my lap so I could turn in my seat. "What did you say?"

"The Wcres might know."

"Why?"

"They keep track of the *others* who enter and leave Patras. I think it's a territorial issue. Like urinating on your border, only more intense."

I opened my phone. "Come on, baby. Please still be here." Yup, I found the alpha's number just where I'd programmed it in. Krios answered almost immediately. When I explained my situation, he couldn't wait to help me out.

"I have a couple of people working the airport. Let me call and find out where your vamps have gone. Back in a flash."

I began laughing before we hung up. I know, such the wrong time. But I was imagining the old wolf streaking through the streets of the city wearing nothing but sunglasses and a pair of Filas, his tongue hanging out like Jack's as he did some mad dialing.

"This is not funny," said Admes, shifting in his seat as if to disguise the worry in his voice. "In fact, I almost wish I had stayed silent. The Weres are angry with us. What if I have set off the firestorm Disa began brewing with the *Sonrhain*?"

I don't give a crap if you guys war for the next two hundred years! I just want to know where Vayl went! Dave must've seen some of what I was thinking on my face, because he said, "Silence kills a lot more often than talk, Admes. You were right to share what you knew."

By the time Krios called we were motoring toward the airport, speeding past square white high-rises spilling light and laughing partyers onto the streets. "The plane is a charter headed for Ljubljana, Slovenia. Two vampires were on it, both of them in a state of high spirits."

"What? Wait a minute—*both* of them were happy?" I clenched my fingers in Jack's thick fur and he swung his head up to look at me. Yeah, a little reproachfully.

"I'm only reporting what my man told me."

I made myself relax. There must be some explanation. I'd imagined her loading him aboard via wheelchair. How else could she force him to travel with her? Cirilai couldn't have sent me a false message, could it?

Disa, of all people, understood the consequences of tampering with Vayl's powers. But she must've found a way to circumvent them. Or he thought he'd found the key to her downfall. Maybe he was just playing along.

Or maybe I was going to drive myself crazy trying to figure this out, in which case my big rescue would end with me standing in a corner, drooling, while I watched an imaginary parade on Venus. Not an option.

"Okay," I said. "I'm not that familiar with Slovenia. Ljubljana's the capital, right?"

"Yes, but I don't think they're staying. He overheard her speaking of renting a car once they arrived."

"What are they going to do there?" I wondered out loud.

"Hold on, I'm getting another call," said Krios.

I turned to Admes. "Does your Trust have any ties to Slovenia?"

He shook his head. Before I could ask him any more questions Krios was back. "My man just remembered something. Before they boarded, she laughingly gave him a coat, telling him they will need to bundle up because it might even be snowing where they were headed. And the male vampire said something like, 'I hope my boys dress better for the weather than they used to.'"

"Oh God." My hand dropped to my lap. I could hear Krios asking for me repeatedly, until Dave finally took the phone from my hand.

"What is it?" asked Admes. Only when he reached out to touch me did I come back to myself.

"Don't," I said, more sharply than I meant to.

"What is happening?" he asked.

Dave hung up, and immediately the phone rang. As he answered it I said, "Disa is taking Vayl to his sons." He and I stared at each other and I felt as if thunder had crashed inside the minibus. My ears rang from the immensity of the realization. Because every genuine psychic Vayl had consulted since his sons were murdered had been vague or stalled him purposely—knowing that the day the three of them met they would all die. "How could she know, though?"

Dave closed the phone. "That was Tarasios," he said grimly. "Niall made him join the chase for Koren. They found her pounding the door to the town psychic's rental house, trying to gain entry. After some intense questioning, she admitted she was trying to get the woman, whose name was Erilynn, to help her discover where Disa and Vayl had gone."

"And?"

"They found her slumped over her kitchen table. Her face was gone. She'd been there for a while, Jaz. The bugs were feasting."

"Why wouldn't anybody check on her before—"

"Last-minute vacation plans with orders for no one to disturb her until early next week. Disa had herself covered pretty well."

I felt my stomach lurch and wrapped my arm across it as if that could keep my insides from banging against each other in the physical version of a bloody scream.

"But—it can't be happening tonight! He's supposed to meet them in America!" I realized I sounded desperate, but couldn't seem to pull it into myself. "He told me a Seer said so."

Dave gripped my shoulder. "Then maybe that's how it'll go down. Disa's conned him before."

"So you're telling me to chill."

"Hell yeah."

I shook my head. "I'm too close to him," I whispered. "It's making me panic when I need to think the clearest."

"Bullshit."

"Huh?"

"I'm sick of listening to your excuses, Jasmine. You can sit here all day and list reasons why you and Vayl shouldn't be together.

Same with me and Cassandra. But there's always the one that outweighs all the rest."

"Which is?"

"Aw, for chrissake, I'm a guy. Don't make me say it."

Oh. "Okay."

Admes sighed. "I wish I had never come on this trip."

"Why's that?" I asked.

"Because, yet again, I feel I might be betraying my Trust. But if it would give you power to fight Disa . . ."

"What do you know?"

"Hamon had been grooming Aine to take his place as *Deyrar*. He might have revealed information to her that would help you understand why Disa has lured Vayl to Slovenia."

I held out my hand. "Dave, gimme that phone."

CHAPTER TWENTY-NINE

Funny what a difference a couple of calls can make. With Niall acting as our go-between, Aine explained that the rites of succession included a moment of sheer ecstasy for the vampire about to become the mask. Like yeast in a bread recipe, the ecstasy was necessary. It acted as a catalyst to the Vampere magic, forcing the mask to recognize a new wearer and triggering it to meld with the new *Deyrar*'s mate.

With a twist, the squares of this mixed-up Rubik's Cube began to align. Disa needed Vayl. Loved him in a sick sort of way. And the binding, this trip to Slovenia, they were all part of the ceremony that would eventually end with his chameleon eyes blinking from that hard wooden shell if I couldn't figure out something, and fast.

Aine said usually the ecstasy involved a bout of sexual bliss, but Disa knew better than to try to take Vayl there. Thus, the reunion. Nothing would make Vayl happier than to reunite with his sons. After which, he'd be dead.

"If I just knew who Vayl's sons are," I said as I hung up the phone. "If only someone could tell me."

"Cassandra might know," Dave said.

"I'm calling her."

But when I woke her up for the second time, clued her in to the gravity of the situation, she couldn't tell me. "I have never gotten a clear look at them," she said. "I'm not sure any Seer ever has. Vayl remembers Hanzi and Badu so strongly, theirs are the faces we see when we try to raise a vision of their reunion."

"Let me think. That means this psychic in Patras, this Erilynn, probably didn't see them either. Which would've maddened Disa. She must've threatened the woman, who would've tried to find a way to survive. So, what did she do? She pulled somebody else's face out of Vayl's head. But who? Vayl doesn't know that many guys. Dave's here. Pete and Bergman are in America. Cole's—"

Cole's somewhere mysterious where Cam just happened to show. Is the world that small? I don't think so. Girls, we have a winner!

"Jaz?"

"Sorry, Cassandra, I think I just figured it out. Cole told me he met Cam while he was working his present assignment. I don't think that's coincidence, do you?"

"No. That sounds—manipulated. Tell me, is Erilynn all right?"

"Not even close. Disa must've been afraid Erilynn would try to find Vayl and set things right. You Sisters of the Second Sight are pretty ethical, after all."

Cassandra sighed. "I'll let the guild know."

"I'm sorry, Cassandra. Are you . . . gonna be okay?"

"Yes, thank you." New warmth in her tone now. "I just—there are so few of us. I always take it personally when a Sister dies."

"I can see how you'd feel that way."

"Thanks."

"Would you—like me to find out about the arrangements for you? That way you could send flowers or something if you wanted."

"You'd do that for me?"

"Uh, yeah, sure." *Assuming Vayl and I survive the next few hours.*

"Jaz, that would be wonderful!"

"Okay, I'll let you know." We signed off and I sank back into my seat, telling myself what an idiot I was to try to have even one relationship, much less multiple ones, when my entire mind should be focused on the task in front of me.

Dave slammed on the brakes. Traffic had backed up now that we'd entered the heart of the city, and his patience had evaporated. As he leaned on the horn he yelled, "Were you just talking about *my* Cam?"

As I nodded he began shaking his head. "It's impossible. He's on the other side of the world. They all are—"

"No, they're not," I told him. "Cole told me he just met up with Cam. If I'm right, they're both in Slovenia. Cole was assigned to terminate a mark who still hasn't shown up. I don't know why Cam's been sent there, but I can guess. Disa's known she needed Vayl all along. I'm starting to think she and Blas got the *grall* to suck at least *that* secret out of Hamon. Knowing Vayl's obsession with finding his boys, she must've decided to manipulate his need to see them one more time. I think she found a way to get Cam assigned to do some training wherever Cole is for the next week or two, just in time for Vayl to make his discovery."

Dave's face looked bloodless inside the van as he took a quick right, rocking Jack into the seat and making Admes grunt. "How could she have the power to force them to split up my unit?"

"Maybe he's just on leave."

"Or maybe I've let them all down. If I'd been there, he wouldn't be standing in the path of octopus-throat right now."

"Your guilt, while attractive in this light, is really starting to piss me off. What do you say you let it go so you can start being the kind of leader they need?"

We stared at each other longer than it was really safe for us to, considering he was driving. Then he smiled. "Sounds like a plan."

"That's the brother I've come to know and occasionally wish I could still kick the ass of. Here, let me check and see if Cole's texted me lately." Yup, he had. In fact, it looked like the message had come while I was talking to Aine.

Cam's done working for the day. We're off to slog some brewskies. Why do they call them Alps anyway? Too short a name for such big, frigging mountains!

I texted him back.

Where are you? If you need to clear the info-share with Pete 1st—do it ASAP. This is vital!

Seconds later I got his reply.

Sorry. If I told you, I'd have to . . . you know.

Shit!

CHAPTER THIRTY

Krios couldn't pull off a charter for me. His guys were ground-crew types, not administration or pilots. But he did suggest someone who could help. My old pal the werebear.

"Kozma, thanks for getting the Range Rover back to me so fast. How are your wounds healing?" I asked as soon as he growled a greeting into his phone.

"Jasmine Parks?" he asked. I heard him sniff, as if he could scent me through the cell signal.

"Listen, I know we already had a deal that made us even, but I need to renegotiate."

"Really?" I was relieved to hear a note of amusement in his voice.

"It's vital that my friends and I get a flight to Ljubljana, Slovenia, like, an hour ago. You got any connections?"

"At this time of night? Only one, and then only because he's my brother-in-law."

"Works for me. Can you two meet us at the airport right away?"

A pause that felt eternal and made my stomach twist so radically I began to suspect internal bleeding. "I think he'll do it. That is, if you can pay." He threw out a figure that would carve a major chunk out of my euro supply. As if I cared.

I took a second to remind myself how to breathe, then said, "No problem."

Which was how we found ourselves strapped into an AStar B2 helicopter. Our relative comfort was due to the fact that the aircraft was designed for touring, its pilot a U.S. expatriate who'd earned his wings in the army. Dooley Green had met and married Kozma's sister the year before — although Kozma made it clear Dooley didn't know about the Were in his extended family and it would be great if that ignorance continued.

Keeping Kozma's secret turned out to be a cinch. Dooley, who flew travelers all around the northern Peloponnese during the day, launched right into tour-guide mode as soon as we took off and only stopped talking twice. Once when we landed to refuel. And again when we finally saw the lights of Ljubljana.

At the beginning of his lecture, which started so far back in history I wasn't even sure people were walking upright yet, I noticed Dave was actually trying to see some of the sights as our pilot described them. He sat with me in the back. We'd brought Jack as well. He shared part of my seat and the empty one to my left. Eventually I would have to convince him he wasn't a lapdog. Definitely before his weight collapsed a major vein. But for the moment I enjoyed his warmth as he lolled across my thighs like a panting, woolly blanket.

Admes had wanted to come, but we'd convinced him to stay with his Trust, whose boundaries still needed guarding. Given the fact that Disa's absence also offered him the chance to spend time with Niall without her interference, Admes decided maybe it would be in everyone's best interest for him to drive the minibus back to the villa.

I gave up on texting and called Cole directly. Having no idea what protocol to follow in this case, I simply said, "Our mission seems to be overlapping yours in a potentially deadly way. Not for you two, I hope. But watch your backs. And your fronts. Okay?"

"Details," he demanded.

"Not many beyond a couple of vampires." I winced. "Including Vayl. But he's not—"

"I knew it! I *knew* that son of a bitch would find a way to blow me out of the picture!"

"Cole! He's on your side. I mean that sincerely. But he's with an evil vamp who's bonded him to her. In a sort of bippity-boppity-I-do type thing."

"Well, how did he let that happen?"

"He didn't intend . . . anyway, I'm sure he's just—"

"Is that why you wanted to know where I was?"

"I know you're in Slovenia near Ljubljana. The lady vamp Vayl's with consulted a Seer, so they have some idea where you—"

"Shit! She probably saw us drinking. Listen, how far away are you?"

"Hours. But so are they."

"Just get here, Jaz. We'll keep moving. Call me when you hit town and I'll tell you where we are."

"Okay."

Three and a half hours later we landed on a sparsely lit helipad and, after paying Dooley his fare plus a generous bonus if he'd stay for the return trip, rushed into the terminal to find ourselves some wheels. Cole wasn't answering his phone. An ominous sign. So we had to find somebody at the all-night car rental counter who could tell us where Vayl and Disa had driven theirs.

It turned out the clerk, a thin balding dude with strangely long fingernails, didn't feel like selling his superior knowledge for cash. But he was partial to the dog's harness. At two fifteen in the morning, we didn't figure we had the time or the resources to haggle.

"Okay, Jack," I whispered to him as I slipped the studded straps off his broad back. "You and I both know the short, skinny freak's going to end up strutting around his bedroom wearing this with a leather thong singing, 'I am the walrus, goo goo g'joob.' I know, gross. But don't feel bad. It made you look like the lead sled dog from that movie *Dominatrix Iditarod*. Don't ask how I came to watch it. There's a reason my work's top secret."

Once the clerk had his bribe, he felt free to tell us Disa had enthused to Vayl about the beautiful scenery that would form the background of his momentous reunion when they reached Skofja Loka.

According to the clerk's map, Skofja Loka was situated eighteen kilometers from the airport, tucked in a valley still blanketed with white, as though winter couldn't quite let go so close to the mountains. I pushed the car as fast as I dared along dark, unfamiliar roads while Dave sat beside me, trying fruitlessly to raise Cole on the phone.

"Well, shit," he said suddenly.

"Yeah?" I asked.

"Cam's got a sat phone. Maybe he'll answer." He did, on the first ring.

"Cam, it's Dave."

Cam was so delighted to get a call from his commander I could hear his voice from three feet away. "No kidding? It's really you? How the hell are ya?"

"More important, how are you?"

"Doing okay. Cole says to tell you reception sucks in the lower part of town, where we've been for the past hour or so. We're headed up to Pub Na Mehelic now." He gave Dave directions, which he passed on to me.

I rolled down the window. As cold as it was, Jack had been banging his paw against it for the past ten minutes. Now he shoved his head through the opening, his tail slamming rhythmically into the seat between Dave and me to demonstrate how delighted he was. And why wouldn't he be? Skofja Loka emerged from the night like a gingerbread town, its quaint old buildings and narrow streets reminding me of something out of Grimms' fairy tales. Which, I reminded myself sternly, often ended in murder.

Mehelic's was a two-story, white-painted structure with the broad dimensions of a barn. *Wow, they take their drinking seriously here,* I thought as I parked in the small lot west of the building. Eventually I realized the second story was an art gallery, at which point all the wine they pushed on the first floor made a lot more sense.

I left Jack in the car. "What can I say?" I told him when he gave me a pitiful stare. "People don't want dog hair in their martinis." We left the window cracked, locked the doors, and headed toward the intricately stenciled front door.

"Aw hell," I said as I walked through, looking back to see if Dave had the same reaction.

He was shaking his head in disbelief. "Is that what I think it is?" he asked.

I had to nod. Our ears were not deceiving us. Somewhere within the depths of the pub, Cole was singing.

I edged farther inside, hugging the brown paneled wall in the hope that he wouldn't see me right away and demand that I join him. Fat chance. The place was as open as a high school gym, with tables covered in yellow vinyl marching in neat rows toward the empty space at the back of the room where Cole stood. Since the place offered no stage he stood on a chair. Crooning into an unlit candle. No microphone. No karaoke machine. Just Cole, belting out the words to Lionel Richie's "Endless Love."

"Two hearts that beat as one/Our lives have just begun," he sang. Then he saw us.

He jumped off the chair, Cole style. Meaning he put one foot on the back and overbalanced it until it tipped gently to the floor, at which point he soft-shoed to our spot, where we stood in mute horror, unable to retreat because the bar, a long, scarred counter that made you think a few guys might've busted their heads against it in the past, blocked our escape. Behind it stood a gray-bearded bartender who seemed to be enjoying the show much more than we were. At least, I thought I heard him chuckle as I whispered, "How drunk are you?"

Cole grabbed me around the waist and danced a few steps with me before I could pull myself free. He said, "I'm as sober as a Baptist on Sunday! But now that you're here . . ." He wiggled his eyebrows cheerfully.

"I thought you were going to keep a low profile!" I hissed. "You sounded so serious on the phone!"

"Well, I realized if this is the last day of my life, I didn't want to spend it cooped up in a closet while I bit my nails and wished I'd taken the time to have at least one deep relationship." He stopped, looked into my eyes. "Okay, I do wish that. In fact . . ." He pulled me into his arms, dipped me until my back creaked. But before his lips could descend to mine I slipped my hand between them. Which meant he laid a wet one on my palm. "Not cool, Jaz," he said. "You're always supposed to kiss the dying man."

"You're so full of shit, *I'm* drawing flies! Where's Cam?"

He lifted me to my feet, nodded to the far edge of the bar. "Over there."

"Where? I can't. Oh." Now I saw him. Well, his feet at least. They rested, upside down, on one of the stools where the bar turned a corner. Occasionally the feet waved back and forth, the heels nudging each other as if to remind themselves of a good joke.

I looked at Dave as he led us toward his sergeant. Every step he took seemed to draw him up straighter, snap his shoulders closer to his back. It was like watching him try on a new uniform. And it fit perfectly.

Upon stopping at the feet, we found the rest of Cam spread out on four more stools, enjoying a back rub from an attractive, brunette barmaid wearing snow boots, a plaid, knee-length skirt, and a white peasant blouse.

"What the hell do you think you're doing?" Dave demanded, the command so prominent in his voice that we all came to attention, including the bartender and an older couple sitting at a table near the door. Luckily nobody else shared the room with us at the moment. I should've felt relieved. After all, we'd beaten Vayl and Disa to the guys. But Dave's irritation at Cam made my stomach clench. This was no time for infighting.

Dave's right-hand man hadn't felt Cole's need to avoid the sauce. The tankard in his hand sloshed ale all over the floor as he jerked sideways and rolled off the stools, still clutching the straw he'd been using to drink from it between his teeth. I would've had to check the instant replay to tell if he hit his butt. Because as soon as he caught sight of Dave he bolted upright, spitting out the straw, throwing the mug to one side as if it had grown spines.

He didn't go so far as to salute, but Cam did say respectfully, "What was I doing? Well, I was availing myself of the local masseuse, sir."

"Are you in the area on business?"

Slow blink, followed by a slight twinkle. Cam was beginning to realize his commander had slogged his way back from the brink. "Yes, I am."

"Then am I correct in stating that you are representing your country by lounging on your face in a bar?"

Cam looked right into Dave's eyes. He pursed his lips, glanced up and off to his right, as if he was solving a physics problem.

"That's about the size of it," he said with a lemme-have-it grin. "In my defense?"

"As if there was one." Dave snorted.

"Cole did say we might die today. So I thought, you know."

"That you'd like to buy it without any kinks in your muscles?"

"Uh, yeah."

"Yes, sir."

"Yessir!" Cam pulled his shoulders back so far the buttons nearly popped off his plaid hunting jacket.

Dave sidled in so close that he and Cam literally touched noses. Cole and I had to move in to hear, which we did as a unit. It was almost like a tights-clad choreographer off to one side had begun a count. One, two, three, four, and shuffle, shuffle, shuffle, shuffle, stop. Shut up. Gape a little but don't interrupt. Because Dave is, by golly, on a tear.

He ripped Cam up one side and down the other. It took three and a half minutes. I timed it. At the end, Cam, who looked even more dangerous without a beard to hide his scars, could barely suppress a grin. But he managed to stare straight ahead as Dave finished.

"And if I ever hear you faced death with your ass pointed to the ceiling fans again, I will personally wrap your face around my fist and mail it home to your mother. You got that?"

"Yessir. Um, sir?"

"What!"

"There's a vampire behind you. Actually, two."

"You think I don't know that? I'm a Sensitive, you dipshit!"

"Yessir."

They don't do "sir" in Spec Ops as a rule. Doesn't really fit their MO. So I figured Cam had just set a world record. But I was glad he'd mentioned the vamps. Because I didn't think Dave *had* sensed them. He was too pissed. Plus, he hadn't developed his abilities the way I had. And *I'd* only just realized we had company.

Despite the fact that we'd been expecting them, Vayl and Disa brought a hush to the room. Part of it was their powers. When they struck you at low boil, like now, you just felt as if you'd been joined by a couple of movie stars. But, unlike the real masters of stage and screen, they weren't regular people underneath all the glitz. If you ran up to them for an autograph, who knew? You might get a soul-shattering kiss that ended with blood on your lips and the feeling that your world had just tipped sideways for good. Or you might get your chin torn off.

Most of it was Vayl. He stood with his feet spread, hands on his hips holding back the heavy coat he wore to reveal a pair of faded jeans and a black silk shirt that made my mouth water. He exuded personality. It practically jumped from his dancing eyes, his smiling lips. Disa, standing slightly behind him, said something that made him laugh out loud.

Cole leaned over and whispered, "Is Vayl high?"

Cirilai had quieted since its initial attack, giving me time to study them both closely.

Looking at her, understanding now what kind of power she can bring to the table, I can practically smell the kedazzle *she's pushing at him. Could it be his resistance has finally worn to nothing? Or is he truly buying this setup? Either story would explain why Cirilai fubarred me.*

I rubbed my left hand with my right and tried to figure out what to do next. Then Disa stepped apart from him, and I felt a glimmer of hope.

Because she had his cane.

I was certain she'd given it to the psychic Erilynn, so that she could read Vayl's past, and his future. But now that I saw it in her hand, I realized Vayl must've been close to the mark too. Shield or weapon, she meant to use it to her advantage. So if I could get it away from her . . .

Disa held the cane like Vayl had when we'd first met her, ramming the tip into the floor as if she was claiming new territory. She twirled it back and forth, her long fingers caressing the blue jewel that topped it in a way that struck me as obscene. The tigers that adorned the wood of the sheath looked wrong to me. Then I realized they were caked in a dark substance that filled in what should be finely carved edges. I didn't need a lab to tell me what it was either.

I pulled Grief, transforming it to vamp-killer mode as I strode forward. I figured the direct approach would work the best. Grab the cane. Take Disa down. Hurt her bad enough that she begged to be released from Vayl. It wasn't a pretty plan, but I could see it working.

Disa took me by surprise. She raised the cane, said, *"Interri lak-kirm tradom!"* and Cirilai struck, spiking into my hand like a deck nail, taking me to my knees.

"Let her be, Disa!" Vayl strode toward me. Lifted me to my feet.

"Keep her away from me, then," Disa replied. Her pout would've been more comfortable on a four-year-old, which is maybe why it dissipated so quickly. But her power, damn, that was fully mature. At least now I knew what had hit me during the battle.

"Wait a second! You knew about the fight with Samos!" I accused her.

"Of course. No one comes through my borders without my knowledge."

"So you twisted Vayl's power through his cane into his ring just when I was at my most vulnerable. You nearly got me and Dave *killed*, you piece of shit!"

She gave me one of her careless shrugs, topping it off with an evil smile as I lunged at her and Vayl stopped me. *He's mine now,* she mouthed as he grabbed me around the waist with one arm while he buried the fingers of his other hand in my hair. He pulled me to his chest and lowered his lips to my ear. "Trust me," he murmured so softly I could almost believe I'd imagined it.

But Cassandra had urged me to follow that same course earlier. So hard to do. Just let go of your fears and totally believe. Especially when you've been burned so badly that the scars still wake you up at night.

"Vayl! How did you find us?" It was Cole. Sounding überpissed. Vayl pulled upright, though he still held me in the crook of his arm.

"It is the most amazing technological breakthrough," Vayl enthused. "It turns out your phone emits a satellite signal that my phone can pick up and locate on its internal map when I punch in a code given to me by the company that made them. The operator was most helpful after I, how do you say, turned on the charm."

Cole clenched his fists. "I am going to kick your ass."

"Now, Cole," Disa said, stepping forward with two small clicks of her heels and one big clunk of the cane. "Is that any way to speak to your father?"

As Cole gaped like a toddler at his first circus, Vayl let me go and turned to Disa, his eyes brightening into high beams as he said, "This is your surprise? Ahh, Disa, after all these years. You have finally followed through on your vow. And the other boy?" His eyes roamed the room. "Let me just savor this moment. There are, after all, so many from which to choose. Will it be David or the bartender? Or one of those two gentlemen?"

He motioned to a couple of men just walking in. One topped six feet by at least a couple of inches. He walked with his barrel of a chest at full inflate, emphasizing the impression that he was a supercilious bastard. The other looked young enough to be his student, a slope-shouldered sloucher whose glaring eyes seemed to question everything they saw. He looked familiar for some reason, but I would've let it go if I hadn't noticed Cole suddenly do an emotion dump and back up to the bar.

Disa put her hand on Vayl's arm, raising a sudden urge in me to strangle her. "My psychic said we would find him in Cole's presence. And that all would be made clear at that juncture. Is it not a blissful feeling to be reunited with your youngest son at last?"

While Disa sweet-talked my *sverhamin*, I moved to Cole's side. Though part of me still watched Vayl as the bitch-queen poured on charm I hadn't realized she possessed, the rest centered on Cole's still, thoughtful stance.

"What is it?" I asked in a low voice, making room for Dave and Cam as they scooted in to hear the conversation as well.

"Those two men who just came in?"

"Yeah," I said.

"The one just sitting down now, the small guy facing us? That's Petrov Kublevsky."

Aha, so that's where I've seen the face. "Didn't he kill—"

"The retired M5 agent Iaine Wilson, yeah. Him among a dozen others we can prove, including, most recently, Larainne Delvan."

"I didn't know she was one of ours."

"No, but somehow *he* did. This is the first time he's been out of Russia since he slit her throat."

"So he's your mark?"

"No. But while I was waiting for mine to show, I spent a helluva lot of time on the laptop. Just saw this guy's mug not five hours ago plastered all over the terminate-on-sight page." *Oh crap.*

Disa screamed, a ladylike shriek of surprise as the cane she'd been holding suddenly leaped out of her hands and burst into green-tinted flame. It flew to a spot less than a foot from my crowd, flipped itself to horizontal, and began to spin.

"What the hell?" asked Cam.

"I don't know!" gasped Disa. "It just jumped out of my hands." She wrapped her paws around Vayl's arm and fluttered her lashes at him. "What do you think it could be doing?"

"Perhaps it knows who my eldest son is?" he guessed.

"What are you up to, Disa?" I demanded.

The glitter in Vayl's eyes told me I was on the right track.

"I am innocent in this!" she screeched. "It's performing on its own!"

"So you've discovered a new variation on Spin the Bottle? Kids don't play that one anymore, you know. They're too freaked about herpes."

"No!" she exclaimed. "Vayl's sword must know something about his son. It's just as Erilynn foretold. She said once we found Badu, Hanzi's identity would be made clear."

"Did you rip her face off right after she spoke those words for you, or did you give her some time to elaborate?" I drawled.

"I have no idea what you're talking about!" Disa's voice began to climb the I'm-getting-pissed scale. The line at her throat was also bright red, just this side of splitting.

"Drop the cane and the pretense, Disa. We both know you're conning him again."

"You interfering little snake!"

"Kill me and Vayl's going to be one sad little vamp. Generally they get that way when their *avhar*s bite the big one, don't they, Disa? And we can't have Vayl sad, today of all days. So what are you going to do?"

Clear, oily fluid began to ooze down her throat. Dave's hand inched toward the Beretta under his jacket. Out the corner of my eye I saw the older couple slink out of the room. Why couldn't all bystanders be that smart?

Deciding I didn't have time for Disa to waffle any longer, I gave the cane a kick. It flipped end over end, the flames extinguishing as it crashed into the ceiling. It plunked to the floor with an anticlimactic bounce that, thankfully, didn't break any pieces off.

Disa threw her head back, the awful brain-colored beak squeezing from her throat. Two black antennae snaked out of the opening it caused and slid up her cheeks, enfolding her temples and forehead in their awful embrace. Then the beak opened and the tentacles erupted from it, just as Blas and Dave had described, like eels leaping from a communal cave. They waved around beside Vayl's head, a horror-movie aura foreshadowing our future if I couldn't break their bond.

To give him credit, Vayl didn't budge a centimeter, though anyone else on earth would've taken one look, screamed like a girl, and begun digging a hole to China. He went as still as if someone had snapped his spine. But I knew better, could feel his powers build like the electricity moments before a thunderstorm hits. *Be careful!* I wanted to scream. *Kill her and you're a goner too!*

"You freaks need to take it outside!" I didn't realize the bartender had pulled a Baikal shotgun out from behind the counter and aimed it at Disa until, from the corner of my eye, I saw Cam yank his Mark 23 from inside his coat. He yelled, "Drop it!" while Dave pulled his own sidearm.

At the same time the *Deyrar* leaped on top of the bar and whipped her tentacles at the bartender's face.

Vayl yelled, "Disa, no!"

I shot her once, winging her, but it was too late. She'd already grabbed the bartender's gun and ripped it out of his hands, though it went off before he released it, showering steel shot into the ceiling. Chunks of plaster peppered our heads and shoulders as the bartender died, the front half of his head severed from his body by Disa's razor-sharp tentacles.

She spun as my bullet hit her, her add-ons waving like sea anemones. "Now you die!" she croaked, jumping easily from the bar.

Despite the fact that fear had turned my intestines to that ooze Dr. Scholl squirts into his insoles, I amazed myself by opening my mouth and saying, "Really, Disa. You're the *Deyrar* of a kickass Trust about to square off with one of America's best assassins, and that's the best line you can come up with? Plus, and this is just my curiosity talking, do you really think Vayl's going to feel ecstatic about anything now? Your plan's a big fat bust. Now that Samos is dead, what do you say you release him from this ridiculous bond and we all go home happy?"

"No!" she screamed, well and truly beyond reason now. "I can force ecstasy on him if I must. I am sure the world wouldn't be seething with drug addicts if I couldn't find one chemical that would put him in exactly the state I require. Which means you are not necessary to either of us now."

She whipped those medusa tails toward me and I reacted instinctively, leaping backward, surprising myself at the speed at which I avoided decapitation, knowing my exchange with Trayton had everything to do with it. I pulled my bolo as Vayl roared in outrage and jumped to my defense. "Vayl, no!" I screamed as he jumped between Disa and me and, for the second time in my life, I could do nothing to stop the man I loved from dying in my place.

I staggered backward against Dave, who grabbed my arm and helped me regain my balance. The boom of Cam's gun sent Disa staggering, but not before she took a second swing at me. Except Vayl was standing where I should've been, and he bore the full force of her attack.

"*Vayl!*" I yanked myself out of Dave's arms and clawed at my *sverhamin*'s back, sure he was only standing because his brain hadn't yet been able to send the rest of his body the message that it was truly dead. My fingers hit hard, unyielding, frozen . . . "Oh, yes!"

Tears ran down my face and I didn't even care that they might later give somebody in the room cause to call me a crybaby. "You *genius!*" He'd raised his greatest power, one he'd only recently acquired, and in a way none of us could properly explain. He'd armored himself in ice.

Everything's going to be okay.

Yeah, I actually thought that.

Idiot.

Cirilai sent pain exploding through my hand, forcing me to pull it into my chest as if it had been broken in six places. No, Disa hadn't pulled this one. The ring's warning rang true this time. Disa's bonding spell combined with her attack on me had ripped away the last bit of Vayl's self-control.

He grabbed her with both hands, tangling one in her hair because it was hard for him to grasp with his digits encased in ice and he needed a way to keep her from running. The other went straight to her tentacles and ripped. The part of my mind that wanted badly to keep a distance thought, *It's kinda like watching a disgruntled electrician tear the cables out of a fuse box.*

But, of course, it wasn't like that at all. And when he didn't stop there, I realized we could be in big trouble.

"Vayl!" I put both hands on his shoulders, though his shirt had begun to shred and the cold burned my palms. "You've got to stop!"

Cole made a sudden move that caught my attention. He'd kept quiet up to this point. Observing the action, watching the CIA's wanted man. Now he drew his Beretta Storm and trained it on him. I looked over my shoulder. Petrov Kublevsky's companion was slumped over his drink, as if he'd had way more than he could handle. But he'd come in after us and our uproar would've made a lifetime alcoholic recall one of his more spectacular blackouts. Kublevsky had risen halfway off his chair before he realized Cole had taken aim at him. At least it seemed that way. But I saw the glint of metal, held close to his chest as he pretended to sit back down.

I yelled, "Cole, he's armed!"

They both fired at once. Cole had won more shooting competitions than his wall had room for trophies. He should've nailed the guy and walked away clean. He had the angle and ample cover. But Vayl and Disa were fighting, wrestling almost, and they rammed into him just as he took the shot.

The shove pushed him right into Kublevsky's line of fire while it threw him off, guaranteeing only that he wounded his target while the bullet that should have zipped harmlessly past his shoulder buried itself in his chest.

"Son of a bitch!" Cam swung his gun off Disa and emptied it into the Russian, who managed to return a single round as he slammed backward into the wall.

I screamed as Cole fell and Cam tumbled into a bar stool before collapsing to the floor.

Dave raced to Cam's side, so I went to Cole. I stood over him like a stone-cold fool who's been clubbed on both sides of the head and can't think what to do. "Vayl?" I whispered. He'd reached down for his cane. But his ice-encased fingers wouldn't close around it.

"What do I do?" I murmured. "This is . . . it's just like the prophecy. Maybe Cassandra was wrong. Maybe you *have* met your sons. And because it was too soon, they've died again."

I gazed into Cole's pain-bunched face, stifling an urge to run a comb through his tousled hair. I turned my eyes to Cam, lying still on his side. When I looked back at Vayl I realized he'd heard. He'd understood. He stared at the two young men at his feet.

When our eyes met I realized he wasn't seeing me at all. "You did this!" he cried, turning on Disa with an expression I recognized because I'd worn it myself only seventeen months earlier. It was the mind-bending combination of grief and rage that had nearly driven me mad.

He slammed his hand against his chest, shattering the armor that covered his fingers, sending ice shards flying from them like poisoned darts. Once again he grabbed for the cane, his hand tightening and twisting even as he straightened. The sheath flew across the room, knocking the napkin dispenser off a table before clattering back to the floor. Disa watched it with unbelieving eyes. "Vayl!" she screamed. "You are *Vampere!* I am your mate!"

He pinned her with dead, black eyes. "You are nothing to me!" He shoved his sword through Disa's heart. Since it was metal it didn't kill her. But, already weakened by her previous injuries, she couldn't seem to hold her feet against this one. She dropped to her knees. He jerked the sword free. As if I could read his mind, I knew his plan.

"Vayl, no!" I cried. "You'll die!" But he was buried in more than ice. He swung the sword with all his might. Not knowing what else to do, I screamed at Dave. "Banzai!"

He turned from Cam, who he'd just helped sit up. *What?* my mind yelled even as my twin and I charged Vayl, both of us going in low. My eyes sought Cole. He too was rising, pulling his shirt open to check out the damage on his bulletproof vest.

"Vayl!" I screamed as Dave and I raced toward him. "Stop! Cam and Cole are alive!"

We hit him just as his sword sliced into Disa's neck. I screamed again as I felt my collarbone crack when it met the unyielding armor encasing Vayl's thigh. The entire floor shook as Dave and I took Vayl down. When he didn't immediately move, I turned to Disa. She was still in one piece, but just barely. The sword had split into her neck and lodged in her spine. She lay in a heap on the floor, the blood puddling beneath her like a filling tub.

I wasn't at all surprised when the face rose from those red waters to blink at me in utter frustration. "She must die," it said.

"No. If she goes, so does Vayl. Give me another choice."

I'd never seen anyone gnash his teeth until that very moment. Not pretty. Especially when done by a blood vision. But finally he realized I wasn't going to budge. "All right, then. There may be one other option. But it is not going to be popular."

Chapter Thirty-One

We took the plane back, since there were too many of us for the helicopter and we were in a helluva hurry. Jack harassed us all the way from Skofja Loka to the Trust, tripping people up, ramming his big shoulders into our legs in a way his grin said was friendly but I began to think was otherwise. As Admes bused us all to the villa, I whispered in Jack's ear, "You don't have to tell me how much this plan sucks. But until you come up with a better idea, it's all I've got."

Trayton and his pack, along with Kozma and the five werebears he could muster on short notice, met us at the Trust's borders, followed us inside the mansion, and provided the numbers we needed to herd everyone into Hamon's hallway. They, more than anything, had convinced the Trust vamps to follow my lead.

"It's this or war," I'd told them flatly. "The Weres have agreed to lay aside their grudges against you, righteous though they are, in return for your cooperation with my plan."

Opening the doors to Hamon's suite again posed something of a dilemma until I decided to summon the vision one last time.

Gesturing with my good arm for Genti to step out of the crowd, I had Trayton and Phoebe hold him as I pulled my knife. "You've got a lot to answer for," I told the shaking vamp. "It's hard to know where to start." I nodded to Aine, who stood near the back of the crowd wearing a dark red veil, her hand steady on Admes's elbow. "But I'm thinking you can give *her* some payback right now."

I directed Phoebe to hold his arm over the case that held the fedora and, with one quick move, slit the sleeve of his fancy blue jacket as well as a foot-long opening in his skin. Phoebe snarled, her silver-painted eyelids crinkling with delight, as the blood poured onto the glass. "Trayton can remember you cheering as he fought," she whispered into the vampire's ear. "Your pain is like candy to me, suckster."

"Put your fangs away," I told her. "You know the deal. You bite somebody, you're going to start a new fight I'm not willing to referee."

She glanced at Trayton, who gestured for her to back off. He returned my grateful nod and added a slow wink that reminded me I wasn't alone in this. I glanced down the line at Cole and Dave, who each gave me a sober nod. So good to have trusted people at my back again. It made even this tonnage easier to bear.

I stared back at the blood. Whispered, "Okay, Hamon. Now would be a good time to—"

He didn't rise this time. Genti's blood simply rearranged itself on the case, taking the familiar form of Eryx's image. Nobody else reacted, which almost made me wish I could give one of them this extra eye I'd grown. Almost, but not quite. *Maybe,* I thought, *maybe Dave was right. I could find all kinds of reasons to bitch and whine about my Sensitivity. About my potential love interest. But if I didn't have either, where would I be?*

"Is it done?" Eryx asked. He blinked, an odd movement that made droplets run down his cheeks like bloody tears. "No. I can still feel the threat to the Trust."

"We're outside your room," I said. "I need your help to get in."

The eyes closed again, the entire face clenching in concentration. Seconds later the barred gate blew open. "Good work," I said, but the face was gone.

I went first, Jack trotting at my side. Hamon had also opened the door to the Preserve. The lights were even on. *What a welcome.*

I led the way to the center of the Preserve, surrounding myself once again with that sense of history you only get when someone a thousand years' gone has crafted the items you currently share space with. But the costumes and shields, the magic bones and blood cups did nothing to help me brush aside the depression that wanted to crush me like a bug beneath its heel.

This is the right thing to do. The only way to save Vayl, I told myself. *And, listen, it doesn't mean anything has to change for him. Or between the two of you.* Before cynical me could rip off a hearty laugh, I poured her a Jack and Coke and shoved her into the arms of a guy who owned a Ferrari. She shut right up.

I took my place beside the mask, which was blinking. *Okay, pretend that doesn't make you want to find the nearest bat and practice your home run swings on Octavia's wooden head.* It helped that I couldn't have held one at the moment. Dave had immobilized my arm on the plane and, now that I was a pack member, Krios had willingly sent a doc to the airport for me in one of those mobile clinics set up inside an RV. He gave me a local anesthetic, a brace, and an urging to visit the hospital the second I had a spare day.

Cole came behind me, carrying the front end of Vayl's litter. I allowed myself a spurt of happiness at the reminder that I hadn't watched him die after all. Cassandra had been right. Which did us no damn good at the moment. My boss had entered some sort of coma state, and nobody could explain to him that his sons were still alive because they weren't Cam and Cole to begin with.

The ice had begun to melt as soon as Vayl lost consciousness. But it had left his clothes a shredded mess. I'd found a thin yellow blanket on the plane, and that's what covered him now, making him look like a sick kid who's spent way too long in the nurse's office waiting for his parents to pick him up from school.

Cam carried the other end of Vayl's stretcher. Despite the pain in my collarbone, I could've danced across the floor to see both his eyes open, though their customary twinkle had been replaced by the grim face he wore in battle. He'd survived the fight only because he'd worn his own body armor, which had covered even more skin than Cole's. Thank God for that, because the shooter's bullet had hit him in the armpit. A death blow to any but a Special Ops trooper who was issued the best of everything.

Genti and his crew followed, guarded by Dave, who'd loaded his crossbow with a Bergman special. Which meant, as he'd reminded them, if any one of them decided to get snippy, they'd experience a repeat of the Koren incident. Only this time we'd all stand and wait until the smartass burned.

Niall and Admes, still escorting Aine, walked around to the side of the dais opposite mine. Disa's guards were flanked by Kozma and his bears: burly, broad-chested men who looked like they spent their weekends braiding saplings into giant slingshots. They carried Disa on a second litter, which Tarasios walked beside, making sure the sword that still impaled her caused no more damage.

Trayton's pack came last, led by Krios, who'd promised to make sure everyone behaved, even the hotheaded dockworker who'd been so ready to war the last time I'd seen him.

Yeah, I hadn't left much to chance.

The second I'd understood what the vision wanted back in Skofja Loka, as soon as I'd realized all the ramifications, I'd pretty much called in all my favors. To orchestrate an event that would force me to betray my basic instinct. Which was to grab Vayl and get him as far away from the monstrosity of a mask at my side as soon as I could. But that, I knew, would kill him.

The guards laid Disa on the floor at the foot of the mask. Cam and Cole had already given Vayl a spot of his own on the carpet beside me. They flanked him in a good imitation of Disa's former shieldmen, though each of my guys held an armed crossbow. The message should've been clear to the assembled Trust members. But I drew Grief and pressed the magic button anyway. Jack looked up at me when he heard the whir of working gears.

"Stay low," I told him. He sat. Well, it was a start.

Admes, Niall, and Aine came to stand beside me. "Are you ready?" asked Niall.

I swallowed the obscenity that lay like salt on my tongue. But I supposed Niall saw it on my face, because he said, "Vayl will be an excellent *Deyrar*. And he should not have to give up his work with you in order to continue the Trust's business here."

I looked at him, feeling colder than I'd be if I were truly dead. "Vayl left this place for a reason. Now we're cementing him to it. If you don't think he's going to be sick and pissed, you don't know him at all."

Cole put his hand on my arm. I appreciated the outreach. Because I knew I was betraying everything Vayl had fought so hard for when he'd separated himself from the Vampere world decades ago. But I'd seen injuries like Disa's before. Vamps didn't recover from them. They simply died more slowly than usual.

Cam and Cole stepped forward to remove the mask from its stand. As soon as they touched it, the keening began, emerging from the mouth of the mask like an opera singer's death scream. Jack began to whine. I shook my head.

Admes and Niall went to kneel by Disa, pulling her into a sitting position so the mask would slide down over her head and torso. "Don't allow any part of your body to go inside the mask with her," I warned them. "I can't predict what would happen, but I don't think it would be good." I looked at my guys. "Ready?" They nodded. "Okay, here I go."

I strode over to Disa, took a firm grip on Vayl's sword with my good hand as I planted my foot in her chest and yanked. She didn't feel a thing. Krios's doc had her on so many painkillers she could've smiled through an elephant stampede. In fact, you might even say she was in a state of ecstasy.

As soon as the sword was free, our men lowered the mask over her, holding it steady so it wouldn't topple over. We heard one piercing scream. And then, with the stomach-churning sound of rending flesh and crushing bone, her entire body began to rise up into the mask.

Cole looked at me, his eyes rounder than the poker chips that sat in my hip pocket. "This is bad, Jaz. Worse than watching all the *Friday the 13th* movies in one sitting. Which I did once."

"This is what she wanted to do to Vayl," I said. I knew it sounded cold, and I was sorry. Not for Disa. She'd dug her plot. But for me. Because I didn't care.

Suddenly the mask's eyes opened. Bored into mine. I felt light, almost separate from myself, like I had those few times when I'd actually traveled outside my body. I put my good hand on the mask to steady myself. The power beat into me, as if the entire Trust had balled up its mojo and thrust it through my chest. And I could hear her, Octavia, speaking to me just like Raoul sometimes did. Only her voice didn't make me feel like my brain was about to shatter. In fact, it spoke so softly I could barely make out the words as they fell like coals from a burning log. However, at last I knew what she wanted.

"Aine needs to go into the mask," I said.

"What?" Dave's voice, its tone telling me I'd just leaped into Ludicrous Land.

Every vampire in the Trust began to protest. Loudly.

I began to speak. But the words weren't ones I recognized. Not English, certainly. Just ones Octavia begged me to repeat. The vampires recognized it at once.

"What's she doing?" Dave demanded. I felt him grab me around the waist. It jarred my collarbone, sending a brain-blowing shaft of pain through my chest and arms.

"Trayton, don't let him pull me off the mask!" I gasped.

I heard the entire pack growl, lifting every hair on my body, and he let go. I kept talking, the words coming awkwardly off my tongue. Would anyone understand? *Octavia, speak up! Slow down! I can't—what was that word?*

Trayton's hand, gentle under my good elbow now, bore me up. His immense trust calmed me, focused me. Octavia's voice came clearer. I repeated her speech exactly.

"What's she saying?" Cole demanded.

Niall's voice, distant and oddly lilting. "Because Hamon was murdered. Because Vayl is unwilling and Disa is undeserving, Octavia can reverse the power of the mask. If Aine wears it now, instead of it consuming her, it will pour all the partners' knowledge into her. She will be able to lead alone for the first time since the Trust was formed."

Leaving Vayl off the hook!

I dropped my hand and, still leaning on Trayton, turned to the vampire holding Admes's arm. "Aine?" I asked. "Are you willing to risk it?"

After a tense, quiet moment when I swore I could hear my own breath moving in and out of my lungs, Aine stepped forward and held out her hands. *Yes!*

By now every vestige of Disa had disappeared into the mask. Cam and Cole picked it up one more time. They walked it to where Aine stood with her arms outstretched as if to give them each a big hug. When her hands contacted wood, she clutched at it, helping them lift the mask and then lower it slowly over her head.

For a minute nothing happened. And then Aine began clawing at the outside of the mask, her fingernails leaving tiny furrows in the wood as they moved from the rounded cheeks to the closed heart-door and off. Still she stood, apparently in one piece. Except for the scratching, which continued pretty much uninterrupted for the next five minutes. Until, suddenly, she screamed.

Admes lunged forward, reaching out for the mask. Cam shoved his crossbow into the warrior's chest. "I wouldn't," he said mildly.

"She's dying in there!"

"She's screaming," I told him. "But she has no means of making music on her. I'd say that's a pretty significant development, wouldn't you?"

"Admes," said a smooth, silky baritone that I'd begun to think I might never hear again. "Tell me you are not threatening my son." Admes raised his hands and backed away as Vayl lifted himself off the floor, using the sword sheath we'd laid across his chest to help him balance as he leaned forward.

I went to my knees beside him, Trayton making sure the move didn't jar my shoulder. "Vayl." I reached out, hesitated, touched the tips of my fingers to his cheek. So cold. He'd need blood soon. And this time I'd make sure it came from me.

I slipped my hand behind his neck. "I thought . . ." I stopped. *Gawd. This is about to be one of* those *moments.* I backed away. And then, *Aw, screw it.* "Don't ever do that to me again, you hear me?" I swung my leg over both of his, wrapped my good arm around his neck, and gave his luscious lips the attention they'd been begging for from the moment I'd laid eyes on them.

When I finally pulled back Vayl said, "We really must do this more often." He looked over my head. "But perhaps without the audience?"

"Agreed. And, uh, about the son thing?" I flipped his collar up and down until he captured my hand in his. "Sorry. Maybe I've developed a new nervous habit. Anyway"—I squeezed his fingers, hoping it would comfort him a little—"we're pretty sure they're not. According to Cassandra, Erilynn couldn't have seen either one of them. And they both seem to have been manipulated to that place by Disa. I doubt she has any contacts in the Agency or the military, so she was probably just pushing her Trust's weight around, which she seemed to be better at than any of us gave her credit for. We underestimated her, Vayl."

He went absolutely still, his face draining of expression. I suddenly felt like I was cuddling with one of those statues you occasionally see perched on park benches. After a moment he moved, but the only sign of disappointment was the slight drop of his chin, the downturn of his lips. "I must stand," he said.

"Of course." Trayton's hand was the one that reached out to lift me off his lap, that continued to hold mine when Vayl rose without looking at or touching me, as much in his own world as the lover in that god-awful poem Eryx liked so much. He stood in his tattered clothes, soaked as a bad surfer, his deep purple eyes taking turns studying Cole and Cam.

Trayton leaned in. "Look at me."

I turned my head, couldn't help but smile a bit as I found myself searching for his gleaming eyes between strands of fine black hair. "What is it?" I asked.

"He's not going to be an easy one to love," Trayton said, with a sideways nod at my boss.

"How can you tell?"

"Because I have a complicated partner myself." He winked at Phoebe, who seemed poised to tear my hair from its roots the moment Krios gave her permission to ditch her post.

Would you chill? I mouthed to her. She looked pointedly at my hand, still entwined with Trayton's. I pulled it free on the pretext of settling Cirilai more firmly on my finger.

Vayl moved closer to me. "What is happening?" he asked, nodding to Aine, who still struggled inside the mask.

I explained as Jack shoved his nose into my thigh, looking for his share of affection. Since he was sitting on my left between Vayl and me, my *sverhamin* helped us both out, crouching down to give the dog a thorough petting.

"I'm sorry," I said as I finished the story. "I knew it wasn't what you wanted. But I couldn't think of any other way to save your life."

When Vayl looked up I felt his power reach out to me as never before. And though he didn't move to touch me, the soft breeze of it caressed me like a cool winter wind. I nearly closed my eyes, the sensation overtook me so completely. But I couldn't relax. Because our work wasn't finished yet.

We were reminded of this when Aine finally stopped moaning, fighting, scrabbling at the mask and stood perfectly still. Blood sprang from the corners of the mask's eyes, ran down its face, and caught in the furrows that Vayl had thought the carver meant as whiskers. It spread outward to the edges of the mask and farther, taking new routes no artist had drawn for it, until lines of red covered it from top to bottom. The mask shivered. Cracked. And fell into pieces at Aine's feet.

Collective gasp as every single creature in the room, human and *other*, discovered that the mask had given Aine a new face. She might have been Disa's cousin. The eyes were Octavia's. Maybe the heart and spine belonged, at least partially, to Hamon's former mate as well. But the rest of the face had definitely been Disa's.

Aine stepped forward. The voice I didn't recognize. Maybe it was hers, given wings now that she had a mouth and a nose to do the work her keyboard had taken over after her injury. "Words of thanks are so inadequate. We are forever in your debt." She wasn't being queenly. When she said we, she motioned to everyone in the Trust. I wasn't sure Genti and his bunch would agree with her, but I was willing to rise above if they could keep their mouths shut.

"Honestly, Aine, this is the best possible scenario for us. Eryx only gave me one other option to Disa's death, and though we were following it, I knew it was going to make Vayl utterly miserable."

"When did you see Hamon?" asked Dave.

"I was having visions of him," I said. "Every time I came across a big puddle of blood, there he'd be."

"Why didn't you say something?"

"It didn't really seem like something a sane person would be experiencing. So . . ."

Aine said, "He came to me inside the mask as well."

"And now?" I asked. "Is he . . . gone?"

She nodded. "He and Octavia both. And the mask"—she looked back at it, now lying in pieces on the floor—"it is shorn of its powers. We will have to find a new way of governing in this Trust."

Aine was looking at Vayl now, and I could see the invitation in her eyes. He must have too, because he began shaking his head before she could get the words out. "My place is in America with my *avhar*. But first"—he looked at Cole and Cam—"yes. Perhaps a trip to my homeland. I believe it is finally time to tie up some very old loose ends. And then I will be able to search for my sons with a new heart." His eyes came to mine. "One that has made room for all kinds of love."

Vayl said more. And Cole made some comment, an angry one I thought, since his hair waggled and spit flew, but my mind began roaring as soon as I heard the word "love" spoken in that possessive tone of voice Vayl only gets when he's talking about what matters to him most. Usually he reserved it for conversations involving his boys. Now he'd added me to the mix.

It's okay. Don't panic. This is a good thing. Like winning the lottery. With fangs.

Inside my head Granny May was cackling like a hen as she

waved her hands, dispersing all the other in-dwellers to their appointed places now that the worst of the danger was over. As I glared at her, waiting for her to whip out the hanky and dry the at-my-expense tears, she shook her head at me and snorted, *You sure can pick 'em, Jazzy. Hey, for an encore, I'd be highly entertained if I had a hobbit for a great-grandchild.*

You pipe down, Gran. I can easily dream up an old-folks' home for you. One that doesn't serve macaroni and cheese or apple pie.

My mind filled with silence. It wouldn't last. Already I could feel the niggling fears that Samos had made too good of a deal with his devil. Cole still needed his answer. My dad's attacker wouldn't lay low forever. And I might do something phenomenally stupid to lose my chance with Vayl.

I met his amber eyes, my heart skipping a beat as they crinkled at the corners.

Or not.

Acknowledgments

This has been the most difficult book to write so far, and it wouldn't have ended nearly so well without the support of my husband, Kirk, who is a constant source of quiet strength. I'd also like to thank my editors, Devi Pillai and Bella Pagan. Funny how one question can open up a whole new perspective on a character's world. Deep appreciation, as always, must go to my agent, Laurie McLean, the great folks at Orbit, and my precious readers Katie and Hope. To the citizens of Patras, please accept my apologies for feeling free to rearrange your architecture. Rest assured I put it right back where I found it after the novel was finished. And to you, my awesome readers, so cool to have you here! Wait till you see what I've got in store for you next!

extras

orbit

meet the author

Cindy Pringle

JENNIFER RARDIN began writing at the age of twelve, mostly poems to amuse her classmates and short stories featuring her best friends as the heroines. She lives in an old farmhouse in Illinois with her husband and two children. Find out more about Jennifer Rardin at www.JenniferRardin.com.

introducing

If you enjoyed BITTEN TO DEATH,
look out for

ONE MORE BITE

Book 5 of the Jaz Parks series

by Jennifer Rardin

May 18, 6:00 p.m.

"Jasmine, do not pull that gun."

Vayl spoke in a voice so low even I could barely hear him, which meant the people in the worn gray seats next to the bathroom door where I stood still had no idea what I meant to do.

"I'm gonna kill him," I growled. My fingers tightened on the grip of Grief, the Walther PPK I kept stashed in the shoulder holster under my black leather jacket. I couldn't see my intended victim at the moment. Vayl had set his hands on the edges of the doorframe, spreading his calf-length duster like a curtain, blocking my view. But I could hear the son of a bitch, sitting near the front, chatting up the flight attendant like she was the daughter of one of his war buddies.

"You do understand what a bad idea this is, do you not?" Vayl insisted. "Even discussing pulling a gun on an airplane could bring the passengers down on you like a mob of after-Christmas-sale shoppers." He fixed me with warm hazel eyes. "I would hate to see you beaten to death with that woman's boot."

He jerked his head sideways, directing my attention toward an exhausted traveler whose fat rolls drooped over her armrests like just-kneaded bread dough. I glanced her way, and as people will do when they feel eyes upon them, she looked back at me. For a split second her pink cheeks and heavy-framed glasses swam out of focus. A lean, dark-eyed face sneered at me from beneath her shoulder-length perm. It said, "Are you certain you know my name?" I squeezed my eyes shut.

You're dead, Edward Samos. I saw your smoke fade into the night. I ground the bits of ash and bone you left behind into the dirt of the Grecian countryside. So stop fucking haunting me!

I turned my head so that when I opened my eyes they fell on Vayl's short black curls, which, I now knew, felt like silk under the fingertips. And his face, carved with the bold hand of an artist whose work I'd never tire of.

"Are you all right?" he asked.

Yeah, sure. For some bizarre reason I'm seeing the last bad guy I assassinated on innocent people's faces. I can't stop thinking about my boss in a totally unprofessional and yet vividly exciting manner. And, at age twenty-five, I am still unable to escape the man who made my childhood pretty much a misery from start to finish. I'm just dandy, thanks for asking!

I picked the part that bothered me least and let loose. "You're the one who allowed my father to come along on this assignment. I told you it wouldn't work. I warned you that blood could be shed. But did you listen?"

"I rather thought you would wait until we had landed in Inverness."

"Who brings baby pictures on an international flight?" I hissed. "If I'd wanted my bare ass paraded in front of all the first-class ticket holders I'd have mooned everyone before we took off!"

Vayl knew better than to tell me the pictures were adorable. Then I'd have had to kill him too. "Look into my eyes," he said.

"What, so you can hypnotize me? No thanks."

He shook his head. "We both know my powers have a minimal effect on you. Come now, my *pretera*. Humor me."

"What's a *pretera*?" I muttered.

"It is a Romani word, meaning wildcat."

"Oh. In that case . . ." I locked stares with the guy who'd started out as my boss and ended up . . . well, that remained to be seen. But the possibilities had begun to make my skin steam. "I can't believe this is happening."

Vayl's shrug reminded me strongly of his European roots. "How do you say? Money talks."

So true. In this case, the bucks had come from Albert himself. "What are we, the Russian Space Agency?" I demanded. "Selling seats on our assignments to the highest bidder?"

Vayl said, "I realize the shock is only now wearing off. I would have warned you, but Pete did not inform me he would be joining us until just before this leg of our flight. Apparently your father felt you would strenuously object to his presence—"

"Ya think?"

"Thus the secrecy surrounding his joining us at Gatwick."

"Because he must've known I'd have thrown him off the plane in Cleveland," I muttered, almost to myself. I realized I'd taken my hand out of my jacket and Vayl had used the opportunity to curl his fingers around mine. I shouldn't see anything romantic in it. He was probably just trying to keep me from reaching again.

I sighed. "Okay, I won't kill him yet. But you get those pictures out of his claws, and keep him away from me, and—"

Vayl slid his hand up my arm, sending trickles of electric awareness shooting through me. Suddenly I couldn't think of anyone but him. A deliberate move on his part, I was sure. "I never thought I would say this," he murmured, leaning in so his lips nearly brushed my ear. "But I would suggest you spend the rest of this flight concentrating on Cole." *Who? Oh, damn, Jaz, would you kick your brain into gear? Your third for this piece o' crap job, remember? The one Pete has decided to fund using your dad's IRA?* I began plotting a revenge so intricate and satisfying I barely heard Vayl say, "I will deal with your father."

"Okay. Thanks. Only, do me a favor?"

"Anything."

"Be discreet, will you? He doesn't know about . . . us . . . yet. And I think I should probably be the one to tell him I'm involved with a vampire."

VISIT THE ORBIT BLOG AT

www.orbitbooks.net

FEATURING

BREAKING NEWS
FORTHCOMING RELEASES
LINKS TO AUTHOR SITES
EXCLUSIVE INTERVIEWS
EARLY EXTRACTS

AND COMMENTARY FROM OUR EDITORS

WITH REGULAR UPDATES FROM OUR TEAM,
ORBITBOOKS.NET IS YOUR SOURCE
FOR ALL THINGS ORBITAL.

WHILE YOU'RE THERE, JOIN OUR EMAIL LIST
TO RECEIVE INFORMATION ON SPECIAL OFFERS,
GIVEAWAYS, AND MORE.

imagine. explore. engage.